Beijing Smog

Beijing Smog

Ian Williams

Matador
9 Priory Business Park,
Wistow Road, Kibworth Beauchamp,
Leicestershire. LE8 0RX
Tel: 0116 279 2299
Email: books@troubador.co.uk
Web: www.troubador.co.uk/matador
Twitter: @matadorbooks

ISBN 978 1788037 372

British Library Cataloguing in Publication Data.
A catalogue record for this book is available from the British Library.

Printed and bound in the UK by TJ International, Padstow, Cornwall
Typeset in 10pt Palatino by Troubador Publishing Ltd, Leicester, UK

Matador is an imprint of Troubador Publishing Ltd

For Serena, Millie and Ollie

Ian Williams is a former foreign correspondent who was based in Russia and then Asia for leading British and American news organisations. He has reported from across China. This is his first novel.

"Online rumours undermine the morale of the public, and if out of control they will seriously disturb the public order and affect social stability."

The People's Daily

"Never believe anything until it has been officially denied."

Otto von Bismarck

– 1 –

The Cyber Guy

The hotel described itself as an intelligent building, the smartest hotel in Beijing, full of sensors to make stuff happen without pressing buttons, but the way Chuck Drayton saw it, the place was retarded.

He called the front desk, which tracked down the general manager, a German called Wolfgang, and he told Wolfgang they needed to work on the intelligent bit.

"Not just once, three times, man. I was up half the fucking night."

Wolfgang said he was sorry to hear that and he'd be straight up, meeting Drayton five minutes later in the executive lounge on the thirty-fifth floor, where the American was standing beside one of its big windows looking for a view. The first thing he told Wolfgang was that the view sucked. He said that it reminded him of one of those over-priced Chinese landscape paintings they sold in the hotel shop, mountains shrouded in mist. Except the mist was smog, thick smog, pierced here and there by the dark shadows of grey skyscrapers and apartment blocks.

He said he could feel his life expectancy shrinking just looking at it.

Wolfgang ordered coffee and said, yeah, but don't you think it's kind of moody, and he apologised again for what he called the hiccups with the technology. He said it was a new hotel and they'd

1

had teething problems with the sensors that were supposed to detect movement in the room and switch stuff on and off.

"There was no movement, Wolfgang. I was asleep," Drayton said. "Then suddenly the curtains open, the TV and the lights come on. I went to sleep last night thinking I'm in a hotel, then next thing I know I wake on the set of *Paranormal Activity*. You get what I'm saying?"

Wolfgang said he got what Drayton was saying and apologised again. He said it was definitely a hotel, and offered a complimentary dinner, lunch, drinks – whatever the hotel could do to make things good; Drayton said he'd take the lot. With a final flurry Wolfgang said he would deal with the matter personally, right now, and excused himself to go and find someone to yell at.

The German had sweat dripping down his forehead as he left. He looked stressed, and Drayton suspected his wasn't the first complaint about the hotel's IQ.

Drayton made a note in his iPhone, a reminder to speak later to the US Embassy security guys, who'd recently given the place full clearance as safe for American diplomats, and tell them that giving a green light to a hotel with a mind of its own, a forty-floor poltergeist, might not be the way to go.

Then he looked again for the maestro. Where the fuck was he? They'd agreed to meet in the lounge at two and travel together to the concert, scheduled for late afternoon, but it was now nearly a quarter to three.

He found an internal hotel phone and called down to the maestro's room, but it went straight to voicemail, meaning that the guy was either on the phone or had it on do-not-disturb mode. Maybe he'd taken a nap and overslept, though the maestro didn't strike Drayton as the type that took naps.

He decided to go and bang on his door, but the maestro's room was on a different floor to Drayton's and the smart lift wouldn't take him there since it wouldn't accept his smart key to get access to the maestro's smart floor. And since the smart lift didn't respond to yelling or to banging on the lift's smart console, Drayton went back to his room and phoned down again for Wolfgang.

A woman on the front desk said Mr Wolfgang was in a meeting, but she had a message from Mr Abramovich.

"He says he'll meet you at the concert and that he's taking the car," she said, and Drayton said that was just great and could she call him a taxi? The woman said sure, only there weren't many around right now and the traffic was terrible.

Drayton hung up and opened a taxi-hailing app on his iPhone. He could see taxis. They looked like rows of termites on his screen. Usually it didn't take long for one to respond, changing colour from white to black when they accepted the fare. Only today the termites weren't nibbling, stuck in little white clusters.

He refreshed the app, but the termites were still stuck. He could barely make out the road below from the window, but at that moment the smog cleared just enough to see what had paralysed the termites. The receptionist was right. The traffic on the ring road was at a complete standstill.

Maybe the maestro hadn't travelled too far, and could still turn around, bring the embassy car back and collect him. He picked up the maestro's business card from his desk: "Alexander Abramovich, composer, conductor and cultural ambassador". Drayton called the cell phone number on the card, an American number, and after three rings the maestro picked up.

"This is Abramovich."

"Mr Abramovich, this is Chuck Drayton. I was surprised to hear you left without me. It's very important we stick together."

But before Drayton could get to the bit about turning the car around, the maestro interrupted him, saying he'd had to leave earlier than planned because of the traffic, and wasn't going to be delayed by Drayton's petty squabbling with the hotel. He said he had a concert to conduct, that this wasn't just music, it was diplomacy, and that you, Mr Drayton, still had a few things to learn about that.

"And another thing," the maestro said, "I want my laptop back."

"Can we talk about that later?" Drayton said, not trusting the telephone line.

"I want it back, Mr Drayton, and you have until tomorrow to return it to me."

"We still have a few tests."

"Fuck your tests, Mr Drayton. I want it back. It was nothing. I overreacted. And anyway, I no longer want to pursue it, and I no longer

3

need you. What I'm doing here is too important to be undermined by your cyber stupidity and paranoia."

Drayton wanted to yell, you were hacked, you moron, and I just hope your pretentious bullshit about cultural diplomacy is being read by somebody who cares more than I do. But the maestro had already hung up.

Drayton decided he'd have to take the metro, and he hated the metro. The nearest station was just around the corner from the hotel. That was the easy bit. When he got there the entrance was packed, and he was swept inside on a human tide, which carried him down two escalators and to a platform on which there was barely room to breathe. The platform had markings, little lanes, for getting off and on the trains, which was encouraging, but meant nothing. As the train approached, the crowd on the platform steeled itself like a team facing off with hated opponents in a grudge football match, and when the doors opened both sides charged. Drayton was carried onto the train by the weight of the crowd behind him.

He'd now almost certainly miss the pre-concert reception at the National Centre for Performing Arts, Beijing's modern egg-shaped arts centre, usually just known as that, the Egg, where Abramovich was performing. Drayton reckoned that at this rate he'd be lucky to get there for the concert itself. Not that he was too bothered, since he found the guy, this maestro, insufferable. He had an ego the size of Tiananmen Square, maybe bigger.

And the loathing was mutual.

The guy's laptop had been hacked soon after he'd arrived in Beijing, there wasn't much doubt about that. He'd opened the machine in his hotel room to find it had connected itself to the internet, the cursor roaming around the screen and doing its own thing, like it had a mind of its own. The laptop was hyperventilating, fan whizzing around and doing all sorts of stuff, but without the maestro at the controls.

He was a childhood friend of the US Ambassador, so he'd taken the machine straight to the US Embassy, yelling and ranting, saying the laptop contained sensitive plans, emails and notes as well as semi-finished compositions. The Ambassador said he'd have specialists look over it, do the forensics, look for digital fingerprints. That had calmed the maestro down a little, but still he ranted, like the future of world peace was at stake.

Like it was all the fault of the embassy.

The first thing Drayton did when he was put on the case was to make sure it wasn't, that nobody at the embassy had been poking around the guy's data. Abramovich had just been to North Korea, part of a tour that started in Russia and would take him on to Vietnam. The way Drayton saw it, the guy had kept some pretty unsavoury company in Pyongyang and Moscow. But nobody at the embassy put their hand up.

He'd hit it off badly with Abramovich from the start, calling his concerts the Tyrant Tour, thinking he was being funny, making a joke of it. But the maestro had called him an idiot, saying that America had lost the moral authority to lecture anybody about anything. He said he was using music to build bridges. That bridges were needed right now because there was a clown in the White House, a dangerous clown, and that he, Abramovich, was the real American diplomat.

Now, a week later, he and Abramovich could barely stand the sight of each other, and Drayton was seething because thanks to this jerk he was stuck on a train that was beyond crowded, four stops from the Egg, four stops too many as far as Drayton was concerned, the crush getting worse at every station.

He didn't think he'd ever be able to get off, but salvation came in the form of a bunch of what he took to be students, who'd clearly done the journey before and lined up in a wedge-like formation as the train pulled into Tiananmen West station, the closest to the Egg. Doors opened, and a dozen heads were lowered, shoulders tensed, before the wedge drove its way off the train; at its arrow-like point a lanky kid with his arms outstretched in front of him was holding an iPad to slice through the crowd. Drayton followed in their wake, thinking it was the smartest use of an iPad he'd seen all week.

Only they swept out of the wrong exit for the Egg, and he had to double back against the tide and into another dark corridor, this one lined with posters and with another barely penetrable crowd. Then he found himself face to face with the maestro, or at least a giant poster of the man, looking grim, about to fire up an orchestra, baton in hand, his chin raised, eyes wide open. Which was pretty scary. The caption said, "A Concert for Resilience and Hope".

Drayton paused for breath under the poster, thinking he could do with both if he was ever going to make it to the hall.

5

At least the forensic guys still had the maestro's laptop. Abramovich had started to have second thoughts twenty-four hours after he'd handed it over to the embassy, seduced by all the bullshit receptions, as Drayton saw it, Chinese officials telling him they were honoured. Privileged. That this was a special moment. An historic occasion for Beijing, for China-US relations, for classical music, they'd said, raising a glass. And the maestro lapped it all up, all the fawning, as if it meant something.

Drayton had trailed along, one reception after another. One Chinese official had told him they were excited to have in Beijing America's greatest living conductor, and a true statesman, performing with a Chinese orchestra for the first time, and Drayton didn't have the heart to say he'd never heard of Abramovich before the guy had arrived in Beijing.

But it all played to the maestro's ego, and he'd said to Drayton that maybe he'd made a mistake, that maybe he'd just been tired and nothing really was going on with the cursor and stuff. And anyway, he said, it really wasn't worth making a fuss over.

Drayton had tried to change the subject, asking Abramovich, "What's with the Leningrad thing? Why are you playing that? It's Russian."

The maestro said that was the point, that music has no boundaries. He said his grandparents on his father's side were Russian, that he'd inherited a passion for Russian classical music, but it was really all about the message.

"On one level the *Leningrad Symphony* is about the defence of that great city during the Second World War, Mr Drayton, but Shostakovich saw it essentially as a tribute to human resilience."

"And this *Shostakooooovik*, he's Russian?"

"He's Russian, Mr Drayton. But if it makes you happier, after the break I'll be conducting the *New World Symphony*, written in New York, and a reflection on America. Neil Armstrong took a recording to the moon. Is that American enough for you?"

Drayton said he liked the sound of that, but why couldn't he put the music by the American guy first?

The maestro said the American guy was Czech, his name was Dvořák, and would Drayton please excuse him. With that he headed back towards a podium, where more tributes were flowing, telling his assistant along the way to please keep that moron from the embassy away from him.

Which would have been just fine by Drayton, but he still had a job to do, and this was bigger than Abramovich. Much bigger.

He continued his slow progress down the corridor and into the Egg, though this time without the help of the student battering ram.

Eventually the corridor opened onto a vast concrete-walled lobby area, the Egg's main glass doors up some steps to one side, the ticket office and cloakrooms on the other. A wall of metal detectors blocked the route down to the main concert halls, though security staff in badly fitting uniforms, frisking people at random, seemed mostly to ignore the madly pinging machines.

No sooner had Drayton been through a metal detector when a group of perhaps twenty police and plain-clothes security agents, some with barely concealed weapons, entered through the main doors. They swept down the steps, shouting to clear out of the way, and forming a cordon around a short balding man with thick-rimmed glasses. The short man just looked straight ahead, walking briskly, or as briskly as people could be cleared from his path. What Drayton noticed most was the way the man's big glasses framed a child-like face. Most people backed away instinctively.

The short man and his escort barged through the metal detectors, since there was no way round them, and the pings turned into one manic high-pitched wail, which lasted well after they'd moved on.

"Who's that?" Drayton asked one of the Egg's security men, who was looking at his metal detector like it might blow up at any minute.

The man just shrugged. Didn't know, and cared even less.

Much to his surprise, Drayton had arrived with twenty minutes to spare before the concert, so he found a bar and ordered a beer, a local Tsingtao, which was lukewarm but went down so well he ordered another, thinking all the time, *who was that guy?* Maybe the maestro was the real deal after all. Drayton hadn't really got a good look, since the guy was dwarfed by his bodyguards, but there was a stern, serious look on that baby face, that was for sure.

A buzzer, a five-minute warning, sounded, and Drayton made his

7

way to his seat, in an elevated section at the back of the hall. The place was packed, but he really wasn't in the mood for this.

The lights went down, and an announcement asked valued customers, out of respect for the artists and the law, to kindly refrain from any recording, videoing or photography.

As the orchestra entered the stage, dozens of smartphones were raised in the air to record, video and photograph. They were joined by still more, as the maestro entered, clad in black jacket and black bow tie, bowing deeply to the smartphones, spotlights highlighting his shiny balding head and round rimless glasses.

Attendants who'd been showing people to their seats scrambled into action. Each had a small laser pointer that they trained on the offending devices, moving the beam up and down. The laser beams were soon dancing all over the auditorium.

The orchestra looked like they'd seen it all before. If the maestro was surprised, he didn't show it. He looked serious and solemn. Just like his poster. And just like the music he was about to conduct.

The smartphones were lowered, driven away by the lasers, or maybe because they already had what they wanted and were now posting online with captions saying, "Hey, look where I am".

Drayton loved those small acts of defiance.

The maestro lifted his baton and the symphony began with a rousing melody from the string section, which Drayton hadn't expected and rather liked. But it didn't last; the Nazis were on the march and so was the maestro, waving his baton as if the defence of Leningrad depended on him alone, the music growing in intensity.

The first movement seemed to go on forever, and as it reached a climax, Drayton felt exhausted, drained. Then he felt a sudden trembling that seemed to rise up through his chair. Those sitting nearby felt it too, and they looked around like maybe the Führer's Panzer tanks had entered the hall and were about to take out the maestro. It stopped, but then started again, which is when Drayton realised he was sitting on his phone, which he'd switched to vibration mode and stuck in his back pocket. Somebody was trying to get hold of him.

The first movement ended, and as throats were being cleared, noses blown and smartphone messages checked, he ducked for the aisle, winding his way towards the exit, his body bent forward like a stressed orangutan criss-crossing the floor of its cage.

"No re-entry once the music starts again," said an attendant, one eye on Drayton, one on the lookout for smartphones.

"That's fine by me," Drayton said.

The security detail, the Praetorian Guard for the little guy, was now huddled in small groups outside the main hall. Other plainclothes security patrolled past the doors of the hall with curly earpieces and big bulges under their jackets.

Drayton reached a quiet corner of the foyer between a pillar and a big gold artwork, a grotesquely contorted head of a buffalo mounted on a wooden plinth, when his phone vibrated again, a call from an unknown number. He took the call, but said nothing, waiting on the caller to speak first.

"Chuck, it's Dave."

"Hey Dave, what's up?"

"We need to talk. We have a breakthrough."

Drayton said that was great, but he was still at the Egg, at the concert, baby-sitting the maestro.

"Fuck the maestro," said Dave. "We have what we need."

Drayton said he could be at the embassy in twenty minutes or so, and Dave said, "No, don't do that. I'll meet you in Tiananmen Square in front of the portrait of Mao. It's more secure."

Drayton left by the main entrance of the Egg. He raised the collar of his thick black overcoat, with matching scarf and thick woollen beanie hat, strapped on a pollution mask and stepped out into the frigid gloom. Police cars were lined up in front of the Egg's titanium and glass dome, with more armed men, and Drayton wondered again who the little guy was and why he needed that level of security.

It took him ten minutes to walk to Tiananmen; he thought the giant square was atmospheric in all the smog. The blurred outlines of the Great Hall of the People to his right. National Museum to his left. Tall street lights, smudge-like, lining the edges. The closer ones had halos of haze, but in the middle distance they faded to nothingness.

He stopped close to the portrait of Mao Zedong, at Tiananmen Gate, hanging above a tunnel into the Forbidden City, the old Imperial Palace. Guards stood rigid in the foreground, and crowds jostled for

9

photographs in front of them, selfies mainly. Drayton took one himself, on his iPhone, and then looked back down the square trying to spot Mao's mausoleum, but it was lost in the smog. He decided he'd pay the old despot a visit at some point, see him in the flesh.

There were a lot of people mingling there. Drayton guessed that was why Dave had chosen this place, figuring there was anonymity in the crowd. But it was sometimes difficult to tell what was going on with Dave, a guy who thought his job was so secret he didn't even have a second name. At least not one he wanted to tell Drayton.

He reckoned it was probably a turf thing too, the Beijing spooks wanting to keep control, wary of the upstarts like Drayton from the Shanghai consulate. It was stupid really, but Drayton never felt particularly welcome at the embassy.

He was beginning to wonder if he'd ever find Dave when he felt a hand gripping his arm, and Dave said, "Hannibal Lecter, I presume."

"Yeah, you like it? I figured it might add a year or two to my life expectancy."

Drayton's big black pollution mask was an all-encompassing studded contraption that covered half his face. He imagined it did make him look pretty scary, that he should keep away from kids, though he thought it more Darth Vader than Hannibal, the Hollywood cannibal. But it seemed to do the job, keeping out the filthy air, though at times Drayton found he was struggling to breathe at all through its multiple filters.

"This one's pretty useless," Dave said, pointing to his own mask. "Maybe worse than useless."

He was wearing a simple white surgical-style mask with the words PM2.5 Mega Blocker printed on the front.

"I think it refers to the tiny bits that do the most damage," he said. "Someone at the embassy bought a whole bunch of them online, while we wait for fresh supplies from Washington."

Drayton said they had plenty at the consulate, smirking beneath his mask, scoring an easy point for Shanghai, which Dave ignored.

"There're a lot of fakes online," Drayton said.

"Yeah, tell me about it," said Dave.

And then he said, "Let's walk", and they headed east away from

10

the square along Chang'an Avenue, the wide thoroughfare running across Tiananmen's northern end.

"I'm really sorry you got landed with this guy, this Abramovich," Dave said. "Sounds like a real pain, but hey, you're the Cyber Guy."

They walked for a while in silence before Dave said they'd got the forensic results back from Fort Meade, and the National Security Agency had confirmed the maestro's laptop had been infected with malicious software, malware that allowed somebody else to take remote control and read his files, messages and emails.

"They were having a poke around when he got back to his room and he saw the cursor dancing all over the screen."

"Why the maestro?" asked Drayton, and Dave said there was some interesting stuff on his computer, that he'd had some quite high-level contacts in China and in North Korea. In Russia too, where he met the President.

"He had some less than flattering things to say about us, the American Government, that is," said Dave. "There was a lot of gossipy stuff, emails, notes to himself, and a pretty full address book. The guy does have some decent contacts."

"I can imagine. And you happened to just stumble upon all this?"

"Well, we were inside his computer. We had to look to see what might be of interest to the hackers."

"Or to you."

Dave ignored that and said, "The key thing, Chuck, is not whether this guy had anything interesting on his computer. It's the pattern, the fingerprints. It's what it tells us about their capabilities. The hackers didn't cover their tracks very well, and Fort Meade says it's consistent with other attacks we've seen against US companies and business people, hoovering up information wherever and whenever they can."

At that moment, a pair of police cars raced out of the gloom of Chang'an, their sirens wailing, lights flashing. Both men instinctively turned away, raising the collar of their thick coats. Drayton pulled down his black woollen beanie hat to just above his eyes.

"You know that building?" said Dave, pointing to the fuzzy outline of the Beijing Hotel, overlooking Chang-an. Then without waiting for an answer he said, "It was from one of those rooms on the left that the famous images were taken. Tank Man. The guy standing in the street facing off against a tank during the 1989 Tiananmen Square massacre. It was right here."

Drayton said yeah, he remembered the photo. He said he'd read that Tank Man had never been identified, that nobody had ever figured out who he was, and he asked Dave whether he thought that could ever happen again.

Dave said from what he could make out, the Communist Party leader seemed in control, locking away his rivals, saying they were all corrupt. And Drayton said the guy was making a lot of enemies. That maybe it was a sign of weakness.

Dave just shrugged, and Drayton said the maestro wanted his computer back, that he was making threats.

"He can have it back," said Dave. "In fact the sooner the better. We've installed a little something of our own in case the hacker returns for another look around his laptop."

"And what little something is that?"

"That's not important right now, Chuck. What matters is that the hackers have left quite a digital trail, and we're close to pinpointing where these attacks are coming from."

"That does sound like a breakthrough," said Drayton. "Where are we talking about?"

And Dave said Drayton needed to get back to Shanghai, just as soon as he could.

*

By that time at the Egg the final movement of the *Leningrad Symphony* was building into a frenzy, and so was the maestro. His face was contorted, grimacing, his arms waving manically as he drove the orchestra on, marshalling the defences of Leningrad.

The little man with all the security was dabbing his eyes, overcome with the emotion of the music. He was seated alone in a box high on one side of the hall, with carefully arranged curtains making him all but invisible to the rest of the audience below.

He was an elderly man, who'd trained in what used to be the Soviet Union. He was hard, uncompromising and feared. Sentiment was not something he was known for, but he did have one private weakness

– for Russian music, especially at its most intense and moving. And none more so than the *Leningrad Symphony*, even if it was conducted by an American.

He saw it as more than just a tribute to the resilience of a city. It was about determination and resolve. It was about strength. All of which he felt he needed now more than ever, to uphold the leadership of the Communist Party which he'd served for almost fifty years. To defend it against the enemies he saw everywhere.

As the music reached its climax, the smartphones came back out, as did the laser pointers. The phones stood firm this time, like the defenders of Leningrad, determined to capture the stirring finale of the symphony.

One laser beam, this one directed from high above the stage, seemed to wander away from the main area of the hall and the main concentration of smartphones, climbing up the steep sides of the hall and into the darkened area behind the curtain. It came to a halt squarely on the forehead of the little man in the box, who seconds later toppled backwards off his chair as a single bullet followed the beam to its target.

– 2 –

Mr China

Anthony Morgan rubbed the train window with the sleeve of his coat, thinking it might have fogged up. But it made no difference to the view; the grey outlines of high-rise apartment blocks remained the same, lost in the thick smog and the fading afternoon light. Behind the apartment blocks, the vague outline of a power station billowed vast plumes of smoke and steam.

The view hadn't changed in two hours, not since the high-speed train from Shanghai slowed, shuddered and then came to a standstill in some faceless suburb of South Beijing.

He phoned his wife, figuring Cindy Wu would know what was going on, what was holding up the train. She usually did. But she said she wasn't sure, that the railway company wasn't saying anything. She said there seemed to have been some sort of security alert, an incident in Beijing, at a big concert hall they called the Egg. She said stations had been closed and that social media was filled with all sorts of crazy rumours. The usual stupid internet stuff.

"And the smog's pretty awful," she said. "I hope you brought a good mask."

They hung up. He didn't need Cindy Wu to tell him about the smog. It had been bad in Shanghai too, but not this bad, and as his train had approached the capital it felt to Morgan like he was passing through a grey tunnel without end.

It was the reason he tried to avoid Beijing. The relentless smog. But he needed to sort out Bud, Bud from Alabama, and he had to do it in person. His reputation was at stake.

He was planning to dine with him early at one of the finest restaurants in Beijing. After that, they were going together to the National Museum on Tiananmen Square, where Morgan had got Bud an invitation to a reception for top foreign business leaders and policy-makers, and hosted by the Prime Minister himself. Trying to make Bud feel important.

He looked at his invitation, requesting the company of one Anthony Alastair Morgan OBE, China Director, MacMaster and Brown. The reception started at seven thirty. Dinner was already looking very tight, and the train still wasn't moving.

Every five minutes or so, a looped recorded announcement said they would soon be arriving at Beijing South and to remember all your belongings. A carriage attendant just shrugged when angry passengers cornered him, asking what was happening. Eventually he retreated to his small cubicle at the end of the carriage, locking the door behind him.

Then Morgan's iPhone rang. It was Bud and he wasn't happy. Ranting, telling Morgan it was no fucking way to do business. Not when you're about to move an entire fucking production line to China. He said it was a big fucking deal, and asked how the fuck the Chinese guy who was supposed to be his business partner could just disappear. What the fuck was that all about?

"You vouched for him, Tony. You said he was solid, that he had the connections to make the deal happen."

Anthony Morgan said weird things happened sometimes. This was China. Calm down, he said, don't worry, there was probably a simple explanation, that he'd figure it out.

"The guy's got a good track record, Bud. He's dependable. He's honest."

"Honest isn't the issue here, Tony. It's whether he can deliver on the deal."

Morgan suggested they talk about it later over dinner, and Bud said, "Sure, let's do that. But we have to sort this out, Tony. I trusted you."

Then Bud hung up.

And Morgan felt like screaming, "Do you think I don't know that?"

Bud was an idiot. But that wasn't unique to him. It was the same wherever they came from. Whether they were German toy makers, British shoe companies or Aussie retailers looking for cheap shirts, most first-time buyers or investors in China didn't have a clue, thinking business could be done just like at home. Except a good deal cheaper. That wasn't really what bothered Morgan, since that was how he made his money, guiding them around the obstacles. He could deal with idiots. Did it all the time.

No, the real issue was his credibility as the go-to man on doing business in China. He was Mr China. He couldn't afford for that to be damaged. Bud was right, it was an issue of trust, and Morgan and his wife had done the due diligence on Bud's Chinese business partner, who seemed to tick all the right boxes, with top-level Party connections. He'd been personally recommended to Morgan by a senior aide to the Prime Minister. But now the guy had gone missing. Just before he was supposed to sign the deal. Just like that.

It was another hour before the train shuddered, creaked and began to move again. Morgan looked out at the smog, the train crawling past the distorted outlines of tall trees, which morphed into monster-like power transmission lines. The whole carriage smelt of soot. His head was starting to ache, a dull pain that seemed to get worse each time he lifted it. Or looked out of the window.

He messaged Bud, apologising because he wouldn't now make dinner, and saying he'd meet him at the reception. Bud messaged back saying he understood, not to worry, that it was no problem. Sounding like he'd calmed down a bit. But Morgan did worry, convinced that Bud would see it as another black mark against him.

He opened his bag on his knee and after digging beneath clothes he found a small silver hip flask, which he opened and from which he took a sip of whisky. He replaced the top, but then had second thoughts and removed it again, a bigger slurp this time.

There were several small compartments in the inner lining of his bag, where he kept a collection of pollution masks, ranging from simple surgical-style devices to thicker and fussier models with bulbous external filters, an array of indecipherable numbers, and names like Dust Busters and Smog Beaters.

The 'Rolls-Royce' of his armoury was a big grey contraption with a replacement filter guaranteeing "maximum ventilation without sacrificing filtration", according to the blurb on the packet. He removed one of those as the train edged into the station.

As he left the train, Morgan noticed the station wasn't as busy as usual, and there were a lot of police, armed police, especially at the exits, watching people come and go. But his mind was elsewhere – on Bud and the reputation he needed to salvage.

There was no sign of his driver, and when he phoned his office they told him that cars hadn't been allowed near the station. So he put on the big grey anti-pollution mask, and left the station, walking through the smoggy gloom for five minutes before finding a taxi.

"Beijing not okay. Air is terrible. Terrible," the driver said before lighting a cigarette.

The traffic moved quickly, and it took just half an hour to get to the museum, or at least a couple of blocks away from it, since Tiananmen Square had been closed off. Morgan paid the driver and walked the rest of the way, wheeling his bag and showing his invitation to get past a line of police, who searched him and his bag at the entrance to the square.

When he entered the main foyer of the museum, the first thing he heard was Bud, well before he saw him, sounding off to a group of executives drinking coffee near the entrance.

"I'm an end game guy. I like to know where we're going. I don't like to circle around," Bud was telling them, and the others were nodding, like they understood that stuff.

It seemed to Morgan like the man was broadcasting to the entire museum, and within five minutes from across the foyer he knew the price of the polyresin he used on his production line, where in Montgomery, Alabama, he went to church and the hassles his wife had faced at the Great Wall the day before.

Then guides arrived, saying there would be a short tour before the reception, which had been delayed because the Prime Minister was running late. They divided everyone into groups, saying they were standing in the largest museum in the world under one roof.

Morgan joined Bud's group as they were led into an exhibition called The Road to Rejuvenation, and a few minutes later they were standing around a glass display cabinet studying a white cowboy hat.

Bud crouched down for a better look, like he was examining a priceless artefact, while the guide said that it had been given to China's then Paramount Leader during a visit to America. She then led the group to another larger display cabinet to look at a chair that the same leader had sat in during an inspection tour to Southern China.

"Deng Xiaoping was the architect of China's reform and opening," she said.

Bud asked the guide about a jacket hung next to the chair, and she said that was the jacket Deng had worn when he sat in the chair.

"Wow," said Bud. "Is that right?"

"Today China is facing a brilliant future of great rejuvenation," the guide said, looking straight at Bud. "The exhibition clearly demonstrates the historic course of the Chinese people of choosing Marxism, the Communist Party of China, the socialist road and the reform and opening up policy."

As they moved on Morgan tapped Bud on the arm.

"I'm glad you could make it along," he said. "Sorry about dinner."

"No problem, Tony. And thanks for getting me on the guest list here. There are some real big hitters. But we've really gotta sort stuff out."

"I'm working on that, Bud, and I already have another potential partner lined up for you."

"And this one ain't gonna disappear on us?"

Morgan laughed that off, saying it was all part of the fun of doing business here and telling Bud to keep the faith, that China was the future. That you had to ride the bumps. You had to be part of it.

Bud then stopped and began looking around.

"If you're looking for anything about the Great Leap Forward or the Cultural Revolution, well they aren't part of official history," he said, trying to sound light-hearted, but making a serious point.

And Bud said, "Sorry Tony, what's that?"

"Millions died, but you'll find nothing here. Nor on the Tiananmen Square massacre of 1989."

"I was looking for the washroom," said Bud, finally spotting a sign. "Tiananmen? That was the riot thing, right?"

And Morgan said yeah, something like that, thinking that Bud would do well in business in China. His hosts would love him.

The museum lined the eastern side of Tiananmen Square, overlooking Mao's mausoleum, in which the Great Helmsman and star of the museum was lying embalmed. Although the square was lit, it was hard to see Mao's resting place through the smog.

The tour ended back in the museum's giant entrance foyer, close to where a series of steep escalators took visitors to its distant and remote corners, and under a statue of Mao and his generals. Mao was in the middle and taller than all the others. He was always taller.

The Prime Minister's reception was in the museum's Central Hall, its walls lined with dozens of paintings on the Communist Revolution, including one that stretched the entire length of its far wall, the founding ceremony of the People's Republic of China. Mao in the middle. He was the tallest again.

The room quickly filled, servers dressed in white weaving their way through Chinese officials and their VIP guests. Trays in their gloved hands were laden with drinks and snacks.

Morgan took a glass of sparkling wine.

"Seventeen metres wide, Tony," said an official who had appeared at Morgan's side and was pointing at the big painting, in front of which a small podium had been set up for the Prime Minister.

"Oh hello, Mr Liu," Morgan said to the official who he recognised as Liu Fangu, a top economic aide to the Prime Minister. "It's certainly big."

"I need to ask a favour of you, Tony," said Liu, and Morgan said sure, what could he do? Liu gently took his elbow and guided him to a quieter corner of the hall under another painting of Mao, this time standing on the edge of a cliff, hands behind his back.

"My son will soon be graduating from university, in computer science," Liu said.

And Morgan said wow, that boy certainly sounds smart.

"I was hoping to find him an internship in finance, maybe in Hong Kong, to get a bit of experience with an international company, like your own."

Morgan said that shouldn't be a problem, that he'd see what he could do.

He wasn't always sure what to make of Mr Liu. He was in

small part responsible for the Bud mess, since it was he who'd first recommended to Morgan the man who was supposed to be Bud's partner, a young entrepreneur doing a lot of high-tech stuff down south. But Liu still had the ear of the Prime Minister, that's what really mattered, and that's why Morgan would help his son.

Then there was a burst of applause as the Prime Minister entered the hall, grinning like a Cheshire cat, waving and grabbing outstretched hands as he made his way towards the podium, onto which he climbed and thanked everyone for coming.

"China is an ancient civilisation with 5,000 years of history," he said. Morgan had lost count of the number of times he'd heard Chinese leaders trot that one out. It was a standard speech-opener, putting the upstarts in their place, reminding the Americans that as history goes, they were not even out of diapers.

Then he said this was a challenging time for Beijing, that lower economic growth rates were the new normal as they tried to rebalance the economy and shift away from investment-led growth to growth driven more by consumers and innovation.

A former US Treasury Secretary led a brief round of applause.

The Prime Minister raised his glass and offered a toast to cooperation and a rosy economic future.

"Hear, hear," said the assembled guests.

Morgan glanced at Bud, who had a wide grin on his face, enjoying the moment and feeling important, like the Prime Minister was addressing him personally, like he had a seat at the top table. Which is pretty much as Morgan had intended.

The Prime Minster said investors would always be welcome and that they and their intellectual property would be protected. He offered personally to address any problems they encountered, which generated more applause.

And then he left. Waving, shaking more hands.

Morgan watched him go. He'd heard the Prime Minister speak before, and thought that this time, behind his platitudes and the indelible grin, he seemed flustered, like his mind was elsewhere.

Morgan left the hall with Bud, suggesting they grab a drink at a nearby hotel, on Chang'an Avenue, just off Tiananmen Square, and Bud said yeah, let's do that, we've got a lot to talk about.

They lined up to collect their coats, and on leaving each guest was given a cloth bag with an embroidered museum logo. The bag contained a book by the Communist Party leader called *The Governance of China*, together with a desk calendar showing the highlights of the National Museum. There was also a bright orange memory stick with the museum logo and containing images of what it called cultural highlights of Beijing.

It took Morgan and Bud ten minutes to walk to the Beijing Hotel, where they sat in a bar just off reception. The bar was backed by a big fish tank, a couple of baby sharks going round in circles. Tall windows looked out onto Chang'an, but the smog was now so thick they could barely see the tall buildings on the other side of the road.

Morgan began to tell Bud about the history of the hotel, about how the famous image from the Tiananmen Square massacre, the man facing down a tank, had been taken from a room in this very hotel. That it was right outside here. But he stopped in mid-sentence, Bud not listening, his attention elsewhere, watching the waiter feeding the sharks, sprinkling some stuff in the water that got them pretty excited. Tank man.

Instead he told him about the smog.

"It can be bad in the winter," Morgan said. "When it's cold, and without much wind. The smog gets trapped over the city. There are a couple of decent phone apps which give regular smog readings."

"I guess this is what you Brits call a pea-souper," Bud said, looking out of the window, where the streetlights had given the smog a yellowish-green tint.

"The good news is that the Government's making big efforts to clean it up, and when the Government decides something in China it usually happens," Morgan said, just as the server arrived with a bottle of Moët in an ice bucket and two glasses.

"What's with the bubbly?" Bud said, as the server popped the cork and began to pour the champagne.

"We're celebrating a great future for you in China," Morgan said. "And how a little setback is not going to get in the way of that." He told Bud he'd been working in China for thirty years, but that it could still be a bit of a learning curve. "You'll emerge stronger. You'll see."

Bud relaxed as the bubbly went down, saying yeah I guess, and he thanked Morgan for his support.

Then he said, "I just don't get it. I thought a deal was a deal. And this was a fucking big deal. An entire production line. And it could have led to more. You may just think of them as garden gnomes, Tony, but we have advanced engineering processes that are world class. 3D printing. We've even licensed some of our processes to the aerospace industry. Imagine that. From gnomes to jet fighters. I was prepared to transfer that stuff over here, to share it. At least some of it. The bits I'm allowed to."

Bud opened his laptop and showed Morgan pictures of one of his Alabama production lines, full of little men with long white beards, one in sunglasses, another on a bike. The next one picking its nose. One more giving the finger. Lasers were moulding the resin. "World class, Tony. Individually tailored gnomes. And it doesn't have to be just gnomes."

Morgan said he had a plan.

"Let's at least get up and running with the lower-end stuff," he said. "I have already lined up a good company that can get you started. A Hong Kong entrepreneur owns it, with factories down south, in Shenzhen. He's reliable. I've known him for years. He'll get you going until we find a full-on partner that can handle the more sophisticated products."

Bud said that sounded encouraging, but the deal needed to be solid. He said politics back home were difficult right now and he was getting a lot of bullshit about shifting jobs to China.

Morgan said he understood, and ordered another bottle of the Moët, changing the subject and asking about Bud's wife and his plans now for the rest of his China trip. Bud said he'd stay for a couple more days in Beijing, see the sights, before coming down to Shanghai.

Morgan asked him what he had in mind and offered to provide a car and driver, and Bud said that would be great, though he wasn't quite sure where to go. He then dug around in the bag he'd been given in the museum, taking out the bright orange *Cultural Highlights* memory stick.

"Let's see what they recommend," he said, inserting the device in a USB port on his laptop. It took a couple of minutes for the computer to recognise the drive. Then an icon appeared on the desktop with the name *Beijing Surprises*. Bud opened it to reveal a list of tourist spots, starting with the Forbidden City and Winter Palace. He clicked on the Winter Palace and a slideshow began, and he said, "Nice pictures." But the slideshow kept freezing, like the memory stick had other things on its mind.

"It's a new computer," said Bud, shaking his head. "I don't get why it's so fucking slow."

Then an alert box appeared on the screen saying a programme it identified with lots of weird letters and numbers was seeking permission to access his computer.

"For fuck's sake," said Bud. "This is so fucking annoying." He clicked the box that said yes, to let the programme in. The laptop speeded up after that, and Bud looked at a couple more slideshows: a famous duck restaurant and a space museum. When he went to close the memory stick window it got stuck again and didn't want to eject. So he just pulled it out.

They drained the rest of the champagne and Morgan said they should meet again in Shanghai and that he was sure things would work out.

"We'll have you up and running in China in no time," Morgan said.

"I'm relying on you, Tony," Bud said, getting impatient with his laptop, which was whirring and refusing to shut down, like it had a lot going on.

"God I hate computers," Bud said. "They can be so fucking stupid."

– 3 –

The Gasping Dragon

The aliens just kept coming, wave after wave of them. Faster than he could blast them out of the sky. The situation looked desperate, but not completely lost. Not yet. Because he was Wang Chu, leader of the resistance, saviour of the universe.

He swung his battleship violently to the right, and then dived before climbing rapidly, guns blazing, taking out several more alien gunships. Take that you sucker! He used a sudden meteor shower for cover, and ducked behind a red planet, just as an alien laser blew a large chunk of it away. Awesome!

Warning lights flashed on his control panel. He'd been hit, but the battle was turning. The meteors had destroyed a big chunk of the alien fleet, and he spun his limping battleship around, emerging from cover for the final showdown.

Then the battery of his smartphone died, and the intergalactic battlefield disappeared, replaced by a blank screen. Shit! He leapt from his chair and towards a power socket that was hanging from the wall, straining under the weight of adapters. He fumbled with the leads, looking for the right one, almost pulling the socket out completely, desperate to get power back in the phone. To get back into battle.

He'd been fighting the aliens for hours. He'd lost count of how many.

This was only the second time he'd left his chair all day. The first was to go to the bathroom, when he simply couldn't hold on any longer. He'd then gone out to fetch noodles for lunch from a local stall, figuring that eating might not be a bad idea either. He could have ordered online. He had at least three apps for that, but had wanted to go outside, to clear his head and finalise his battle plan. To push the aliens out of his galaxy and move to the next level of the game.

By the time he'd got back with the noodles his eyes had been watering and he had a scratchy throat. The sooty air outside was so bad he could taste it.

Waiting for his phone to charge was agonising and he fidgeted awkwardly in his seat, which was beside the room's only window, overlooking a cluttered courtyard. Though all he could see through the smog was the vague outline of the neighbouring apartment block. Its dark red wall and jumble of wires, window bars and pot plants had become a kind of surrealist smudge.

His smartphone returned to life with a chorus of buzzes and beeps. He made another lunge for the socket, grabbing his phone like some hungry predator smothering its prey, then sitting on the floor beside the socket, keeping the phone plugged in, not wanting to jeopardise the victory that was so close.

The battlefield reappeared, but he immediately threw the phone to the floor with a groan. The game hadn't saved his settings, so he'd have to start the battle all over again. It was beyond annoying. He'd seemed so close to winning. So close to the next level.

He sat for perhaps five minutes, his head in his hands, before picking up the phone again, deciding to see what was trending online and finding a video of a Tibetan mastiff dog that a zoo had tried to pass off as an African lion.

A report alongside said the zoo had sent the original lion elsewhere for breeding, replacing it with the mastiff, which does have a furry brown coat and bit of a mane. But they were exposed when their lion started to bark.

Another dog was being passed off as a wolf.

It had already been shared hundreds of thousands of times.

Only when somebody posted a digitally enhanced picture of a local Communist Party leader, with a hairy mane and a caption, "Real or fake?", did the censors step in, and posts started disappearing, replaced with a message saying the connection had been lost. Access denied. Deleted by the unseen but all-watching hand of the internet police.

But the story was already out there, embellished by rumours of llamas dressed as giraffes and a labrador posing as a donkey.

Wang reposted the original story to *The Gasping Dragon*, his Twitter-like account, which had more than 100,000 followers.

He shared another video of a man who'd released a box of bees in a crowded metro station after security had prevented him taking them on the train. He thought that was pretty funny too.

He then saw a series of photos and a video, spreading fast. Going viral. Armed paramilitary police running. Others pushing, looking angry. A row of armoured vehicles, shot from a distance. Ambulances. Frantic-looking paramedics pushing a stretcher trolley. It was hard to tell what was going on, since many were blurry, shot and then uploaded with unsteady hands. Smartphones on the move.

In the background of several was the vague outline of a vast egg-like roof, its dome floodlit and just about penetrating the thick smog.

There was a video too, which already had hundreds of thousands of likes. It showed a balding older man, a foreigner, wearing a dinner jacket and bow tie, red-faced and shouting, demanding to be allowed out of somewhere that looked like a hall. There was a stage behind him full of abandoned musical instruments. The hall looked full, but everybody's attention was on the foreigner, round rimless glasses hanging from one of his ears, and waving around what looked like a little baton. Police wrestled him to the ground.

Wang shared the video to *The Gasping Dragon*.

He then went back to the photos, intending to share them too, but they'd been deleted. The internet censors were erasing them almost as quickly as they were being posted.

Then the screen of his smartphone went black again and the phone started quacking at him, sounding like a demented duck. It was the ringtone he'd assigned to his mother, whose name appeared across the screen. He hesitated and then pressed the red button that rejected her call. He felt a momentary sense of relief, but that quickly turned to guilt. He knew he should have picked up, her third attempt that day, but he didn't know what to say to her.

He opened a messaging app and saw eleven marked as new. Three were spam, investment schemes promising massive returns on money Wang didn't have, and which he deleted. Two were from a university tutor and marked "URGENT. PLEASE READ", while the rest were from his mother.

He deleted the messages from the university without opening them. They weren't the first warnings he'd received from his tutor and he knew pretty much what they'd say, chasing work he hadn't done, and giving him yet another final deadline.

He then sat looking at the unopened messages from his mother. He scratched his knee and tried to control a sudden trembling in his right foot. It was a nervous reaction usually triggered by any communication from his parents.

He opened the most recent message, which began with the familiar question about why he hadn't been in touch or returned her calls. His mother then asked about his girlfriend, saying she couldn't wait to meet her. Was she the one he would settle down with? When was he going to bring her home? It was a long and rambling message, going on to say she was so pleased he had so many job offers and that studying in America sounded fantastic too. It was good to have options. She said she was so proud that he was making the most of his studies, grasping opportunities never available to her or his father.

The foot tremor got worse, so did the itch. There was no girlfriend, and there were no options. The graduate job market sucked. Studying in America was his dream, but a pipe dream unless he could raise some serious cash. And that assumed he could even get the grades, which at that moment seemed like a distant prospect. He'd made it all up to humour his parents.

It wasn't as if he could deflect their attention onto a brother or sister, since he had neither. He was an only child, a product of China's one-child policy, and his parents had invested all their hopes in him. He got that. At least he did when he thought about it, if he thought about it at all. Which wasn't very often. Mostly he just saw nagging.

He pressed Reply, wrote "Hi Mum", and then for five minutes sat looking at the screen. He couldn't think of anything else to write, so saved the empty message to drafts. It would have to wait until he felt more inspired. Or creative.

Instead he joined a university chat room that was running an online competition for the ugliest snowman.

Beijing had just had a heavy snowfall, and Wang voted for a bug-eyed creature made of three big snowballs stacked on each other. Its out-sized head had dark shadows around small eyes made of bottle-tops, a carrot nose and a receding hairline, the colouring created from a liberal layering of mud.

For good measure he posted a picture of the Prime Minister alongside the snowman with the caption, "Spot the difference", thinking they really did look similar.

Which then started an online trend, with each new ugly snow creature accompanied by some official or celebrity it most closely resembled. The thread was terminated and the chat deleted by internet censors soon afterwards, but only after Wang had commented online that they should be careful because the ugly snowmen might take offence at being unfairly likened to government officials.

He looked again at the one that looked like the Prime Minister and thought he had a problem with his screen because the snow wasn't white, but more dirty grey. But then he remembered this was Beijing snow, and he figured the snow picked up a lot of filth and toxins from the smog on its way down, before it settled on the ground. He shared that thought online too, together with a picture of a pair of disfigured zombie hands he'd grabbed from a movie poster.

"Beware of the toxic snow!" He then wrote, "I went outside to have fun with snowballs and came home a zombie."

Then he found a video that seemed to have been taken by a passenger from an aircraft window. It showed a baggage handler lazily throwing boxes and bags onto a conveyor belt to the aircraft and mostly missing, the contents spilling all over the floor, and the man not giving a shit. Funny.

He was alone in a two-room fifth-floor apartment he shared with two other students in a shabby low-rise block in a district called Haidian, in the north west of Beijing, the university district. This is where he called home, though for the most part he lived in a wild online world beyond the screens of his computers, where he could conquer just about any world he wanted, or at least have a fighting chance at doing so.

He was tall and thin, topped by a mop of unkempt black hair and large black-rimmed glasses. On the rare occasions he did get to see his mother, she would tell him how unhealthy he looked and declare that he was incapable of looking after himself and needed a woman in his life, either her or the elusive girlfriend. Perhaps both. And as annoying as Wang found the lecture, his mother was not entirely wrong.

He was wearing a thick black coat and a pair of fingerless gloves, the coat to keep him warm, the gloves to leave his fingers free to work his keyboards. A chunky radiator heated the room, but as the Beijing winter began to bite it struggled to counter the bitter cold that seeped in through a badly fitted window frame.

Once he'd regained control of his trembling right foot, he put both feet up on the ledge below the window. He placed a battered laptop on one knee, while at the same time he pummelled the well-worn keys of his smartphone. There were broadening cracks on both screens.

The laptop was a Lenovo think-pad, which used to be called an IBM before the Chinese company bought the American computer-maker. At least that's what it said on the case. Wang's model had been revved-up, souped-up and generally customised in every imaginable way, with the finest software that could be copied.

The smartphone was new, but with plenty of mileage. It was a local model that looked a lot like an iPhone, but at a fraction of the price.

The main room was lined on two sides by bunk beds, with sheets hung along the side of each bed for privacy, and also to shield those who chose to sleep from those who didn't, from the bright lights of computer screens working into the night.

In the small kitchen, a sink was overflowing with used plastic lunch boxes and disposable wooden chopsticks. Hardened slithers of noodle clung to the boxes and to the sink.

Wang looked out again at the smoggy smudge beyond his window, raised his phone and took a photograph. He then strapped on a soiled surgical-style mask, extended his arm, raising his eyebrows in a look of horror and took a selfie, which he uploaded to his *Gasping Dragon* account.

He removed the mask and threw it towards the sink, but it ricocheted off a lunch box, scattering several cockroaches that had taken up residence inside. It was a PM2.5 Mega Blocker, a small logo said so on the front, and it was one of the products Wang sold through an online shop he ran with his roommates.

The name of the mask referred to the tiny and deadliest particles of air pollution, able to penetrate deep into the lungs and blood stream, and leading to heart attacks and premature death, or so said a report he'd read, which he'd copied for the sales blurb, together with warnings that Beijing's toxic air routinely reached levels multiple times the maximum recommended by international health experts.

He thought that was a good sales pitch and the mask had sold well, at least initially. Unfortunately, Wang's PM2.5 Mega Blocker was neither mega nor much of a blocker. The shop was being bombarded with complaints that it didn't work. The roommates had a consistent approach to complaints. They ignored them. And after firing up his Lenovo, Wang began to delete the latest crop from their website.

One buyer moaned that she might as well hold tissue paper to her mouth, which made Wang smile, since the Mega Blocker was largely that: tissue paper. There'd been so many complaints the roommates had decided to remove the mask from the shop, at least for the time being.

The masks were made at a small Haidian workshop from which Wang and his roommates frequently sourced their products. There were few things that could not be copied or concocted by its feisty owner, a man they called Fatso.

Wang and his roommates didn't have a lot in common, but if there was one thing they did agree on, it was the need to make money. Lots of it. Wang had been telling the truth when he'd told his mother that he wanted to study in America. That bit he hadn't made up. What he didn't tell her was that he still had no offer of a place and no money to pay for it.

The problem for the roommates was that the greater their entrepreneurial zeal, the further they seemed to fall into debt.

Smog-protection gear had seemed a no-brainer. It had become big business since the smog became smog. For years the Communist Party had described it as fog, a weather issue, or a foreign conspiracy on account of a small air quality sensor on the roof of the US Embassy which tweeted regular and scary updates.

Mostly, though, they'd called it an internet rumour.

Until it became so bad it could no longer be denied.

For Wang and his roommates, masks had been the easiest smog business to get into, though sales of air purifiers were also booming, as were pollution apps, which had become standard on any smartphone in China, where a check on smog levels was now routine most mornings.

Wang looked at the screen of his phone, where a pollution app used as an icon the face of a woman with a mask. The badge on the icon said "428", which it described as hazardous. "Stay indoors", it recommended. The smog index had a scale of one to 500. When it exceeded 500, the air became too bad to be measured.

There were more beeps from his phone. More alerts. The Communist Party had made a rare online statement in response to the weird security images he'd seen earlier, saying there was no truth in stories of what it called "something going wrong in the capital". Not only were these rumours, they were scurrilous rumours.

In Wang's online world that meant they were probably true – or at least a little bit true. That *something* must have happened. Even though the images had largely been deleted, the Party's denial fired up the online rumour mill.

There'd been a terrorist attack, a bunch of machete-wielding Islamic militants on the loose. The roof of a hall had collapsed, trapping hundreds of people. There'd been an industrial disaster, a factory exploding. Poison gas had seeped in during a concert. A senior government official had been assassinated. There'd been a coup attempt.

It had happened at the concert hall known as the Egg. Or possibly the airport. A luxury hotel maybe. The city's main railway station. Possibly all four.

Wang felt inspired. So he did a quick search online and found an old photograph of American tanks in the Iraqi desert, preparing for an assault on somewhere called Baghdad. He added a caption saying the People's Liberation Army was crossing the Gobi Desert and bearing down on Beijing and posted it to *The Gasping Dragon*.

He then took a glass cup to his kitchen for a refill with hot water, and was pleased to find there was still life in the congealed tea leaves that had been sitting for two days at the bottom of the glass.

He was feeling creative now, so quickly went back to his phone, wanting to have some more fun. He opened *The Gasping Dragon*, and wrote:

Under cover of the smog aliens have landed and taken control of Zhongnanhai.

He looked at the words for a while. Zhongnanhai was the name of the Communist Party's leadership compound next to the Forbidden City. He knew that any reference to that place risked being quickly deleted by the internet censors, who seemed to be busy that day.

So he opened a file of clip art and replaced the word Zhongnanhai with a small picture of a cigarette, since this was also the name of one of China's best-selling brands. Then he looked at it again.

Under cover of the smog aliens have landed and taken control of

He liked that, and was about to share it when he got worried about aliens, thinking that might get blocked too. So he went back into his clip-art file and settled on a picture of a stick alien, with which he replaced the word 'alien' in his post.

"That should work," he said to himself. He looked again at his creation, smiled and then shared it.

Under the cover of smog *have landed and taken control of*

Wang slumped down in his chair, closed his eyes and within moments was asleep.

While he slept, precisely one hour twenty-seven minutes and fourteen seconds later, an internet censor who knew a thing or two about cigarettes deleted his post. But by then it had been shared more than three million times.

The alien had escaped.

– 4 –

Airpocalypse Pale Ale

Chuck Drayton liked to tell anybody who would listen that the old mansion housing the US Consulate in Shanghai had once been the home of drug dealers and torturers. And he reckoned he could learn a thing a two from both when it came to convincing American businesses about the threat from Chinese hackers.

He left the consulate through a series of clanking and pinging security doors leading out onto the tree-lined streets of the city's old French Concession, wishing they'd all get hacked because maybe then the fuckers would take him seriously.

He needed a beer after the disaster that had been his afternoon.

He crossed the road, shaking off an old shoeshine man who chased his feet, trying to land a dollop of paste, and passed the nearby mansion that housed the Iranian consulate, right next door to the local branch of Hooters. He thought about slipping in there, maybe catch a mullah or two letting their hair down.

The thing about the French Concession was the choice. Sure there was Hooters, and plenty of other tacky places, but there were also a whole host of cool boutiques, cafés and restaurants inside the rows of French-style mansions and shophouses.

Plenty of simple places too, with local food.

It took him five minutes to reach a pub, a microbrewery run by an enterprising guy from Minnesota, where he took a seat in a corner and ordered a pint of Airpocalypse Pale Ale. The beer was usually called Shanghai Wallop, a hoppy little brew, but they changed the name on polluted days and gave discounts linked to the air quality readings, which had reached unhealthy levels. Thirty per cent off.

It was a gimmick, but it brought in the crowds. Air purifiers humming in the corner helped too.

The consulate that morning had organised a seminar on cybercrime, and had invited a bunch of American business people based in Shanghai, as well as executives visiting from the States for some big trade fair and conference.

They could have held it at the consular section, but that was a soulless place above a shopping mall on the Nanjing Road, the city's main shopping street. It had been Drayton's idea to use the mansion, which had history. They'd like that. It was more secure too, behind tall walls and even taller trees.

And they'd recently had it renovated, bringing in American contractors, to preserve the beauty and get rid of the listening devices, at least the ones they could find.

It had been built in 1921, French Renaissance-style, and was at first home to a big British trading company that had once grown rich shipping opium to China. During the cruelty and madness of the Cultural Revolution it had been a centre for what the Communist Party called "political education", which to Drayton meant large-scale fingernail extraction.

The turnout at the seminar had been pitiful. Twenty people, mostly looking like they'd rather be somewhere else.

Still, he'd tried to grab their attention straight away, shock them a bit, saying that cybercrime was an epidemic costing the world economy US$600 billion every year.

"Think about that," he'd said. "And the bad guys are always one step ahead with this stuff."

He'd told them that in China cyber spying against US companies seemed like part of government policy, that copying was easier and cheaper than inventing.

"We're witnessing the biggest theft of knowledge ever," he'd said, telling them there were two types of American company: those who'd been hacked, and those who'd been hacked but just didn't yet know it.

He'd told them they had to look at everyday stuff in a different way. That a car wasn't a car anymore. It was a computer with an engine and four wheels. A smartphone was a computer that happened to make calls. It was the same for connected cameras, fitness trackers, kettles and fridges. Even pacemakers and toys.

They were all computers, and they were all online.

"All of them can spy on you. Some of them could kill you," he'd said.

He'd looked around at blank faces, at least those not looking out the window at the consulate's rock garden and carp pond.

"And you want to know who's most vulnerable? Just take a look at the Communist Party's five-year plan. The last one named energy, healthcare and steel as areas they wanted to develop. And guess what? That's where we saw most US companies hacked. And suddenly Chinese companies are coming out with technology which looks a lot like ours."

He'd paused for questions.

One lonely arm at the back; its owner had identified himself as a man called Bud from Alabama. He'd asked whether this wasn't all a bit paranoid and whether a good anti-virus would do the trick. Drayton had said that a little paranoia wasn't a bad thing, and that an anti-virus looked at known threats, not new ones. And that it was the unknown ones that were really worrying.

Bud and another man then left, saying thanks, but they had a meeting to get to. Drayton had said no problem, he fully understood, but hating them for walking out on him like that and thinking about fingernail extraction, thumb-screws or something worse.

He'd ploughed on.

"Now they're talking about green tech, renewables, defence, health. And you know what that means?"

More blank faces. At least they'd had no phones to play with. They'd had to surrender them as a security measure on the way in.

"If you are into any of that, or any advanced technical processes for that matter, then you've got to bolster your cyber defences. And even if you're not into any of that, you've still gotta be vigilant."

He'd told them if somebody stole from you something physical, cardboard files say, then you'd know about that. Maybe the thief hits you on the head and runs off. You'd certainly be aware of that. But with cyber you may never know it's gone, at least not for months or longer, only after your plans have been copied, and some Chinese company has brought your Big Idea to market before you.

"And even then, it's hard to prove who stole it," he'd said. "Digital forensics is tough."

He'd then gone through a bunch of defences, like *never* opening attachments you're not really confident about, and absolutely avoiding memory sticks, since they're the most common ways of passing on an infection. He said both might contain malware, the weapons that can take over computers, suck out information. He'd explained about using a VPN, software to disguise where you are at and access banned sites.

"And cover the camera on your computer. They can take over that too," he'd said, asking them to tell him about their own experiences, but just seeing more blank faces.

"You won't make this go away by pretending it isn't happening," he'd said to the group, which appeared to be doing its best to pretend his talk wasn't happening.

He'd just felt like screaming, come on, guys, have you not listened to a fucking word I've said?

He ordered another Airpocalypse Pale Ale. Forty per cent off this time, since the air quality reading had just passed another fifty-point threshold. He'd be drinking for free soon if this continued.

He'd asked how many of them used encryption, and they just looked at him like he was speaking some ancient language or was describing a mind-bending drug. He'd said to think of encryption as like Ironman or the Hulk. Pretty menacing, but basically on your side. Which got a smile or two, kind of deranged smiles that got Drayton thinking that maybe they'd been popping their own mind-benders.

He'd finished his talk with another plea to share their experiences, absolutely confident they wouldn't. They might whinge to the consulate or the Chamber of Commerce privately, but he knew that few would want to jeopardise their relationship with Chinese partners who in many cases were the ones ripping off their secrets.

And if they had been attacked they wouldn't want to advertise their cyber stupidity to rivals or clients.

It made no sense to Drayton.

Right at the end, as a kind of experiment, he'd asked the group how many of them did social media. Facebook, Twitter, LinkedIn, Instagram, that kind stuff. Just a handful of arms went up, and with no great enthusiasm. Sure, they were an older crowd, but when they didn't even do social media, how would they even begin to grasp the threat from bad guys breaking into their computers?

He was sure glad that was over, and now tried to focus on his beer and a sorry-looking plate of fries. Then his iPhone rang, the *Mission Impossible* theme. At first he ignored it, switching the phone to silent, and went back to the beer. But moments later the phone rang again, and this time he took the call.

"Hey Debbie babe, what's up? Must be kinda early over there."

"Yeah, it's real early, Chuck, but every other time I've tried you your phone was off. It's always off, or else you just don't pick up."

Drayton said sorry, he'd been busy, and if it was about the house, the roof stuff, then to go ahead and get that fixed and he'd get the money over by the end of the week.

"That's what you said last week, Chuck, and these roof guys they want to see money up front before they start climbing up there."

She said the roof would never have been damaged if he'd sorted the trees, cutting them back, like she asked, that it was an accident waiting to happen. She said that all it took was one winter storm, the branches hammering the roof.

Drayton said, sure, he'd deal with it, but that he really needed to go now, that he was in the middle of something.

"Oh yeah, and what's her name? The wife of a Chinese Government minister this time, or are you sticking with the Germans? You cooking up another diplomatic incident there, Chuck? Just let me know before I read about it in the papers."

Drayton did his best to laugh that off, telling her about the beer that was going down in price because of the shitty air, but she cut him off and said, "Fuck you, Chuck."

"You have a nice day too," Drayton said, but by the time he got the words out she'd already hung up.

They'd been separated for more than a year, Debbie still living in the Maryland house they'd once shared. She sent the big bills his way, and he always dragged his heels on paying them. It had become a kind of ritual. And every conversation they had, whether it was trees, the roof or whatever, always came back to Berlin. And Berlin had been a mess, that was for sure.

They'd been together in the German capital, where Drayton was doing a grunt political job at the embassy. She had elderly parents back home, and when her mother fell ill she'd returned to the States, leaving Drayton in Berlin alone, which was when the trouble started.

Soon after Debbie left, he'd met the wife of the German Energy Minister. She was a couple of years younger than Drayton, but almost twenty-five years younger than her husband. And she wasted no time in telling Drayton that she found the Minister a complete bore.

She busied herself with charities that organised field trips for disadvantaged kids. The embassy also gave support, sponsoring competitions and awarding the winners free trips to the States, figuring it might also help relations with the Minister, who was considering buying American turbines for a new generation of gas-fuelled power stations.

Drayton was told to stay close to the wife, which he did, joining her and one group of kids on a field trip to the Black Forest, equipped with specially donated US-made energy-efficient tents and stoves and low-water solar-powered showers. But there was nothing energy saving about Drayton's encounter with Frau Schoenberg in her tent at the end of the second day's trek and after one and half bottles of Riesling, and which left the breathable, self-inflating mattress and groundsheet flattened and in tatters.

Unfortunately for Drayton and Frau Schoenberg, the kids quickly realised what was going on. It was hard to ignore, and a good deal more entertaining than the trekking. And they knew a valuable story when they saw one.

Frau Schoenberg's husband, the Energy Minister, had political enemies, and there was strong opposition to the turbine deal. So it wasn't long before the story of his wife's romp through the Black Forest with an American diplomat in tow was front-page news in Germany's tabloid newspapers, together with grainy photographs of the couple checking out the low-water solar-powered shower together, and apparently liking what they found.

American newspapers picked up the German stories, beginning with the *New York Post*, which is when Debbie first discovered her husband's recently found attraction to the great outdoors. He was soon on a plane back to Washington DC in disgrace, and she was consulting her lawyer.

That had seemed to put an end to a hardly promising diplomatic career, as well as his second marriage.

He'd been given a pen-pushing job on the Asia desk at the State Department in DC, which wasn't busy and gave him plenty of time at his computer or on his phone, learning the digital ropes, though mostly shooting people and blowing them up in the latest versions of *Grand Theft Auto* and *Global Offensive*. He'd taken a course in coding, computer programming, thinking he could then make his own games and maybe come up with the next blockbuster. It was just a matter of creating sufficient mayhem. That sort of shit. He'd done another in cyber security, because that sounded cool, and he figured it was the kind of stuff that might give him a way out of government service and into a real job.

When the State Department itself got hacked and somebody hauled off a pile of payroll data, Drayton was on hand with some practical advice, much along the lines of the things he'd told the seminar at the consulate that day. He instantly became an expert, the go-to guy on cyber security, since nobody else had a clue, and was despatched within weeks to China, the digital front line as far as the spooks were concerned, and where they suspected the payroll data had ended up.

Inside the consulate, Drayton was known simply as the Cyber Guy. Which was kind of cool at first. But he soon learned it meant everything and nothing. They all agreed that what he did was extremely important, without quite understanding what that was. And he reckoned that when his co-workers couldn't grasp it, what hope was there of convincing American businesses to take him more seriously?

He finished his beer, paid and headed back towards the consulate, making another call as he walked. It just rang out, so he called again. This time Sakura picked up, saying, "Yes, hello", sounding real formal, before slipping back into Japanese, continuing some other conversation.

He just loved that accent, and listened for a couple of minutes before saying, "Hey Sakura, it's me, Chuck, how you doing?"

She ignored him for a while longer and then she said, "Chuck, hi. I can't really speak now. I told you I have a trade delegation in town today and not to bother me. I'll get back to you."

He said yeah, let's talk later, and maybe they could get together that evening, have some fun. It had been a tough day.

"I'm busy this evening, Chuck. I have stuff going on. I'll call you when I'm free."

Then she hung up.

It was like, get off my case, I'll see you when I want to see you.

She worked for a Japanese business group, and he'd been seeing her for a couple of months, but it was mostly on her terms and when she wanted. The way Drayton saw it, a bit more engagement wouldn't do any harm, but then after the Berlin mess and all the crap he was getting from Debbie it mostly suited him just fine.

He loosened his tie as he walked. It was a cool day, but he was more used to an open neck. He'd put on a suit for the seminar, which he hated to do, dusting off an old two-piece that he hadn't touched in weeks, discovering that he could barely get into the trousers, which he put down to too much Peking Duck during his visit to the capital. Or all those stupid banquets while he was looking after that maestro.

He made a mental note to get a bit more exercise. Maybe start walking home from the pub. Still he didn't think he was in bad shape for a man of forty-one. He much preferred a well-worn sports jacket, black jeans and an open-neck shirt, figuring he was going to set his own dress code, because isn't that what cyber guys did? He'd grown his hair a bit too, brushing it back, thinking that was a geekier look. The glasses with their thick black rims might have to go next. They were decidedly pre-cyber.

He arrived back at the consulate with twenty minutes to spare before a National Security Agency briefing, to get the latest on the hacking stuff, enough time to collect some papers from his office at the back of the old mansion. He then headed down a stairway that led to the wine cellar that was now the secure communications room, the Bubble Room. It was behind two heavy metal doors with biometric scanners. One read his retina, another his thumb and forefinger. Security cameras and motion detectors monitored the stairs.

The room was long and narrow, a rectangular table running down the centre with chairs around the table. There were more chairs along the walls, where the original brick of the cellar had been covered with a special membrane to block electronic signals. Several big screens hung at the front of the room, though only one was live, showing another conference table at which two men and a woman were taking seats. A sign under the screen read, "Fort Meade", the NSA.

There were three others in the room with Drayton. The CIA's Shanghai Station Chief, a liaison officer from the FBI and the man called Dave, who'd come down from Beijing and still had only one name.

While they were waiting to get started, Drayton asked Dave about all the fuss at the Egg, whether they'd figured out what had actually happened that evening.

"Nothing. Absolutely nothing. At least that's what the Ambassador was told by his Chinese Government sources," said Dave.

"They told him nothing, or they told him nothing happened?"

"Both, I suspect."

"But there were photos online of armoured vehicles," Drayton said.

"The Ambassador says they're probably fake," Dave said. "One even showed tanks in a desert, but they turned out to be frigging American tanks. In Iraq. He called it the internet rumour mill on steroids."

"But *something* happened," Drayton said.

"Bomb scare maybe. Perhaps a technical thing. Who knows? But the Ambassador's satisfied it wasn't a big deal."

"All pretty odd though."

"The funniest thing was the maestro," Dave said. "Went ballistic when they stopped his show at the interval, then wouldn't let anybody out of the hall. There's a video online. Take a look."

Drayton said he'd seen it and almost felt sorry for the guy.

"Well, you're gonna love this," said Dave, tapping a file in front of him as the picture on the big screen flickered a bit then stabilised. They all confirmed they could see and hear each other.

One of the men in Fort Meade said digital forensics was an inexact science, that a lot of the attacks on American businesses had been routed through computers in Canada and Europe, which was a challenge. But he said the hackers hadn't covered their tracks well.

He said the digital fingerprints on the maestro's computer were the same as those they'd found on bigger attacks, but even clearer, that the hacking came from the same source. Then he showed a picture. It was fuzzy, but it was clearly a face, a thin middle-aged face with closely cropped hair. Military-looking. Staring at the camera. Dave had a copy in his file, which he passed to Drayton.

"This is one of our hackers," said Dave, looking smug, enjoying the confusion on Drayton's face.

"Before we returned the laptop to the maestro we added a bit of our own spyware, which we embedded in a file we created called *Notes on Ambassador Meeting.*"

The woman on the Fort Meade screen then said the decoy, as she called it, had worked well. She said that when the hackers went back into the maestro's computer they couldn't resist opening that file, which then infected the hackers' computer, taking control of their camera.

"So this is our man?" said Drayton, looking at the photograph.

"Well, one of them," Dave said.

"Cool," said Drayton. "Does the maestro know?"

"He doesn't," said Dave. "I don't think he was in a mood to be helpful. But he probably won't notice. His computer's a mess. He doesn't even have the most basic security. And we can delete the decoy remotely if we need to.

"And there's another thing," Dave said. "The maestro had photographs on his computer that shouldn't have been there. He's into some pretty weird stuff. Likes to party, dress up and take a bit of discipline when he's not waving his baton around on stage."

"He kept photos like that on his computer?" Drayton said.

"Actually they'd been deleted, but we recovered them pretty easily. Let's just call it an extra insurance policy should Mr Abramovich feel like complaining."

And for the second time that evening, Drayton almost felt sorry for the maestro. Almost.

Then one of the men on the Fort Meade screen showed a bunch of spiderweb-like drawings, and there was more techno-talk about routing and IP addresses. Drayton nodded like he understood. Then the NSA guy said the bottom line was they'd traced the attacks to a building in an area at the north end of the Bund. Satellite images showed it to be a white low-rise, maybe a warehouse, in an old neighbourhood close to the river. He showed the images on the screen.

"We think this is where we'll find our man. We need you to find out more about that place, Chuck. We think we know what they're doing there. But who are those people?"

– 5 –

@Beijing_smog

There were definitely ships on the river below because he could hear their horns, some short and sharp, others a deep-throated growl. And it seemed to Anthony Morgan that they were all sending the same shrill message to clear out of the way as they steamed blindly into the gloom.

His luxury apartment was on the twenty-fifth floor of a block called the Lucky Bund View, on the banks of the Huangpu River, in Shanghai's financial district. His floor-to-ceiling windows looked out across the river to the city's historic Bund, the riverfront sweep of grand colonial era buildings that had been the financial heart of old Shanghai. But that morning it didn't feel particularly lucky, and as for the view, the river was lost in the smog, and he could barely make out the closest of his towering neighbours.

He'd moved from Beijing to Shanghai because this was a better base for his business, closer to his clients, but also to escape the smog. But the smog had followed him there.

His was one of the most prestigious addresses in the city, largely because of that view, a US$13,000-a-month view, a deal-making view, and worth every cent as far as Morgan was concerned. The windows were the focal point of the dinners and receptions he hosted, where he would tell his guests about how that view represented the past and the future of this great city. Indeed, of China. And how every ship along that magnificent river, that throbbing commercial artery, was a building block.

"You can't afford not to be part of it," he'd say, as servers in pristine white jackets refilled champagne glasses. He'd tell his guests how in just twenty-five years the very spot where they were standing, the district of Pudong, had been transformed from swampy farmland to a forest of skyscrapers, on track to become the world's leading financial centre. And his guests would stand there nodding, enthralled by that view, and charmed by Cindy Wu, his Chinese wife and business partner, looking elegant in a long shimmering black dress, jewellery glistening around her neck.

Together they ran the China office of MacMaster and Brown, a company with Scottish roots, which had been doing business in China for 135 years. The company started as Hong Kong-based traders, but with the opening of the country had evolved into a sprawling organisation with offices in London, New York, Hong Kong and Tokyo, and offering what its glossy brochures described as "bespoke business and investment services".

After thirty years in China, Morgan liked to think of himself as a guiding hand for businesses. And whether it was identifying partners, finding factories for outsourcing production, or providing more discreet financial advice, he was regarded as the finest of Old China Hands.

Publicly, he was evangelical about the China Miracle, and could reel off the statistics without missing a beat: nearly 700 million people pulled out of poverty in two decades; average annual incomes up from US$200 to US$6,000 in just twenty-five years; the largest number of billionaires in the world. Where else had that ever been achieved in such a short period? And whether it be steel, platinum, cars, champagne or movies, if China wasn't already the world's biggest market it soon would be. He'd tell his dinner guests again, "China is the future. You need to be part of it."

Most of all, he and his wife were regarded as the best corporate investigators in the business. He had the insight and experience and she had the connections.

That's what had brought Bud to them, and Bud had a lot of money to spend. His company was one of the largest employers in

Montgomery, Alabama, his products ranging from garden gnomes to light fittings. His production processes were state-of-the-art, and now he was looking to shift a good chunk of that production to China. Morgan and his wife had given him the full Lucky Bund View treatment. They'd found him a partner, but the partner had disappeared and was now rumoured to be caught up in a corruption investigation.

Bud had every right to be annoyed. He was under pressure at home, facing a lot of hysteria about jobs lost to China. But Morgan felt he was now on top of the Bud problem. The trip to Beijing had gone well. He'd calmed the guy down. They'd take things a step at a time, starting with the gnomes at a factory down south that Morgan trusted well.

Bud was now busy seeing the sights with his wife in Beijing, chauffeured around in a MacMaster and Brown limo. Morgan had instructed the driver to give regular updates and to pay for everything. And the driver said Bud seemed happy enough, though he shouted a lot. Morgan said Bud always spoke like that.

He would give Bud the five-star treatment in Shanghai too.

Morgan walked across his vast dining room, past a heavy teak dining table so big that on smoggy days when he didn't want to go outside he'd strap on a pedometer and walk round and round it, use its perimeter as an exercise track. He reached a rosewood drinks cabinet with shiny gold handles, which he opened, and poured himself a large Jack Daniels. He closed the cabinet, but then decided the large Jack Daniels wasn't large enough, and opened it again for an extra splash.

Several US$1,000 air purifiers hummed quietly but reassuringly in the background, guaranteed, so the American manufacturer claimed, to filter out even the tiniest of toxic particles.

He lifted a remote from the dining table and turned on his television, a 52-inch, state-of-the-art, ultra-thin Panasonic, which dominated one wall in an adjoining lounge area. He caught the top of the news, CNN leading with the Shanghai smog, the anchor saying that airports and schools were closed, hospital emergency wards overrun with children and the elderly with breathing problems.

The anchor began to interview a Chinese environmentalist, who was saying something about empty government promises, but never finished because the censors cut the signal and the screen went black.

Morgan could never understand why they did that. CNN and the BBC, the big news channels, weren't available outside diplomatic compounds and hotels. Cutting the signal whenever it got interesting about China just irritated people. But then he guessed that might just be the point, so as you didn't forget who was in charge.

He quickly flicked through other channels, looking for CNBC, the business network. The censors didn't have time for the business stuff, not watching too closely, finding it boring maybe, and he wanted to catch a re-run of a chat show he'd been part of, doing what he did best: being reassuring and sounding positive about China's future.

By the time he found it, the show had reached the bit where he was telling the anchor how it was important not to overreact to the smog, that there were of course environmental challenges, which the Government understood. And that for investors there would be many opportunities in green energy.

The discussion moved on to the economy, the jittery markets, the anchor interviewing a New York-based analyst who said China's accumulation of debt was the fastest in history, that it dwarfed the run-up to the 2008 global economic crisis. He said that China had too many empty homes and factories and that when the music stopped the world economy would come tumbling down.

Then it was Morgan's turn again, and he said, "There's certainly a lot of scaremongering out there. This should not blind us to the long-term strength of the Chinese economy and the ability of the Government to deal with the challenges." He said that although China's rate of growth was slowing, it was still the envy of the world.

He thought he sounded reasonable, measured. The sort of responses that had made him a regular on the business chat shows. And he thought he looked good. A new pair of glasses with tortoiseshell frames, a little designer stubble, the closely cropped hair – at least what was left of it.

He then sat down at a laptop computer that was open on an antique desk below the window, placing the whisky down beside it. He was putting together a monthly newsletter, the *MB China Report*, for the 12,000 select subscribers – now including Bud from Alabama – who each paid US$1,700 a year for Morgan's insights into the Middle Kingdom. He began to write:

The Chinese economy and financial system are fundamentally strong. The leadership is committed to reform, to put the economy on a sounder footing. Market volatility is only to be expected.

He liked that. It was crisp and clear. But he quickly ran out of steam, not sure where to take it next. So he checked his emails, finding a new one from Geraldine MacMaster, the chairman of MacMaster and Brown, and the great-great-granddaughter of its founder.

She confirmed the date of the company's annual strategy meeting in Hong Kong, saying she'd be flying in from New York a few days before. She said she was looking forward to hearing his take on the Chinese economy, because she was hearing some pretty scary things, like it was a mess, an accident waiting to happen.

Morgan emailed her back, saying there was a lot of hysteria about China right now, and he cut and pasted a couple of the more reassuring lines from the *MB China Report*, saying he'd give a fuller presentation in Hong Kong and that China's leaders knew what they were doing.

"The Chinese economy is not about to fall off a cliff!!!" he wrote, sounding confident, emphatic.

Only he no longer believed it.

He tapped on an icon on his iPhone, a picture of a badger, and the app opened to show a map with the animated animal, a big stripe on his head, sitting on Shanghai and then burrowing into the ground before popping up in America.

The app was a VPN, a Virtual Private Network, which gave him an IP address, a digital identity outside China, a disguise, as well as allowing him to access usually blocked sites, like Twitter and Facebook.

Like the badger, he was tunnelling out of China and beyond the reach of the internet censors.

In that other world lived Morgan's alter ego, an anonymous Twitter account under the name of *@Beijing_smog*. At last count he had

338,439 followers, and he shared with them his private and darker thoughts about the future of China:

Now China's financial capital is gasping for breath. Like nuclear winter. They blame weather. What bullshit. Pollution is pollution.

Then for a while he worked in tandem, jumping between his two worlds. First his newsletter on his laptop:

Ironically, China's environmental challenges could provide investors with opportunities in several sectors. There can be no doubt about the Chinese Government's resolve to tackle the environmental challenges.

Then back to the phone, tweeting:

Brief walk outside this morning. Eyes stinging. Hospital emergency rooms reported full. Schools closed. No doubt this toxic air is a killer.

Then to his laptop again:

China has embarked on an ambitious multiyear rebalancing of its economy. It's a positive endeavour that in the long run will be a win-win for everybody.

And then he was back on *@Beijing_smog*:

China miracle is over. Built on shaky foundations. Debt out of control. Leaders hapless. Once motor of world economy, could now bring it down.

His concentration was broken by another deep and long growl of a ship's horn, and he thought he made out the distant outline of a dredger sitting impossibly low in the water. A ray of sunlight penetrated the smog, and for a moment it illuminated like a spotlight a row of paintings on his living room wall, colourful characters from Beijing Opera. A large chandelier above his dining table sparkled before the sun disappeared as quickly as it had emerged and a city of twenty-four million people again retreated into silent gloom beneath his windows.

He picked up a birthday card from his desk. He'd just turned fifty-four. It was from his only son, Robert, fourteen years old and at an elite boarding school in England. It was late, but at least he'd sent one. Cindy Wu had given up a long time ago. Most greetings had arrived by email, the majority from hotel loyalty and frequent flyer programmes.

Then he picked up a photograph from the top of a Chinese cabinet, a sunset shot from a beach in the Cayman Islands, close to a villa he owned there. There was another on the beach, the three of them, Cindy, Robert and him, taken a couple of years earlier. They looked happy enough, smiling to the camera, but already he and Cindy had been growing apart, and it was shortly after that she'd moved back to Beijing, saying she needed to be closer to her elderly parents. Their relationship was now largely one of business.

They could still put on a display of the happy couple when they needed to, for Robert or for clients, but that was becoming a harder act too. They'd need to ham it up again for Robert's next visit to China, fast approaching, which he'd need to discuss with Cindy. Robert was due to stay with her in Beijing first, but they hadn't discussed plans beyond that. He'd not seen Robert for nearly three months, which he regretted. The boy was growing up fast.

There were other photographs on the cabinet. Another villa in Phuket, Thailand, the town house in Central London, the ski chalet in Verbier, Switzerland. They were the things that still motivated him. China had been good for them. It had made them rich and it had kept them together, and looking at those photos encouraged him to press on with the *MB China Report*. But the relentlessly upbeat message was becoming harder to generate.

He picked up his phone and began to trawl through social media sites on the Chinese version of Twitter. On one he followed, called *The Gasping Dragon*, he found a video taken by an air passenger of a baggage handler lazily throwing boxes onto a conveyor belt to the aircraft and mostly missing. And another story about a zoo trying to pass off a dog as a lion, which he thought was funny. He shared them both to *@Beijing_smog*.

Then he came across another posting on the same site, which took him a while to figure out.

Under the cover of smog 🛸 *have landed and taken control of* 🚬

He thought it was pretty clever. And after a few moments he shared that too.

"They might as well be aliens," he said to nobody in particular.

– 6 –

The Moment On Time

Wang Chu waved a teapot at the server, while being chased through a temple by a pack of crazed monkeys that wanted to eat him. The server took the pot out of his left hand, while with his right Wang continued to play the game, working his smartphone, tilting it back and forth and up and down, as he was chased through crumbling doors and around tall pillars until he stumbled over a rock and a monkey sank its teeth into his back.

That ended the game and he flung his phone onto the table in front of him. Only then, very briefly, did he glance up at the server, who was entering the kitchen, pot in hand, for a refill with hot water.

"Try the zombies. Awesome," said Liu Wei.

"What's the difference?" Wang said.

"No real difference. Crazed zombies just make a change from crazed monkeys. They all get to eat you in the end."

Wang agreed that was awesome and downloaded the zombies.

It was mid-morning in The Moment On Time, which called itself a coffee shop, but mostly served tea. Its owner, who called herself Lily, got mad if anybody pointed out the tea thing or tried telling her it should be The Moment *In* Time. She'd call the place whatever she wanted to call it, and most customers learned quickly that it was best not to get on the wrong side of Lily.

Wang and his two roommates sat at a table, their table, in the corner of a raised platform near the window and beneath two fading posters. One was for the movie *Easy Rider*, the other a Cultural Revolution propaganda image of happy workers and soldiers.

Wang Chu, Liu Wei and Zhang Jun were all computer science students, in their last year at one of Beijing's most prestigious universities, and The Moment On Time was their home from home. Part classroom, part office and part rest house. Though mostly it was their portal to the online world, somewhere to pass the hours on their smartphones and laptops. Just occasionally they'd order something to drink or a snack, though never often enough for Lily, who patrolled the tables reminding her customers that she ran a coffee shop and not a flophouse.

The coffee shop was in a busy side street, above a small Haidian clothes store. It was close to a railway line, and when the smog allowed for it, the coffee shop's tall windows looked across at the constant flow of packed trains between downtown and this, Beijing's student heartland.

There were around twenty wooden tables, and on each was a small lamp, more for effect than any light they provided. Round red lanterns hung from the low ceiling, arranged around two clunky overhead heaters, which were working overtime to keep the temperature bearable.

Wang decided he'd save the crazed zombies for later and instead began hopping between Twitter-like accounts he followed.

He shared a picture of a pair of security guards asleep in their chairs at the front door of a bank, and a report about a man who'd pocketed millions of yuan by setting up a fake branch of the China Construction Bank, complete with card readers, passbooks and three teenage girls working at the counter.

He shared another about an investigator looking for fake goods and collecting fines when he found them. Only the investigator was an imposter.

"Get this," he said to Liu, "there's a story here about a guy hunting fakes who turns out to be a fake."

But Liu ignored him. He was sitting at an open laptop computer, updating their online store, adding a range of caps with images from the latest *Star Wars* movie, which had been a big hit, and removing any last references to the PM2.5 Mega Blocker anti-smog mask, which hadn't.

The roommates had decided it was far better for now to stick with what they knew best: knock-off caps, T-shirts and bags. Though they'd yet to make money on any of them.

Liu Wei was twenty-three, a year older than Wang. He was shorter but broader, with closely cropped hair hidden under a yellow baseball cap with a picture of Daffy Duck on the front. He began browsing other online shops, checking on the competition.

"Hey guys, you won't believe this, but there's a shop here selling canned clean air. No kidding. Says they come in different flavours."

"No way," said Wang. "How does that work?"

Liu said he wasn't sure, but guessed you just sniffed it to get a reminder of what real air tasted like.

Wang said that was really cool and what *did* real air taste like? He said that maybe that was a business they should get into.

"It must be a gimmick. It can't be for real," Zhang said. "No way. It must be a scam."

And Wang said, "We should definitely get into that."

Zhang Jun, their other roommate, was a tall, darker boy, who was the same age as Wang. He was now bent over his smartphone playing a card game, occasionally flicking back his hair, which hung down almost to his eyes. He switched from time to time to a dating app, on which he appeared to have found a match.

He told Liu and Wang the match was stunning, but he thought the photograph might be a fake because everybody faked their photographs.

His was a random picture he'd lifted from a magazine, some minor television celebrity. He said he couldn't possibly meet the girl, even if she wasn't a fake, because then she'd know he was.

"So what's the point?" asked Wang.

And Zhang said the fun was in finding the match, not meeting her. That would be far too embarrassing. Best keep it online.

In The Moment On Time that passed for serious conversation. The few words spoken were usually ignored. For the most part Lily's customers lived in the world beyond their screens, fingers and thumbs frantically working their keyboards.

Mostly they communicated in grunts, without ever looking up, preferring to send each other text messages, even when they were sitting around the same table.

Wang found a bunch of angry posts about a reality TV show, some sort of talent contest, that had been pulled from air after a record three million people voted for a woman dressed as a duck singing a cheesy old Chinese love song and dancing with her pet dog.

That had attracted thousands of comments asking what had really upset the authorities, the duck or the vote? One posting had a photograph of China's Communist Party leader alongside the duck woman and with a caption, "Who got the most votes?" It was quickly deleted by the censors, but only after Wang had shared it.

Then the internet went down.

There was a collective groan across the coffee shop. A flustered-looking Lily immediately pulled the power lead out of the router, thinking that rebooting would solve the problem.

She knew her customers would suffer most things in silence. The coffee machine going down, the hot water heater for the tea, even the heating. But a temperamental internet link was something else. She suspected they'd probably drink dishwater just as long as they could get online. The mood could quickly turn ugly. It could trigger a rebellion, especially as a new coffee shop had just opened around the corner, claiming to have super super-fast broadband, whatever that meant. They'd even hired a couple of kids to hand out flyers right outside The Moment On Time before Lily chased them off with a torrent of abuse and a couple of well-aimed coffee cups.

Lily rarely lost her cool, but she knew what was at stake, and she rushed around offering free drinks and assurances that her internet outage was just a teething problem with a new router that really was much faster than anything anybody else could offer.

Wang took a pen out of his pocket and began to doodle on the cream-coloured shade of the lamp on the table in front of him, mostly calculations about the number of *Star Wars* caps they should ask Fatso to make for their online shop in order to at least break even.

Throughout the coffee shop the lampshades had become canvases for drawings, ramblings and other graffiti, usually to pass the time while the internet was down.

As the outage continued, and lacking anything better to do, more conversations broke out, a low-level murmur across the room, that was so unusual that Lily looked up too, momentarily neglecting the router that she was still trying to nurse back to life. She had the internet provider on the phone now, and was following instructions that made little sense to her.

Wang asked his roommates whether they'd heard anything about graduate job fairs coming up, since they were getting close to that season. And Zhang said no, he hadn't seen any schedule.

"But don't hold your breath," said Liu Wei, who was staring at the dead screen of his laptop, as if by concentrating hard enough he could bring the internet back to life. "Don't expect so many jobs this year. And starting salaries will suck because of the economy."

"The economy seems to be holding up," Zhang said. "They're predicting six percent growth this year. I read it online. Not as good as before, but still pretty healthy."

"My dad says it's all made up," said Liu. "They say whatever figure they want to say."

Wang nodded. Liu's dad was some big-shot government official. Liu had once boasted that he advised the Prime Minister on economic stuff. He'd know.

Zhang looked back down at his dating app, which was still showing no signs of life. He was the more academic of the three, which is to say that he mostly attended class and did the work assigned to him. He was smart in a nerdy kind of way. His grades were scarily good, and he could find his way around computers like nobody else Wang knew.

Wang thought again about his parents. The guilt returned, as did the itchy knee and the trembling foot. The internet was still down, but he was able to access the draft reply to his mother and the only two words he'd so far managed to write: "Hi Mum".

Then he went back to her original nagging messages. How could he answer her questions about the non-existent jobs and girlfriend without digging himself deeper into a hole? He was twenty-two years old, but his mother was treating him like one of the children at the kindergarten where she taught in the far northern city of Harbin. Perhaps it was best to ignore her, at least for now. Or blame the weather. Tell his mother that his girlfriend hated the cold, and he'd have to postpone the visit until the summer. But then she'd offer to come to Beijing. She'd done that before.

And Harbin was cold. Very cold. To him, it made Beijing seem like the tropics.

Both of his parents were from the same small town in the more temperate south of China, where they'd met and married young. Pretty much as they assumed Wang would too. They'd moved to Harbin when Wang was eleven. It had been a sudden, abrupt move. They'd never told him why, but his father had a teaching job in Harbin's Communist Party School, one of a vast network of schools run by the Party for its members.

His father had never really explained to him what he did at the school, what he taught, not talking about it much, though Wang had never really asked. It just didn't seem that interesting.

He closed the draft message without adding anything to it, and told his roommates that he'd decided to study in America.

"You know air pollution is killing 4,000 people a day in China. Lung cancer rates are soaring. The soil's toxic too. And imagine what that does to the food. Northern China is becoming uninhabitable," he said.

Zhang said he'd read online that Delhi was now worse than Beijing for smog, and Wang said that didn't make him feel any better, and was that even possible?

"And how are you going to pay for that, for America?" Zhang said.

"Our businesses will come good, you'll see," Wang said, not sounding particularly confident.

Lily then came off the call with the technician and rebooted the router again, having put in the new settings. The internet came back to life.

"We're up. We're back online," she shouted, with a mixture of triumph and relief.

There was brief applause, then silence, just a hardly noticeable clicking and tapping of keyboards. A silence so sudden and abrupt it was as if somebody had flicked a switch, as they all went back into their online worlds.

Zhang re-opened his dating app, with its gushing profiles of would-be matches, which he thought were mostly as fake as his own. A world of make-believe.

Liu opened an online share trading account he'd just set up, which he was beginning to think was much like that too. Except real money was at stake.

Wang went back to his *Gasping Dragon* account to which he shared a video of a man from Nanjing who was living like he was a goat, crawling around and bleating like one and eating grass. Then he posted pictures from the coast, a beach near Tianjin where the bay had been taken over by green algae and kids were swimming in the stuff, looking like sea monsters. Maybe they were monsters. He shared that thought too, together with a stick alien wrapped in green slime beside a statement from the local Communist Party leader pledging to clean up the beaches.

But he soon got bored, and he said to his roommates, "I'm going to see Fatso about the *Star Wars* caps."

And Liu said, "Good luck with that", knowing the big man would be less than happy with all the unsold masks. "Tell him we need them by Monday. If he's still talking to you."

Wang crossed the now-packed Moment On Time coffee shop, down the narrow wooden staircase, through the clothes shop and out onto the street, where a light snow was falling.

He walked past several noodle stalls and a newspaper kiosk, where he could just about see the seller swaddled in a thick coat and scarf behind piles of magazines. On the road in front, a taxi driver had his bonnet open and was trying to return some life to his crippled vehicle, cigarette hanging from his mouth.

There was a high-pitched siren and flashing lights ahead of him, where a barrier came down across the road. A train was coming.

He took cover under the awning of a mobile phone shop close to the barrier, and while he waited he went back online, returning to the crumbling temple, dodging and for the moment outrunning a pack of crazed zombies.

The train passed and the barrier was raised. Wang crossed the line and entered a narrow alleyway full of parked bicycles, which he somehow navigated without taking his eyes off the screen of his smartphone, where he was still keeping the zombies at bay, ducking through doorways and down steps that disintegrated beneath him.

Fatso's door was squeezed between a coat shop and a packed dumpling store, a lunchtime crowd spilling out into the alley. A woman swore at Wang as he almost knocked a box of steaming dumplings from her hand. He didn't hear her. Didn't even notice. Because the zombies were now closing in and he was trapped, tangled in creepers and dense undergrowth on a path that went nowhere.

He used his right elbow to press the buzzer on Fatso's door, his fingers still working the screen. There seemed no way to escape the wrath of the zombies.

Nor of Fatso.

Wang was jolted back into the real world as Fatso answered the door with a look that was every bit as scary as anything Wang had been running from in the game.

"What do you want, Wang?" said Fatso, wearing just a soiled vest in spite of the weather and lighting a cigarette.

"I need to talk to you about caps."

"And I need to talk to you about those fucking masks."

– 7 –

The Colonel

The server said she was sorry about the smog, but didn't he think it was kind of moody. She asked Chuck Drayton whether he was enjoying the view, if this was his first time in the city, and did he know they'd just been voted the coolest bar in Shanghai.

To Drayton that was four questions too many, and as for the cool bit, that would usually be good reason to avoid the place.

So he ignored the questions and just ordered another mojito because that seemed like the kind of thing you drank in a bar like this, telling her to go easy on the sugar this time, and where was the change from the last one. Lost in the smog maybe?

The view didn't really exist, at least not like the one on the back of the menu, Drayton wondering how long they had to wait for a clear day like that.

Still, the server had a point. It was moody.

The bar was at the top of one of the tallest and swankiest hotels in the city, at the northern end of the Bund, looking directly across at the skyscrapers of the Pudong financial district on the other side of the Huangpu River, with the Bund way below to the right, with its sweep of old buildings. Ships moved slowly along the river in-between. He could barely see them, but the deep guttural blasts of their horns penetrated the bar and provided for Drayton a welcome break from the dreary soul music.

The Pearl Oriental TV Tower, at the centre of all the Pudong glass and metal, was lit up like a Christmas tree, changing from blues to yellows and pinks. Its massive spheres sparkling like disco balls. It was dusk, and the lights were fuzzy through the smog. The whole sky above seemed to glow.

Drayton took his drink and climbed a spiral staircase to a circular outdoor terrace on the very top of the building, where he took a stool at a tall table near the wall. He reached in his pocket for his pollution mask, but then changed his mind, figuring that probably wasn't the coolest thing to wear in a cool bar, that it didn't really go with the mojito.

He'd have to suffer.

The terrace had a series of high tables next to small open pavilion-like structures with padded seating on the floor. Tall heaters were sprinkled around the terrace, and at the centre of it all a steaming Jacuzzi, in which three girls lounged, bubbling champagne in hand. Which got Drayton smiling. In the middle of winter, for fuck's sake.

It was early evening, but the terrace was busy, small groups mainly, young and straight from work, hunched over their smartphones.

But one group was different. There were around twenty of them, celebrating, spread over two of the pavilions and several tables, which were weighed down with bottles of champagne and expensive spirits. They'd been there most of the afternoon. Kids mostly, late teens, early twenties Drayton guessed. Flash, expensively dressed and loud.

Drayton opened the camera on his iPhone and took some photos of the view: Pudong, the Bund, the river, a panorama, during which he lingered on the party crowd, on a boy with spiky gelled hair and dark glasses who appeared to be at the centre of it all, and on an older man who looked strangely out of place, but who from time to time would place a paternalistic hand on the boy's shoulder.

One of them shouted, and they all raised their glasses.

"Huizhi. To Huizhi."

They knocked their drinks back in one. Drayton noticed that two kids appeared to be sleeping in one of the pavilions. Another was throwing up.

They then struck up a heavily slurred rendition of 'Happy Birthday', and the boy at the centre of it all raised a champagne glass, took a lengthy gulp and climbed fully clothed into the Jacuzzi followed by two of the girls. The older man smiled, an awkward smile, and sipped from a small porcelain mug. He was drinking tea.

Everybody was taking photographs of the Jacuzzi, so Drayton joined in too, taking a couple more of the older man for good measure. Getting a closer look, and thinking how formal and stiff he looked beside the kids.

The birthday boy climbed out of the Jacuzzi and the whole group gathered round; time for a birthday photo, looking for a server to take it for them. But the server had gone downstairs for a mop to clear the puke. So Drayton volunteered. Allow me. Taking photo after photo as smartphones were handed his way.

Ending with several more on his own phone.

A glass of champagne was thrust into his hand.

"Thank you. Thank you."

"You're very welcome. Happy birthday," he said, raising the glass, clinking it with the boy called Huizhi, and then looking directly at the older man. He was medium height, mid-forties Drayton guessed, maybe slightly older, with closely cropped hair. Military-style. It was the shape of the face, a long thin face, showing no emotion, that was most distinctive. Just like in the fuzzy computer photograph of the guy poking around in the maestro's laptop.

Only he didn't look much like a hacker, not like Drayton imagined one anyway.

Then the man looked straight at Drayton, and for a moment the two men locked eyes before both looked away.

Drayton retreated to his table and then back down the spiral staircase to the downstairs bar, which was inside and warmer. He took a seat where he could watch the staircase.

The mojito had been too sweet again, so he decided to order a beer because they couldn't mess that up. The server from earlier started to make her way over, then thought better of it, leaving him to a miserable-looking guy with a face that said he didn't give a shit about the view. Which was absolutely fine by Drayton.

"Thanks," he said, when the beer arrived.

"Quite a party upstairs."

The server nodded, saying nothing.

"That Huizhi, quite a character. Comes here a lot, I guess."

"Yeah," the server said, no longer mute. "Chen Huizhi. He likes to party."

"Rich kid, hey?"

The server didn't reply, just looked around the bar. They were all rich kids.

The smoke in the bar was almost as thick as the smog outside. Another government smoking ban failing. Nobody was about to tell these kids to take their habit outside.

Drayton had quit smoking a couple of years earlier, and now he hated it with all the zeal of a religious convert. But all the same this was another of those little acts of defiance of the rules that he found mildly encouraging, just like the smartphones at the maestro's dreadful concert.

He paid for the beer, then opened an air quality app on his iPhone, so he could see what he was breathing. There was a ton of these to choose from, but the one he liked best was called Airpocalypse. It was funny, somehow finding plenty of humour in the disaster that was Chinese pollution.

Airpocalypse opened and after a few seconds a big yellow window appeared with the figure 375, and below that the words "Air Soup" and an image of a man in a mask. Drayton loved these guys. The figure meant the air had improved a bit from earlier, but for the tiny dangerous bits that did the most damage it was still hazardous, still fifteen times what experts said was safe, and that wasn't funny.

There was banging from the spiral staircase, somebody slipping, almost falling over as they tried to make their way down. It was one of two girls clinging to the arms of the birthday boy, the older man following behind, face set in stone.

The boy was still in his wet clothes, black jeans and a tight grey pullover over a black T-shirt, designer casual. He was still wearing his dark glasses, a cigarette hanging from the side of his mouth. He was carrying his shoes, as was one of the girls who'd been in the Jacuzzi with him. She had a towel around her shoulders, and was wearing a short black dress, wet and clinging to her.

The older man was wearing a dark windcheater over a white polo, which struck Drayton as classic bureaucrat-issue.

They walked down a long corridor lined with wooden wine racks and took the lift to the lobby. Drayton followed, taking the next lift, down a glass tube looking out over a barely visible city, descending through the smog.

The kids were unsteady on their feet, clinging to each other as they crossed the lobby, but with a bit of guidance they managed to negotiate the hotel's revolving door and out to its covered drop-off and pick-up area, the boy handing a sodden piece of paper to the concierge.

The boy then detached himself from the girls and went over to the older man, who had been standing to one side, putting one hand against the window to steady himself, neither of them noticing Drayton, who was now sitting the other side of the darkened window, looking out. They talked for a while, the older man smiling for the first time, putting his hand on the boy's shoulder again, patting him, then pointing to where a red Ferrari was pulling up behind them.

A bellhop got out of the driver's door, leaving it open, before walking around the car and opening the passenger door towards which the two girls staggered before tumbling inside, the bellhop closing the door with a look of complete indifference.

With a wave to the older man, the boy got into the driver's seat and revved the engine like he was on the grid at Le Mans. The wheels span and the car lurched forward towards the road, onto which it made a screeching right turn, forcing an oncoming taxi to brake and swerve.

The bellhop and the concierge glanced at each other with an expression that said to Drayton that they'd seen it all before, though he suspected that neither would be entirely upset if the Ferrari veered into a lamppost.

Soon after the Ferrari left, a black Audi pulled up, a licence plate of red and black text on a white background. Military. The concierge opened the rear door and the older man climbed inside, on the phone now.

The car turned left out of the hotel and headed north.

Drayton left the hotel on foot, making a call. The number rang three times before somebody who didn't speak picked it up.

"Our friend is on his way," were the only words Drayton spoke. Then he hung up.

It started to rain, more of a heavy drizzle really, which suited him just fine. He bought an umbrella from a woman selling them in the street outside the hotel, and pulled his hood over his head. With the big black pollution mask he felt suitably anonymous.

The area he headed into was one of the last around the Bund still to be developed, and was a jumble of new office buildings, apartments and construction sites, mostly close to the river, side by side with weathered warehouses and narrow lanes of dilapidated shophouses, some boarded up, waiting for demolition.

The roads were now quiet and dark, most of the light coming from the Pudong skyline, which loomed like a giant from across the river. He entered a shabby building with a hostel sign at the front, squeezed between a noodle shop and a motorcycle repair centre. He waited just inside the door and looked back down the street from where he'd come.

A police car with flashing lights passed slowly along the road in front.

A voice from the gloomy interior of the hostel asked what he wanted. Drayton said he needed the washroom and the voice said it was at the back.

Drayton walked towards the back of the building, but before he found the washroom he passed another half-opened door that led out to an alleyway behind the hostel. He went out into the alleyway and followed it to where it joined another road, where he waited.

A pile of black trash bags rustled and pulsated by his left leg, so he kicked them, then jumped back as rats spilled out in every direction, some across his shoes. He kicked at the rats, still coming out of the bags.

"For *fuck's* sake."

He hated rats.

A woman looked from a window down the alley, asking what was going on.

He decided he was done with being cautious and, satisfied he wasn't being followed, walked deeper into a maze of old narrow streets until he came to a fading white low-rise building, set back from the street. It could have been a warehouse at some point, but no longer carried any signs identifying it.

It could easily have been dismissed as another abandoned building, if not for the array of antennae and satellite dishes on the roof, and a heavy sliding metal door at the front, watched over by a cluster of security cameras. The door led to what looked like a courtyard beyond.

Drayton walked past the building, bringing his umbrella down low against his head, turned another corner and entered an old office building, where he took a lift that creaked its way up to the top floor of the twelve-storey building.

He left the lift and walked to a door with a plaque outside reading SHANGHAI TT LOGISTICS. He unlocked the door and let himself in.

The outer office was deserted. It was sparsely furnished – just a reception desk and a coffee table with sofa and one other chair. There were some shelves with guidebooks to Shanghai, gathering dust, and a single picture on the wall of the Bund at night.

There was also a fish tank; most Chinese offices had fish tanks, only this one had no fish, just an inch of fetid green water.

There was another door behind the reception desk, on which Drayton knocked twice, twice again, then three more times before he heard heavy bolts being slid open.

"Hi Chuck. Everything okay?"

"Fine, Dave. How's Team Panda?"

"We've had a busy day. Lots of comings and goings down there."

The room contained two sofas, an armchair and two tables, one with an overflowing ashtray and empty coffee cups. There was a case of beer beneath the table.

The other longer table had on it two cameras with telephoto lenses, binoculars and a laptop. It was close to a window that looked down on the entrance to the white warehouse-like building, and with glass adapted to prevent anybody seeing into the room.

"Just like in the satellite photo, hey?" said Dave.

"Yeah," said Drayton. "Now tell me about the Colonel."

The man called Dave handed him a camera and he played back a series of shots of a black Audi arriving at the white gate, the gate sliding open, and the car driving inside.

The gate stayed open just long enough for the camera to catch the older man from the birthday party getting out of the car and being saluted by two men in military uniform. Then the heavy gate slid shut again.

The time on the last photo was 20.23.

"That's nearly seven thirty in the morning DC time," Drayton said. "He's working American hours. Makes sense."

"This guy we're calling the Colonel, what do we really know about him, Chuck?" said Dave.

"Right now, not a lot," Drayton said. "But I'm working on it."

– 8 –

Shadows on the Bund

Anthony Morgan left his Lucky Bund View apartment as the sun should have been rising, but the sky was grey, everything was grey. It was as if the whole city had been drained of colour, the neighbouring towers of Pudong just shadows in the gloom.

He'd slept badly. It wasn't just the Bud problem. Clients were becoming cautious about China, and he needed to convince them to keep their faith in the Chinese economy, to keep their investments flowing, and with them the fat fees he charged because he was their guiding hand. He was Mr China. But that was becoming a bigger challenge by the day.

Still, this new client, this American called Drayton, seemed promising. The call had come out of the blue, Drayton introducing himself as the US Consulate's commercial guy, looking for some due diligence on business partners for American companies. He said it needed to be discreet, which was fine by Morgan, but dawn on the Bund discreet seemed a bit much.

He decided to take the ferry across the Huangpu, but quickly regretted it as he stepped in a deep puddle crossing the road that separated his luxury apartment complex from a low shed-like building from which the ferry left every half hour.

It wasn't cold, but there was a chilly damp after heavy overnight rain, one of those damps that penetrated every seam of his coat. At least it had cleared some of the smog. He'd checked his air quality app before leaving, which gave a reading of a still-dangerous 256. He chose a mid-range pollution mask.

There were five other people waiting for the ferry. A young boy and his mother and another young couple were all bent over the screens of their smartphones, which glowed brightly in the dark of a damp waiting room.

Outside, an older man in a leather peaked hat was standing under posters saying no smoking or spitting, with helpful cartoons of both. He lit a cigarette and cleared his throat, a long high-pitched retch, and spat into a trashcan.

The crossing was quick; Morgan had taken it dozens of times, but it still enthralled and sometimes alarmed him, the way the ferry picked its way through the heavy river traffic.

Even this early in the morning it was more like watching a freight train on a railway line than a river, a seemingly endless passage of ships sitting so low in the water that they looked like they might submerge, submarine-like, at any moment. Morgan guessed that some of them did. Most were weighed down with what looked like sludge or sand, and were at times three abreast.

The river was fast-moving and the ferry seemed to struggle against the tide, steaming parallel to the passing ships until it spotted a small break in the traffic, powered up, and went for the gap.

Morgan left the ferry, and climbed stairs to a wide walkway beside the river, alongside the old buildings of the Bund, or rather their darkened silhouettes.

His client had asked to meet near the old Customs House, and bells rang from its clock tower, almost invisible in the gloom.

He began to walk north towards the bells, passing joggers, some in masks, some jogging backwards, which Morgan had never quite been able to figure out. Two men were trying to launch an enormous kite, as big as them, eagle-shaped.

A bigger group of older people were moving slowly, rhythmically, raising their hands, twisting, turning and bowing in unison. Further along, women in bright tracksuits were dancing to traditional Chinese music, fans in hand. Another group were prancing up and down, round and round to Chinese pop.

Dawn on the Bund.

"What a fucking circus," said a voice from behind him.

He turned to face a tall man in a black coat and scarf, collar turned up, a head of thick black hair swept back and wearing a big black pollution mask.

"Chuck Drayton. Nice to meet you."

"You too," said Morgan. "A little early."

"Nothing like a bracing early morning stroll on the Bund, Tony. Or is it Anthony?"

Morgan said Tony was fine, and Drayton said to call him Chuck.

They began walking north, Morgan saying he knew a good place for coffee and maybe breakfast. That it was quiet and private.

Drayton said he liked quiet and private.

"Tough doing business in China, I imagine," said Drayton.

Morgan said it could be, and Drayton said the consulate had just been dealing with one pain-in-the-arse American businessman, now in a Shanghai hospital.

"An accident?"

"Yes and no," Drayton said. "He was in Ningbo, at the airport, walking towards his gate and on his phone, texting, when he got hit by one of those ridiculous electric buggy things, speeding around a corner, and moving a bunch of Chinese VIPs who couldn't be arsed to walk. Broke three ribs and fractured his ankle."

"Wow. I guess there's a compensation issue."

"You could say that. Police kept the guy's passport and refused to give it back until he coughed up US$5,000 in compensation for damage to the buggy."

"So, did you sort it out?"

"Well, here's the thing. We *did* sort it out. Or thought we did. But you know what? This businessman says, no, he *wants* to pay compensation to the people who nearly killed him because he doesn't want to rock the boat, doesn't want to risk losing a contract he's close to getting with some local state-owned company."

"That's too bad," Morgan said. "Stuff happens in China. But it's an important market. Sometimes you have to be pragmatic."

And Drayton said that wasn't being pragmatic, that was being stupid.

Morgan let that go, though it did strike him that for a diplomat this guy Drayton wasn't particularly diplomatic. It was a good story though, which he'd pass on later to followers of @Beijing_smog.

They passed another smaller group, men and women this time, dancing, twirling slowly to a haunting piece of music. One of them gestured to Morgan to join them. He smiled and waved. Maybe next time.

"Go on," said Drayton. "I won't tell Mrs Morgan. Bet you can do that twirly stuff."

"Used to," Morgan said.

"I hear you and Mrs Morgan are good. The best corporate investigators in China," Drayton said.

"Thanks. We've been here a long time," said Morgan, a little puzzled since he couldn't remember telling Drayton about his wife. But he let that go too. The American must have done his own due diligence about MacMaster and Brown.

"I'd love to meet her."

"Who?"

"Your wife. Must have some great contacts."

"I'll see what I can do. Though she's been pretty busy."

"I can imagine," Drayton said.

He had zero intention of giving Drayton direct access to his wife, precisely because her contacts were so good. It was the way they worked on investigations. He dealt with the clients. And, anyway, he resented the implication that it was his wife who did the work. Sure, she got the raw data, but it was he, Morgan, who gave it context, provided the analyses.

They crossed an old metal bridge over a small river off the Huangpu and entered a baroque-style hotel called the Astor House, Morgan telling Drayton it dated back to the 1840s, just after the first Opium War, founded by a Scottish merchant.

"Oh yeah?" said Drayton, who'd stopped just outside and was looking back down the street, towards the bridge.

"You okay?"

"Thought I saw someone I knew," Drayton said.

He followed Morgan into the hotel, a doorman in white uniform holding the door open for him.

71

"Let me show you something," Morgan said, leading Drayton down a corridor off the ornate lobby. The corridor was lined with photographs, a history of the hotel that was also a history of the city. A plaque said Ulysses Grant, Albert Einstein and Charlie Chaplin had all stayed there.

"So we're in pretty good company," Drayton said.

The long photo-lined corridor was book-ended by two little massage places.

"I assume they're a recent addition. Or is that where Ulysses went for a rub down?" Drayton said.

Morgan said he really liked the place. That it was tired and weathered, but full of charm. That sooner or later it would be taken over and renovated and turned into some super-luxurious place, which would kill the charm.

Drayton didn't seem to be listening. He was looking inside one of the massage places, which was open in spite of it being so early, though he couldn't see anybody on duty.

"Just curious," he said. "You like a massage?"

"Sometimes," Morgan said, looking a little embarrassed.

They took a table in a dining room. Drayton said he thought it resembled an opera house, with its marble pillars, high roof and stuff, and asked when the fat lady was going to sing. There were even little high-up balconies surrounding the hall and a series of big chandeliers.

Morgan fetched two coffees from a long table at the back of the hall. The machine spluttered and hissed, but eventually filled the cups with something the machine described as espresso.

When he got back to the table, Drayton asked him, "What's with the OBE?"

"That was a few years ago," Morgan said, brushing it off, but loving the moment. He always did when he was asked that question and had a chance to flaunt it, affecting an air of modesty.

"It was no big deal," he said. "It was just for doing my best, for services to British trade. It was presented by the Queen."

Drayton said yeah, he'd seen the photographs in the MacMaster and Brown promotional stuff. In the company reports.

"Commander of the Order of the British Empire. Pretty

impressive," Drayton said. "You don't have any problems with the Chinese with all that empire stuff? I mean they're always droning on about the gunboats and the opium. All that national humiliation stuff. The way your empire snatched Hong Kong."

Morgan said the Chinese rather liked British pomp and royalty.

The American ignored that and removed a brown envelope from an inside pocket. He gave two sheets of paper to Morgan, one giving brief details of a chemical company based in a city called Nanjing, the other a Shanghai-based insurance company, both of which he'd grabbed at random from a database at the consulate's commercial section the day before. He said both were looking to snap up some US companies.

"We just want to know if they'll make good partners," Drayton said, and Morgan said that should be pretty straightforward. He said it wasn't always clear where a lot of Chinese companies got their money and who ultimately owned them, but that he'd get the answers.

"That's why we've come to you, Tony," said Drayton.

In reality the American didn't have a clue what the cement and insurance companies were up to, and cared even less, but he figured that requesting the extra research would boost his credibility with Morgan, help his cover.

"You're the best," he said, pouring on the flattery before he got to the real reason for the meeting.

"And there's one more thing," he said.

"Sure. What's the deal?"

"Can't really be sure at this point. Technology, broadly."

Drayton took several photographs out of the envelope and laid them one by one in front of Morgan. The first was of a spiky-haired youngster in dark glasses. He appeared to be in some kind of bath with two girls. All were fully clothed.

"He's into technology?" said Morgan.

"Yeah, but he likes a dip in a Jacuzzi from time to time. You know these tech types," Drayton said, laying down two more photographs of the boy in a bigger group, champagne glasses in hands, smiling.

"It was his birthday," Drayton said.

Then three more pictures. The kid getting into a car. The car driving off. A tight shot of the licence plate.

"Nice car," Morgan said.

"Ferrari. Kid's name is Chen Huizhi. And this, I believe, is his father."

Drayton placed three more photographs in front of Morgan. The older man at the party, looking serious, uncomfortable in the crowd. Then with the kid, his hand on his shoulder, looking a bit more father-like.

"And his father, what's his story?"

"That's what I'm hoping you can tell me, Tony. There's money there, but we're not sure where it's come from."

"And you have somebody wanting to do business with these guys."

"Yes, you could say that."

"That's not much to go on. What do you need?"

"As much as you can get."

Drayton put the photographs back in the envelope, which he handed to Morgan, who went to put it in his bag.

"And there'll be a decent bonus with this one, Tony. This one's a bit more sensitive than the others."

"Dawn on the Bund sensitive?" Morgan said. "I'll see what I can do."

"That looks a barrel of laughs," Drayton said, pointing to a booklet with the title *Golden Road, Golden Age,* which Morgan had taken out of his bag and briefly placed on the table.

Morgan said it was the title of a conference he'd be attending later at the Shanghai Stock Exchange, about China building regional economic links. He said he was to be a keynote speaker.

"Bit of a casino that stock exchange if you ask me," Drayton said. "What are you speaking about?"

"Addressing foreign investors mainly, telling them to keep their nerve, that emerging markets can be volatile. To have faith in the long-term future of the economy here."

"And you plan to say all that with a straight face?"

Drayton picked up the booklet, quickly thumbing through it, and said, "Golden age of bullshit if you ask me."

– 9 –

Fatso

Fatso rolled up his soiled vest so it perched just above his bare belly and pulled out another cigarette from a crushed packet in his back pocket.

"Warm enough for you?" Wang asked him.

Fatso ignored the question and lit the cigarette from one of the bright red bars of an old electric heater, which Wang thought you could probably use to smelt steel.

"You know smoking killed a million people in China last year," Wang said. He told Fatso he'd read it online, posted by some doctors, so it might even be true.

"So, did they count them all? How do you know it wasn't the air that killed them?" Fatso said, pointing to the window, which was steamed up because of the heat in the second-floor room.

"With cigarettes I have a choice. With the air I don't."

"And they've banned cigarettes from the coffee shop again," said Wang.

Fatso laughed, like that was the stupidest thing he'd heard all morning.

"Oh yeah? Wear this," he said throwing at Wang a mask from an open box, which was one of about a dozen piled against the wall, and all full of unsold PM2.5 Mega Blockers.

"You ordered them. They're your masks," he said, throwing some more. "You hear that?"

"She comes back, I've seen it before," Wang said, thinking he was talking about the old television in the corner, which was showing a rerun of some family drama, a woman throwing pots and pans at her in-laws, screaming, then storming out of the house.

"No, not that. *That*," said Fatso, walking to the window and opening it, giving them a grandstand view of another drama unfolding at the railway crossing, just beyond the bicycle-clogged alleyway below. The barrier was down again and an angry crowd looked like they'd given up on waiting for the train.

Cars were honking horns and bikes were edging closer to the barrier. But as far as Wang and Fatso could see the real threat came from a group of women who'd already climbed over the barrier and were moving closer to the track, egging each other on.

Two policemen in thick, badly fitting coats blew whistles and yelled at them. But the women just got bolder and yelled back. Fatso said it was the most entertaining thing he'd watched all week. One woman was carrying a small child and was now right in the face of one of the cops, screaming, as they bombarded each other with spittle and steamy breath.

"He's going to hit her. I swear he's going to hit her," said Fatso, getting excited, as the policeman took one step back, like he was getting ready to lunge at the woman.

But quickly several other women flanked her. To Fatso they looked like a row of gunslingers from one of the B-grade American westerns he liked to watch when he wasn't catching a rerun of a mindless soap.

And, like gunslingers, their hands were poised over their pockets, ready to draw.

Only, their weapons were their smartphones.

The policeman appeared to blink, retreating a few steps. Then something was said by one of the women, which Wang and Fatso didn't quite catch, but the cop did and he just snapped, yelling and then lurching at the woman with the child, pushing her back. She fell to the ground, as did the child, screaming.

The gunslingers were quick to the draw, and half a dozen smartphones were already rolling.

The child grabbed the policeman's hand and sank in its teeth. The cop screamed and kicked the child. By now there were phones raised right along the barrier. It could have got a lot worse, only the train came, a piercing blast of a whistle announcing its approach. Now both sides had to retreat.

No sooner had the train passed, and more than twenty videos were being uploaded to the web and would soon be shared by millions.

"Bastards," said Fatso. "They should have thrown the cops under the train. They think they can treat you like shit."

"They can treat you like shit," said Wang.

Fatso pulled his smartphone from his pocket and waved it in Wang's face.

"There's something changing in this country," he said. "It's getting harder for them to trick us. Much harder."

Wang just shrugged. "So do we have a deal?" he asked, coming back to the masks. And Fatso said sure, let's do that, deferring the money for the masks for a share in profits on sales of the *Star Wars* caps.

"You think they'll sell?" he asked.

"Of course," said Wang, telling him *Star Wars* was huge in China.

Fatso cleared his throat and spat into a waste paper basket beside the boxes of masks. He'd get them made, he said.

Wang told him he'd read that 70% of stuff sold online was fake. Fatso said he doubted that.

"That means 30% is genuine. That can't be possible."

Fatso said he wanted to buy some shares.

"I think there may be money to be made on the Shanghai stock market."

"But it's just collapsed."

"That's my point, Wang. I can't see the Government letting it go lower, or they'll have more of that," he said, pointing towards the railway crossing.

Wang told him his friend Liu Wei had a share trading account, but that Liu's dad was some big-shot government official, doing lots of economic stuff, so Liu pretty much knew what was going to happen before it happened.

"That's ideal," Fatso said. "Why else would you buy shares?

"And another thing," he said. "I want to set up one of those websites to give investment tips."

"But you don't know anything about investing."

"That's beside the point. I can learn."

Fatso told Wang he was thinking of getting a diploma in advanced stock market strategy from the Mid-America University of Advanced Finance.

Wang said he'd never heard of it.

"You don't seem the studious type," he said. "How long's that going to take you? One, two years? Is it online, or do they have a campus here?"

"It takes about ten minutes, just fill in some stuff online and send 500 yuan. They send you the diploma. Saves all that studying. For an extra fifty, they'll arrange a graduation photo with one of those flat boards on your head and a reference from the Dean."

Wang agreed that it saved time.

They shook hands on their deal, and Wang gave Fatso the spec for the caps. Then he headed back down the stairs and through another room where a woman, much younger than Fatso, sat at a printing machine that hissed and spluttered and gave off more heat than the electric bar heater upstairs.

Wang assumed this was Fatso's wife or mistress or something, since she was always around. He'd never been introduced though, and Fatso wasn't about to do the formalities this time either.

She was turning out replica football shirts with a logo for Liverpool Football Club, which Wang had read would soon be playing some exhibition games in China.

"Nice," he said, picking up a shirt. Fatso ignored him. So did the woman.

"Your friend, this Liu, he's doing okay with his stock market stuff?"

"Up and down. How's business for you? Looks like you have a lot going on."

"A man should fear fame like a pig fears getting fat," said Fatso, a saying he seemed so proud of he repeated it.

It was an old saying, which Wang had heard from his father, usually as a warning that nobody should think himself bigger than the Communist Party.

Though from Fatso it was more of a 'butt out and mind your own business'. He had his own very small circle of trust, if he had one at all, and Wang wasn't in it. That's how he survived.

Fatso went back upstairs and left Wang to find his own way out.

Back on the street, the traffic was flowing again, and the policemen were snarling at a vendor, accusing her of setting up a stall selling earphones for smartphones too close to the railway barrier. As Wang passed, the vendor yelled something at the cops, but then thinking better of it, moved back a few feet.

Wang looked back down the alleyway towards Fatso's place. On the face of it, his stock market idea seemed a little ridiculous, but Fatso was smart – not academic smart, but street-smart.

He'd got money, of that Wang was certain, compensation for the old house he'd been forced out of by one of the many new developments that had changed the face of the city, ripping the heart out of old Beijing. Fatso's had been a traditional house, a hutong home, and he'd appealed to various international heritage organisations to keep the developers at bay. Foreign television teams had visited his area, and he'd told them he'd resist until the end.

And resist he did. At least until he was happy with the compensation.

He'd never seen the romance of outside toilets and Qing Dynasty plumbing, and the money he'd squeezed from the developer bought him his three-storey shophouse with plenty of change to spare. Or so Wang suspected.

He reckoned his own landlord was playing a similar game. He'd sounded the guy out and just got bland answers that all was well, that he'd never sell up, which just convinced Wang that his shabby low-rise was probably doomed. The buildings all around were slated for demolition. Some had already been pulled down.

It felt sometimes like his home and university were in the middle of a construction site. Two of the city's subway lines had been extended to the area, and with them had come a building frenzy. Malls and high-rises were sprouting all around. Old neighbourhoods were being flattened.

The University had benefited too, with some new faculty and research buildings, though it felt to Wang like a bad consolation prize for all the disruption.

Not that the dreary apartment he and his friends rented had much appeal. There was nothing Qing Dynasty about its leaking roof and creaking plumbing. It was the convenience that mattered to him, cheap and so close to University.

A long road leading to his University, and to his apartment, was lined with a high wall to hide the construction. It was covered with murals. Satellites, space rockets, a ballistic missile, computers, an aircraft carrier. A slogan written in large characters said they were building a civilised society. The Chinese Dream.

Wang knew there'd been a few holdouts, fighting the developers, but it seemed a lost cause.

He took his phone from his pocket, put in his earphones and zoned out. He was on autopilot, along a route home that he knew so well he could navigate just about every obstacle without ever looking up from his screen. He opened a game trying to line up rows of colourful blob-like animals on a grid, clicking and zapping until he had three in a row to win points.

Closer to his apartment block, part of the wall had been screened off and workmen were trying to paint over graffiti. The graffiti was of a stick alien, not the best drawing, but it was definitely a stick alien. Just like Wang's stick alien. It had been spray-painted on the wall, over the top of the slogan about the Chinese Dream, and the workmen were now obliterating it.

Not that Wang saw the graffiti. And he would barely have noticed the workmen at all had he not almost fallen over a tin of their paint, looking up briefly as one of them swore at him. His mind was on the blobs he was trying to line up on his phone.

Three policemen in heavy coats stood close by, supervising the paint job. They watched Wang as he passed. One of them told him to pay attention and look where he was going, saying it in a sneering sort of way. Wang grunted, a pissed off sort of grunt. Though it had nothing to do with the cop, whom he hadn't even heard. It was because he'd just failed to match three yellow birds and was stuck at level thirty-one of his game.

He reached his apartment block just as two more policemen were leaving from its main entrance. One of them asked Wang if he lived there, and when he said yes they showed him two photographs –

grainy black and white computer printouts. They looked to Wang like they'd been taken from a surveillance camera up on the main road, and they showed what appeared to be an old man spraying something on the wall.

"You know this man?" said one of the policemen.

"Why, what's he done?" said Wang.

"I'm the one asking the questions and I asked you if you know him."

Then the second cop said the old man was a vandal who'd destroyed state property.

"Oh, yeah?" said Wang. "Never seen him before."

Wang entered the dark stairwell of his apartment block and began to climb the stairs, stopping on the first-floor landing and looking out of a cracked window as the cops headed across a piece of cleared land towards another block. Going door to door.

The old man in the photographs was well known in the neighbourhood, a holdout, the last person still living in one of the condemned blocks nearby, which he was refusing to leave. He'd always seemed friendly and harmless enough to Wang, though not to the developers. Wang wasn't about to give him away, though he suspected it wouldn't be long before someone else did.

He continued up the stairs, back on his phone, and by the time he reached his door he'd matched three frogs, followed by three foxes. Then with a ding and a chirp, the game told him he'd now reached level thirty-two, and awarded him twenty happy coins.

– 10 –

Myopia

Wang Chu was woken by what sounded like the clanking and rumbling of heavy machinery. He sat bolt upright in the chair in which he'd dozed off and spent the night clinging to his laptop and smartphone. There was a loud crunch and a thud that made his room shake, followed by a long straining sound and the crash of falling glass and bricks.

He thought that maybe this was an earthquake and he ran out of his room, through his small kitchen and onto a landing where Zhang Jun and Liu Wei were already at the window looking out at a row of diggers and small cranes, lined up like in the photograph he'd posted of American tanks in the Iraqi desert.

The early morning smog had drained the scene of most of its colour, and the machines were just dark shadows, the diggers raising their long arms, demolition balls swinging from the cranes, as they prepared for a final assault on a small apartment block, already half flattened.

Police in riot gear were lined up alongside the diggers, and one cop was talking into a loud hailer. It was hard to hear clearly since it kept screeching, but he was telling somebody to come out, that this was his last chance, and threatening to bury him under the rubble.

Wang assumed they must be talking to the old holdout, the old man still refusing to leave his condemned home, the graffiti man. Moments later the man appeared at the main door of what was left of his block, wearing pyjamas and holding a placard high in the air, defiant.

The old man began to shout, but was smothered by cops, all over him like hungry animals, pinning him to the ground, and then dragging him towards a police van. But they couldn't completely subdue him and his angry words cut through the cold morning air.

"The developers are the criminals! The developers are the criminals!"

The cops pushed him into the back of the van, stuffing him in like a bag of trash into a garbage truck. He was beginning to cry, sobbing now, "Criminals, criminals. The lot of you", his voice trailing off as the door was slammed behind him.

The van pulled away and passed a wall, the graffiti wall, freshly repainted with a picture of a spacecraft and the words "Building the Future" and "Rejuvenating the Nation" in big characters. The riot police retreated, and the diggers and cranes moved in for the kill, the demolition balls swinging and the long arms of the diggers clawing the remaining walls of the old man's building.

By the time Wang and his roommates left their own place, thirty minutes later, heading for The Moment On Time coffee shop, the nearby apartment block was a pile of concrete and twisted metal. The old man's ancient box-like television, crushed and half buried, was the only obvious evidence that he'd once lived there. That, some scattered flowers and a card from well-wishers. Liu went over and picked up the card. The message inside read, "Keep up the fight", and next to the characters was a crude drawing of a stick alien.

Liu also saw the placard the old man had been holding. It was face down in the rubble. From his own building it had been hard to make out what it said. He turned it over to see another scratchy drawing of an alien, with the words "Keep your hands off my home".

Wang hadn't noticed. He'd just taken a call from Fatso, who was telling him that the first of the *Star Wars* caps should be ready ahead of schedule, but there'd been a slight mess-up and they'd all be with the guy in black with the funny mask.

"Darth Vader. That's fine. Don't worry. He's probably the best known of the characters," Wang said, telling Fatso that the most important thing was speed.

Fatso then told Wang he'd had another idea, what with the smog being so bad.

"We rebrand the masks," he said.

"What, paint them black and call them Darth Vader, or something like that?"

Fatso said that wouldn't work. "3M, you can't beat 3M. They make the best masks."

He said the useless PM2.5 Mega Blockers that for weeks had been sitting in boxes at his place would become useless 3M PM2.5 Super Mega Blockers, with the addition of a small piece of plastic on the front with the 3M logo. The plastic nodule would be designed to look like a filter, but would be just solid plastic. Fatso said he could sort the plastic pretty quickly and bring in a team of migrant labourers to stick them on every mask by hand. It wouldn't take more than one afternoon.

He seemed pretty excited and, once he'd hung up, Liu and Zhang agreed that rebranding the masks was a great idea. That Fatso could be pretty smart after all.

The smog was so bad that morning that it had stopped registering on the air quality apps on their smartphones. It had gone off the scale. As they walked towards a main road past their University and to The Moment On Time, the tall buildings which lined it resembled ghostly shadows; cars with fuzzy headlights passed beside them.

A long banner across the University's main entrance read, "Building an Ecological Civilisation". It was another slogan from the Party leader, in giant characters, which had been put there when he visited the campus to open some new buildings and plant some trees. But it was only visible from close up because of the smog. Wang took a photograph and posted it to his *Gasping Dragon* account with a brief caption:

Nice idea, when are they going to start?

"Did you ever find out what that is?" said Liu. "The ecological civilisation thing?"

Wang just shrugged.

He'd asked one of his tutors, partly as a joke and partly because he was genuinely curious. The tutor had asked the professor who ran the

Computer Science Department, who'd checked with the University's Communist Party office, which ran everything. They'd passed it on to the Party's district office. Which is where the trail went cold and after two weeks the tutor had summoned Wang and told him he was an idiot and that the answer was obvious, though without saying what the answer was.

Wang assumed that his tutor never got an answer. Shortly afterwards, the professor had been accused of a lack of ideological rigour, and had his permission cancelled to attend upcoming academic conferences in Europe and America.

A small digger was trundling across an area below the ecological civilisation banner that used to be a lawn, but was being prepared for replanting.

"What happened to the grass?" Zhang said.

"It didn't like the paint," said Liu. He told his roommates that there'd been such a bad drought before the visit by the Party leader that the grass was a kind of brown. So the University had given it a coat of high gloss green.

Once the visit was over, the grass died completely.

"Too bad," said Wang. "Grass should really be green."

It took around twenty minutes to reach The Moment On Time, where they took their usual table by the window, Wang and Zhang working the keyboards of their smartphones. Liu opening his laptop and logging into his share trading account, letting out a deep groan as soon as he did so. The market was crashing again.

Liu then said that China was going blind, and soon most Chinese wouldn't be able to see beyond the end of their nose. He said he'd seen it online, quoting a bunch of experts.

"China's got an epidemic of myopia, can't see stuff in the distance, because we spend too much time indoors and looking at screens."

"Oh yeah?" Wang said, without looking up from his smartphone, where he was back trying to line up colourful blob-like animals and earn some more happy coins. "I don't really see that."

"Very funny," Liu said, "but this is serious."

And it then struck Wang that the smog was so bad most days that he might not notice if he was going blind.

Wang then noticed that several of the regulars had started wearing masks inside the coffee shop, and it was true that even indoors the air didn't smell good.

Lily had brought a small air-purifying machine. At least that's what she called it. Wang suspected it was a fake, and it sat lonely in one corner, spluttering and wheezing, struggling to cope. He was convinced that what came out of it smelt worse than the air that went in. But fake or not, there was keen competition for the tables nearby.

And they all knew better than to complain to Lily.

Wang then opened another game, and was soon racing on a hoverboard. He was a hooligan caught red-handed spraying graffiti on a train. He was riding a board called Panda, racing down a metro line and along the roofs of trains, chased by a grumpy train inspector and his dog.

He was trying to grab gold coins out of the air and at the same time stop the board from crashing. But the board, with its two big panda eyes, slipped as he sped round a corner, trying to avoid an oncoming train, stretching for a coin, the snarling dog at his heels.

He crashed and Panda exploded just as another message came through from his mother asking if he'd read her earlier ones and why he didn't answer or return her calls.

His knee began to itch again and his right foot trembled worse than ever. He tried planting it firmly on the ground, pressing hard and hoping nobody would notice. There was no way of avoiding it, he'd have to answer. So he opened the draft reply with the lonely words "Hi Mum", and wrote:

Great to hear from you. I am so sorry it has taken so long to write. I am working very hard, with so little time to myself, because I am determined to get the best results.

My girlfriend Eu-Meh is really looking forward to meeting you. She's smart and intelligent and a beauty queen, but very busy with studies. She's from Shanghai, but has family in Australia. Like me, she's hoping to study in America.

We will try and get to Harbin during the Spring Festival.

Please say hi to Dad.

Your loving son, Chu

He then attached a photograph he found online of a Chinese-Australian beauty queen called Yang Eu-Meh and pressed send.

No sooner had it gone than he had second thoughts, thinking that was way too much detail, that he was digging himself even deeper into a hole, and wondering if the photo was really necessary. But it would keep her happy, keep his mother off his back, at least until the Spring Festival. He'd at least bought himself time.

He then went back to hopping between social media sites, seeing what was trending. One online campaign had gone viral, people posting selfies wearing pollution masks and the word "Why?" written on the front. Hundreds of thousands had joined in, figuring there was safety in numbers and that wearing a mask made them tougher to identify.

Wang posted one of himself wearing a PM2.5 Mega Blocker that was soon to become a 3M PM2.5 Super Mega Blocker, adding the online address of their shop.

Others posted doctored pictures showing various monsters in the smog. Wang added his own: the stick alien lurking in the haze behind shrouded buildings.

He then opened a video-sharing site and found at the top of the trending list a grainy video of an old man being dragged by police across a piece of wasteland. It took him a while to recognise the scene he'd witnessed that morning. It was silent and shot from a nearby window, moving in and out of focus before the shot was lost completely as the person making the video ducked behind a curtain to avoid being seen.

Which to Wang made it all the more chilling. He was about to show it to Liu when the video disappeared from his screen and was replaced with a lost connection alert. It had been deleted.

Zhang was reading a story about a collision in the South China Sea between a ship belonging to the Japanese coast guard and a Chinese fishing boat it was trying to chase off near some disputed islands.

The Japanese had accused the Chinese of illegal fishing, of plundering the area of endangered species and damaging rare coral, which Zhang said was ridiculous.

"The endangered species are Chinese. The coral too."

Wang just said, "Yeah, sure."

Zhang could get quite excited about that sort of stuff, and when he did Wang mostly ignored him. As did Liu. The patriotic bloggers, as they called themselves, and which Zhang liked to read, were the loudest on the web, mostly unbothered by the censors and often with official encouragement. China claimed all the South China Sea as its own, saying it had a right to the lot, and the latest collision had brought the nationalists out in force demanding that the entire Japanese fleet be immediately sunk, that Tokyo be nuked or worse. Stuff like that.

Wang reckoned the patriotic bloggers were just about the most stupid people on the web, though there was plenty of competition for the title.

And that gave him an idea.

The area that China claimed was within what it called a nine-dash line, surrounding the entire South China Sea. Why not claim a bit more? So he wrote a post to a top nationalist website saying the claim was being extended to a 351-dash line encompassing the entire Pacific Ocean. Quoting an unnamed Party leader, he said that Ming pottery had been discovered on an island called Alcatraz, showing the presence of early Chinese settlers and therefore giving Beijing an indisputable historic right to the island and the entire ocean leading to it. He said all Chinese maps were being immediately updated.

He wasn't entirely sure where Alcatraz was, but once had watched a movie about the place, which was pretty cool. It had been some sort of prison, and China needed prisons. He shared that thought too.

He then searched for Alcatraz and found the movie he'd watched. It was called *Escape from Alcatraz*, and he'd picked up a pirate copy a while back in a nearby market, but had since lost it. He copied the movie poster, a picture of a Hollywood actor called Clint Eastwood looking out through a crack in a wall, and he replaced Eastwood's face with his stick alien. He shared that too, with a caption:

Right historic wrongs! Return Alcatraz to the motherland!

He then went back to the hoverboard, the one called Panda, which had recovered from its fiery crash and was soon being chased again, this time by an entire pack of snarling dogs. He was starting to get the hang of it now and kept their snapping fangs at bay until he got bored again, closed the game, and looked back out of the window, at the thick smog.

He began to think again about myopia and whether he might be losing his eyesight, but just didn't know it yet. That one day the smog might clear, but stuff would still be all fuzzy.

"Hey Zhang," he said, "what can *you* see when you look out towards the railway line?"

But Zhang was no longer paying attention. He was taking selfies.

Wang kicked him, and asked him again; this time Zhang told Wang there was no smog, the visibility was perfect, and that he was almost certainly going blind.

Which is when Wang noticed for the first time that Zhang was wearing glasses.

"I didn't know you wore those," Wang said. "Myopia?"

"No. Vanity mainly," Zhang said handing over the glasses, which had no lenses, just the frame, which Zhang said he thought was pretty cool, telling Wang that the selfies were for the dating app, since he'd now decided to use a genuine photograph rather than the one of the celebrity he'd grabbed off the web, just in case he did decide to meet his match.

Wang said that sounded smart.

He then typed 'myopia' into a search engine, still worried, and not finding Zhang's joke particularly funny.

As well as stuff about eyes he found the other definition: "a lack of imagination, foresight, or intellectual insight". And that prompted him to join the online discussion, suggesting government officials might be particularly at risk. He shared that thought to his *Gasping Dragon* account, and alongside posted his stick alien on which he painted an outsize pair of spectacles with thick black lenses.

– 11 –

Shanghai Bull

Anthony Morgan thought his talk at the Shanghai Stock Exchange had gone well. He was a true friend of China, said the Deputy Chairman of the Exchange, standing in for his boss who'd been detained on the eve of the conference for unspecified breaches of Party discipline.

Foreign investors had praised him too, calling his talk sober and realistic, a breath of fresh air in the face of all the negativity and hysteria.

"Great work, Tony," said one former top US Treasury official.

The mood had been upbeat, and Morgan had set that tone.

He left the conference, and had just climbed into a cab for the Bund, heading to lunch with Bud from Alabama, when his iPhone rang. The voice at the other end said that it was the office of Mr Fang, and that Mr Fang needed some more investment options, real estate preferably, in America. And he needed them urgently.

Morgan asked whom he was speaking to, but the man ignored him, repeating that it was urgent. Morgan said he was putting together a number of options for Mr Fang including beachfront and city centre properties, as well as farmland. East and west coast, and some in the Midwest. Morgan asked what were Mr Fang's preferences and budget. The man said that Mr Fang would look at the lot, that the budget was big and the priority was speed.

"And another thing," he said, "Mr Fang wants to buy a football team."

"Any particular football team?" Morgan asked, a little taken aback, not having a clue about football. "Are we talking American football or English?"

The man from Mr Fang's office said he'd check, but thought it was the one with the round ball, the English game, and that he'd prefer a top club, second division or above.

"Mr Fang likes football," the man said. And then he hung up.

Mr Fang, who also called himself Michael, was one of Morgan's newer clients, based in the southern boom city of Shenzhen, next to Hong Kong, and to whom Morgan provided what MacMaster and Brown described as wealth management services.

Mr Fang represented a consortium of investors. Rich investors. Everything else about him was a bit hazy. But the way Morgan saw it, the guy had a lot of wealth to manage and was in a hurry to find a home for it, and at the end of the day what else was there to know?

Mr Fang was uncomplicated, unlike Bud. Sorting that idiot from Alabama had been an ordeal, but it was worth the effort, to keep his own reputation intact. He'd not yet found out for certain what had happened to Bud's original business partner, but the new partner he had in mind was solid, dependable, a Hong Kong guy with a bunch of factories in the south. One of Morgan's oldest business associates.

Still, he was uneasy about the lunch.

But when he reached the restaurant, a new place in a plush hotel on the Bund, he found Bud in good spirits.

"Go ahead, get the quotes from the guy down south, but I'm not sure I'm gonna even need a new partner," Bud said, telling Morgan that a Chinese company had made a bid for his entire business. "They want to buy the whole thing, the whole fucking thing, and they are offering stupid money. All cash."

Bud said the offer had come out of the blue, and that the company was well informed.

"They seem to know a lot about me. About the business and our technologies. I mean really detailed stuff that I didn't really know. They've done their homework. I was quite surprised." He said the

91

Chinese company had asked him for a whole ton of additional stuff about his plans.

"They are especially interested in the technology."

Morgan said that was good news, that technology was often the deal clincher, but to be careful about what you give them in advance. He said he'd be happy to do the due diligence, check them out. And this time it was Bud's turn to brush that off, saying US$250 million in cash was about as diligent as you could get.

Bud said he was staying on for a few days to try and close the deal, but to keep him up to speed on the guy down south. Morgan thought the offer to buy out Bud's entire business sounded odd, but he kept that thought to himself and didn't push the issue. Bud was happy, and that's what counted. If this new deal collapsed then Bud only had himself to blame.

The restaurant served what it called "Chinese fusion". Morgan wasn't sure what that meant, other than an extra zero or two on the bill. But the wine, two bottles of it, was good.

Bud said he'd been to a seminar at the US Consulate that was beyond tedious. Something about computer hacking. "I only stayed for a while. Those people are paranoid. You know what I mean?"

Morgan said he knew what he meant.

Bud was so loud it was as if he was broadcasting to the whole restaurant. Morgan wondered if there was anybody in there who hadn't heard Bud's plans. And it struck him that you didn't really need to break into computers to steal his business secrets.

When they left, Bud said he wanted to visit the bull on the Bund, get a photo with it. Feeling good about himself now.

The raging bull sculpture was a replica of the famous Lower Manhattan bull, and created by the same artist. The Bund had been the financial heart of old Shanghai, and the Chinese bull had been installed in front of that famous facade, a universal symbol of financial muscle, but also of Shanghai's ambition to take on the world.

Bud grabbed the bull by the horns, flashing a V for victory, while Morgan took a few photographs on Bud's smartphone.

"I think you're right to remain bullish on China, Tony," he said in his deep southern drawl, before his car arrived and Morgan waved him off.

Morgan looked again at the bull. The thing he'd always found most interesting about it was its enormous testicles. With its backside raised towards the Bund, it was what you noticed first, or at least Morgan did.

As did a bunch of kids, who began to photograph each other grabbing the bull by its balls. Morgan raised his iPhone and took a photograph of them, thinking that was maybe a better way of looking at Bud's latest China deal. And at a good many others too.

He then took a mid-grade pollution mask from his pocket, coughing before he put it on. He didn't wear them in front of clients or officials, fearing it might somehow be seen as a reproach, showing a lack of confidence in China.

He still had a while before he was due to meet his wife, Cindy Wu, at her favourite teahouse in the old French Concession. So he decided to walk.

The sun had broken through the haze for the first time in days, which brought out the wedding photographers. Brides and grooms posing in front of the Bund's old buildings, brides in flowing wedding dresses, grooms in dinner jackets and bow ties.

They pouted, laughed, smiled and jumped on cue.

It was a cold day, and the trick seemed to be to get in as many photos as possible before the smiles became a grimace and bare shoulders sprouted goose bumps. At which point friends were on hand to put them back into thick coats, to warm them up before the next set of photographs.

One couple was wearing colourful pollution masks. Designer masks. Morgan liked that and took a photo. Another one for *@Beijing_smog*.

He walked up Nanjing Road, packed with Saturday shoppers, and through People's Square, where there was a very different picture of marriage from what he'd just seen down on the Bund.

The pathways through the centre of the park, around an artificial lake shaded by tall trees, were packed. Shanghai's marriage market was in full swing. Hundreds of mostly older people stood behind open umbrellas, which served as noticeboards on which were taped photographs and profiles of their children or grandchildren, trying to find them partners. Desperate to have them settle down and have a child, maybe two now that was allowed.

Others, whom Morgan assumed to be commercial marriage brokers, had taped together dozens of laminated profiles and draped them over fences and bushes.

Crowds moved slowly along the lines of umbrellas, looking over the profiles, photographing some and stopping from time to time to talk. To get more details. They were mostly older too.

Missing were the kids themselves. The ones in the photographs. Most would be single children, children of China's one-child policy, and Morgan wondered whether they even knew they were being marketed like this. Which got him thinking about his own marriage to Cindy Wu, which in its own way had been arranged, a kind of marriage of convenience.

They'd first met more than thirty years earlier and were married six months after that. He was a young businessman, a pioneer back then as China first opened up. Her mother was a prominent scientist involved with the country's young space industry, her father a senior Communist Party official with links to the country's early revolutionary leaders.

Morgan had first met the parents, at a reception for a visit of the then US President, Ronald Reagan, and they'd got back in touch soon after, introducing their daughter, seeing the young Englishman as a good catch in spite of their Chinese establishment background.

A reformist mood was running through China back then, the mid-eighties, which was brutally brought to a close with the Tiananmen Square massacre in 1989. Both Morgan and his wife had retreated to the UK for a while after that, until they figured it was safe to come back and resume business.

Her Chinese name was Wu Jinting, and she'd joined him at MacMaster and Brown as his translator and guide. Until they both began to understand the value of information in a society where nothing was certain or clear, and the authorities all too often made up the rules as they went along.

And as the country opened up and the economy boomed, everybody wanted to be part of the China Miracle, and the value of insight and information grew with it. Morgan and his wife rode that wave. And they were the best.

And even though the skyline of a city like Shanghai had been transformed, Morgan reckoned the rules of doing business remained as clear as the smog that all too frequently blanketed those towering skyscrapers.

He was walking in the old French Concession now, his favourite part of Shanghai. An oasis. Almost like it wasn't China at all. And it gave him the feeling again, a feeling that had been growing stronger in him, that it was time to cash in and leave. But he felt trapped. Trapped by all the money he was making. China was like a drug to him. It was hard to quit the habit, even while his fears grew that it might destroy him. That any day it might all come tumbling down.

He hadn't talked to Cindy Wu about that, not in those terms, uncertain how she'd react. He knew she was as worried about the future as him. Maybe more so. But she had family here. And anyway, he wasn't sure what the marriage meant anymore. Maybe leaving China was what would save it.

And he thought again about Mr Fang. He'd not yet told Cindy Wu about his dealings with Fang either. The man had money to burn. All that property he was after. A football team. What was that all about? He didn't know and didn't really care. More and more he saw Mr Fang as his last big killing. The final ticket to a comfortable life beyond China.

Daylight was fading fast along the Concession's tree-lined streets, lights going on in the restored mansions and old shop fronts from a different era.

He and Cindy Wu had agreed to meet in a narrow three-storey teahouse, or *Maison de Thé* as it called itself, a teashop on the ground floor, tea and cake served on the top floors.

He climbed the stairs to the first floor to find his wife sitting in her usual alcove, the most private area, glass teapots and a small cup on a traditional wooden tray in front of her. The walls were lined with big old metal tea tins, wooden birdcages hung from the ceilings, without the birds. Mellow jazz played in the background.

He could see why she liked the place.

His wife greeted him business-like, a kiss on both cheeks, which seemed appropriate, since they were in a *Maison*. Then some small talk about their villa in Thailand and their son's schooling in the UK and his visit to China. Cindy Wu said she'd meet Robert when he landed in Beijing and he could stay with her for a few days. Then she'd bring him to Shanghai.

Morgan said that sounded fine.

A server came over and refilled her pot, then decanted it into another, and then into the cup. The server said it was a green tea with a hint of flower from Hangzhou. Morgan ordered the same.

He looked at her and wondered whether it was just boredom, familiarity maybe, that had driven them apart. There'd been no serious girlfriends since she'd left to live in Beijing, nothing like that, but plenty that weren't so serious, and there was barely a city in China where he hadn't rustled up company, usually at commercial rates. And he wondered whether she knew. Whether she suspected.

As with his business dealings, he was always cautious and discreet, but if Cindy Wu could dig out all that stuff on officials and business people, what couldn't she find out about him?

She had a small box in front of her full of index cards, preferring that to computerised records. She'd divided them into current investigations and then subdivided them into different aspects of each case, including education, family, business, and Party links. There was a special card for the personal stuff, the indiscretions, real and rumoured. It was usually the fullest card of them all.

And Morgan wondered whether one of them had his name on it.

She was always well organised, always had been. And once Morgan's tea had arrived they began to run through the active investigations, mostly background checks on prospective business partners, Cindy Wu giving a brief commentary as they went, usually in terms of eggs.

"He's a bad egg. I'd be very careful here. This one's a good egg. This one's got no real business record, but he's well connected with the local government."

For each completed investigation, she'd compiled and printed a document, summarising her findings on a cover page, followed by more detailed background, translated from Chinese to English where necessary. Both of them preferred to deal with hard copies, real paper, from years of doing it that way.

At first they'd been surprised how easy it was to get hold of personal information in China. The flip side of an authoritarian system was an almost complete disregard for privacy, and they'd discovered that everything from bank records to household registration files were readily handed over for a small fee or sometimes just by asking.

And rumours could be found everywhere.

Rules had been tightened, which meant that sorting the eggs took a bit more money and leverage than before.

But Cindy Wu had plenty of both.

Morgan asked her about Bud's partner, the guy who'd disappeared, and she said that had come as a shock to her too, that her contacts had told her the guy had got caught up in a corruption investigation.

"But I thought he had impeccable Party connections," Morgan said.

"He did have connections," Cindy Wu said. "But they turned out to be with the wrong faction of the Party."

She said the investigations were getting tougher and he asked why.

"It used to be more straightforward, just a matter of judging the quality of connections. You know, whether Dad's in a position to help with contracts or the wife's in the Party. But the anti-corruption crackdown has complicated things.

"They dress it up as being anti-graft, but it's an old-fashioned purge. It's about power."

She said that it was hard to explain, but even purges had rules. Now all the certainties had gone. She said there'd been nothing like this since Mao.

"Nothing or nobody is out of bounds. It makes it hard to figure out who'll disappear next," she said, sipping tea and tapping the card file box with long fingernails, painted purple. She said there were all sorts of rumours around, about a power struggle in the Party.

Morgan said that maybe they really did want to get rid of corruption, to clean up the system. And that had to be a good thing.

And Cindy Wu said, "Sometimes you just don't get it Tony. Corruption *is* the system.

"What we're doing, it's not as straightforward as it used to be."

Morgan said that he understood, though Cindy Wu doubted that too.

"So what else have you got for me?" she said.

"These are from a new client, an American guy," Morgan said, handing her two plastic folders: the Nanjing chemical company and the Shanghai insurance outfit. "Due diligence stuff mainly, on companies looking to make investments in the States."

She looked at them and said neither should be a problem.

"And there's this one," he said. "Same client, but more urgent."

He placed a third file on the table beside their tea cups, first taking out the photographs of the kid at the party and of the older man, and laying them on the table in front of Cindy Wu.

"Background?" she said.

"Kid's name is Chen Huizhi. Rich. The client thinks the older man is his father, so I guess he's a Chen too."

"And that's it?" she said, lifting the photos as if she might find something else underneath, something that might give her a bit more to go on. Then she placed them back on the table.

"The client says they're into digital stuff, computers, and wants whatever background we can get on both of them. And there's one more thing."

"What's that?"

"Kid's into Ferraris."

He handed her two more photos. Chen Huizhi getting into the car and a tight shot of the licence plate.

She sat for a while looking at the photos and then said, "This really isn't a lot to go on."

"I know," said Morgan. "But the client is paying well. Very well."

They sat in silence for a while, both of them sipping tea, and then Cindy Wu said, "Tony, Ferraris aren't good."

– 12 –

Shanghai Dumplings

"I do not believe it. I do not frigging believe it. They've gone for the noodles. They've gone for the frigging noodles."

"Relax, Tom. Maybe they want a change."

"But they always go for the dumplings. Every day they order the dumplings, Dick. Come on, order the dumplings, you twats. Order the frigging dumplings."

But the twats ordered the noodles, beef with pepper, some spicy chicken and a bunch of vegetables.

"Ah shit," said the one called Tom, pushing his laptop away.

Tom and Dick were the latest additions to the surveillance team in the office of Shanghai TT Logistics, or The Facility, as they now liked to call it. They were fresh out from Fort Meade, National Security Agency analysts, travelling under the guise of visiting businessmen, and they'd arrived with a pile of computers, and various odd-looking accessories, which they'd set up in the room overlooking the white low-rise building in the North Bund.

Not that they'd really introduced themselves. Just Tom and Dick, which Drayton suspected weren't their real names. Nothing more. He wanted to ask if Harry would be arriving next, but wasn't sure they'd find that funny.

Tom was fluent in Mandarin and all sorts of computer stuff that

Drayton didn't come close to understanding. He'd been staring at the online menu of a local restaurant, from which the shadowy characters in the white building ordered their takeaways. And mostly they did order dumplings, the speciality of the place, and mostly they ordered online.

Tom and Dick had hacked into the restaurant's website and so could monitor the orders being placed real-time. They'd also infected the menu with malware, some bug they'd developed back at Fort Meade, so that when the guys from the white building clicked on the dumplings they got a whole lot more than soggy pastry and pork.

"They'll be downloading a code," Tom had told Drayton. "And that should give us a foothold in their computer system."

Drayton asked about the malware they'd used on the maestro's computer, to get the photograph of the Colonel, and they said that one was programmed to self-destruct once they had the photo. They said they weren't taking any chances. Tom said the dumpling bug was much smarter, smiling at Dick in a knowing sort of way.

Drayton said that was really neat, and made a mental note never to order takeaway food online. He asked Tom what happened once they got the foothold with the new smart bug, and Tom said they'd take a poke around, but that he wasn't entirely sure because it was new and untried. The guy was pretty excited by his new bug. Which was why he was so pissed when they ordered noodles.

"Should we infect the noodles?" said Dick.

Tom said no, we don't want to overplay our hand. These guys are cyber experts too.

They watched from the window as a deliveryman on a motorcycle arrived at the main gate. He was wearing a bright red jacket, "Dumpling King" in big black characters on the back. He retrieved two bags from a red box on the rear of his bike, and handed the food to a uniformed guard.

"I was hoping we'd have some better news for Washington today," said Dick, looking at his watch. "Conference call is in an hour."

"I can deal with that," Drayton said. "I need to be back at the consulate anyway."

"Sure, if you don't mind, Chuck."

Drayton didn't mind, in fact he was pretty keen to get away, finding the atmosphere of the room tense and stuffy, the geeks far too serious. To make matters worse they'd run out of beer. These NSA guys were strictly mineral water only, making Drayton feel bad each time he cracked a Tsingtao.

Drayton reckoned they'd both had a sense of humour bypass. Maybe that was a qualification for all this stuff. Personalities need not apply.

Tom thanked him again and coughed, a deep hacking cough.

"Jesus, I haven't had a cough like this in years. Is the air always this bad?" he said.

"It gets worse," Drayton said, picking up his coat and mask, and making for the door. "Get yourselves some good masks. There are a couple of apps you can download too, give you the air quality real-time. I can send you the link."

Tom said thanks, but don't worry. That wouldn't be necessary. They weren't the kind of guys who downloaded anything from anybody.

Once out on the street he followed a routine they'd set up, heading north along another narrow cluttered road lined with old shophouses. He then cut back towards the river, beside an empty block of land that used to be more shophouses but was now enclosed by a fence plastered with pictures of the ugly office tower they planned to replace them with.

Drayton instinctively raised his collar and adjusted his hood and mask as a police car, lights flashing, raced past him. Then another. He reached an abandoned riverside warehouse with a narrow alleyway running beside it, where he stopped and sent a brief message on his phone, just the word "smog". The signal that he was ready to be picked up.

Five minutes later a green Toyota taxi pulled up in front of the warehouse and Drayton climbed into the back seat.

"Good afternoon, Mr Drayton."

"How you doing, Cyril?"

"I am doing good, though the car takes a bit of getting used to. It's not like driving the consulate limo."

"But it is discreet, and discreet is what we need."

"Probably need a few more dents then, if you really want to blend in. All Shanghai taxis have got dents," said Cyril, in a slow, languid delivery that irked Drayton. He'd arrived with the NSA guys, who said they needed a trusted driver and a vehicle that wouldn't get noticed.

Cyril was Cyril Chow, a Chinese-American, and this guy didn't give much away either, though he did have a family name. He sure knew his way around Shanghai, and Drayton wondered whether he also planted bugs in online dumplings.

"You certainly know the streets here, Cyril man. Been here before, I take it?"

Cyril just said that Shanghai wasn't that complicated a city to find your way around.

"Do me a favour, Cyril, and just slow down here a little. I'm curious about what's going on, all these cops."

The police cars that had swept past him had joined several more and a couple of vans outside an office block they were now passing on their left, on the river bank. The building was maybe seven or eight storeys of dark red brick, and pretty rundown. There was a neon sign, high up and reading, "Shanghai Glorious Shipping Company". Though it was tough to read through the smog, and not all the neon was working.

As they passed, two cops were carrying an elderly man to one of the vans. He was wriggling and shouting. There was a big group of people inside the main lobby, chanting and yelling. The police were yelling back, were trying to get them out of the building. There was a loud crash as a window smashed.

"Pretty feisty bunch," Drayton said. "Wonder what that was all about. Did you catch what the old man was shouting?"

"Hard to tell. It was a tough accent, from the west of China I'd say. Something about children, killing children," Cyril said.

"That's not good," said Drayton, intrigued. He asked Cyril to swing around the block again, but Cyril said that wouldn't be smart, that he didn't want to get noticed, that they should get back to the consulate.

The traffic was heavy and it took forty minutes to reach the French Concession. Drayton's phone rang twice as they crawled along the Concession's tree-lined streets. The *Mission Impossible* ringtone, his ex-wife Debbie. He ignored the calls, switching the phone to silent. The ringtone made Cyril laugh, and Drayton was about to tell him that the grief he was getting was no laughing matter, but he thought better of it. That wasn't the sort of private detail you shared with a guy from the NSA, at least not knowingly.

And he knew what the calls were about. Debbie had already emailed him to say the roof problem wasn't just a little leak from the blow from the tree, but was structural, and that was a big job, an expensive job. And guess who'd have to pay for that.

Which made him think about Sakura. She didn't give him any of that grief. Though right now she wasn't giving much of anything at all.

She was number two at the Shanghai branch of the Japan External Trade Organisation, and Drayton had met her a couple of months earlier at a reception at the consulate, one of the rare moments when he was wearing his official Economic/Commercial Officer hat, or at least trying to, doing his best to avoid serious conversations since he knew very little about either economics or commerce.

It turned out that Sakura found the reception as tedious as he did, and told him that. Then she said it was hard to figure out what was going on with US policy on Asia. Or on anything else for that matter. Drayton just smiled and offered to fetch her another glass of wine, getting one for himself too, because diplomacy these days was a good deal easier after a couple of drinks.

Sakura then suggested they escape to a bar in the Concession, near her place. Which they did, talking some more in the bar, small talk mostly. Drayton hadn't said too much about himself, largely because she never asked. And she was as guarded as him, though he did learn that she was from Nagoya, spoke fluent Mandarin and was perhaps a couple of years older than him.

She was tall, slim and wore dark-rimmed designer glasses and dark blue suit, with a skirt just above her knees. And she was available, because that's what she told him, out of the blue, after two more glasses of wine, and they immediately left for her small apartment, tastefully decorated with Japanese prints and furniture, above an old shophouse.

She fetched some warm sake from the kitchen together with something to snack on. Maybe meat. Possibly fish. But definitely raw

– and chewy. He thought he heard snoring coming from the kitchen, but not like snoring he'd ever heard before. She said that was Bobby, sweet, sweet Bobby.

"Is he your only child?" Drayton had asked.

Sakura said, "Good gracious no," sounding very English. "He's a dog. A beautiful pug."

Then, just as Drayton thought things might get interesting, she told him to leave since she didn't want to wake the pug. She said she also had a call scheduled with Tokyo, and was working early in the morning.

Drayton said he hoped to see her again, and she said sure, but to please keep the noise down as he left because Bobby was a light sleeper.

Though it had been a strange evening and ultimately a bit of a letdown, he was intrigued by Sakura, and especially the bit about being available. But she had her own priorities. And right now Drayton didn't appear to be one of them, since she wasn't returning his calls or messages.

His journey back to the consulate took him past her office, and he thought about having Cyril drop him there, but he was already running late for the conference call, and she'd hate him turning up at the office. She didn't even like him ringing her there.

He messaged her again, saying let's get together, maybe tonight, have some fun, but there was no reply.

Cyril stopped the old taxi a few blocks from the consulate; when Drayton said he was running really late and couldn't Cyril take him straight there, Cyril said that wasn't smart, wasn't protocol.

Drayton jogged the rest of the way, which probably wasn't protocol either, but neither was turning up late.

Once inside the compound, he crossed to the old mansion and down the stairway that led to the wine cellar that was now the secure communications room, the Bubble Room. He went quickly through the retina check, which opened the first door. The scanner on the second door accepted his forefinger, but twice rejected his thumbprint. He wanted to hit the thing. See if it recognised a fist. But then he remembered the security cameras watching him and decided that might not be such a great idea. He tried for a third time, which worked, the scanner having second thoughts and accepting reluctantly that the thumb belonged to Drayton.

The security stuff could be tedious, but it also gave him a buzz. It made him feel part of something bigger, something sexier, and something altogether unexpected. He'd be the first to admit that for a Cyber Guy his qualifications were less than stellar. He'd been in the right place at the right time, and had found his way to Shanghai more through luck than judgement.

But now he was a real player, rubbing shoulders with the spooks, at the heart of US-China relations.

"It's in San Francisco Bay for Christ's sake. How can Alcatraz be part of China?" said a voice from Washington DC as Drayton entered the room, taking a seat by the wall. "It's 6,000 miles from Beijing."

Somebody at the table in the Bubble Room – Drayton thought it was the consulate's political guy – said it was all over the internet. That it had first appeared on some nationalist website, but had gone viral, quoting a top Party source.

There were about a dozen people in the Bubble Room talking to five large flat screens, all of them feeding live video and audio from identical conference rooms in the States. Everyone sitting around long tables, badly lit. From left to right, little digital labels under the screens said State Department, White House, CIA, NSA and FBI.

The Beijing embassy was coming in on an encrypted audio line.

A State Department voice said that since the Alcatraz stuff went viral, there'd been a ten-fold increase in Chinese tourists visiting the island and several what he called annoying incidents: graffiti, and Chinese flags being planted. One tourist had chained himself to the bars of a cell, refusing to leave until America recognised China's incontrovertible rights.

The White House voice said he'd put it on the tentative list for the President's visit, but the embassy should lodge a strong protest with the Chinese Government. Get some clarification.

"The President doesn't want to look stupid," he said.

"No, we wouldn't want that," said one of the figures on the NSA screen, asking what they all made of the picture, the doctored *Escape from Alcatraz* movie poster, Clint Eastwood as an alien.

"We should check that out. Might help us find where the thing came from originally. Think you can look into that, Chuck? You're the Cyber Guy. Chuck, you there?"

And Drayton said yeah, he was there, and he'd get onto it, not really knowing where to start.

It was midday in Shanghai, eleven in the evening on the US east coast. Drayton thought they all sounded surprisingly alert, though if somebody had nodded off it wouldn't be the first time.

It wasn't always easy to see who was talking. Not only were those distant rooms badly lit, but there were frequent glitches, which Drayton assumed was because of all the encryption stuff they needed to make it secure.

Then a woman on the White House screen asked about the cyber operation.

"The President's a dealmaker," she said. "He needs information to confront them with, so we can draw up some ground rules on this. Is Chinese cyber spying still rampant? Is it falling? Or is it just getting cleverer, more targeted?"

The NSA screen said it depends, but possibly all of that.

"How's Team Panda doing? Tom, Dick, are you there?" said a man from Langley, the CIA.

"The guys are at The Facility," Drayton said.

"Okay, talk to us, Chuck. Seems like you guys are making a bit of a meal of things," said somebody from the FBI screen.

Which wasn't entirely inaccurate, what with the dumpling bug, but he wasn't about to go into details of the operation, just telling them it was coming along fine.

"We're close," he said, sounding more confident than he felt.

"We need names, Chuck. We need to know what they're doing. We need to know who's in there. And preferably before the President's visit," said another voice from the NSA link.

"Got it," said Drayton.

And a voice from the White House screen said, "Okay. Good. Keep us posted. Anything else we should think about for the President's visit?"

"Well, the human rights situation is looking a lot worse than it has for a long time, lots of lawyers arrested," said another voice from around the conference table. "There's a big crackdown underway."

And the consulate's economics guy said, "There's also the market meltdown. Some people think the economy here's an accident waiting to happen, and that could have a big knock-on effect on America and the world economy."

But the meeting was already breaking up, screens going blank.

Drayton left the Bubble Room and as he climbed the stairs, his iPhone came back to life with a beep, the signal blocked down below. It was a short encrypted message from the one called Tom, which Drayton unscrambled.

They've ordered the dumplings

– 13 –

The Professor

The wide road that ran from Wang Chu's University to The Moment On Time coffee shop was lined mostly with colleges and research institutes, announcing themselves with large signs and logos, which he used as subliminal landmarks as he walked without ever taking his eyes off the screen of his smartphone.

He knew them all by heart, except for one. A drab grey twenty-storey building was set well back from the road behind a high wall with broken glass embedded in the concrete on top. It was in the centre of a large compound along with several smaller buildings. There was no sign, just a number. And the building didn't appear on any map.

Liu said he'd heard it was a secret prison. That once you went in, you never came back out. Zhang said it was where they took corrupt officials. He said it was the headquarters of the Party's anti-graft enforcers.

To Wang it was mostly a nuisance, slowing down his journey to the coffee shop, since whatever they did in there, they seemed to be doing a lot more of it. He was always getting held up. It was worse than the railway crossing near Fatso's place, as the sidewalk and road in front were repeatedly closed while fleets of black cars and vans with darkened windows swept in and out, often accompanied by wailing police cars and bikes.

The last time it happened Wang was playing a game on his smartphone, back in the temple being chased this time by monkeys and zombies. He'd walked straight onto the rigid outstretched arm of a paramilitary guard, who was blocking the sidewalk, blowing a whistle. Wang was knocked backwards and slipped, dropping his phone. He sprained an ankle, but it could have been a lot worse. The phone could have been damaged. Luckily there was just another crack to the screen. He could live with that.

It was a creepy building, that was for sure, but the roommates wouldn't have given much more thought to it, had not one of their University's most popular professors suddenly disappeared.

*

After Wang's collision with the arm, he'd limped on to The Moment On Time, where he began to play another game. This time he was a medieval king riding a tall stallion, leading an army of thousands across a misty plain. With a few taps on his screen he upgraded his weapons and closed in for a final assault on his enemies, now fleeing the battlefield. He was just a few clicks from world domination.

His concentration was interrupted by an argument on a nearby table, where a couple wearing nearly identical dark padded jackets and beanie hats had just sat and ordered tea. They were trying to keep their voices down, but not doing a good job of it.

"It was a stupid thing to do," the boy said. "Think of your parents. Your career."

The girl snapped back, calling him a coward and said you had to stand up for what you believed in, that the students had to support Huang Guangbi. She said it wasn't fair, what had happened to him. She said that the Professor was one of the most honest men she'd ever met and the accusations against him were rubbish.

The boy told her she was talking nonsense. That fairness and honesty had nothing to do with anything. It's just the way things are, he said, and there was no point in making a fuss. He shook his head, and she looked away before both pulled out their smartphones and retreated to the comfort of the world beyond their screens.

Professor Huang Guangbi taught urban planning at the University, or at least he used to. A week earlier he'd stopped giving classes. It was as if he'd abandoned his job. Just like that. Students who went to his office expecting a lesson found books and files still open on his desk, a half-filled tea cup, but no Professor. The department said they had no idea what had happened.

Three days later a short statement on the university website said the Professor was being investigated by the Communist Party's Central Committee for Discipline Inspection, the graft-busters, for what it called "serious disciplinary offences". It gave no further details, but everybody knew that was usually Party-speak for corruption. Wang said that maybe the Professor had been in one of those vehicles with darkened windows they'd seen sweeping into the building that didn't officially exist.

His disappearance triggered an unusual wave of online support from students, even a small placard-waving protest outside the University's administration office.

Wang assumed the girl had been one of the fifteen-odd students on the protest and that's what she was fighting with her boyfriend over. He'd watched the protest himself, though from a distance. The protesters had been more than outnumbered by plain-clothes security agents, videoing them.

Wang also knew that what made the Professor so popular was not so much his command of urban planning, which was beyond dreary, but the debates and discussions he allowed after his classes.

As darkness fell, students would gather in ever-growing numbers in his fourth floor classroom in an older block in the far corner of the campus, and talk about the nature of democracy, free speech and corruption. It was rumoured they openly discussed the 1989 student movement and the Tiananmen Square massacre, though Wang didn't know for sure, since it wasn't something he ever went along to.

To him, politics was best avoided, at least openly. It would only bring trouble. He didn't think it had anything to do with him. The way he saw it, why should he care when he couldn't do anything about it anyway? If he thought about it at all, it was as something to poke fun at online, in the relative freedom and anonymity of cyberspace, where nothing seemed particularly real.

As he saw it, the boyfriend was right.

He glanced again at the girl, just as she stood, calling the boyfriend a spineless idiot, and spilling what was left of her tea. The boyfriend seemed to shrivel in front of her, keeping his eyes firmly on his smartphone, at which the girl took a swing but missed. Then she stormed to the stairs leading out of the coffee shop, nearly taking out two tables on the way.

The Professor's reputation went beyond the University. He also had a popular blog, with almost a quarter of a million followers. He was a lawyer by training, and he argued online and in his after-hours talks that if the Party was serious about ending corruption and upholding the rule of law, as it claimed, then it needed to be accountable to its own laws and its own constitution.

He always sounded so reasonable, like he was just defending Chinese laws. He was also a member of the Party, and Wang suspected that was why they found him so dangerous and had gone after him, using the catch-all of a corruption investigation as an excuse.

There'd been an online petition in his defence too, which had been signed by hundreds of students. But not the roommates.

"What difference can it make?" Zhang said. "And anyway, how do you know it won't come back to bite you?"

For once, both Liu and Wang agreed that Zhang, boring and cautious Zhang, did have a point. And Zhang said it wasn't just the Professor. Something weird was going on, and not just on campus. They should be careful. He said the Professor's blog had been deleted, and that it wasn't the only one. Dozens of others had gone too, part of a crackdown on what the authorities called rumour mongering.

Wang said he'd heard that several bloggers had been arrested for the same reason, including two that he followed.

"What do you suppose the Professor did wrong?" said Zhang.

And Wang said, "What does it matter?"

It seemed to Wang that corruption was part of the job description for any Party official, though he conceded that Professor Huang Guangbi wasn't like your average Party member. It was hard to think of him doing anything dishonest.

Then Wang said, "I was seriously thinking about joining the Party."

"Seriously? The Party? You?" Liu said.

"They'd never have you," said Zhang.

Wang said he did try, once; sent a letter, but didn't get a reply.

"I've heard they choose you. You don't choose them," Zhang said.

Wang said that Party membership had seemed a good route to easy money. The others agreed. All Party officials enriched themselves, but things were certainly getting trickier now.

Zhang said that some local governments had stopped making decisions because officials were terrified they'd be accused of corruption. He said he'd heard it from his father, both his parents having mid-ranking government jobs in a small town near Shanghai.

"Did you know that half a million officials were punished last year?" Zhang said.

Wang said he didn't know, but that was a lot of vacancies.

"But there's no point if you can't make money anymore," he said.

Zhang said the Commission, the graft-busters, were trying to improve their image, that they'd been sponsoring concerts, where performers sang and danced and did sketches about corrupt officials. One had been broadcast live on television. That they were trying to be more open.

"More open about disappearing people?" said Wang.

Zhang ignored that and said, "They've even got a website with a link for reporting corrupt officials. It crashed several times on its first day, there was so much demand."

Wang said that was cool.

Then Liu began to groan. Another of his investments had gone bad and he had his head in his hands. He said this one was a solid investment, or at least it should have been. His dad, the big-shot government official who advised the Prime Minister, had tipped him off that the company was about to do a deal with an American partner, from somewhere called Alabama, who was going to shift most of his production to China.

"So what happened?" Wang said.

"The guy, the owner, he just disappeared, so the share price has crashed. Just like that. He was a young guy. Into tech mainly. Nobody at the company can say what's happened to him, though there are online rumours he's been arrested."

"Bit of a casino that stock market if you ask me," Zhang said.

"Nobody asked you," said Liu, irritated and thinking Zhang was just being smarmy again. He threw a teaspoon at him, which ricocheted off the table and hit the abandoned boyfriend on the leg. The boyfriend looked up, perhaps thinking the girlfriend was back for another round of argument about the Professor. Liu caught his eye and apologised.

Wang then searched for the website of the Communist Party's anti-corruption outfit, the one that called itself the Central Commission for Discipline Inspection, curious about how they were trying to give a cuddly face to the business of disappearing people.

The site had all the design flair of a funeral announcement or the menu in the university canteen. You didn't have to be a computer science student to recognise that.

He opened it and began to watch a recording of one of their shows, which he thought was so bad it was almost funny. Then a man appeared on screen and said that the Commission would go after what it called "tigers and flies" – high-ranking officials as well as low ones. The man was described as Head of the Commission, its top graft-buster, and he looked uncomfortable, his delivery stilted. Like he hated doing it, being in the limelight like that. Trying to sound reasonable.

But it was his appearance that was most striking to Wang. He was a short man with a balding head, but a curiously round and child-like face. His most distinct feature was a pair of thick-rimmed and slightly tinted glasses that were so big they dominated his face. He showed no emotion.

"So this is the guy who does all the disappearing," Wang said. "What a creep. I don't suppose he has too many friends."

*

The protests against the Professor's disappearance quickly died down. Few people had really expected them to make a difference anyway, and the university chat rooms had reverted to their usual torpor.

Wang could see no further mention of the Professor. It was as if he'd never existed. The old posts had been deleted. Those who'd taken part in the small protest outside the University's administration building had received a summons by the university authorities. They called it an invitation to tea, where they were reminded of their duty to parents, family and university. That rules were rules. They were told to think of their careers.

The girl who'd argued with her boyfriend about defending the Professor had continued to come to the coffee shop, though this time alone, taking a seat in the corner, which she had made her own.

The Party had contacted her father, who owned a small factory on the coast and threatened him with a tax investigation, so she'd promised him she'd concentrate on her studies. For the good of the family. Challenging the authorities does nobody any good, her father had warned her. You can do nothing for the Professor.

From where Wang and his roommates sat, she looked subdued, like the spirit had been sapped from her, just working the keyboard of her smartphone. They never knew her name, never bothered to find out. That would have been to get involved far more than they wanted. They just called her The Girl In The Corner.

– 14 –

Funny Money

For the most part Tom and Dick preferred to stay at The Facility or else in their five-star hotel further down the Bund. Or in Cyril's taxi, travelling between the two. Shanghai was just a backdrop, to which they paid little attention. The world that mattered to them lived beyond the screens of their laptops.

But the dumpling bug, which they had so lovingly nurtured and eventually delivered, seemed to have gone AWOL. At least that's how it seemed to Drayton.

"When does the bug start talking?" he asked Tom, and Tom said the bug was a worm and worms were complicated, especially this one; that it needed time to replicate, to spread through their network, learning as it goes, concealing its tracks.

"Wow," said Drayton, "that's some worm. So you're saying it's kinda burrowing away, getting familiar. But when does it feel sufficiently at home to start spouting names and stuff?"

"When it's ready," Dick said, without looking up, sounding protective about the worm and irritated with all the questions.

A bit of irritation was fine by Drayton. As long as it got the message across, that they weren't on vacation here. As he saw it, he was the one getting all the flak in the Bubble Room, while these guys sat around spouting geek-speak and waiting for their baby to come home leisurely like and say, "Hey guys, look what I've got." At least that's how Drayton imagined it.

An investigation that had seemed so promising was getting bogged down.

And there was a lot of pressure from the Bubble Room. The President's visit was getting closer. There's a window here, he kept being told, to put pressure on Beijing over all this cyber stuff. We just need names, they kept telling him. We need to know, who is the guy in the photographs? And who's he working with?

He left The Facility, putting on his black Hannibal Lecter pollution mask, and walked towards the river, messaging the word "smog" to Cyril, the signal to meet him with the old taxi at the rendezvous point. He called Morgan as he walked, wanting to press him on the Colonel, see how he was doing and what he'd learned, remind him that it was urgent, but the Englishman didn't pick up.

He then messaged Sakura, and was surprised to get a quick reply, saying she was at home and why didn't he come over. Which made him smile. She'd ignored his messages for a week, and now it was like, get over here now. He checked the time. It was early. He had three hours before the midday conference call in the Bubble Room. He messaged Sakura back saying he'd be there in half an hour.

Cyril was already pulling up as he reached the alleyway by the abandoned warehouse, two fresh dents in his rear door.

"Nice one, Cyril. You were serious about blending in, man. You had an accident or did you take a hammer to it?"

Cyril ignored the question and said the smog was bad, but it was moody. The way it hung over the river. Drayton thought that was so fucking stupid, all that moody bullshit, and that the next person to tell him that deserved to be thrown in the cesspit of a river, along which they were soon driving.

But he wasn't about to tell Cyril that, because he needed the guy to drop him near Sakura's place, in another part of the Concession, which probably wasn't protocol. So he just said that yeah, the pollution reading was bad, "hazardous" according to a smog app on his iPhone. He held the phone out to Cyril to take a look, since there was a cute little cartoon of a man with a mask and the word "Yuk".

"This is a great little app," he said.

116

And Cyril just said, "Oh yeah", without taking his eyes off the road, like he might get some sort of viral infection just by looking at a Chinese app.

But Cyril was good about dropping him near Sakura's place, Drayton saying he needed to deal with some consular business, and turning down Cyril's offer to wait.

Her apartment was on the second floor of a small colonial-era shophouse, which he entered through a side door and then climbed the stairs. She opened the door wearing a grey woollen bathrobe, her hair pinned up and cradling the black and white pug she called Bobby, and which Drayton thought was just about the ugliest dog he'd ever seen.

Sakura lent forward presenting Drayton with one cheek and then the other. He kissed both, and then she held up the dog for him, pushing its permanently creased face right towards his, a dripping pug tongue stretching towards his nose. Just before contact, Sakura's smartphone rang and she retreated into the apartment to take the call. Drayton followed her in, grateful for the timing of the call and closing the door behind him. He sat on a low sofa in the darkened room, blinds still closed.

She finished the call and asked how he was, but before he had a chance to answer, she said it was a pain not being able to get to the office, since she had a lot of work on, but there was some sort of protest against Japan, right outside the office. She said it had started the day before, and they'd already burned two Toyotas – a Prius and a Lexus – as well as a Kia SUV. She said the mob, maybe 200 of them, arrived by bus, and the police had just looked on. In fact, she said, it seemed like the police knew the protesters really well.

"Yeah, that makes sense," Drayton said. "And Kia's Korean."

"And the two Toyotas were owned by Chinese businessmen," she said.

He asked what the protest was about and she just shrugged, saying it was something to do with the South China Sea, about Japanese islands that China claimed. There'd been some sort of collision between ships.

Then she said, "Where's Alcatraz?"

"San Francisco Bay. Just off America. Nowhere near Japan."

"That's what I thought. It's just that some of the placards the protesters were carrying said 'Hands off Alcatraz' and things like that."

He started to tell her about the nationalist blogs that had gone viral, and that maybe the nationalists were a bit out with their geography, but she'd already gone to the kitchen and Bobby had climbed onto the sofa and had his nose in Drayton's crotch. He stood up, pushing the pug away, went to the window, and started to open the blinds.

"Don't do that," said Sakura, pushing him back to the sofa, straddling him, saying that she didn't have long, her hands now pressing where Bobby's wet nose had been moments before. She kissed him so hard that it felt to Drayton like a suction cap had been fitted around his mouth and his tongue might be torn out at any moment.

She paused for air, removing her bathrobe. He pushed himself forward and began to kiss her neck, her ear lobes, hands massaging her back, trying to gain the initiative, slowing things down. But she pushed him down again, hands on the belt of his trousers, pulling at it so hard that Drayton yelped. She ignored that, maybe thinking it was the pug, and after a brief struggle with his trouser buttons, he was naked from the waist down.

Then she was back on top and he was still trying but failing to slow things down, wanting to pace himself. But she was on a sprint to the finish. There was a lot more yelping, a kind of duet between Sakura and the pug, before she lifted herself off him and said, "Oh, you've finished." Sounding disappointed, and looking at his crotch like it was something a little distasteful that Bobby had dragged home.

"Well, yeah," said Drayton. "It's been a while."

Without another word, Sakura went to her bedroom and Drayton heard the whoosh of the shower starting up. He began to get dressed, the pug jumping back onto the sofa and making another lunge for his crotch. This time he pushed the dog away with a bare foot, but it snapped back, biting his toe. Drayton shouted, a pained sort of, "Arrrhh fuck!" and kicked the dog again, which yelped, this time a terrible high-pitched yelp.

Sakura came rushing back to the living room, a towel wrapped around her, and said, "Baby, darling, what happened?"

Drayton said, don't worry, it's just a scratch. I'll be alright. But Sakura wasn't talking to him. She went straight to the dog, saying "Baby, my baby", and a bunch of other stuff in Japanese, before picking the dog up and taking it to her bedroom, ignoring Drayton.

She returned to the living room five minutes later, in her work clothes, and talking on her smartphone. She ended the call and told Drayton she had to get to the office because the protesters had gone and there was a ton of work to do. She said to Drayton to let himself out, and then she left, blowing him a kiss.

Drayton sat for a couple of minutes before he noticed the crumpled face of the pug, eyeing him from the kitchen door. He threw a cushion at it and then left, deciding to walk to the consulate, grabbing a coffee along the way, and thinking about Sakura and how that really hadn't been his best performance.

He'd wanted a relationship that was uncomplicated and straightforward, especially after the Berlin mess, but it would be nice if she showed a bit more interest in him, was a bit more engaged. She'd never once asked what he did at the consulate. Not that he could ever tell her, but it was the principle. And she should get rid of that fucking dog.

After a few blocks he'd developed a sharp pain in his toe, the one bitten by that pug, and soon his entire foot was aching. He'd have to get that checked out. By the time he reached the consulate he was limping, and the first thing he was asked when he arrived in the Bubble Room was whether he was okay.

"Yeah, sure, it's nothing," he said. "Stubbed my toe."

"You need to be careful with injuries like that, Chuck. They can turn nasty," said the consulate's FBI guy, who was sitting at the conference table with a bunch of papers in front of him.

Drayton said thanks, that he'd take care of it.

There were six people around the table and another four around the walls, where Drayton took his usual seat and watched the screens come to life: the State Department, FBI, CIA and NSA joined by the Treasury Department, another cloned video conference room, three people around another table.

The President's visit was top of the agenda, a woman at the Bubble Room conference table running through the draft schedule for the Shanghai end of the visit. Somebody on the CIA screen asked about progress on the cyber stuff, whether the operation was any closer to getting names, because they really needed names, everybody looking at Drayton.

"We'll get them," he said. "We're close", knowing that he was starting to sound a little repetitive. So he was relieved when the satellite link wobbled a bit. The pictures kept fading and going to static. The sound wasn't good. An encryption issue, said the tech guy.

That served to blunt the inquisition, and by the time the system was fully restored and all screens were up and running, they'd moved on to economic stuff. Which he stayed for because nominally at least he was Economic/Commercial Officer.

The FBI screen took the lead, a woman with small round glasses saying there was a lot of hot Chinese money flowing to the US, looking to buy American companies, but that the hottest money was into US real estate. Cash buyers with wads of dollars. In fact, she said, they've got so much cash they seem willing to outbid anybody if there's a place they really want. She said there'd been a sudden surge and it seemed like people were desperate to get their money out of China.

Treasury then got defensive, saying foreign buyers helped buoy the real estate market, that we shouldn't scare them away.

"We are putting new measures in place to stop abuse," said a man who was hard to identify since the lighting in the Treasury's conference room clone was even worse than the others. He was just a darkened shadow at the far end of the table.

"But naturally we're concerned about illicit money flows into luxury real estate," said the shadow. He said they were working on identifying and tracking secret buyers, the ones using front companies, shell companies, to hide their identities. Usually in the Caribbean.

The woman on the FBI screen, which was much better lit, then raised a big poster-sized picture of a seaside resort, which looked pretty plush, bathed in sunshine, beach in front. Surf.

"Hawaii," said the woman. "Just sold for US$220 million – all cash – to a company called Rising Phoenix Holdings, which is registered in the Turks and Caicos Islands. But I'm guessing Chinese controlled. And we could show you dozens of others. We are talking wealthy, secretive buyers in a hurry," she said.

The FBI's man at the Shanghai consulate then handed out a thin file to each of those in the Bubble Room. He was another Economic/ Commercial Officer, at least that's what it said on the Diplomatic List, and Drayton wondered whether there were any real ones at the consulate.

Half a world away, the FBI said that Beijing was tightening controls over money flowing out of the country, that in theory there was a US$50,000 a year limit per person on what Chinese can take out, but there were a ton of ways of getting around it.

"You can launder through Macau casinos, do lots of tricks with dodgy invoices out of Hong Kong. But that's China's problem. We just want to have a better idea who we're getting as neighbours and where they're getting their cash from."

She said they'd tracked a number of big recent transactions to a group of companies based in Shenzhen, the southern boomtown next to Hong Kong, one of which appeared to be linked to the Phoenix company and to others in Hong Kong and Macau.

"Funny thing is, they call themselves trading companies, but it's not clear what they trade, nor who owns them. We'd love to know more about those companies."

A man from the NSA said they could maybe poke around a bit inside their systems, but a woman from the State Department screen said best hold back on that. We don't want to be caught breaking into computers, just as we're condemning China for doing just that.

"So we shouldn't do it?" said the man from the NSA.

"We shouldn't be seen to do it."

The woman from the FBI said that maybe this required a little more traditional legwork, since there had to be Western advisers, bankers, involved. Guiding the money along. Managing stuff.

And Drayton said, let me help here, I know a guy.

"That's great. Go for it, Chuck. You take ownership of this. But don't take your eye off the operation at The Facility."

Drayton said no, he wouldn't do that, suddenly feeling very good about himself again, and momentarily forgetting about his aching toe.

*

Drayton reached Morgan on his iPhone on the third attempt, and Morgan said he was at a reception at the Pentagon, which for a moment threw the American.

"It's a new shopping mall in the south of Shanghai," Morgan said, giving him the directions how to get there and saying he could meet in an hour.

Drayton messaged Cyril, who picked him up in the old taxi at a rendezvous point a ten-minute walk from the consulate and headed south on an elevated highway, knowing where to go. No map. No sat nav. And not for the first time, Drayton wondered who this guy was who knew the city so well. This NSA trusted driver. And as usual Cyril was giving nothing away.

"I've read about this place, this Pentagon," he said. "It's a knock-off of the Defence Department's Pentagon only bigger. And a shopping mall."

"Jeez," said Drayton. "Is there nothing they won't copy?"

"They've got a copy of an English town right here in Shanghai, with statues of Winston Churchill and Harry Potter. There's also a fake Austrian Alpine resort and a fake Jackson Hole. That one's just outside Beijing. And you know what? I read they're pulling down a big slice of old Lhasa in Tibet and replacing it with a copy because they think the copy looks better."

It took them forty minutes to reach the Pentagon. It was vast, bigger than the original and largely empty.

Cyril dropped Drayton in a deserted car park, saying to message when he was ready to be picked up, and Drayton had to walk around two of its five sides before he found a door that was open and had signs of life.

Only one section seemed to be fully operating, and even here the shops were largely deserted. There seemed to be more shop workers and mall security, standing around, than shoppers. He found the coffee shop where he'd agreed to meet Morgan, ordered a latte and took a seat in a far corner, where he started to read a copy of Morgan's latest newsletter, the *MB China Report*, thinking, do people actually pay to read this stuff?

Morgan joined him ten minutes later, panting, and saying sorry, he'd got lost on his way over, that it was a big place. He ordered a cappuccino.

"Just reading your report, Tony. Interesting. Just so I'm clear, what you're saying here is that there are two economies in China: the one that's a bit wobbly, and one that's gonna save us all?"

"Something like that."

"And the wobbly one is stuff like steel, shipyards, where they've got way too many filthy factories. And property, all those ghost cities and empty houses. And this economy is gazillions in debt, because they've built all sorts of shit that nobody wants."

"Well, broadly speaking," said Morgan, nodding.

"And the saviour is what you call the 'innovation and consumer-driven economy'. You mean inventors, entrepreneurs and shoppers?"

"That's not a bad summary," Morgan said.

"And you think the Communist Party's gonna make all this happen?"

Morgan said he was sure China's leaders knew what they needed to do, but sometimes they were not too great at communicating it.

"I'll tell you another problem I have," Drayton said, closing the report. "It assumes the Party leader actually wants to reform stuff. But I see a guy who's maybe a few fries short of a Happy Meal and who just wants control. That's all he knows. Communist Party control. He's terrified of instability, anything that might threaten one-party rule. And all these reforms you talk about, they mean mixing things up a bit, easing the reins, some pain in the short term."

"I think that's being a bit bleak," Morgan said.

"Look at this mall, Tony. Where are the shoppers?"

And Morgan conceded they might have gone a bit overboard on malls.

"Overboard is an understatement," Drayton said. "I read this thing saying they poured more cement in China in three years between 2011 and 2013 than was poured in the US in the whole of the twentieth century.

"What are you doing here anyway? Not shopping," Drayton said.

"One of the developers is a client of mine."

"Well, that figures," Drayton said. "How're my investigations going?"

Morgan said they were coming along fine, that he'd have the full reports soon, but so far they'd found no evidence that the Nanjing chemical company wanted to buy anything in the States and the Shanghai insurance outfit seemed to have stopped trading.

"Is that so?" said Drayton. "What about the Ferrari kid? Chen Huizhi and his old man."

"Still working on that one, Chuck. I did say you hadn't given us much to go on. And some of our usual sources seem very reluctant to speak."

"I'm under a bit of time pressure on that one," Drayton said. "So whatever you can turn up would be helpful."

Morgan said he understood, and the American said there was another thing.

"What's that?"

"Real estate. A couple of Shenzhen-based companies looking to buy in the US. My clients want a bit of background."

Drayton showed him a sheet of paper from the files with the company names and Morgan nodded, saying, "We've acted on their behalf, helped them with one or two transactions. Handled some investments."

"You know I had a feeling you might have done. Are they sound?"

"Well funded, but very private."

"Naturally. Anything more?"

"There is an issue of client privilege on this one, Chuck. I'm sorry."

"I'm sure there is. Which means I will pay you a little more. And ensure that the good name of MacMaster and Brown is not dragged into any federal investigation should the source of their funds be anything less than kosher. You get what I'm saying?"

Morgan sipped his coffee, thinking.

He'd been hoping to make a lot of money out of Mr Fang. But he couldn't see any real reason why he couldn't play both sides. And, anyway, Drayton was giving him no choice.

"They have a lot of money looking for a home right now," Morgan said. "And they are in a hurry. We've been looking for real estate for them in the US. In St Kitts too."

"St Kitts? The tiny speck in the Atlantic?"

"The Caribbean. If you invest half a million dollars there you get a passport. It's called the St Kitts Citizenship by Investment Scheme."

"What's the point of that?"

"A St Kitts passport gets you visa-free access to the States."

"In through the back door. Well, that's absolutely great," Drayton said. "Who are they?"

"I don't know for sure."

"You don't know for sure? But you're their fucking banker."

"It's because I'm their banker," Morgan said. "Discretion is important."

"Oh yeah," Drayton said. "But so is fraud and money laundering."

"Well, there's a point man I deal with, a guy called Fang who calls himself Michael. He represents a consortium of investors, government officials mostly."

"And this Michael Fang – the bagman – what's his real name? I mean his Chinese name."

"I'm not sure."

"You're not sure of his name? Is that another discretion thing?"

Morgan ignored that and said, "They want six St Kitts passports."

"Which you're helping to facilitate?"

"Possibly," said Morgan, sipping his coffee. "To get the passports Mr Fang will need to provide rather more personal information on his investors than he's been willing to do so far."

"Like real names," Drayton said. "Because I'm guessing that even the good folk of St Kitts need at least a name, a photo and a tiny bit of background before handing over a passport."

"Mostly they want cash," Morgan said. "But yes, basically you're right."

Morgan said he was going to Shenzhen at the weekend, to meet Fang, but that they still hadn't fully committed to the scheme.

"They take their privacy very seriously," Morgan said.

"I am sure they do," said Drayton. "You know what, I think I might be down that way too this weekend. I fancy a change of scenery."

Drayton handed him back his report and said he was looking forward to the next one.

"I got lost with all the statistics. Not that I've ever met anybody who trusts official statistics anyway. Seems to me they are political, not economic, conjured up as needed."

Morgan said that was why most economists had their own ways of measuring economic activity.

"Which is precisely my point," Drayton said, making to leave and

125

saying to keep in touch and not forget the Ferrari kid and his dad. That was still the priority.

Morgan said sure he wouldn't forget, asking Drayton where he'd be staying in Shenzhen, and the American said don't worry, I'll find you.

"I admire you, Tony, trying to make sense of stuff that makes no sense. To me it's about as clear as Beijing smog."

– 15 –

Robert

Cindy Wu had done a good job. She always did, and the way Morgan saw it she should have been pleased with herself. But instead she was worried. Angry even, saying, "I don't like this, Tony. What are we getting into?"

Morgan was looking through her research, three neatly bound documents that she had placed on the table in front of him. They were sitting in the coffee shop of a luxury hotel in Pudong, Shanghai's financial district, where Morgan was attending a conference about the internet. Cindy Wu had met him there on her way to the airport for a flight back to Beijing. He'd been staying at their apartment nearby; she elsewhere, with friends. Which had become their usual pattern.

"I'm not bothered about those two," she said, referring to the Shanghai insurance company and the Nanjing chemical business. "It's as we thought. One's gone bust and the other's not far off. No way are they interested in buying anything in America. I don't know why this client of yours even asked us to look at them."

Morgan had already given the preliminary results on those companies to Drayton, and he said yeah, that it did seem a bit of a waste of time, but maybe the client just wanted to be certain, not understanding China, the usual stuff.

She then took the third, thinner, document, and placed it on top of the pile, and said, "It's this one I'm worried about. This isn't usual at all, Tony."

The heading on the cover page was "Colonel General Chen Shibo", and underneath were three photographs. One was of a man in full military uniform, presumably the Colonel General himself, the second of a much younger man in an open-neck shirt and trying to look serious, but not doing a very good job of it, which Morgan took to be the son. The photographs were much more formal than those Drayton had given him, and at first he struggled to recognise either. The third photograph was of a red Ferrari. He recognised that.

"The father's military. Top military. Secret military. And from what I can tell, very well connected politically. The son's a waster. But the businesses are all in his name through a string of Hong Kong and offshore companies."

She said the information was pretty sketchy, that many of her usual sources had been very reluctant to help. She said the Colonel General's biography had suddenly gone blank about three years back. Before that he'd been into computers, logistics mostly, heading a unit that bought and sold for the army.

"Logistics is always a big money spinner, lots of opportunities for a bit of private enterprise on the side, which is presumably where his money comes from, the money the kid manages, though I can't say I'd want him in charge of my cash."

She said she was still waiting for one or two sources to come back to her, trying to get more recent information on the Colonel General. So the report was still a bit preliminary.

"There was a lot of push back, Tony. It was tough."

"Looks pretty good to me," said Morgan.

"You said it was urgent, Tony. You also said we were getting paid well for this. It had better be very good," she said, repeating that she was worried, handling stuff like this. That it could come back to hurt them. Especially now.

Morgan changed the subject, thinking his wife was being over-dramatic, and asking what time their son Robert was arriving from the UK. She said he was on his way, that his flight got into Beijing late that afternoon. She said she'd timed her flight from Shanghai back to the capital to get in a couple of hours ahead of him, and that she'd wait for Robert at Beijing airport.

"He wants to stay in Beijing for a while, then come to Shanghai."

She asked about her husband's plans.

Morgan said he was travelling to Southern China, to Shenzhen, to get the new partner lined up for Bud, though he may no longer need one. Maybe see one or two other clients.

He said he would then be going to Hong Kong, and that he'd be back after a week.

She placed the three files back into a brown envelope, handing them to her husband, and said, "Promise me you'll be careful. This could be dangerous in the wrong hands."

"How's that?" said Morgan.

"This is a very powerful man," she said, tapping the envelope. "I have a very bad feeling about this."

The coffee shop was quiet, and they'd chosen a table on the far side, nobody close, Cindy Wu lowering her voice as a man walked by, taking a nearby table.

She showed Morgan the front page of the *People's Daily*, the Communist Party mouthpiece, which carried what it called a report card for the Communist Party's corruption busters, the Central Commission for Discipline Inspection, saying that in the last year alone nearly half a million people had been punished for what it called "discipline violations", including ninety top officials. It vowed that no matter who they were, "tigers or flies", there'd be no hiding place.

She said the graft-busters mostly operated in the shadows, with their own courts, their own prisons, their own rules. That they could grab anybody they want.

"They're making a lot of enemies. Look at who's been targeted. Not only in the Party, but top officials in the army, state-owned companies, even private ones. They've virtually declared war on Shenzhen."

"We do a lot of business down there," Morgan said. "You know there's a real clamour to move assets out of the country."

"I'm sure there is," Cindy Wu said. "While they still can."

She said the crackdown was going further still, that labour rights lawyers and other social activists were being targeted. That the Party was shutting down even the most limited space for criticism.

She said that only online was there still room to breathe, but even there she said the Party was tightening the noose.

"People who can are looking for a way out of China, for them and for their assets." She said the graft-busters were the most powerful unit of the Party and had become the leader's personal enforcers. She said there was even a rumour of a showdown between his faction and another loyal to the Prime Minister.

"I really think there will be a backlash," she said, tapping the newspaper. "Maybe it's already started."

Beneath her long purple fingernails was a picture of a man described as the head of the Central Commission for Discipline Inspection, the Party's chief graft-buster. He had a balding head and a round face, child-like, but serious. And cold. Not an inkling of emotion. He was wearing an enormous pair of thick-rimmed and slightly tinted glasses.

They sat in silence for a while, and then Cindy Wu stood to leave, pointed to the brown envelope and said, "I would be very, very careful with that, Tony."

She looked anxious, more so than he could remember in a long time.

*

Morgan went into the conference, where China's top internet official was addressing an audience of executives from Western tech companies about the promise of the Chinese market.

He sat at the back of the hall fiddling with his iPhone.

The official, the head of the Cyberspace Administration of China, was reeling off statistics. Nearly everybody in the country owns a smartphone. Nearly 700 million internet users. The world's largest online community. The value of e-commerce on course soon to reach a trillion dollars a year.

"The door is always open to Western internet enterprises, as long as they do not hurt the national or consumer interest," said the man whose day job was running the Great Firewall, the Party's internet censorship machine, and the most extensive system of online control yet invented.

But he knew his audience's interest lay elsewhere, and recited a bunch of figures that he said showed that Western companies gained half their profits from the Chinese market.

"China has an open and fair internet," he said. "China manages cyberspace under the rule of law. In other words, we manage the relationship between freedom and order. We have to provide a healthy environment for the young."

And at that moment order and health got the better of a web posting Morgan was reading on his iPhone, more speculation about a power struggle in the Party. It went blank. He tried to turn on his VPN, but struggled to make the connection. He could open the *People's Daily*. No surprise there. It was reporting that 200 websites had been shut down and ten bloggers arrested for "lies and speculation" and "fabricating and spreading rumours".

"We welcome you," said the internet official, reaching the end of his speech, which was greeted with warm applause from the Western tech executives.

One young American executive turned to Morgan and said, "That's really encouraging. Amazing growth. You really can't afford *not* to be part of this. I mean the law's the law. You have to respect that in any market. I think we can do business here."

Morgan smiled, thinking about the kids on the Bund grabbing the bull by its balls, and saying sure. That's good. Let's chat later. There are many ways that MacMaster and Brown can help you find the right partner and get established here.

Tech was a new business for Morgan, but a promising one. The internet official had been right, it was an enormous and growing market. But Morgan also knew that the price of entry would be a large pair of online shackles and the keys to back door access to their systems and technology in the interests of order and health.

It wasn't that the tech executives weren't aware of this, at least in part. It was more that they didn't really care. They saw it as a price worth paying. For entry to the market.

To Morgan, they were deluding themselves. But it was also for him a very profitable delusion; as the conference came to a close, he traded business cards back and forth between smiles and handshakes, and set up coffee meetings and two lunches for the days ahead.

He then sat back in the lobby, waiting for his car and going back on his iPhone. His VPN was working again.

Xinhua, the state news agency, had announced that the head of the Government's statistics office was the latest official under investigation for the same "serious discipline violations" as hundreds of thousands of others. He shared the link to *@Beijing_smog*, tweeting:

China's leading writer of contemporary fiction is rumbled. Did he exaggerate too much or not enough?

*

Chuck Drayton was at Sakura's apartment when his phone rang. He'd got the summons early afternoon, Sakura telling him to come over because the protesters were back in front of her office and she was at home and wanted to have fun. Like now, right away.

She said she was lonely because Bobby the pug was at the vets after developing some kind of fever, and Drayton wondered if that had anything to do with his toe. His own pain had become so bad that he'd gone to see the consulate's doctor, telling her a stray had bitten him while his shoes were off and he was having a shoeshine. It was a convoluted story, but the best he could do and better than the truth. He'd immediately regretted it after the doctor insisted on a series of rabies and tetanus shots and handed him a cocktail of antibiotics.

He'd not gone to The Facility that day, where progress was still slow and he was starting to find Tom and Dick and all their techno-rambling a bit tedious. When Sakura messaged he was nearby, at the consulate. He still took a taxi over, not wanting to put too much stress on his foot. He was limping when he reached Sakura's place, telling her he'd stubbed his toe on the sidewalk and asking about Bobby, trying to sound sympathetic, while hoping all the time that it was nothing trivial.

Her blinds were shut and the apartment was in near-darkness again, which is the way she seemed to prefer it, like she had something against the sun. She was wearing faded jeans and a white T-shirt, her hair down this time. She ignored his question about the dog and his explanation about the limp, pulling him by his belt and falling backwards onto the sofa, Drayton on top this time.

"Hey baby, mind if I just get rid of the coat?" he said. She ignored that too, keeping a firm grip on his belt and kissing him so hard that the question trailed away and the two of them rolled off the sofa and onto a rug that smelt of the pug. It was then that Drayton's phone rang for the first time. The phone tumbled out of his pocket, but Sakura was holding him so tightly that he couldn't have reached it, even if he'd wanted to.

The next time his phone rang his trousers were around his knees. He was trying to pull her T-shirt over her head, but his coat was so twisted it was acting like a straight-jacket. He could see the face of his phone this time and recognised Morgan's number.

"Shit," he said. "Sorry, I really gotta take that call."

She continued to hold him tight and they grappled like a pair of wrestlers before he broke free, grabbing the phone and sitting on the sofa. By that time, the ringing had stopped. Drayton pulled up his trousers and said, "I'm sorry, babe. I have to return the call."

He left Sakura's apartment and went to the street outside, calling Morgan, who immediately picked up.

"Sorry, Tony. You caught me in the middle of something," he said.

"I have the report you commissioned," Morgan said, getting straight to the point.

"That's terrific, Tony. Our friend with the Ferrari-loving kid?"

"That's the one. I can scan it and email it over to you."

"No. Don't do that. I prefer a hard copy," Drayton said.

"Sure," Morgan said. "Where and when do you want to meet?"

And Drayton said, "I'll let you know", feeling like he'd already said more than he'd wanted to on an open telephone line.

When he returned to Sakura's apartment she was sitting at a small table, her clothes back in place and with a pot of green tea and two small cups in front of her. She was reading something online, on her phone, and ignored him at first before asking what was so important that he had to run away, go outside, just as they were getting into things. He said sorry, embassy stuff, and went to take her hand, which she pulled away, getting to her feet. She picked up her coat and headed out of the door, saying she had to go to the vet, that Bobby had taken a turn for the worse, and for Drayton to let himself out.

After she'd left, he punched air, a triumphant punch, because that was the second piece of good news he'd heard in the last five minutes.

Then he left the apartment, wiping dog hairs off his coat, keen to see what Morgan and his wife had turned up.

*

Morgan had just arrived back at his Lucky Bund View apartment and poured himself a large Jack Daniels with ice when his phone rang. He pulled it out of his back pocket and crossed to the tall windows. The smog had lifted enough that he could now just about make out the Huangpu River below.

There was no number identifier shown on the screen, and he said, "Morgan here."

It was Cindy Wu. She was crying, desperately trying to control herself.

"Has he been in touch with you? Has he contacted you?" she said.

"Has who contacted me?" Morgan said.

"I waited at arrivals, at the airport, where I told him I'd be," she said between heavy breaths. "He was definitely on the flight. I checked."

"You mean Robert? Something's happened to Robert?"

There was silence at the other end of the phone as Cindy Wu struggled to get the words out.

"Cindy, Cindy. Calm down. Talk to me. What's happened to Robert?"

"He never came out, Tony. He never came through," she said. "I don't know where he is. It's like he's just disappeared."

– 16 –

The Girl In The Corner

It took a while for Wang Chu to notice that The Girl In The Corner was no longer in the corner, and at The Moment On Time coffee shop word quickly spread that she'd killed herself.

"She threw herself from the roof of her dormitory building," said Wang.

"It wasn't the roof," said Liu Wei. "It was from a window."

While another student on the next table said they were both wrong, that she'd hung herself in a cubicle in the washroom.

Her ex-boyfriend wasn't much help, since he was now denying ever having been her boyfriend and was avoiding the coffee shop.

Zhang said they were all silly rumours and that perhaps she wasn't dead at all, but had been expelled because of the protest in defence of the Professor. Perhaps it had all been too much for her and she'd just left.

"But there's definitely something weird going on," Zhang said.

What they did know for sure was that the University had threatened to expel all those who took part in the protest, and had warned their families. It had also stepped up what it called patriotic education and ideological guidance and warned against what it called "pernicious Western values".

Soon after the protest, the University had announced that all students were required to attend extra classes in Marxism and

Theories of Chinese Socialism. It said they were expected to take the classes seriously and that there would be tests. It warned students against listening to music, watching videos or doing anything else on their phones during the classes. Sleeping was expressly banned, and surveillance cameras were installed in some classrooms.

There were special lessons for those who'd taken part in the protest or signed the online petition and deemed to be in most need of attitude adjustment.

Like most students, Wang and his roommates regarded the University's periodic ideology campaigns as a bit of a joke, but one of those things you went along with. The University usually didn't take it too seriously either. Sure, the rules this time seemed a bit tougher and pretty stupid, like having to actually attend the lectures, but the way the roommates saw things, it was best to go through the motions and get it over with.

But it had quickly become clear to them that The Girl In The Corner was in no mood to be lectured to by the Party and wasn't about to have her attitude adjusted.

Wang and his roommates had attended the first lecture, on the contribution of the Communist Party to the development of China, during which they all stayed awake, though Wang did manage to see off some more zombies on his smartphone, and Liu was able to monitor the stock market, though that proved more depressing than the lecture.

Afterwards, questions were handed out, starting with multiple choice. The first one asked:

Which of the following statements best describes the Communist Party's achievements?

It gave five options:

a. *The unparalleled combination of Marxism with China's reality*
b. *Leading China through a long struggle to prosperity and happiness*
c. *Representing the common interests of all Chinese*
d. *Leading the social and spiritual development of all Chinese*
e. *Forging the Chinese Dream*

Wang had looked at Zhang, who'd looked at Liu.

"Is this a trick question?" Liu mouthed silently to the others. To which Wang shrugged, put up his hand and asked the lecturer, who said it was a stupid question.

That got the hall laughing, but not the lecturer, who banged his fist on the lectern, and corrected himself saying it was Wang's question that was stupid, not the test. He said they could choose more than one answer and if they had half a brain they'd realise that all five were right.

And with that helpful guidance, Wang, Zhang and Liu ticked all five. The next section asked for further thoughts on how the Party was enhancing the lives of the people. None of the roommates could immediately think of an answer for that, so not wanting to get it wrong they left it blank.

The Girl In The Corner had been sitting at the back of the hall. She found that section far too tempting to ignore, and she did the unthinkable. She gave an honest answer:

The Party can only truly command the respect of the people when it gets out of their bedrooms and allows them a completely free choice to have children. When it constructs buildings that don't fall down. When it stops poisoning the air and soil. When it stops robbing and bullying the people.

The roommates knew what she'd written because she later shared her answer in university chat rooms and online, where it spread rapidly before it was deleted. The Girl In The Corner had then received another summons by the university authorities, and was again threatened with expulsion and ordered to do an additional set of ideology classes. This time her invitation to tea had a far bitterer taste to it. Wang had heard that the tone was nastier and that the police had been involved, telling her that she might be charged with subverting state authority. Her businessman father was briefly detained as part of what was described as a corruption investigation.

Among the students in The Moment On Time there was a grudging sense of respect for her spirit and her bravery. Though most saw it as good reason to have nothing further to do with her, not wanting to be seen as guilty by association. Nobody could argue with what she'd said. It was stating the obvious. But Wang and his roommates agreed that she was being unnecessarily reckless and provocative.

"What for?" said Zhang. "What does she seriously expect to achieve?"

Wang agreed. "What's the point?" he said.

The Girl In The Corner had become more withdrawn, and at a time when she needed support, she was shunned. The one exception was Lily, who was mostly rushed off her feet, but had spent what time she could at that table in the corner, with the girl. Lily recognised strength and decency when she saw it. She respected defiance. She'd talk to whomever she wanted to talk to, and didn't give a hoot what anybody thought.

While The Girl In The Corner had appeared to be down, she wasn't out. She wasn't through yet, and not content with criticising the Party, she took aim at her fellow students. She condemned them as a bunch of cheats.

Her latest results had been poor, well below average. But she had a simple explanation: that she hadn't bought the exam papers and answers in advance, and she went back into the student chat rooms and attacked the cheats, who included just about everybody who could afford to buy them.

And she attacked the university authorities for sitting back and letting it happen, only caring about the results and not how they were achieved. She said it simply wasn't fair.

For Wang, fairness was relative. He saw fairness as being about maintaining a level playing field on which to cheat. Buying the answers to exams had become routine, and the accusations from The Girl In The Corner were just sour grapes.

For a while selling exam answers had also been one of the services offered by their online shop, Liu buying the papers and answers in advance from a contact he'd made at one of the testing agencies and selling them at a small mark-up. But like most of their businesses, it hadn't made much money. The market was too competitive. It was saturated. There were too many sources at the test agency selling too many papers.

"She just can't afford to buy the answers," said Liu. "Her father must have cut her allowance because of all the shit she's causing him."

Wang agreed. And Zhang said, "What's the big deal? Everybody cheats."

It was soon after this that The Girl In The Corner disappeared.

The rumours became increasingly outlandish. That she'd been pushed to her death after an argument with an official. That a security guard had tried to rape her. That other students had tried to silence her over the cheating allegations. That she'd been taken off to a secret prison and charged with subversion.

Her parents arrived on campus, and were spotted sitting tearfully outside the administration building, asking anybody who would listen what had happened to their daughter. The university authorities refused to see them, as if it was really none of her parents' business.

Zhang stuck to his theory that she might still be alive. Perhaps she'd just run away. Liu said she'd definitely killed herself. Wang agreed with Liu and said that probably she was definitely dead, that it was a tragedy, but one she'd brought on herself.

Then the university authorities intervened, clarifying everything but nothing. The Computer Science Department was among those that gathered their students and told them not to spread rumours and not to talk to anybody outside the University about "certain events", though without ever saying what those "certain events" might be.

Which vindicated just about everybody's favourite rumour.

Even when The Moment On Time was busy, nobody took the table in the corner, her table, as if ghosts inhabited it, as if by avoiding the table they could avoid the subject. All except Lily, who was the most visibly upset by the rumours, and told anybody who would listen that they were all spineless and that the missing girl was worth more than the lot of them.

Mostly they ignored her, thinking it was just Lily being Lily, but knowing deep down that she was right. Most of her customers quickly zoned out. The coffee shop went back to its default setting, heads buried in computer screens and the barely audible tapping of keyboards.

Liu opened an online card game. He'd promised his roommates that he'd stop looking at the trading account, or at least no more than once a day. He had no more money to invest, and just sitting there staring at the screen wasn't going to bring the market back up again.

Zhang went back to his dating app, where he'd now had second thoughts about using a real photo and was choosing from a bunch of Olympic athletes to use instead.

Wang opened a game where he was breeding dragons, building a dragon city. Some were already in training for his dragon army, and he was waiting for a new batch of eggs to hatch. He'd already reached level five, but he thought it was a boring game. It took too long to get to the fighting bit.

So he opened his *Gasping Dragon* social media account and shared a video he'd taken earlier that day: a young woman in high heels and fur coat walking past the campus with what looked like a new Louis Vuitton handbag, which he suspected was a fake, since it resembled one they sold in their online shop. Either way, it was fresh out of its wrapping and behind her was a big university hoarding with the words "Core Socialist Values". Nice.

The next thing he knew, Lily was poking him in the back and he guessed from the serious look on her face that she hadn't come over to see the video. He told her they should be able to settle their bill by the end of the week. But she hadn't come over because of the roommates' lengthening tab either.

"The girl, the one who would sit in the corner?" Lily said.

"Which girl?" said Wang, not wanting to go there and now just wanting to hide, desperate to get back to the world beyond his screen.

"The one who's disappeared. Well, her parents hired a lawyer and the lawyer was threatening to sue the University, demanding to know what happened to their daughter."

"And?"

"And now the lawyer's disappeared. What do you know?"

"I don't know anything," Wang said. "Why would I know anything?"

"And you two?" she said to Liu and Zhang, who ignored her, keeping their eyes on their screens.

"What is it with you guys?" said Lily, starting to get angry. "There's a real world out there you know. It's not all online. And it's not nice."

But it wasn't a world the roommates wanted any part of. Not then. As far as Wang was concerned if it didn't happen online, it didn't happen at all. It was safer that way.

But Lily persisted.

"He was supposed to be a hot-shot lawyer," she said.

Liu finally replied, saying, "Maybe that's why he disappeared."

Lily turned, slowly shaking her head, and returned to her counter thinking these boys are beyond pathetic.

Zhang looked at his roommates and said, "These are weird…"

"Yeah, we get it, Zhang," Liu said, interrupting him. "These are weird times."

He was about to say something to Wang, but Wang had received a call.

He was a pale boy, and it was hard for Liu to imagine him getting any paler. But Liu was sure he could see the little colour his friend had rapidly draining from his face. It was like he'd just seen a ghost.

"What's up?" said Liu, after Wang hung up.

Wang said it was a summons from the University authorities.

It was an invitation to tea.

– 17 –

An Invitation to Tea

There were two things Wang Chu found most surprising about his invitation to tea. First, they'd phoned him on his spare phone, an old and battered Nokia with a pre-paid SIM, which he used mostly for the online shop.

He rarely gave out the number to anybody else.

Second, the invitation was polite.

That didn't make it any less unnerving, but he had always thought the University authorities would make any summons as nasty and humiliating as they could. Instead the voice on the phone asked him how he was doing and when would work for him?

The voice didn't introduce itself, but said it was from the office of his supervisor, who wanted him to join her for tea to discuss his academic progress and other issues.

Since the voice appeared so accommodating, Wang asked it if he could possibly have details of those other issues, to better prepare for this important meeting.

The voice said it was so glad he could make it and hung up.

As far as Wang could recall, his supervisor was an older woman whose name was Deng. Or maybe Jiang. He'd have to check. She was responsible for overseeing his academic and personal development, always at hand to give guidance. At least that's what she'd told him at their first meeting shortly after he'd started university. He'd not met her since then.

To Wang's mind she was part tutor, part nanny and distinctly part-time.

Which had come as a bit of a surprise to him at first, as had the general torpor of university life after all the blood, sweat and tears to get there. The entrance exams had been brutally competitive. But he soon settled into a university routine that seemed to him to be built around an agreeable understanding that students pretended to work while teachers pretended to teach.

Supervisors mostly avoided those they were supervising, unless they really had no choice, which was why Wang found the invitation to tea so puzzling and worrying.

"It's got to be the work stuff," he said to Liu Wei, who'd offered to walk with his roommate to campus, to help calm him down, but he just seemed to be making things worse.

"I've just fallen too far behind. What else could it be?" Wang said.

"Selling fake stuff online maybe? Selling exam answers?"

And Wang told him to stop messing around, that it had to be something serious.

"You suppose it's about the Professor?" Wang said, thinking again about The Girl In The Corner and the Professor who'd disappeared.

"But you didn't take part in the protest. We didn't even sign the petition," Liu said. "Perhaps you should have taken the ideology courses more seriously," reminding his roommate that supervisors were also in charge of political and ideological education.

"I took it as seriously as everybody else," Wang said.

"Which isn't saying a lot. Remember the exam? You asked if the question about the Communist Party's achievements was a trick question. And there was the ecological civilisation thing, when you asked what it meant and they got mad."

"They were jokes."

"Yeah, and since when has the Communist Party had a sense of humour?"

Liu was right. The lecturer had got mad at him in the ideology exam. And his tutor had been angry over his questions about ecological civilisation. Perhaps that was why he'd been summoned.

But then that made little sense either. They were just silly questions and who cared about ideology? No, it had to be his work. He'd been a little negligent, but then who hadn't?

Liu left Wang at the main university entrance and wished him luck. "Just don't disappear until we've paid off the coffee shop bill."

Wang told him that wasn't funny, taking a mock swing at Liu, who ducked, then waved and walked off towards their nearby room.

His supervisor's office was in the far corner of the campus, on the ground floor of a low-rise administration block, red brick with peeling white paint around the windows. Wang missed it, walking straight past, doubling back when he reached another exit from campus and realised his mistake.

He was panting and five minutes late when he entered a small room to one side of the lobby, where an elderly woman wearing a big black poncho-type woollen top was watering an emaciated-looking plant, which was just about clinging to life.

"Good afternoon, Mrs Jiang. Sorry I am a little late."

"She's in there," said the woman, without turning, just gesturing to another room with her little blue watering can.

Wang, relieved he'd at least got the name right, removed his coat, under which he was wearing a jacket and tie, dressed to impress. It was the first time he'd done that for a while.

He knocked and entered the other room, which seemed bigger, possibly because it was so empty – just a big desk on one side and on the other a pair of crumpled sofas around a stained coffee table.

There was a single poster, for an academic conference, two years old, on one of the stained whitewashed walls.

Mrs Jiang rose from behind the desk. She was a tall severe-looking woman, her hair pinned up and wearing what struck Wang as a rather dishevelled grey jacket. She wore a pair of oval, rimless glasses, and appeared younger than Wang remembered.

They shook hands and she gestured towards the sofas, where they sat, one sofa each. She was carrying a file, which she placed in her lap.

"You are looking well," Mrs Jiang said. "How are you finding the landscape architecture course?"

Wang said he was fine thank you, and that he was studying computer science.

Mrs Jiang looked at the file, then back up at Wang and rebooted.

"You are looking well. How are you finding the computer science course?"

"It's challenging at times, and I have been a little slow with some recent assignments, but generally I am coping well, and really enjoying it thank you, Mrs Jiang."

He was about to blame the missed deadlines on a sickness in the family, possibly his own sickness or even a computer virus. Perhaps all three. But somebody interrupted him, clearing his throat, a long piercing retch.

Wang looked round to see a man sitting in a chair at the back of the room, near the door, which was now closed. The man lit a cigarette and sniffed. Wang turned back to Mrs Jiang, who ignored the man, making no attempt to introduce him.

"How are your parents?" Mrs Jiang said.

"They're fine, thank you. Still finding the winters a little cold in Harbin, but doing very well."

"Your sister?"

"I don't have a sister."

Mrs Jiang looked back at the file, then across at the man, then at Wang again.

"Your parents must be very proud of you, Wang. As is the University. You are a good student and you have a great future ahead of you. You have a lot of responsibility, to them and to us."

Wang thanked her again and said he appreciated the opportunity he'd been given, as he began to wonder where all this was going. Her appraisal of him and his future seemed, well, a little generous, and he began to wonder if she was reading from the correct file.

Mrs Jiang glanced at the man, who cleared his throat again, though this time more of a gurgle than a retch.

"Such a promising future," Mrs Jiang repeated. "We would not want you to do anything to jeopardise that. Neither would your family."

Wang heard movement behind him, and then saw that the man, who was heavily set and wearing a black ski jacket, had moved to one side of the room, closer to the sofas, from where he was taking photographs of Wang with his smartphone.

Mrs Jiang continued as if he wasn't there.

"You are at a crucial time in your course, Wang. You should never forget your responsibilities."

Then they sat in silence. The ski jacket retreated to the back of the room, wheezing and sniffing. Mrs Jiang continued to ignore the man and was again leafing through papers in her file.

"If it's about the exam, I can explain," Wang said.

The ski jacket stopped wheezing and Mrs Jiang looked up from the file.

"The exam?" she said.

"Yes, the ideology exam, the bit on the achievements of the Communist Party. When I asked the lecturer whether it was a trick question, it wasn't out of disrespect, but because I genuinely thought it was."

"A trick question?"

"Yes. Because you see it was multiple choice and all the answers seemed to be right because as you know the Party has so many achievements. That's why I asked if it was a trick question."

At mention of the Party, Mrs Jiang looked over Wang's shoulder towards the ski jacket, who was wheezing again. She looked longer this time, as if she was expecting the man to say something, which he didn't.

"If it's about Professor Huang, I accept that it was wrong to question the judgement of the University authorities or the Party. Though I didn't take part in the protest or sign the petition."

"The petition, Wang? The protest?"

"Yes, in support of the Professor who disappeared and is under investigation for violating Party discipline," said Wang, aware that he was rambling and regretting ever having mentioned it.

"Wang, this is China. People don't just disappear. At least not without very good reason," Mrs Jiang said, looking again at the ski jacket. "You know the Party always acts in the best interests of the people and corruption is a cancer that needs to be cut out wherever it occurs."

Wang said that was the point, that many people felt Professor Huang was a decent and honest man, but immediately regretted having said it.

"I really can't recall a Professor Huang having ever worked at the University," Mrs Jiang replied. "If he did exist, he doesn't anymore, and issues like that, real or imagined, are best put behind us. You have a promising future to look forward to. That is the most important thing, Wang."

"If it's about the ecological civilisation thing, I really was just curious."

"The ecological civilisation thing, Wang?"

"Yes, I asked my tutor what it was."

"Well, isn't that obvious?"

This time the silence was longer and Wang began to wonder whether the invitation to tea included any tea. He was about to ask, when there was a screeching and a clanking as the ski jacket, still seated, pulled his chair over to the coffee table, where he sat looking at Wang before lighting another cigarette.

"Do you believe in aliens?" the man said in a rasping voice that Wang at first struggled to understand.

"Aliens, Wang, do you believe in them?"

"Aliens?"

"That's right. Aliens. Little stick men with pear-shaped heads and big eyes."

Wang said you couldn't completely discount the possibility of some form of life out there in a distant world, thinking that perhaps this was a sort of test. He said they'd even found signs of water on Mars, which could support a living organism.

"Is that so?" said the man, like he'd never heard of Mars and cared even less. He leant forward until his face was inches from Wang's, his breath reeking of stale tobacco.

"Not Mars, Wang. Here. In Beijing. Maybe on campus."

Instinctively, Wang looked towards the window, as did Mrs Jiang, who was now looking very uncomfortable, and seemed keen to avert her gaze from the dreadful man who was clearly in charge. The light was fading, and the smog hung like a blanket outside the window. The view was barely distinguishable from the room's grubby whitewashed walls.

The ski jacket just kept looking at Wang.

"And another thing," the man said, followed by a long silence.

"Yes," said Wang.

"Online rumour-mongering is expressly forbidden by law."

Wang said he understood the need to respect the truth, but sometimes it was difficult to distinguish what was real and what was not, especially online.

"That's not for you to decide," said the man.

At which point the woman in the black poncho entered from the small adjoining room with the tea. She carried two mugs, each filled with hot water, leaves floating on the surface. She gave one to the man and the other to Mrs Jiang.

The man took a sip, spitting leaves onto the floor and wiping others from his mouth using the sleeve of his jacket.

Wang had been there for more than half an hour now. He still didn't fully understand why, though was increasingly convinced it must be because of the exam. Perhaps this was another ideology test.

The man lit another cigarette, throwing the empty packet on the table. He was smoking Zhongnanhais.

"It's important to respect historical reality, Wang," the man said.

And Wang said he was sorry, but what was that exactly.

"Did you learn nothing in your ideology classes, Wang?" Mrs Jiang said, with no great feeling, perhaps thinking that as his supervisor she needed to participate. "Historical reality is whatever the Party says it is."

Wang thanked her and said he'd perhaps overlooked that bit, but would apply to resit the exam just as soon as their meeting was over.

Then the man took a folded piece of paper from an inside pocket, which he opened and placed on the table in front of Wang. It was a computer printout, a picture of a snowman alongside a picture of the Prime Minister and a caption, "Spot the difference".

"Looks familiar?" said the man.

Wang went to pick up the paper. It wasn't a great copy and he didn't immediately recognise it as his posting. He wasn't sure what to say, wanting a better look, to buy some time, but the ski jacket snatched it back.

"It should be familiar," the man said. "You posted it in a university chat room."

The man then took a long drag on his cigarette and cleared his throat so loudly that it made Mrs Jiang wince. "You really think they look the same?" he said, but the question trailed away and was engulfed by another lengthy retch. Wang thought the man was beginning to sound a lot like Lily's malfunctioning espresso machine in The Moment On Time.

The man took another sip of tea, cleared some more troublesome tea leaves and tried again. "Tell me about it, Wang."

Wang was genuinely confused. He posted a mountain of stuff online. It was how he spent most of his day. He needed a better look, but when he leant over the man pulled the piece of paper closer to his chest, like he was protecting a valuable hand of cards.

Then, ever so slowly, he turned it towards Wang, like he was revealing what he thought was a sure-fire winner.

Wang said it was a picture of a snowman next to one of the Prime Minister, and the man told him not to be so stupid, that he could see that for himself and that if Wang valued his place at university he should stop giving stupid answers.

"What does it mean?"

"What do you mean what does it mean?" said Wang.

"I mean what does it really mean?" the man said, getting angry.

Wang said it didn't mean anything, that if he had posted it, he'd done so as a joke. That it wasn't meant to be serious.

"Precisely," said the man. "You were trying to undermine the credibility of the Government and the Party. Because do you know what, Wang?"

Wang said he didn't know what.

"We should respect our leaders."

"It was a joke," Wang said.

The man then sat back, looking smug, and nodded slowly. He looked at Mrs Jiang, and she nodded too.

"I'm really sorry," Wang said, figuring that at this point it was best just to apologise, even if he still wasn't entirely sure what for. "It really was just a joke."

"Like in your last ideology exam, Wang? Like your pointless enquiries about the meaning of ecological civilisation? A joke like them?" Mrs Jiang said, coming back into the conversation.

149

The ski jacket leant forward, blowing smoke laced with tiny pieces of tea leaf into Wang's face, like he'd been watching too many bad gangster movies.

"Does it look like I'm laughing, Wang? Is she laughing?"

Wang looked at the man, then at Mrs Jiang.

He said no, it didn't look like they were laughing.

– 18 –

The Workshop of the World

Morgan hardly slept. He was worried sick. He'd rung the airline in Beijing and London and it had told him what it had told his wife: that Robert had been on the flight, and he'd got off the aircraft when it landed in the Chinese capital.

But Robert had never reached the arrivals hall. He'd not met Cindy Wu. And he wasn't answering his phones, neither his UK number nor the China one he used whenever he visited.

Perhaps it was a customs or immigration issue. Morgan was sure his son had the right visa, all the paperwork he needed, but still there might have been some sort of airport mix-up. He tried to be rational. That could happen. He tried ringing the airport, but when the call was eventually answered he could find nobody willing or able to answer his questions. He was passed from one official to another, before they just hung up.

He'd said to Cindy Wu, "We should call the police, call the embassy. He's a child. How can he just go missing like this?" And his wife had said to leave it with her, that neither would be useful. She asked him to give her time to work her contacts.

Morgan knew that made sense, but it didn't make it any easier.

He heard nothing more from her until shortly before dawn, and when she phoned her tone had completely changed, saying to Morgan, "Everything's fine. He's fine. It was a mix-up like we thought."

"What sort of mix-up?" said Morgan, feeling enormous relief, but also confused and angry, wanting a fuller explanation.

"Nothing. Just some confusion at the airport."

Morgan asked what sort of confusion, and she just said, "Don't worry yourself, Tony, I have sorted it." She said she was tired since she'd been up half the night and would fill him in later. She asked if he was still going down south that morning.

He said he'd been planning to cancel the trip, what with Robert going missing, and Cindy Wu said again, "It's sorted." She said he should go ahead with the trip.

Morgan asked to talk to their son, but she said he was asleep, that he was jet-lagged and the whole experience had been exhausting for him.

Then she said to Morgan, "About the research I've been doing, Tony, who's the client?"

"Which research?" said Morgan, surprised since she never asked about clients. It was a sort of unwritten rule. The client side of the business belonged to him. That's how they worked. And she usually preferred not to know more than the generalities.

"The Colonel, the military guy and his son. I am still digging, looking for the more recent information you asked for, and it would help to know more about the client."

Morgan hesitated before saying, "He's American. Concerned about investors looking to buy in the US."

"You told me that, Tony. What's his name, and who does he work for?"

"His name's Drayton, Chuck Drayton."

"Drayton with a y?" she asked.

"That's right," Morgan said.

That was followed by another long silence before she asked him again, "Who does he work for?"

"He's a diplomat, deals with commercial stuff at the US Consulate in Shanghai."

"A diplomat?" she said. "So we're working for the US Government? What have you got us into, Tony?"

Then she said she had to go and hung up, and when Morgan tried to phone her back her phone was busy. He tried three more times before leaving for the airport, going straight to voicemail on each attempt, before giving up, figuring that she was probably sleeping. He'd try her again when he got to Shenzhen, when he'd get to speak to Robert too and get the fuller story about what happened.

His wife was stressed. They both were. He understood that, but she'd get over it.

*

Morgan's aircraft left Shanghai three hours late because of the smog. That was annoying enough. But then it turned back an hour into the flight because a passenger had tipped a bowl of scorching noodles over a flight attendant.

All Morgan had heard from the relative comfort of his first class compartment was a lot of shouting and screaming from beyond the curtain, and when they got back to Shanghai a short, stocky woman with a face redder than the Shanghai Airlines seat covers was offloaded in handcuffs by the police, a male companion in tow.

While they waited on the ground Morgan tried phoning his wife again. This time the phone rang, but she never picked up. Then he phoned a man called Sam Ching, who was supposed to meet him in Shenzhen, to find that Ching knew more about the air rage incident than he did.

"The woman didn't like the noodles," Ching said.

"She didn't like the noodles?"

"She wanted rice."

"And?"

"The rice was finished."

Ching told Morgan the woman pushed over the flight attendant before throwing the noodles in her face.

"That's crazy," said Morgan.

"I know," said Ching. "They never carry enough rice."

Ching told him it was all over the internet, that perhaps a dozen people had recorded it with their smartphones and uploaded the photos and videos just as soon as the aircraft landed back in Shanghai and they had a signal.

It was a hazy afternoon in Shenzhen when Morgan's aircraft landed, but not nearly as bad as the smog Morgan had left behind in Shanghai. He felt more relaxed. Mellowed by several gin and tonics. He tried to telephone Cindy Wu. Her phone rang, but she still didn't pick up. He tried Robert's two numbers, but they went straight to voicemail and he left a message on both.

"Hey Robert, it's Dad. Sounds like a bit of a pain at the airport. Looking forward to seeing you. Call me when you can."

Then he tried to concentrate on the business he needed to sort in Shenzhen. Bud's gnomes and the deals with Mr Fang.

He was soon sitting comfortably in the back of Sam Ching's black Mercedes van, sipping ice cold water, Ching telling him that business wasn't too great down south.

Ching was from nearby Hong Kong, but also held a Canadian passport, which he called his insurance policy for when Beijing destroyed Hong Kong, scrapped the freedoms it had promised when the place was handed back to China by the British. He thought that was bound to happen.

He said Beijing didn't like anything it couldn't control.

He was hard-nosed and practical, and had a Hong Konger's sense of superiority towards the mainland Chinese, whom he regarded for the most part as crude, uncultured and corrupt.

Ching was Morgan's age, but looked ten years younger. He was medium height with a full head of greying hair parted at one side, and he was well built. He was wearing dark jeans and a beige padded sleeveless jacket over a dark blue shirt.

His face seemed to have fixed on it a permanent smile, or perhaps a smirk.

Morgan had been working with Ching for almost ten years. He was his eyes and ears in the south, where he owned a string of factories, and acted as a broker for many more. If Morgan needed something, Ching could usually make it happen.

Between gin and tonics, Morgan had spent most of the flight south doodling on a Shanghai Airlines sick bag, which he now had in front of him, looking like a deranged game of snakes and ladders. At the top, underlined three times, was the title, "Still the Workshop of the World".

It was an outline of the next edition of the *MB China Report*, which he'd seen as a kind of travelogue across the area where the China Miracle began, and where it would continue, or so he'd tell his readers. He knew those statistics by heart too: three quarters of the world's toys, umbrellas and mobile phones, more than half its shoes and electrical appliances, all produced here.

Now bold new industries were emerging, like drones, robots and 3D printing. Sure there was a bit of a downturn, but the future looked good. Shenzhen was now leading China's latest economic transformation. At least that's how he'd tell it to readers of his report.

But as they drove north, the shuttered shops and lifeless factories told another story.

"It's bad," Ching said.

Ching had been doing business in Shenzhen since well before the handover of Hong Kong. He'd been a pioneer when China first opened up, and Shenzhen had been the first of China's Special Economic Zones.

He still had the pictures in his office of the area when it was rice paddies and swamplands. Now Shenzhen was a city of ten million with a sprawling hinterland of tens of thousands of factories from which just about anything could be sourced.

Ching regarded himself as a decent man working in a corrupt system. He would tell Morgan that he never paid a bribe or cut corners unless it was entirely necessary. Which gave him a lot of leeway, and anyway Morgan preferred not to know those details.

Ching said he'd not known things this bad in a long time, and as they drove he pointed out the shells of factories that had closed, places that had made shoes, toys and light fittings. At one, the gate was blackened, the nearby guardhouse burned down.

"The owner just closed the place, locked the gate and left," he said. "From Taiwan I think. Workers broke back in, angry, demanding to be paid. But the guy had taken all the money with him."

He said there'd been a lot of unrest, strikes and stuff, and the police had arrested a whole bunch of labour rights activists. Rounded them all up. Not that Ching was a big fan of labour rights, which he saw as a contradiction in terms. But he liked the Communist Party even less.

He said the local government was in denial.

"They keep saying it's all part of a plan to get out of low-end manufacturing and into high tech, like robots. But I don't see no robots. Just a lot of empty factories that can't sell anything anymore."

He told Morgan that one of his companies had made a small loss over the last financial year, but when he went to file the accounts with the tax office they told him a loss wasn't acceptable.

"So we changed it to a small profit. That's how they do their statistics here," he said. "It's about what's politically acceptable, not what's real."

And Morgan made a mental note to post that thought later to *@Beijing_smog*. He crumpled up the sick bag. He'd need to rethink that as well. At least a bit.

Their van then turned onto another wider road lined with factories, through a gate and parked in a small claustrophobic courtyard surrounded by tall, grey and mostly windowless buildings.

They left the van and took a battered service lift, which clanked, jolted and shuddered as it scraped its way up the lift shaft. Every floor had its own factory, and the sliding metal door opened first at a manufacturer of dental equipment. A high-pitched whine made Morgan cringe and involuntarily he ran his tongue along his teeth to make sure they were still there.

Ching's factory, one of several he owned, was on the eighth floor, the lift opening onto a corridor of white, scuffed walls. A woman sat painting her nails behind a reception desk, alongside an empty, stained fish tank. There was a worn leather sofa and a small coffee table on which sat an old cracked teapot and three dirty cups.

A tall glass cabinet with sliding doors displayed a selection of the factory's products: phone cases, tripods, selfie sticks and other simple electronic accessories. There was a map of China, a white board that was no longer so white and a battered projector.

They sat at the coffee table, and it was then that Morgan told Ching that he had a client from Alabama who was looking to shift production to China, wanting to make a bunch of garden gnomes from a good quality polyresin.

"You know, smiling old guys with white beards, to stick in the garden," said Morgan, showing him a picture.

"Wow. Pretty ugly. Pretty scary," Ching said.

Morgan told him they were meant to be comforting, and were very popular.

"Look pretty scary to me," Ching said.

Ching looked at the pictures and sketches and said that wouldn't be a problem, that he'd get some quotes. Nothing was ever a problem for Sam Ching.

He led Morgan down another dark corridor lined with sparsely furnished offices with signs saying Marketing, Sales, Engineering and Finance. They were mostly empty.

Then onto the vast and harshly lit factory floor, where several hundred mostly young women, wearing yellow polo-shirts, jeans and sneakers were bent over long tables, with a conveyor belt running alongside each table, assembling selfie sticks, extendable arms for taking smartphone photos.

Boxes were piled high against a door marked Emergency Exit.

Ching pointed out to Morgan where he thought he could install new machinery for the gnomes. And Morgan said the Alabama guy was a serious player, that he wanted to shift a lot of his production to China to cut costs. That gnomes were just the start.

"I need a good price, Sam, but we have to keep an eye on quality. I don't want a repeat of the Freeport thing."

"It was a dog, Tony. A fucking dog."

"The dog had a name, Sam. It was called Honey."

It had been in many ways a freak accident, but it had become a big political issue in the city of Freeport, Illinois, and a rallying point for opposition to outsourcing to China.

Honey, an over-weight Labrador that newspapers would later call "adorable, loving, loyal, like another child", had choked to death on a small nut that came loose from a chandelier, fell and landed in her food.

The dog's owner had bought the US$600 chandelier from a local mall, which had bought a batch of them from a wholesaler for US$350 each. The wholesaler had paid US$200 per item to a Hong Kong trading company, which in turn paid Sam Ching US$37 per chandelier.

Anthony Morgan had brokered the deal, but the fallout never reached him or Ching personally. The supply chain was too complicated.

But fallout there was. An Illinois election was approaching, and Freeport had other issues with China, which was blamed for a string of factory closures, including a local car parts plant that was dismantled and shipped to Shanghai, the workers asked to train those who'd be replacing them.

So the nut, once discovered, had become the "killer nut from China" in local media.

Honey was then stuffed by the State's finest taxidermist, making an appearance alongside the Governor at a nationally televised press conference.

"China is not only taking our jobs," he thundered, banging his table. "They are killing our pets!"

"I hear you," said Ching to Morgan. "But you're squeezing me. You want to pay me less and less. Then you complain about quality issues."

And he did have a point.

Morgan told him this Bud from Alabama had money. That he'd pay a fair price.

They looked out of a stained and cracked window at a drab, rundown building across the road. There was little to distinguish it from its neighbours. But Morgan recalled that last time he visited, it had been busy with crowds of mostly young men and women who all had one thing in common: they had missing limbs or other terrible disfigurements.

"What happened to the hostel?"

"Police closed it down," Ching said. He sounded almost sorry, which came as a surprise to Morgan, since Ching was forever complaining about the place, a refuge for workers who'd been maimed while working in the area's factories, lawyers fighting an uphill battle for compensation. It was as if he saw the hostel as an accusing finger, pointing directly at him.

Now he said, "They weren't doing no harm. Just standing up for their rights." He said there'd been a big raid on the place, lots of police and paramilitary. "To take away a bunch of invalids, for God's sake."

He said they'd barricaded themselves in, and showed Morgan a series of photographs he'd taken on his smartphone of the place surrounded. There were defiant posters in the windows, home-made sketches mostly. A worker on crutches. Another with patches over her eyes. There were others that didn't look human, more like aliens. Stick aliens.

A final photograph showed a man being dragged off by police. Ching said he was one of the hostel organisers, who'd lost a foot in a metal processing machine and broke the other resisting arrest. He was still carrying a stick alien poster as he was hauled away.

Morgan asked for a copy of the photo. One for *@Beijing_smog*.

Then they went back to the Mercedes van, Ching saying he wanted to show Morgan something else, so he could understand what was going on in the area, and they drove for fifteen minutes until they came to an area where development petered out and gave way to patchy farmland and a small settlement.

Which is when Morgan looked at his phone, swearing under his breath as he saw that he'd missed two calls from Cindy Wu. His phone had been on silent mode for the flight and he'd forgotten to switch it back. He went to call his wife's number, but then decided to wait. It wasn't a conversation he wanted to have in front of Ching.

And he couldn't leave the van. There were rocks all over the road ahead and the burnt-out shells of two cars and an excavator. There was a strong smell of burning. Several men stood alert like sentries under a cluster of lychee trees.

They eyed the Mercedes suspiciously. Ching got out, telling Morgan to stay behind the darkened windows of the van, and went to talk to them.

When he returned to the van, Ching told the driver to head back the way they'd come, saying to Morgan, "They're playing with fire around here."

He said there was a big landfill site just up the road, which the local people said was dangerously unstable, and was being used to dump construction waste by a developer with strong local political connections. The usual story. He said the people around there had tried to block the entrance and had clashed with the police and thugs working for the developer.

Morgan looked back as they left, at one of the burnt cars – a police car. There was an image engraved on its charred door. It was another stick alien. Ching saw it too and said the alien had been getting around, that it seemed to have been adopted by just about everybody down here with a grudge against the Government.

"And that's a lot of people," he said as they drove away.

– 19 –

Dot-com Billionaire

Wang Chu said he'd decided to become a dot-com billionaire, and Liu Wei asked him when that might be because Lily was giving him a hard time about their unpaid coffee shop bills.

"Seriously," Wang said. "I've made up my mind. I'm going to start my own business. Mine will be the internet's next Big Idea."

"Which is?"

"I haven't had it yet. But I'm working on it."

The summons from the University, the strange meeting with Mrs Jiang and the fat creepy guy in the ski jacket had shaken him. Mostly he was confused and depressed by it, still not sure why they'd called him in.

Liu agreed it was probably about ideology, Wang not taking it seriously enough. Whatever the reason, Wang was convinced it had badly damaged his already faltering prospects at university, even if they didn't kick him out.

He needed a Plan B.

He needed to strike out on his own. And internet start-ups were the future.

Wang said he'd just been to a talk at the University given by Mark Zuckerberg, the American who set up Facebook, who was visiting China, and it was really inspiring.

"Who?" said Liu.

"Zuckerberg. You know. He runs the American version of Renren. And he says he'll be giving his fortune to charity."

"Why would he do that?"

"To make the world a better place. To cure all the world's illnesses."

"How's he going to do that?"

Wang said he wasn't entirely sure, that this Zuckerberg was speaking Chinese, or trying to.

"It wasn't great Chinese. But at least he tried. And he has a Chinese wife. Said he had to learn Mandarin so he could speak with her parents."

Wang said Zuckerberg had also been jogging in the smog in Tiananmen Square without a mask, and Liu said in that case he must be really confident of knocking out a quick cure for heart disease and lung cancer.

They were walking from the University to The Moment On Time, passing a statue of Mao that stood in front of a rival university, its arm outstretched and pointing in the direction of the coffee shop, which Wang always found helpful on smoggy days, getting some guidance from the Great Helmsman.

"The zombies were awesome by the way."

"What zombies?" Liu asked.

"*Temple Run*, the zombie version. The one you said to download. It was cool. You were right. Thanks. The crazed zombies, they still get you in the end, but I'd had enough of the crazed monkeys," he said.

"You're welcome," Liu said.

They stopped at the railway crossing near the coffee shop, because the barrier was down and extra police were there to prevent anybody impatient from slipping through. They'd been given little red flags to wave.

Wang told Liu there'd been a big confrontation there, people trying to force their way across, a cop pushing over a woman with a child.

Liu said he'd seen it on a video-sharing site.

"These guys are idiots," he said, pointing to the police.

Wang said he couldn't see the one who'd done the pushing, and Liu said he'd probably been promoted.

This time the wait was shorter. A goods train rumbled through and the barrier was raised, creaking like it might come crashing back down at any moment.

Liu said you couldn't even get Facebook in China, and that maybe that was why this Zuckerberg was in town, sucking up to the Party.

"It won't work," he said. "How can you trust a man who can't see smog and wants to talk to his mother-in-law. How's that inspiring?"

"Well then look at Jack Ma," said Wang. "He was just a teacher and now he's the king of e-commerce. He built Alibaba from nothing. Now he's a billionaire. Richest man in China."

"You sure? I thought the richest guy was into property."

Wang said the new rich were all dot-com guys. That was the future. Property was yesterday, the bubble was bursting. There was too much of it. And he said he was through with going to pointless job fairs.

The graduate job market was worse than anybody could remember.

Wang said the future was in internet start-ups.

He said you couldn't even make money working for the Government anymore.

Liu said the road to riches still lay through the Party, and Wang said he wasn't so sure and that he wanted nothing to do with the Party or the Government. Not after all his trouble at the University.

Liu said he thought that was naive.

"You suppose Jack Ma would last one day if he didn't toe the Party line? Or Zuckerberg will be allowed to operate here if he doesn't follow their rules. Nobody's bigger than the Party."

Wang said that a bunch of places had opened in Haidian, not far from the University. They were called spaces. Incubators. For developers to work on new tech stuff.

"You go there and talk about ideas and where to raise the cash, where to get the backing, that kind of thing. It's pretty cool."

Liu asked why you'd talk about ideas in front of other people.

"Suppose somebody else stole your idea, then what would it be worth?"

Wang said it wasn't like that.

"These people don't steal ideas," he said.

And Liu said that everybody stole ideas, and maybe if Wang hung around there long enough, in one of those incubators, then maybe he could walk away with a few as well, saving him a lot of work.

Wang ignored that and said, "They even invite people who've started successful businesses to come and talk, and say how they did it."

He said it was just like Silicon Valley, in America, except right now it was centred on just three or four coffee shops and an apartment or two in a street north of the University.

"We should talk to Lily, tell her to set aside some space in her place for an incubator."

"She'd love that," Liu said. "She'll think you want to turn the coffee shop into a glorified crèche, and you know how she hates having children in there.

"And any case," he said, "we still have her bill to pay."

"Maybe we should talk to Fatso. He's got a ton of space at his place," Wang said.

"What does Fatso know about internet start-ups?"

"Not a lot, for sure, but the guy is sharper than he looks. Fatso wants to go into finance. He's thinking of getting himself a diploma so he can do all that stock market stuff, give advice on where the market's going."

"That's not difficult," Liu said, his thumb pointing downwards.

He said he wouldn't want to take advice on the market from Fatso.

"That's his point," Wang said.

"What's his point?"

"That there are so many people out there, claiming they know everything, but really know nothing. Fatso can't be any worse. He might even be better."

"Tell him he can talk to the students, as a successful entrepreneur," Liu said.

And Wang said he wasn't sure that was such a good idea, since churning out knock-offs might not be everybody's idea of a digital start up.

They agreed to talk to him all the same. Maybe raise it with Lily as well.

They were in the coffee shop now, joining Zhang at their usual table near the window. Lily came over, not looking happy, and they ordered tea. Wang asked her if she'd heard of an incubator. She said she had Americano, latte and cappuccino and if they wanted a fancy coffee they should go elsewhere, though only after settling their bill.

They decided that Fatso might be the better option.

Liu logged into his trading account and found the market had picked up. He was smiling for the first time in days, saying the Government had intervened, buying shares to prop up prices after a big riot outside the Shanghai Stock Exchange.

"People don't like losing money," he said, telling his roomates that brokers had been arrested for selling shares, and journalists detained for negative reporting about the market.

"It's a market. Aren't they supposed to go up and down?" said Wang

"It's a Chinese market," said Liu. "The Party wants prices to go where it tells them to go."

Liu then told Zhang about Wang's plan to become a dot-com billionaire, and Zhang said great, just keep clear of robots, especially in orange robes.

"So why's that?" said Wang, and Zhang told him that a new artificial intelligence programme at the University had been shut down and the Director arrested after they made a politically incorrect robot.

Zhang said it was all a misunderstanding.

The programme had been launched by the Party leader himself on a visit to the University. A model programme, he'd called it, part of China's new innovation economy, and Zhang, one of the stars of the Computer Science Department, had been asked to join.

Their first creation was a robot monk, which had been installed in a Tibetan temple. It was four feet tall, dressed in orange robes and able to answer questions about Buddhism, interact with its surroundings and chant and play music.

"It was a cutting-edge way of explaining Buddhism," said Zhang, and it was praised immediately by Party officials, who saw a lot of promise in friendly and compliant robotic monks.

Zhang said there'd been a few teething problems, and one day it burst into flames.

"Self-immolated? That's pretty realistic,'" said Liu.

"It was a problem with the circuits," Zhang said, not seeing the funny side.

He said the real problem came when the robot got attitude and attacked another visiting Party official, hitting him with a prayer wheel and telling him to get out of the temple, not being friendly at all. And certainly not compliant.

Which Liu thought was really funny.

"I want one," he said. "We can put it at the door of the coffee shop."

"But how did that happen?" said Wang. "It was supposed to be a robot."

Zhang said the Director, the one who'd now been arrested, thought at first it had been hacked, but then decided it was just acting rationally.

"These are intelligent machines. They learn from their environment. They are designed to be sensitive and responsive."

"So they decided life for Tibetan monks sucks. And it's all the Party's fault." said Liu, laughing again. "That seems pretty smart to me."

Zhang ignored that, and said to Wang, "So what's your Big Idea?"

"He hasn't got one," said Liu.

Wang said that wasn't strictly true. While he didn't yet have *the* Big Idea, he had written his first app, and he was close to putting it up for sale on a couple of app stores.

"Wow," said Zhang. "So what is this app that's going to make us all rich?"

"It's a game. The money's in games," Wang said. "You want to see?"

They moved their chairs either side of Wang, who clicked on a small icon on his phone.

The screen was filled with a picture of Tiananmen Square, the entrance of the Forbidden City with its big portrait of Mao Zedong at the top. There were a series of buttons at the bottom and a number box for the score.

"There are three modes," Wang said. "Night, day, and smog." He swiped the screen to move between modes, saying the smog mode was probably more realistic, and that the final version might have more locations.

He touched another button to start the game and, slowly at first, stick aliens started appearing from under the portrait of Mao, spilling onto Tiananmen Square.

"This is where it gets fun," he said. Another button controlled a hand holding a fly swatter, which appeared at the edge of the screen, and by repeatedly touching the button the swatter swiped the aliens from the screen, complete with a high-pitched whooshing, and a sound like a racquet hitting a tennis ball.

"Nice," said Zhang, and Wang passed him the phone to let him have a go.

"It's pretty straightforward," Wang said. He told them you scored points by whacking as many aliens as possible. There would be several levels, but he'd not quite worked that out yet.

"What are the little bags they're carrying?" Liu said.

"That's money. You'll eventually get more points for whacking the ones stealing the most money, but that's something else I have to work out."

He said he was also looking at options to shoot the aliens or run them over with a car.

"Cool," Liu said. "You should really get this out there. How much are you going to charge?"

"I think it will be free at first, then I'll charge for add-ons. That seems best. Get people into the game, then offer them extras."

"What are you going to call it?"

"*Whack an Alien, Cleaning up Tiananmen Square*. Something like that. It's almost ready to go."

"Well, the sooner the better," said Liu, who wasn't smiling anymore. He was back at his screen, the market falling now.

"The Government must have stopped buying," he said. "Or else they didn't arrest enough brokers."

Wang played some more with his game. He was pleased with it, but it wasn't an instant answer to their money issues. It might take time to take off.

He whacked a few more aliens, wondering how else he could improve it, thinking hard about maybe adding an optional boot to kick them off the screen, until a piece of paper hit him on the head, thrown by Liu.

"Wang, promise me you'll get that game out, I mean soon."

And Wang said not to worry, that he was almost ready to go live, and that he was convinced there were a whole lot of people out there just itching to whack some aliens.

– 20 –

Mr Fang

The next time Morgan got to speak with his wife he was in his Shenzhen hotel room, just after breakfast, on the second day of his trip down south.

She rang him just as he was cleaning his teeth, an electric toothbrush in one hand and with a mouthful of paste. The first thing she said was that Robert was feeling much better, but when Morgan asked to speak with his son she said he'd gone to the coast with his grandparents. That he'd just left. She said it was good for him to get away from the smog and cold of Beijing. That it would be a good break.

Morgan spat the toothpaste into the sink and said, "I'll try and call him later."

But Cindy Wu said that wasn't going to be possible since Robert had left both of his phones in Beijing.

"Don't worry," she said. "I will get him to call you just as soon as he can."

Then she asked about Morgan's schedule.

"How's your day looking?" she said.

Which surprised him, since she never asked about his day, at least she hadn't for a long time, and he just said, "A lot of meetings. Factories, clients. The usual stuff."

He said he'd pretty much confirmed the new partner and factory for Bud from Alabama, should Bud still want to go ahead. He was just waiting for a few technical details and the full quote, but that shouldn't be an issue, since he knew this partner well.

Cindy Wu said that was good to know. And then she said, "And Drayton. What's the latest on our American client?"

Morgan said he'd be catching up with him at some point, though wasn't exactly sure when. He asked his wife whether she had anything more for him on the Drayton project.

She said she was still working on it and then told him again that Robert was fine. That he shouldn't worry and that she'd get the boy to call his father later.

Then Morgan's hotel room phone rang. It was the concierge, who said his car was ready and did he need a hand with the golf clubs? Morgan said he'd bring the clubs down himself and then went back to his iPhone, telling Cindy Wu that he had to go, that a client was waiting.

"Drayton?" she asked.

"No, not Drayton," he said. "Another one."

Then he hung up and hauled his golf clubs out to the lift and down to the lobby. He was halfway to the hotel's revolving door when his phone rang again.

"Golf's off," said the man from Mr Fang's office.

"Golf's off?" said Morgan.

"Golf's off."

"And lunch?"

"Lunch is on. One o'clock at the Golden Phoenix Restaurant, at Magnificent Gulf View. Mr Fang will see you there."

Then the man hung up, just like that, and Morgan was left standing in the middle of the lobby, phone in one hand, balancing the bag of clubs with the other and with a car warming its engine outside, ready to take him to a game that now wasn't going to happen.

He'd been looking forward to the golf and a long lingering lunch at the club's lakeside restaurant overlooking the first hole.

He went to the concierge, gave him the clubs to store and said he might need the car later, but wouldn't be going anywhere for now.

Then he rang Sam Ching.

"Yeah, what?" said Ching, which is how he mostly answered the phone. Though he changed his tone when he realised it was Morgan, who asked him if he knew the place he'd just been summoned to.

Ching offered to take him over there, saying Magnificent Gulf View was a big new development along the coast, beyond his factory. He said it was a vast place, but pretty much deserted. Another crazy development. A ghost city. And he said it was construction waste from that place that was being dumped in the landfill beyond the protest they'd seen.

"There's really a restaurant there? Really?" he said. "I thought there was nothing there but empty buildings."

An hour later they were driving east in the black Mercedes van, Ching suggesting a detour, to check out the golf club, the Eternal Springs Country Club.

The club covered fifteen square kilometres, its eighteen-hole golf course sprawling around low hills and artificial lakes, the clubhouse with spa and restaurant at the heart of it. One of the finest in southern China, they claimed. Membership cost a quarter of a million dollars.

But when they got there the main gate was shut and chained; two security guards sat nearby, smoking. A light haze hung over deserted hills, but Morgan could see that trees had been planted where a month earlier there'd been fairways designed by Gary Player. The nearest bunkers had been filled with earth.

One of the security guards told Ching it was an illegal development.

"So what's happening?" Morgan asked Ching.

"It's illegal," Ching said.

"What's illegal?"

"Golf's illegal."

Morgan didn't really get that.

"Since when?"

"Since 1949, or thereabouts."

Ching told him that Mao hated golf, said it was bourgeois and when the communists came to power he banned officials from playing and had all the courses dug up.

"Then they banned it again, must be at least ten years ago. Said that was to preserve arable land. Farmers were getting pretty angry too, seeing their land stolen for golf courses."

"But there've been hundreds built since then," said Morgan.

"Yeah, but they call them country clubs, or resorts, which just happen to have a golf course. Same thing, different name."

"You know a lot about golf."

"I know a lot about communists."

Morgan said he guessed it must be part of the Party's anti-corruption crackdown, too many officials cutting deals on the fairways.

"I'm not sure about that," Ching said. "Some have been shut down. But plenty are still open. Depends on connections. That's why I'm surprised about this place. Owned by a big developer, close to the local Party, which is how they got the permissions and were able to throw so many farmers off their land."

Ching said the people he spoke to thought the Communist Party leader in Beijing was just getting rid of his rivals, reshuffling the assets, and that he was targeting officials in the south. But Ching said it was a dangerous game, that he was making a lot of enemies.

That sounded to Morgan a lot like the warning from his wife. Ching was well connected down south and good at reading the political mood. You had to be, to survive and thrive as long as he had in the jungle that was the factory business in southern China. That's why he was so valuable to Morgan.

And Morgan wondered where Mr Fang fitted into all this.

They drove east, close to the coast for a while, and through another district of factories, and then more drab egg-box-like shophouses fronted by a clutter of noodle restaurants, print shops, an open-fronted tea house with pool tables. Beyond one hill a power station belched out smoke so thick that Ching's driver was forced to put on his headlights.

Then more construction sites. Row upon row of tall apartment blocks, each wrapped in scaffolding and green mesh, framed by impossibly tall cranes, none of which appeared to be moving. In the distance, through the smoke, they looked like a marching army of grotesque monsters. War of the Worlds.

Morgan opened his window and took a photograph with his iPhone. He posted it to *@Beijing_smog,* and he tweeted:

171

Construction addiction. 70m empty homes. Ghost cities. Kicking the habit could be fatal. How much longer can they defy economic gravity?

Though the latest draft of the *MB China Report*, which he was continuing to work on, would be calmly reassuring. The Party's mandarins are aware of the challenges. They can rise to it. Keep investing. You can't afford not to be in China.

They were approaching Magnificent Gulf View now because that's what it said on more hoardings along the roadside, with computer-generated pictures of a gleaming glass city of tall buildings and lakes, between which families relaxed, children ran with balloons in hand.

But beyond the hoardings Magnificent Gulf View was like a deserted film set, rubbish blowing in the streets between the shells of buildings in various stages of completion. Two workmen sat on a pavement on one corner eating noodles from plastic boxes. They were the only construction workers to be seen, and they pointed their chopsticks up the road when Ching's driver stopped and asked for directions to the Golden Phoenix Restaurant, which was written on the side of the noodle boxes.

The restaurant had no sign, but two cars, one a BMW 7 series, Mr Fang's ride, were parked out the front of the only plausible candidate, because this building was almost complete. A driver was asleep in the back of the 7 series. They were the first cars Morgan had seen in Magnificent Gulf View.

Morgan got out of the Mercedes van and Ching said he wanted to have a further look around because this was surreal, and to message when Morgan was through with lunch.

Morgan climbed a narrow staircase to the first floor, where a door opened into a large dining room, with small windows but fierce strip lights, the walls lined with paintings from Beijing Opera. A few people were sitting around, bent over bowls of steaming noodles, which seemed a speciality.

Morgan recognised one group of thickset men who always travelled with Mr Fang. One in particular was hard to forget. A bear of a man with closely cropped hair and a long pink scar from beyond his hairline to just above his right eye and wearing an orange ski jacket. He pointed with his chopsticks to a curtained-off area on the far side.

Morgan followed the chopsticks and pulled back the curtain.

"Ah, Mr Fang, good to see you."

Mr Fang was on the phone, and didn't look like he was happy with the conversation. There was hardly an acknowledgement for Morgan, just a downward flick of the wrist with the big silver Rolex, telling him to sit. He had gold rings on most of his fingers, except the little finger of his left hand. That finger was missing.

A server had followed him in, and Morgan pointed at Mr Fang's noodles and tea. He'd have the same.

This sure wasn't the Eternal Springs Country Club, where he'd have ordered the filet mignon, always rare, and one of their finest bottles of Bordeaux. Instead Morgan waited for his noodles and for Mr Fang to finish his call.

Morgan removed a file from a small shoulder bag he was carrying and shuffled some papers.

Mr Fang rubbed his dull sunken eyes. His face was red and getting redder, but this was from anger, not from any claret. And there was no lakeside view to calm him down, just a rather faded portrait of a pasty-faced opera singer.

Fang ran a hand back and forth through cropped hair and fiddled with a heavy gold chain, which he tucked into a white polo shirt.

When he'd finished ranting he put his phone face down on the table.

"So, tell me."

Morgan told him he was sorry they couldn't meet at the club. Made a joke out of the noodles, which had just arrived.

Mr Fang said he was sorry too. The club was facing some paperwork issues.

Morgan opened some spreadsheets and started his presentation. The cash balances were good. Investment income was strong. He recommended closing one of the three accounts based out of the Turks and Caicos Islands, perhaps opening another in Hong Kong or London.

MacMaster and Brown provided the nominee shareholders and management for the offshore companies.

Fang said to tell him about the real estate, sounding impatient, and Morgan said the purchase of the Hawaii resort was now complete, all cash through Rising Phoenix Holdings, one of the Turks and Caicos companies.

"These are the others I'd recommend," he said, putting another file on the table containing glossy brochures: a beachside condo development in California, a ranch in Ohio, a big new development in Palm Springs, refurbished apartments on Central Park, New York.

He said prices were high, but Fang said that didn't matter, and without even reading the brochures he said that he'd like to move ahead with them all except the ranch. He didn't like farms.

Morgan said he was still working on the football club, though prices were high with patchy returns. Fang sniffed and wiped a hand across his nose. He told Morgan that price and returns weren't important. That it was speed that mattered.

Morgan then asked if Fang and his partners still wanted to move ahead with the St Kitts passports, and now it was Fang's turn to put a file on the table. It contained a summary page and seven sheets of A4 paper, one for each applicant. There were names, photographs and some brief biographical detail on each.

It wasn't much, but more than Morgan had ever received from them before, and enough, he imagined, to satisfy the St Kitts immigration authorities.

Morgan said he'd arrange the payments from the offshore accounts, half a million dollars per applicant into a local St Kitts account. They could decide later how to invest it, just as long as it stayed in the country for at least a year.

Then Mr Fang stood up, picked up his phone and left, followed by the man with the scar and several others from the main part of the restaurant.

Morgan poked at his noodles and phoned Ching, who said he'd be outside in ten minutes.

He really didn't know quite what to make of the meeting, or the venue. Mr Fang sure seemed desperate to get money out of the country. Which was just fine by Morgan.

He'd always known that Fang was the frontman for a syndicate of local officials, which he presumed was now feeling the heat and seeking salvation in US property and St Kitts citizenship. And Fang had done what he'd never done before: provide at least some details of the people he represented.

The private client business, or wealth management as they preferred to call it, was one of MacMaster and Brown's most lucrative.

Morgan's alter ego, *@Beijing_smog*, regularly denounced crooked officials, but as their investment adviser he was always scrupulously detached. How and where they got their money was not his concern.

There was a saying in the world of private banking: 'Know your clients'. Which made Morgan smile as he sat there, hand on the file he'd been given, thinking that he would finally get to learn their names.

– 21 –

Hand-Job Machines

As they drove back towards Shenzhen, Sam Ching gave Morgan a brown envelope and said, "Big winner this one, Tony."

Inside was a photograph and drawings of what looked like a vacuum cleaner on adjustable legs, with an opening at the front that resembled the head of a toilet plunger, with a hole in the middle. A caption described it as an "Automatic Sperm Extractor – Mark 2".

"Hand-job machine," said Ching. "Could be big in America."

"I'm not sure it's going to catch on," said Morgan.

Ching told him it was super silent and had seven different speeds, and that two Chinese hospitals were already taking a look.

"For fertility treatment," he said. "And that's a fast-growing market."

"What's with the mark 2?" Morgan asked.

"The Japanese have a model, so I don't want confusion."

"So you copied it?"

"Adapted it, Tony."

Ching was never short of ideas, Morgan would hand him that. And the man could switch his production line overnight: selfie sticks one day, garden gnomes the next. So Morgan had no doubt Ching could make the thing. He just doubted any self-respecting American male would trust his member to a hand-job machine "Made in China".

Anticipating that, Ching pointed to the small print, which said, "Made in Hong Kong".

"You're going to make it in Hong Kong?"

"Package it in Hong Kong."

"Is that legal?"

And Ching looked at him as if that was just about the most stupid thing he'd heard all day.

When they reached Morgan's hotel, Ching asked him to take a proper look at the Automatic Sperm Extractor – Mark 2, and said there was some additional technical information in the envelope.

"It really is a good market," Ching said. "Promise me you'll at least take a look, Tony."

Morgan said sure, he'd look, and put the envelope into his bag. He reminded Ching about the quote on garden gnomes, saying that was urgent.

Morgan got out of the van, saying thanks for the ride, and Ching shouted after him, "Hand-job machine, Tony. Hand job. It's the future." Morgan quickened his pace towards the lobby, absolutely sure everybody anywhere nearby was looking at him.

It then took Morgan what seemed like an eternity to cross the cavernous hotel lobby, weaving around fat marble pillars and huddles of buyers back from a trade fair, buses depositing wave after wave of them at the hotel's revolving doors.

His hotel was new, built to service a series of hangar-like exhibition halls built nearby, but convenient as well for Ching's factories. Large chandeliers hung from a distant ceiling, and one wall was lined with tall mirrors and built-in television screens looping kitschy videos. A log fire. A coral reef. Mountains.

What it hadn't quite mastered yet was service, and dazed and overwhelmed bellboys ping-ponged between the buses, yelled at in dozens of languages as they juggled overstuffed boxes of samples from the trade fair.

And to cap it all, the concierge seemed to have lost Morgan's golf clubs.

He ordered a gin and tonic in a packed corner bar, hearing Russian, Arabic, German, some kind of Scandinavian, an African dialect or two, and several varieties of English.

Some were first-time visitors, overwhelmed by what they'd seen.

"Can you *believe* that place?"

"Two hundred *thousand* exhibitors!"

He knew what a buzz these trade fairs could be. You could spend days walking through halls the size of several football pitches and lined with everything from televisions to toys, to shorts, socks, shoes and Christmas decorations. He was hard-pressed to think of anything you couldn't find there.

Morgan also knew how a buyer's day was organised. From hotel to bus to fair to lunch to fair, then maybe to a company showroom before the bar and dinner, maybe with a supplier, and always at a good restaurant. Maybe a bit of karaoke. From one air-conditioned space to another, chilled face towels and iced water always at hand before the serious drinking began later.

Rarely did buyers get to see the factories themselves. Those who did ask to visit would be politely told it wasn't convenient or the production line was undergoing maintenance. Most preferred not to know the conditions under which their products were manufactured, or else they employed middlemen like Morgan to be their buffer with the factory bosses, paid to provide assurance that things were absolutely fine. That it wasn't a sweatshop.

He signed for his drink and headed to the lift. In spite of the buzz he knew that the numbers of visitors and exhibitors were well down this year. Ching had told him, and Ching knew. Things were getting tough for China's exporters.

He admired the enthusiasm of the buyers, especially the first-timers. Once upon a time that had been him. But years of working in China had taught him to be very cautious.

Ching was just about the most solid, dependable and honest man he'd met down there. A man of principle. But everything was relative. Especially trust, and especially in Shenzhen.

He'd been stung early on in his business career after handing to a factory owner the full spec for some garden furniture, a really funky design. Pretty original, he'd thought, only to find that within a month the market was flooded with cheap knock-offs.

The factory owner had not only copied the design, but also set up a parallel production line, right out the back, churning out the copies under his own brand and right under Morgan's nose.

Even after Morgan had discovered the scam there wasn't much he could do. The law wasn't clear, and nobody enforced it anyway. The factory owner just shrugged, as if to say what do you expect?

The lift was packed with buyers from Hong Kong, who all appeared to be talking at once. He could tell they were from Hong Kong since they all had restless fingers, which meant that every time the lift stopped and its doors opened, several index fingers made a lunge at the close button. The one that got there first jabbing away as if each lost millisecond was lost business. Maybe it was.

You had to have your wits about you simply to get out, which Morgan did, at the twenty-fourth floor, where he went to the business centre and copied Mr Fang's documents, the information for the St Kitts passports. He also copied the document from his wife about the Colonel and his Ferrari-loving son, placing the copies together in a brown envelope. He put the envelope in his bag.

Morgan put the bag over his shoulder and took the lift up to thirtieth-floor bar. He ordered another drink, a vodka-soda this time, went outside and walked down to the darkened end of a long open-air terrace looking out on a new area of the city.

He tried to activate his VPN, so that he could share some more material to his @Beijing_smog Twitter account. But his VPN refused to work.

"They're fucking with you, man."

It was Chuck Drayton, by his side with a beer in hand, telling him that VPNs were being blocked now, particularly on smartphones.

"They don't want you accessing what they can't control," Drayton said.

"Can they do that, technically I mean?"

"They can try. It's a challenge for the VPNs though. Have to keep coming up with new addresses, fresh ways to tunnel out of China, keep one step ahead. You should install a couple more of them. Have some back-up."

Morgan said it was stupid. Business people needed to be able to access information. He waved his glass in the direction of the growing numbers of buyers now spilling onto the far end of the bar.

"China's going to lose business."

"You think the Communist Party gives a shit," said Drayton. "They want to do business on their terms or not at all. You know that."

Drayton said the US Embassy had complained to the Foreign Ministry.

"And what did they say?"

"Not much. They said Chinese internet was run in accordance with Chinese laws. Which seems to mean blocking anything they don't agree with."

Drayton said he'd been looking after Mark Zuckerberg, who was visiting China, doing some university talks, speaking Chinese to the students.

"The Facebook boss? He speaks Chinese?" Morgan said.

"Badly."

"So what's the point?"

"He thinks that if he makes the effort with the language, and tells them about his Chinese wife, then maybe they'll lift the ban on Facebook in China. He told the students that he first learned it so he could speak to his wife's family."

"Seems a lot of trouble to go to."

"He told them he likes Chinese culture too," Drayton said.

"What did the students make of it?"

"Not sure if they understood frankly, but they lapped up the soppy stuff all the same. He never mentioned a word of politics, so they'll probably invite him back."

Morgan said, "Who knows, they might even let Facebook in."

"For speaking Chinese? I doubt that. Maybe if he puts the Communist Party in charge of everybody's privacy settings, makes the Party a default Friend to all, so they can scoop up or block everything they want, any time. Maybe then they'll let him in."

"So I guess you told Zuckerberg that."

"Not in so many words, Tony, because you know at the end of the day I'm just a lowly public servant. He did tell me afterwards that he likes a challenge, though."

"And what did you say?"

"I said, 'Mark, you've got one'."

There was a piercing cackle of laughter from the far end of the terrace as more buyers, several drinks into their evening, came out onto the terrace.

"So how was your Mr Fang?" Drayton said.

"A little strange, I'd say."

Morgan told him how he'd switched the venues for lunch, had seemed a bit desperate. Didn't say much.

"And still wants a little slice of Caribbean beach and a bunch of American property?"

Morgan said yes, that's what he was most interested in. Said to go ahead and buy without even looking at the details and not caring about the price.

"And the documents, for the passports?"

Morgan took a brown envelope from his bag.

"It's all here, I think. The basic info on those who want citizenship of St Kitts, even a summary page. I've not looked at it in detail, but it appears to be a kind of who's who of Mr Fang's associates."

"Perfect," Drayton said. "And the Colonel?"

"It's in here too," Morgan said, patting the envelope. "That's still a bit of a work in progress, since there's not too much recent stuff on the father. Plenty on the son though."

"I can imagine," said Drayton, taking the envelope, folding it lengthways, and putting it into an inside pocket of his jacket.

Drayton asked Morgan what his plans were now, and Morgan said he was heading over to Hong Kong for an annual company get-together and a big rugby tournament. And Drayton said he expected the rugby might be more fun and wasn't that a bit like American football.

"Yeah, a bit," said Morgan. "But without all the armour."

There was no sign of a server, so Morgan told Drayton he'd go inside for a refill, but by the time he came back, drinks in hand, the American had gone.

Morgan had another drink and treated himself to a steak dinner washed down with two glasses of Bordeaux.

Then he decided to go for a massage, a little place he knew called the Pink Lady, close to the hotel, where he asked for his regular masseuse who called herself Mimi.

She was tall, from northern China. Not the best masseuse by a mile, but Morgan thought she was sweet and attentive. He had a hot shower, and then lay naked on his front while she pummelled his back like some not-so-prime buffalo steak that needed a good amount of tenderising. Drowning him in oil too.

181

Then he turned over, wondering how the next bit would unfold. She was always a little unpredictable. That's why he liked her, though right now she seemed to be in a hurry, and after a couple of half-hearted stokes to the thigh, she just grabbed him.

If before she'd been tenderising a steak, now she was working his member like she was milking the last and most stubborn cow on the farm. Morgan winced, grabbed her wrist and slowed her down. She seemed to get into a better rhythm after that.

But it was erratic. There'd be moments of almost hysteric activity, then nothing. The action just stopped. He opened an eye and saw one of Mimi's hands round him, while the other was holding a smartphone, texting.

He exploded, though not perhaps in the way she'd been expecting. He leapt off the bed yelling that it was the worst bloody massage he'd ever had. He got quickly dressed, his clothes clinging to the oil and telling her she should be concentrating on the job in hand, not the bloody phone. He refused to pay.

She looked at him as if she didn't understand a word of that, which mostly she didn't, saying it was her sister on her way to town. He said he didn't care who it was, and left the room, slamming the door behind him.

As soon as he left the massage place his phone rang. It was Drayton, who sounded agitated.

He'd just landed back in Shanghai and was at the kerbside outside the airport, waiting for Cyril to pick him up in the old taxi to take him to The Facility. He'd just taken a first look inside Morgan's envelope.

"Tony, man."

"Yes, Chuck."

"What the *fuck* is an 'Automatic Sperm Extractor – Mark 2'?"

– 22 –

Happy Birthday to Wang

Lily brought to Wang's table a large brick-like slab of chocolate, which she described as a birthday cake. It was topped by two small flickering candles and an arrangement of leaves, real ones possibly. It was hard to tell, but Wang reckoned it must have been a while since they were part of any living plant.

"It's from them," she said, nodding towards Zhang and Liu, who each raised a hand, very briefly, without looking up from their screens.

"Happy birthday," said Lily, with no great enthusiasm, before telling Wang it had been a month since the roommates last settled a bill at The Moment On Time coffee shop. Wang thought she might repossess the cake at any moment, but instead she went straight back behind the counter to add it to their lengthening tab.

He blew out the candles and then hacked away at the cake, passing crumbling slices to his roommates before starting on a piece of his own. It was hard going, and he thought about asking Lily for a hacksaw, but then thought better of it. She wouldn't see the funny side.

It wasn't a very happy birthday.

He opened a message app to find several new ones from his mother, wishing him happy birthday and inviting herself to Beijing. She said she was planning on coming anyway, during her break at the kindergarten.

She thanked him so much for the lovely photograph of his girlfriend Eu-Meh, saying she was gorgeous, and sending her love. Wang's itching knee and trembling foot returned, worse than ever. He'd regretted sending the photo of the Chinese-Australian beauty queen almost as soon as he'd hit the send button, figuring it would make his mother even more determined to meet her, which it had.

He sent a brief note back thanking her for the birthday wishes and saying he'd pass on her love to Eu-Meh. He said he'd just been offered a place at one of the most prestigious universities in America, near New York, to study business and computer science, thinking that might provide a distraction from the girlfriend. He ignored the bit about her visiting Beijing.

The American offer was true, or almost true. He'd applied to a whole bunch of American colleges and now had his first offer of a place, which had arrived by email just that morning. It was from a college somewhere in a state called Iowa, which he hadn't heard of and couldn't remember having applied to. He checked on a map and found it was in the middle of the country, though pretty much in line with New York. Which was close enough.

The reason why he struggled to remember his applications was that he'd never made them, not in person anyway. He outsourced the whole process, hiring a company to write his application essays and provide fake letters of recommendation from teachers. Zhang had completed the English proficiency tests on his behalf.

So when Wang told his roommates about the offer, Liu congratulated Zhang instead.

"Well done," he said. "Good job. Have you ever thought about applying for yourself?"

Zhang shrugged. He didn't want to leave China. Liu was planning to stay put too, or maybe go to Hong Kong, at least for now. He was hoping for an internship with a big Western finance company, and his father, the big-shot government official who advised the Prime Minister, would fix that for him. His father knew all the major foreign financial outfits, and none could operate without his approval.

Liu said they should offer the college application service through their online shop, but he knew that Zhang was the only one of the roommates with the academic and language skills to make it work, and Zhang didn't want to go there. He didn't mind helping out his roommates, but he didn't have time to make a business of it.

Having somebody else do his applications seemed pretty sensible to Wang, since he struggled with English language and couldn't think of a tutor who'd give him a real reference. Though he did worry that colleges might check up or ask to interview him on a video link.

"No way," said Zhang. "They just want your money."

Which was another issue, since Wang didn't have the cash to pay the roommates' lengthening tab at The Moment On Time, let alone American tuition fees.

Alongside those from his mother, his smartphone had several messages and three missed calls from Fatso, and he knew they weren't to wish him a happy birthday. After an initial burst, sales of the rebranded 3M PM2.5 Super Mega Blockers had slumped. It wasn't so much the quality this time, but the competition. The market was now saturated with cheap masks, mostly as shoddy and ineffective as the Super Mega Blocker. That meant complaints were more evenly spread.

The *Star Wars* caps weren't selling either, and in Fatso's workshop the piles of boxes of unsold caps were now competing for space with those of unsold masks.

"Let's face it, nobody wants to wear a Darth Vader cap. Maybe we should have concentrated more on the other characters," Wang said.

Zhang agreed and said they'd maybe been a bit hasty, and that who wants the Dark Lord on his head. "It's bad luck, bad *feng shui*. We should have thought of that."

Which is when Wang said, "We should get back into the other business." He said they'd left it long enough and it was sure to make more money than their online shop.

For a while neither Liu nor Zhang answered him.

Then Liu said, "Which other business?"

"Come on, Liu. You know. Nobody needs caps. I mean really *needs* them, but everybody needs help figuring out computers."

"Oh, that business. No way. Not yet," Liu said.

For a while the roommates sat in silence, working their keyboards.

Wang shared a video of some air-rage incident on a flight from Shanghai to Shenzhen, a woman tipping her scalding noodles over a flight attendant because she wanted the rice and they'd run out of rice. Then he went back to the game that matched blob-like animals on a grid and where he was stuck on level forty and running short of happy coins.

Zhang was on his phone watching the latest episode of *Stranded in Another Time*, a science fiction series about a time-travelling farmer whose fridge turns out to be a portal to different worlds. The series had been banned, at least briefly, after the Party accused the producers of distorting historical reality. Zhang wasn't quite sure what that meant, but in the latest episodes the farmer seemed a good deal less keen on finding freedom and justice in faraway lands, and was always pleased when his fridge brought him back to China.

Liu burrowed deeper into his share trading account. From time to time he banged his fist on the table beside his laptop and emitted a deep groan, which sounded to Wang like a distressed donkey. It so terrified Lily that she almost dropped a tray of small jugs, each containing a single leaf, which she was distributing around tables.

Wang picked one up. The leaf was a sorry-looking specimen, and he began to ask whether it had been breathing too much Beijing air. Lily cut him short and said she thought they were cool, that she'd got the idea from a lifestyle magazine story about New York cafés and didn't really care what Wang thought.

"Wang's going to study in New York," said Liu.

"Really?" said Lily, perking up, and thinking that if Wang could afford to study abroad, he might soon be able to pay off his tab. "In New York City?"

"Well, Iowa," Wang said.

"Iowa, New York. Nice," Lily said before moving on to the next table.

Zhang's science fiction programme came to an end, and he said, "You know Wang's got a point. The money would be useful, from the other business."

Liu said sure, he couldn't argue with that. It would be useful. His share trading losses were hurting. Their landlord was chasing them for months of back-rent. But all the same the other business was too much of a risk right now. And he'd promised his father.

"Don't you guys realise, we could have been kicked out of university, arrested even?" he said.

Wang said he doubted it would have come to that.

"We might even have got a job out of it, I mean a proper well-paid job with the Government or a big company. That's how people get noticed. Everyone's trying to break into everyone else's computer these days. There's a lot of opportunity out there."

But he agreed that things could have been a whole lot nastier if Liu's father hadn't pulled strings on his son's behalf.

The other business was what the three roommates called a computer consultancy, offering advice to companies on tightening up their online security.

They offered to help fix computer flaws, but with a twist. The offer of help came only after they'd broken into a company's system or website in order to expose the flaw they then offered to fix.

Though all three were studying computer science, their security business didn't really have much to do with skills they'd picked up in the lecture halls.

They used simple hacking tools, easily and cheaply bought online, and more than enough to crack poorly defended websites. They targeted smaller companies, since they usually paid up, no questions asked, to get their websites back and for a dubious package of security software.

The roommates had quickly discovered that computer security at most Chinese companies sucked. A majority used pirated software, which didn't even get basic security upgrades or patches. The smaller ones were the worst.

"They're sitting ducks. Sitting ducks," Wang had said. And for a while their business went well. It was a competitive business, but they didn't charge a lot, were always polite, tried to sound constructive, and after the initial anger at getting hacked, most of their targets were prepared to chat and eventually pay up, realising that this kind of thing was best kept secret, because what would customers think if they knew your computer systems were full of holes?

Wang would remind them about that. He liked to think that everybody won.

Sometimes it even led to extra business, like when a company they'd just hacked thought, hey, we could use these guys, and asked them to hack the computers of a rival company, to create a few problems for them, maybe see what they're up to.

The roommates' problems had started when they hacked the website of a stock brokerage company based in Shenzhen, right beside Hong Kong. It was small, but making money because the stock market then was still booming.

The way Wang saw it, that was a time you could probably have sold shares in Lily's dead leaves in The Moment On Time.

He had made the initial hack, and defaced the company's home page with their signature banner of big characters saying "You've Got a Problem" next to an image of a bug with a speech bubble saying they needed better security. They usually provided an anonymous chat address. Though sometimes they'd leave that out, and make contact themselves by phone, using the details on the hacked website.

Occasionally Wang liked to customise the message with a little cartoon, and the Shenzhen broker when he opened his hijacked website was confronted with the banner, the bug and a drawing of a fat guy crying over his steaming laptop. For good measure, Wang defaced a home page picture of the head broker by drawing on it a pair of glasses and a big moustache.

He had this idea that all brokers were fat.

Fat or not, the broker refused to pay and got really mad. He accused Wang of extortion and went to the local police. Though the cops knew nothing about computers and cared even less, they had their own investments to protect, most of them made through that very brokerage.

The head broker also offered the police a bounty for tracking the extortionists, which they did.

That's when in a panic the roommates turned to Liu's dad, whose influence more than trumped that of the fat broker, who called off the police after a visit from the Shenzhen market regulator, who said he was investigating complaints about illegal share dealings.

"No way can we get back into that right now," Liu said. "Best wait for the dust to settle."

Which surprised Wang because Liu was usually the gung-ho one among the roommates. But he just sat there fixated on the screen showing his share trading account.

"Did it bounce back?" Zhang said.

And when Liu ignored him, Wang said, "The money, Liu, did you make it back?"

Liu was watching the lights flashing on the screen of his laptop as share prices swung violently, though the trend was mostly in one miserable direction. Down. Liu had invested cash the roommates had borrowed to pay Fatso for the first batch of *Star Wars* caps, which is why they were taking a closer interest than usual.

He'd invested it all in a company that was about to win a big government deal. Another tip from his father, who'd even put some of his own cash his son's way. But the deal hadn't happened. And that was strange.

"Sounds like a scam," said Zhang.

Liu shrugged. The whole market was a scam. That wasn't the point.

"The market will bounce back," he said with no great conviction. "The Government will step in again. They don't want investors getting angry."

Wang hacked at the birthday cake, offering another slice to his roommates. Neither took one. They both looked worried. While their businesses had always struggled to make money, he couldn't remember a rough patch quite as bad as this.

But where Liu and Zhang saw pending disaster, Wang saw hope. As he saw it, there might be a silver lining to his friend's stock market agonies. Bad might turn out to be good and very bad might be very good if that's what it took to convince Liu that it was time to get back into the other business.

– 23 –

Dipsy

It was always nice to be back in Hong Kong, and when Morgan woke, the sun was rising over a hazy Hong Kong harbour. He pulled back his curtains, giving him a grandstand view of the Star Ferry ploughing back and forth to Kowloon.

He ate breakfast in his hotel room before showering and getting dressed, looking at himself in the full-length mirror and thinking he really did look ridiculous. But hey, it was the Rugby Sevens weekend.

He took the lift downstairs and crossed the lobby. Anthony Morgan the Roman Centurion, wearing tall gold boots, a short crimson tunic and robe, all topped with a gold helmet with a red plume. He was carrying a small shield. He'd get over the embarrassment after the first glass or two of champagne. It was getting to the stadium that was the awkward bit. It always was.

He walked just about as fast as the boots would allow, out to the taxi line, where the concierge greeted him, deadpan.

"Hong Kong stadium, sir?"

It was early, but the concierge had already sent a caveman, ironman and two lobsters in that direction so far that morning.

His red taxi took the familiar route onto Harbour Road, then followed the waterfront into Causeway Bay, where an elevated highway lined with towering office blocks and hotels swept inland towards Happy Valley.

Which is when his iPhone rang. He pulled it from a small pouch in the belt of his tunic. It was Cindy Wu telling him that Robert was there and wanting to speak to him.

Morgan felt enormous relief, but at first Robert said nothing.

"Hey Robert, you there?"

"Yes," his son said eventually.

"So how are you?"

"I'm fine."

"So what happened?"

"I'm fine."

"Well, that's great. So good to know. I'm really looking forward to seeing you in Shanghai."

And Robert just said, "Yes. I'm fine." And then, "Here's Mum."

Morgan thought he heard other voices, a heavy door swinging closed. But he couldn't tell for sure. There was a lot of noise on the street outside the taxi.

"Where are you?" he asked.

"At home," said Cindy Wu.

"Robert's not very talkative."

"He's a teenager," she said. "That's how they talk. If you found the time to speak to him more often, then you'd know."

Then she said, "About Drayton, has he asked you to do anything else for him, apart from the research on the Colonel and his son?"

Morgan said there was another project, but he was deliberately vague with his wife, preferring to keep the Fang business to himself. He said he'd be seeing the American at the rugby.

"To give him the files?"

"That's what he's asked," said Morgan, and he told her about their arrangement, what Drayton had told him to do.

"That's a really strange arrangement," she said.

And Morgan said, "Yeah, I guess. But he's a strange guy."

She told him to take care and then hung up.

Morgan looked out of the taxi window as they got closer to the stadium: at the rundown tenement blocks, washing hanging from windows, a jumble of shops lining the streets beneath them. He felt uneasy about the call, the stilted conversation with his son.

And about Drayton.

He didn't need his wife to tell him that the Drayton stuff was strange. And he did have a plan. The memory stick was in his pouch beside his phone. He'd deliver it as they'd arranged and then later, when Drayton had seen what was on the stick, he'd confront the American, demand to know what he was getting into. What he was really getting into.

When he arrived at the stadium, ticket touts were already out in force.

"Tickets, mate? Buy, sell?" in heavy London accents.

A group of tourists from mainland China were there too, near the gates, on the lookout for ridiculous costumes with which to grab a selfie. They stopped Morgan, but then almost immediately deserted him for a group of big unshaven men in drag, possibly the pop group, Abba. It was hard to say.

Morgan dug out a pass from beneath his tunic and entered the stadium, which was already filling at nine in the morning. Some qualifying games had started. He took a long escalator to the executive floor of the west stand, a wide orange-panelled corridor hung with photographs of some of the ageing stadium's finer sporting moments.

The corridor was lined with corporate boxes, a roll-call of Hong Kong's elite companies, for whom the Sevens was a must-do networking weekend, a chance to entertain clients and staff.

Each box reflected the personality of the company. Some were austere, all business; others had a theme. The MacMaster and Brown box was squeezed between those of a Hong Kong investment bank that was so drab Morgan wondered why they'd bothered, and a fashion house, which was hosting a beach party.

The MacMaster and Brown theme was Roman, and there were two slaves at the door, a huge muscular Chinese man and an impossibly thin young woman, both from a local model agency. Geraldine MacMaster, who greeted Morgan just inside the door, thrusting into his hand a much-needed glass of champagne, had personally vetoed initial plans for two women as inappropriate.

MacMaster, the company's chairman, was fresh in from New York for their annual strategy meeting, which they always timed to coincide with the rugby, one of the biggest weekends in the city's social calendar. It had become a tradition.

She was dressed in a blue silk knee-length tunic, tied over one shoulder, a broad silver sash around her waist and silver sandals. She had a crescent-moon circlet around her head, and on her back was a quiver of arrows.

"Artemis!" she said, before Morgan could ask. "Goddess of the wilderness, mistress of the moon, symbol of untrammelled womanhood."

"Isn't she Greek?" asked Morgan, and MacMaster shrugged, seeing that as a minor point of detail. "You know Mr Yang? We've just promoted him. Deputy Head of China Research, based here in Hong Kong."

Morgan shook the hand of a young, pale Chinese boy, who looked fresh out of college, and was dressed in what seemed to Morgan like a designer gladiator outfit. All it needed was a Gucci label.

"Tony Morgan. I run the Shanghai office."

"I know."

Which pretty much killed the conversation, until MacMaster said, "Mr Morgan is one of our company's real treasures. He has been the backbone of our China business for years."

By which time Yang had been distracted by something more interesting on his smartphone, and moved to another part of the room, which was already beginning to fill, some spilling out from the main enclosed reception area to the open seats in front, where at some point they might get to watch a bit of rugby.

"He's working out, then?" said Morgan.

"Well, yes, so I'm told. He's quite a find, pulling in the business, at least for now, if that's what you mean," said MacMaster. "Though I personally find him hopeless at his research job and insufferably arrogant."

Yang Xinmai, who'd adopted the name Donald, had been employed under what the company called its Sons and Daughters Programme. His overriding asset was his family connections. He was the son of the head of one of China's most influential economic think tanks, close to the Finance Minister himself. And in the year since he joined, MacMaster and Brown had won a series of lucrative contracts to advise leading state-owned companies on overseas asset purchases.

And Morgan knew that if you walked into most of the boxes lining the executive floor you'd find many other versions of Mr Yang. They were rarely popular among their colleagues, but regarded as necessary for doing business in China.

Or at least they used to be. Morgan had his private and growing doubts. With the corruption crackdown proceeding with all the subtlety of the big Fijian prop forward who'd just that moment floored a tiny Portuguese winger, he knew that today's asset could easily become tomorrow's liability.

But he said to MacMaster, "There's an intern I'd like us to take on here in Hong Kong in the summer. He's the son of Liu Fangu, a top economic official in Beijing, part of the Prime Minister's inner-circle."

"Well, if we must," MacMaster said, with no great enthusiasm.

"He's studying computer science at a top Beijing university. Sounds smart. And I think it will help us in the current environment."

And MacMaster said, "We have to talk about that environment, Tony. I'm looking forward to your presentation."

Morgan looked at his watch. It was almost one o'clock. And following Drayton's instructions, he left the box and took the escalator back down to the ground floor near the entrance, which was now heaving. He headed to a Cathay Pacific Airways stand where flight attendants wearing different uniforms from over the years were posing for photographs.

The big yellow Tellytubby was standing with its back to Morgan, curly antenna on its head, watching a game. Morgan tapped it on the shoulder and as agreed slipped the memory stick into a small pouch-like pocket in the left side of the costume. The Tellytubby disappeared into the crowd without turning or saying a word.

Morgan returned to the box, and another glass of champagne. He walked out to the seating area, to watch the second half of a game between England and Wales. England were winning ten points to five, but there'd been a lot of silly mistakes by the English.

It was a beautiful day. Not too hot, not too cold. And the air had cleared. A cloudless blue sky above the tree-clad hills behind the stadium, pockmarked with soaring apartment blocks. The higher up, the more expensive to live in.

He was relaxing now, moving on to a gin and tonic, settling into the game, when his iPhone rang, vibrating in the pouch on his belt. It was Chuck Drayton.

"Where the fuck were you?"

"What?" replied Morgan, almost choking on the lemon in his gin and tonic. "I was there, one o'clock as agreed. The memory stick's in your pocket."

"I am here now, Tony, waiting. One ugly green Tellytubby standing beside some gorgeous Cathay Pacific trolley-dollies. And I have nothing in my pocket."

"Green? You were yellow. I mean I gave it to a yellow Tellytubby."

For a moment there was silence at the other end of the phone, then a sharp intake of breath.

"Tony, I'm Dipsy. The green fucker. You gave it to La-La."

"Chuck, you said a Tellytubby. You didn't say which one."

At that moment, there was a huge roar from the crowd. The final whistle. England had beaten Wales. Music began blasting around the ground: "Sweet Caroline, good times never seemed so good..."

And the crowd chanted, "So good, so good."

In the packed south stand, one drunken mass of humanity seemed to move and sway in unison. Which is when Drayton and Morgan both saw them, near the top of the stand, towards the left and briefly captured on a giant television screen: a group of more than a dozen Tellytubbies, jigging their bloated bodies to the music.

Without a further word, Drayton shut down his phone, barged past two men dressed as priests, spilling a jug of beer they were sharing, and nearly collided with a woman dressed as a banana as he headed towards the south stand.

Beneath the stand, the floor was sticky with spilled beer as crowds milled around bars, ordering beer by the jug. Kim Jong-un staggered past, beer in hand, escorted by a detachment of North Korean soldiers. Two judges told Kim he was as guilty as hell. A ballerina, or boozy ballerina according to a big and quite accurate label on her outfit, was slumped against a wall. Captain America was throwing up in a wastebasket.

And it was only one thirty. *Jesus*, Drayton thought, ploughing through a group dressed as whistle-blowing Australian lifesavers and spilling another beer, this one out of the hand of a nun.

"May the wrath of God be upon you," she slurred.

Drayton ignored her and headed up a set of stairs and towards the area of the stand where he'd seen the Tellytubbies. He was caught in the crossfire of beer cups between a group dressed as surgeons and Kim Jong-un's guards, who were back in their seats.

Halfway up the stand, a group dressed as bowling pins blocked the path. He pushed one, who fell into another, and then another, like bowling pins do. And soon they were splayed over several seats, covered in their own beer.

He had the Tellytubbies in his sights now, but as he drew closer the Tubbies all stood on their seats and pulled down their costumes, exposing a dozen Tellytubby arses to the crowd, which roared with approval and threw more beer.

Drayton grabbed at the nearest La-La, but its suit had no pocket.

"Hey man," said La-La. "What's up?"

But before Drayton could reply he was pushed from behind by several vengeful bowling pins, then pulled by the Tubbies, who set about ripping the Dipsy suit from his back, wanting to bring another Tellytubby arse to the party.

Then the south stand's security guards barged into Tellytubby land, deciding that the Tubbies had crossed a line with the arse stuff.

By this time Morgan had another drink in his hand and was waiting for the next game. The rowdy scenes in the south stand seemed little more than the usual for the first Saturday of the Sevens. But then he sat up in his seat.

Was that Drayton? Surely not. But it sure looked like him.

Several security guards were surrounding and escorting out of the ground a man dressed only in a skimpy and shredded pair of briefs. As they walked along the touchline, the crowd rose to its feet, cheering the guy and showering him and his escort in beer.

Though Morgan couldn't hear it, the man was angrily protesting.

"I'm a diplomat. I'm a fucking diplomat."

The security men ignored him. They'd heard and seen it all before. Priests, Supermen, nuns, clowns, airline pilots. Diplomats. Sure.

The next game was getting underway now, China against Korea. China scored the first try. Few people seemed to be paying attention, though if Drayton or Morgan had cared to look high into the east stand they would have noticed another La-La. This one jumped to its feet and cheered when China scored.

Then it left. Out at the front of the stadium, a group of tourists asked for a photograph. La-La told them to fuck off before climbing into a van with dark windows, which headed back towards the harbour and a People's Liberation Army facility in a part of the island that still went by its former colonial name of Admiralty.

– 24 –

The Video

Geraldine MacMaster didn't take an active management role these days, but she tried not to miss the company's annual strategy meeting in Hong Kong, where her great-great grandfather had founded the company.

Her family still held a controlling stake in MacMaster and Brown. Which is why, looking from her hotel window at the hazy harbour view, she was more than a little troubled.

It was shortly after dawn, two days after the rugby weekend, and she had hardly slept. The journey from her home in New York was tough at the best of times, and the sixteen-hour flight and a thirteen-hour time difference seemed to get harder each time she did it. It took her days to get over the jet lag.

So she left the hotel, thinking a walk might clear her head, and anyway, she had time to kill before the meeting, scheduled around a working lunch, to be followed by a harbour cruise on the company boat.

Andrew, her chauffeur, who was already on standby with the company limo, intercepted her. She told him she wouldn't need him until later.

The meeting was going to be difficult enough as it was. There were tough questions about China, which still accounted for half the firm's business, but now she'd have to sit through Morgan's presentation while trying to keep a straight face, not knowing quite whether to laugh or cry. What was the man thinking?

She walked north on an elevated walkway, then boarded a tram, climbing its narrow stairs to the upper deck, and took a hard plastic seat beside an open window. It was already busy, and the tram screeched and rattled through the central business district before ending its journey in the crowded streets of Sheung Wan in the western part of Hong Kong Island.

It was more instinct than planning that had guided her to an area she associated so much with her youth, growing up in the city, exploring these narrow alleyways and streets lined with shops overflowing with sacks of dried seafood, from squid and scallops to snakeskin and seaweed. She found the smell overpowering, but reassuring. The timeless Hong Kong.

She looked for, but couldn't find, an old teashop she remembered that specialised in dried chrysanthemum, so settled for a coffee in a market area that wasn't so timeless and had been transformed into a mall of boutique shops, cafés and stalls.

Outside, another tram rumbled past. It was the MacMaster and Brown tram. They'd turned two of them into mobile billboards, advertising their private banking. "Making your dream a reality," it said. "Nobody serves you better." There were images of smiling faces, young and old, an impossibly sincere-looking banker looking over the Hong Kong skyline, a private jet. It made her feel embarrassed, not proud. She thought it was horrible.

But she was no longer involved in that sort of day-to-day decision. She saw herself more as the company's conscience. A guiding hand from afar. And on that morning all she could think about was the stupidity of ego-driven men and wondered how she could best protect them from themselves.

She told herself not to jump to conclusions. Morgan was an idiot. What other way was there to look at it? That *thing*. And she wondered who else had seen it. She'd always thought of Morgan as such a gentleman. Now this. Was it blackmail, extortion, some sort of revenge? She'd have to confront him with it.

The video had arrived as an email attachment. The subject line said simply, "Anthony Morgan – Urgent". The sender used a Gmail account, which was a jumble of letters and numbers. No name.

There was no message either. Just the video, which she had opened without thinking, to find herself looking at a grainy image of a poorly lit room with whitewashed walls and a single narrow bed on which a man was lying naked on his back.

The picture kept losing focus, but then stabilised. A slim young woman was standing by the bed. She looked a little bored, but it wasn't her face that drew MacMaster's attention, but what she was doing with her hands, one of which was moving rather erratically around the man's private parts, while the other held a phone, which appeared to be taking most of her attention.

It was only when the man looked up and angrily threw a towel at the woman that she realised that, good God, that's Morgan. There was no sound on the video, so it was like watching an old silent movie, which somehow made it all the more compelling. And sordid. Morgan appeared to be shouting. He was certainly shaking, waving his arms all over the place, before storming out of shot. The young woman continued on her phone, and seemed oblivious to all the fuss.

MacMaster finished her coffee, then took a cab to the Wanchai skyscraper where the company had its China headquarters, and where the meeting was being held.

The lift from the ornate main lobby to a second lobby on the forty-sixth floor took precisely thirty seconds. She'd timed it, and hated every second; it always made her feel nauseous.

Another lift took her to the sixty-eighth floor, and the company's offices. She was the first into a conference room with panoramic views of the harbour, over which the morning haze was beginning to lift. Other than the view, the room was barren and soulless. Writing pads, pencils and bottled water had been arranged at a dozen places at a long rectangular-shaped table.

A projector and screen linked to a laptop computer were at the ready.

The receptionist brought her tea, and she sat, looking at the harbour, thinking, making notes. No, this was not going to be easy.

She'd considered talking to Morgan before the meeting, get it over with, but there were already several others in the room before he arrived. She'd have to talk to him afterwards.

There were teas, coffees and a few pleasantries, everybody saying how really good it was to see everybody else, sounding like they meant it, before the meeting began at midday, on schedule. MacMaster sat at the head of the table, the Director of Finance on her left, Chief Executive Officer on her right, and the heads of the company's regional offices spread around the table. All of them, apart from MacMaster, were men.

The CEO and finance guy gave brief presentations. The figures were mostly good, though projections cautious. China was perhaps the biggest uncertainty. Tony?

He waited as sandwiches were delivered to the table with bottled water, juice and more tea and coffee.

"It's true there is a lot negativity on China," he said. "And there are certainly challenges. There's a lot of debt in the system. It's hard to calculate how much, but we think it's manageable. And there's a lot of over-capacity. A lot of money's fleeing the country too. There are concerns over growth, the exchange rate. The property bubble's bursting. And the ongoing anti-corruption campaign has injected further uncertainty."

"That's an awful lot of negativity," MacMaster said. "How do we know the debt is manageable when we haven't a clue what it is? What do we really know about what's going on with China's economy?"

Morgan avoided a direct answer, saying it was at times like this that clients turn to us, that they value our insights. He said that China's financial system was still fundamentally sound, and that Beijing had the tools and the skills to reform the economy.

"And that's what we're telling our clients?" MacMaster said.

Morgan took a sip of coffee and nodded. He said not to forget that economic growth rates, though falling, are still the envy of the world.

"But do we believe the figures?" MacMaster said. "Can we believe any official statistics? From what I can make out, they're about as real as the DVDs and handbags in their markets. If they don't like the figures they seem to suppress, abolish or massage them."

"*Massage* them Tony," she repeated, holding Morgan's gaze for what seemed to her like an eternity before looking away.

"It seems to me that China's leaders live in a sort of alternative reality, a parallel universe in which black is white, white is black and the truth is whatever they say it is," she said.

MacMaster then asked the finance head on her left what contingency plans he had if it did turn out that the Chinese economy was like Greece and Lehman Brothers on steroids and the China Miracle ended in one big train crash.

"We're selling up," the finance guy said. "Discreetly, of course. Getting out of a lot of our mainland investments and shorting the Hong Kong and Taiwan markets, especially Chinese companies or any with heavy exposure to the mainland economy."

"So if I understand this correctly, we are betting against the Chinese economy, while telling our clients to keep ploughing their money in because all will be well?"

The finance guy said there wasn't really a contradiction here, that they were just being prudent and responsible, hedging their position.

Morgan said that client trust was the most important thing. That it was MacMaster and Brown's job to offer them assurances during this choppy period, to look for opportunities in the new consumer and innovation economy that China now wanted to build.

"Isn't there a bigger issue here?" MacMaster said. "I've always felt there's a bit of an unwritten deal between the Party and the people. The Party delivers growth and the people let them get on and govern without any irritating demands for democracy. But what happens when they stop delivering? What happens when the music stops?"

Morgan ducked that one too, just saying there was a lot of music still to play, putting on a smile that MacMaster was starting to find really annoying. Morgan said they shouldn't get too carried away by property and stock market wobbles. "Markets in China can be a bit of a casino," he said.

"I don't think so, Tony. Casinos have rules," said MacMaster, looking at Morgan, a benign smile on her face, and thinking that maybe he was a bigger idiot than she'd thought. But it was time to move on to the reports from the other regional heads, who rattled off summaries of their positions with few questions asked. Then MacMaster proposed they move to the limos to take them to Stanley, on the far side of Hong Kong Island, where the company boat was moored, and where they would be joined by other staff for the harbour cruise.

As they got up to leave, MacMaster asked Morgan to wait.

"Can we have a quick word?"

Morgan said sure and sat back down.

MacMaster waited for the rest of them to leave the room.

"I have received a video," she said, stumbling over the words.

"A video? A blockbuster, no doubt."

"Well, of sorts. It's about you. Or rather of you."

"Of me?"

"Yes."

She looked out of window, no longer able to hold his gaze. "And a masseuse."

Morgan could feel the blood draining from his face. He felt dizzy. He stretched for some water, but stopped after he realised his hand was shaking.

"A masseuse? Doing what?"

"Well, she was on the phone. At least, in part."

MacMaster handed him her smartphone, the video ready to go. He watched the grainy images.

"Well, this is a little embarrassing," Morgan said.

MacMaster said it was not up to her to judge his private life, what he chose to do in his own time, but she had to consider the interests of the company. She had to protect MacMaster and Brown. She said the video had arrived by email. Just the video. And she asked if he'd received any threats or messages at all that might explain the motive for this.

"What do they want?" she said.

He said he had no idea, that he'd received nothing, and was anybody else aware of this?

"Nobody, Tony. Not yet. Perhaps we should report it. Though it's hard to say to whom."

Morgan asked for a copy, and she immediately emailed it to him. He said he suspected it was something personal. A silly thing, and could she please keep it between themselves for now and leave him to look into it?

She said she'd do that. At least for now, and they left to join the others.

Morgan said he needed the bathroom, and once inside and confident he was on his own he called a number, his fingers still shaking.

The call went straight to voicemail.

"Chuck," he said. "Morgan here. We need to talk. It's urgent."

– 25 –

Lamma Island

Drayton had messaged Morgan to meet at a quarter before noon the following day, outside pier number four on the harbour front, right in front of the IFC Tower in Central Hong Kong.

Morgan arrived five minutes early and found the American already there, sitting on a concrete bench between students shovelling noodles from plastic lunch boxes. He was reading a newspaper and drinking coffee.

The first thing Drayton said was that the coffee tasted like it had just been scooped from the harbour, and what was it with all those judges he'd seen walking through Central in wigs and robes like pallbearers at a funeral, except without the coffin.

"They're lawyers mostly, protesting against the death of justice," said Morgan. "Against interference from Beijing. It's an important principle for Hong Kong."

"Oh yeah?" said Drayton. "You really think Beijing meant all that stuff about leaving Hong Kong to do its own thing for fifty years? It's not in their DNA. They want to control everything."

Morgan changed the subject. He said the video had come as a real shock, sent to his boss for Christ's sake. And when she told him, at a company meeting of all places, it had been the most embarrassing thing he'd ever had to sit through."

"Well, I can see that, Tony. But let's not talk here."

"Where are we going?"

"We're going for a hike."

They boarded a ferry to Lamma Island, just off Hong Kong, climbing to an upper deck so fiercely air-conditioned it made Morgan shudder, and then out the back to an open area of metal seating but with a nice breeze. Drayton thought it would be more private out there, but by the time the ferry left at noon it was packed.

They sat mostly in silence. Drayton tried to read his newspaper, but every time he opened it the wind gusted and he almost lost it over the side. He gave up.

The ferry hugged the coast of Hong Kong Island, heading west along a wall of tall office buildings and scrappy ramshackle apartment blocks, a mountain rising behind.

"Don't know how they do that," Drayton said, pointing at an impossibly narrow building, clad in bamboo, that was under construction, squeezed into the wall.

Once out of the harbour and into open water the ferry wove between cargo ships at anchor, then juddered and bounced as it hit the wake of ships on the move, Lamma Island lying ahead of them, three tall chimneys of a power station towering over its main village.

They left the ferry down a wind-swept pier and along the village's narrow main street, lined with restaurants and small shops, before turning inland onto a steep path towards the centre of the island.

Drayton said a friend of his had moved to the island to be closer to nature.

"Nice apartment, with a bird's eye view of the power station," he said. "Sits around all day drinking beer and smoking weed from what I can make out. Calls himself a writer."

Morgan said he could see the appeal of the place, power station aside.

After fifteen minutes they reached a sandy cove where they took a table in a largely empty open-air restaurant and ordered two cold beers.

"So, you've become a porn star? Cheers!"

"I really can't see anything funny in this, Chuck."

"Can I see?"

Morgan gave Drayton his iPhone, and Drayton then watched the grainy action unfold, zooming in and telling Morgan he thought the woman was cute and what was her name?

"Mimi, at least that's what she calls herself."

"A regular?"

"Sort of."

"Which means?"

"Three or four times, I guess."

"And the name of the place where it's at?" said Drayton, asking him to write it down on a napkin.

"No threats? No demands?"

"Nothing."

"Not the best customer service. Any idea what was so important on the phone?"

"She said it was her sister coming to town, that she was arranging to meet her."

Drayton then took from his back pocket a silver slab of something. It was his iPhone wrapped in several layers of kitchen foil, which he carefully opened. He transferred the video to his phone using Bluetooth, wrapped it again and put it back in his pocket.

Then he pulled out a very old Nokia on which he made a call, very brief, passing on the name and location of the massage place. Nothing more, not even a greeting, and hung up.

They left the restaurant and continued on a path that now rose steeply to a lookout area close to a temple. There was a small drinks stall and Morgan suggested they get some water. Drayton said that was a good idea and ordered two more beers.

They sat on a wooden bench with a panoramic view of the power station.

Drayton asked whether he had the documents with him and Morgan said no, he wanted to talk first. He said he was worried, and so was his wife. That they wanted an explanation. He said the people Drayton had asked about, the Shanghai guy with the Ferrari-driving son, the Shenzhen syndicate too, these were very powerful people.

"What are we getting into here, Chuck?"

"We're just trying to protect American investors," Drayton said.

"And we appreciate your help. And we're paying you well, and into whatever dodgy account you name, Tony."

"Which I appreciate. But that's not really the point."

"So what's the point?"

"The point," said Morgan, "is that this could be dangerous for us, for our business. These people are well connected. It was tough to get the information. The Shanghai guy, he's military, top military, with some special unit, but also has a lot of other stuff going on, investments in China and abroad, all channelled through his son to keep it clean."

"Tony, I'll level with you. There is a bigger picture here, which I can't really explain right now. I just need you to trust me. Your name, your wife's name will be fully protected."

Drayton said they really needed to talk about security. The mess up in Shenzhen, that stuff with La-La at the rugby, it really wasn't cool. He said he'd come up with a more secure way of communicating and gave Morgan a business card.

Morgan looked at the card.

"Shanghai TT Logistics. I thought you worked for the embassy."

"I do, Tony. Think of it as a sort of subsidiary, an affiliate. The important thing is it provides us with a better way of communicating."

"What does the TT stand for?"

"Nothing in particular, but if it makes you feel better you can think of it as Tellytubbies."

Drayton told him there was a web address on the card and once he'd got to the website he should log in.

"The login is 'login', the password is 'pa55word', using the figure 5 instead of s. You think you can remember that?"

Morgan said he thought he could.

"Once you're logged in you can upload the documents to the site. You can also write emails to me, only don't send them."

"Don't send them?"

"No, save them as drafts. I have access to the same site, so can pick up the drafts, as well as the documents. It's more secure."

They walked on, then stopped, breathless, leaning against an information board beside the path, the "Bugs of Lamma Island", listing all the creepy-crawlies you were likely to come across on a hike.

"Look at this. They trying to drive people away?" said Drayton.

"Chuck, I do need to know more."

"It's all here, man. The ones you tread on, the ones that bite you. Maybe we should have bought some spray."

Then he said, "Everything's cool. Let's go and get ourselves some seafood."

They entered another village of seafood restaurants lined with tanks and buckets overflowing with live shellfish, crabs and swimming fish of all shapes and sizes, though they didn't strike Drayton as being in the best of health.

"What's the name of that big fish at the top that's got the tank to itself, the one with the pout, the big lips, looks like it's been clonked on the head?" Drayton asked.

Morgan said it was called a Humphead Wrasse.

"Beautiful fish. Elegant, stately. And endangered," he said.

"Tasty too. I imagine," Drayton said. "Maybe the Communist Party will come to its rescue."

"How's that?"

"Haven't you heard? The Party's already saving the sharks."

Drayton said he'd read it in that morning's newspaper. Shark fin sales in Hong Kong had collapsed, and Hong Kong was where most of the trade happened.

"You know why?"

"Tell me," said Morgan.

"It's the corruption crackdown. Shark fin soup is off the menu. No more big banquets for the comrades, chomping on endangered species. Bad for the comrades, but good for the planet's wildlife."

They looked for the quietest restaurant, where a server recommended the Grouper, saying they were wild and tasted better than the farmed fish.

There were two in one small tank and one was lying motionless on its side.

"Is that live fish still a live fish?" asked Drayton. "Or maybe it's sleeping."

The server poked it with her net and it twitched. It was still a live fish. Drayton said they'd take the other one, which had a few more vital signs. The server fished it out with her net, but as Drayton and

208

Morgan headed to a table by the water, she dropped it back in the tank and quickly scooped out the one with the twitch.

Morgan took the farthest seat, his back to the water, and Drayton asked him to swap.

"You don't want the sea view?" said Morgan.

"I want the restaurant view, Tony."

Drayton's old Nokia rang, and he took the call. Just listening, not saying a word. Then he hung up.

"Your massage parlour, it's closed. Boarded up. Neighbouring noodle place says the police closed it down two days ago. Nobody's heard of a Mimi."

Morgan said he wasn't sure if that was a good or a bad thing.

"Might mean nothing. There's a big crackdown on that kinda service right now. But anybody contacts you, you tell me, man."

Morgan said he would, and then asked Drayton, "What's with the phones?"

Drayton put the iPhone wrapped in kitchen foil and the ancient Nokia side by side on the table. "Smartphone, dumb phone. You're in China. It's good to have one of each, Tony. My iPhone has State Department encryption for what that's worth. The kitchen foil's a bit of extra defence, blocks radio signals, so you can't be tracked."

He tapped the old Nokia.

"And this, this is the one I love best. Makes calls, messages if you're lucky. Nothing else. Pre-paid card. Anonymous."

They stopped talking as the server came to the table with the fish, steamed in soy sauce, together with a bowl of fried rice and two more beers. She told them not to forget to eat the meat in the cheeks of the fish because it tasted special.

Once she'd gone, Drayton said he was still worried about La-La, that fucking Tellytubby. But they just had to hope that inside the outfit was some drunken Aussie rugby fan who, even if he'd found the memory stick, wouldn't be able to understand the stuff anyway."

"Well, that's the thing," said Morgan.

"What's the thing?"

"That information, about the military guy and his son, about the syndicate, it wasn't on the memory stick."

"It wasn't on the memory stick?"

"No, I wanted to talk to you first. I was worried. My wife was worried."

"So what was on the memory stick?"

"Well," said Morgan, "it was the full technical specification for the Automatic Sperm Extractor – Mark 2. I think you're already familiar with it."

Drayton started to laugh.

"So La-La has the hand-job machine."

Morgan nodded, and Drayton said, "Tony, I love you."

*

The first thing Morgan did when he got back to his Hong Kong hotel was to scan the documents using an app on his iPhone. He called them *The Colonel* and *Mr Fang*, and then uploaded both to the Shanghai TT Logistics website, following Drayton's instructions. It was surprisingly straightforward.

Once the upload was complete he felt an enormous sense of relief. He'd done what he'd been commissioned to do. He'd fulfilled his side of their contract and would be in no hurry to do any more business with Drayton. It was as if a burden had been lifted.

Then his phone rang, Sam Ching's name on the screen.

"Hello Sam. What's up?" he said.

But it wasn't Sam. It was Sam's wife, Su.

"He's gone, Tony. They took him away."

She was sobbing and garbling her words. Morgan told her to calm down, slow down, take a deep breath, and tell him what happened.

She said she'd been visiting Sam in Shenzhen. Then she started crying again.

She was from Hong Kong, like her husband, and Morgan knew she hated the mainland, but felt she had to go from time to time to keep tabs on Sam, not trusting him with the factory girls. She had good reason for that, and Morgan's initial thought was that she'd caught her husband doing something he shouldn't.

She said they'd been woken before dawn by banging on the door, so hard she thought they were trying to knock it down.

"I opened it slightly, with the chain on, and they just pushed their way in," she said. "Snapped the chain, and pushed me aside, Tony. Demanded to see Sam."

"Who are *they*, Su?"

"Wouldn't say. Refused to give IDs. But one guy was in uniform. Police. The others were in plain clothes, big guys."

She said they sat Sam at the dining table, one of them on each side, two opposite, another two looking around the apartment like they owned the place, picking up photos, books and stuff. Throwing things around. No respect.

"What did they want, Su?"

"They told me to stay in the bedroom, but the door was open a little, and I could see they had some papers, drawings and pictures mostly, and they kept waving them around in front of Sam, asking what it was. What it *really* was."

"What did Sam say?"

"I think he thought it was some sort of anti-counterfeit operation, you know, that maybe they were investigating fakes. Maybe looking for a bribe. He kept telling them that it wasn't a copy, that it was his design. He said that if there was a problem they could sort it out in a friendly manner."

"Since when have the police been bothered about fakes?" said Morgan.

"That's what I thought. Made no sense. And, anyway, they ignored that and just kept on at him, getting angry, asking what *is* it?"

"Did you see the drawings?"

"I didn't get a real good look, but it looked like some sort of vacuum cleaner on short legs, with a funny hole in the front."

"Oh," said Morgan.

"You okay, Tony?"

"Yes, sorry, Su. Lost the signal then. What did they say next?"

"Just kept banging on and on, getting angry, demanding to know what it did."

She stopped, sobbing again.

"Then… then Sam got really mad. He just snapped."

"What happened?"

"He yelled at them, Tony. You know what he's like when he loses his temper."

Morgan said he did.

"What did he yell, Su?"

"He said, 'It jerks you off, you fucking moron'."

"Oh."

"And then they hit him so hard, Tony. Cut his face and mouth, a lot of blood. He fell on the floor and they kicked him. Then they grabbed him by the arms, one big guy on either side, locked his arms behind his back, hurting him, and they took him out to one of two black Audis."

She said Sam was barely conscious.

"What did you do?"

"What could I do? I was so frightened I couldn't speak. I was shaking, couldn't get no words out. Just stayed, frozen, in the bedroom."

She said that as soon as they'd gone she headed straight for the crossing to Hong Kong. Wasn't going to spend another fucking minute in that place.

Morgan asked her if she'd reported it to the authorities.

"Tony, they are the fucking authorities."

Morgan told her it must be some sort of horrible misunderstanding, you know how things are sometimes in China, that he'd sort it out.

And she told him he was a good man, that she really appreciated that.

But he had no idea where to start, what to do. He suddenly felt very sick.

After they'd hung up, he just sat staring out of the window, towards the main highway through Central, where the protesting lawyers and judges were still marching. Crowds along the roadside were applauding as they passed. Which is when Morgan noticed that at the front of their march they were carrying a single large picture, like sometimes happens at funerals. Only this one was a picture of a stick alien.

He took out his iPhone and photographed the passing protest, zooming in on the alien. He opened his Twitter app and went to upload the photo to *@Beijing_smog*. It was then he saw that he had a Twitter message, a private message. The first surprise was that it addressed him personally. The account was supposed to be anonymous. The second shock was that it was from Cindy Wu. He'd never told her about the account.

The biggest shock was what it said.

Stay in Hong Kong. Do not come back, and do not try and contact me or Robert. Robert should be fine. My parents are helping. Cindy

– 26 –

The Hack

It was hard to say what finally brought Liu around. He'd been sitting at their usual table at The Moment On Time, staring out of the window at a dirty grey nothingness, smog so thick it had again gone off the index and was no longer registering on their smartphone apps.

"Let's get back into the other business," he said.

Wang wasn't sure he'd heard him right, and said, "Which other business?"

"The computer security business. You guys are right. Let's get back into it."

Possibly it was their worsening debts and the sorry state of their other business ventures. Maybe it was the stock market, which was now so bad Liu had completely stopped looking at his trading account. Though Wang suspected Liu's change of heart had more to do with what had happened to his father. The big-shot official who advised the Prime Minister was now an ex-big-shot official. He'd been suspended from his job.

Liu was shocked when he heard. They all were. But his father had calmed him down, saying that it wasn't a big deal, calling it a misunderstanding. That he'd be fine, saying there were many things going on in China right now. Things he couldn't talk about.

Liu didn't quite get that.

Liu worried about the internship his father had arranged for him, thinking the company might change its mind now that his father was no longer pulling strings in Beijing. The job was with an international finance outfit called MacMaster and Brown, which he'd never heard of, but which looked like it had a lot going on. He'd only just received the formal offer in a personal letter from their China Director, a man called Morgan. He wasn't sure exactly what he'd be doing for them, since nobody had ever asked about his skills or qualifications and there'd been no interview, but the post was in Hong Kong, and Hong Kong was ideal.

His father had tried to reassure him, saying he knew the company well, but Liu had still felt compelled to check out a couple of big graduate job fairs, as a back-up, just in case. He'd been to one that morning, and Wang had asked him to pick up anything that might be interesting.

Which turned out to be nothing. Liu had returned empty-handed, telling his roommates that the whole thing had been beyond depressing. He said the jobs sucked, those that were available, that the starting pay was dire and that one recruiter had told him that it was the worst graduate job market ever.

He showed them photographs he'd taken of a vast hall that had two rows of narrow desks down the middle. The recruiters sat shoulder to shoulder behind the desks, hundreds of students swarming in front of them, wads of résumés in their hands.

"The photo's a bit fuzzy," Wang said. And Liu told him that was the smog. *Inside* the hall, can you believe it? He said it had been freezing outside, but sub-tropical indoors, which was way over-heated. He said it stunk of sweat and the recruiters were rude and bored. It had taken him fifteen minutes to get to one desk and then, when he got there, the woman behind it just walked off.

And whether it was a money thing, worry over his job prospects, or simply because he no longer felt bound by any commitments he'd made to his father, Liu had decided the computer security business might just be their salvation.

The roommates were all wearing thick coats and hats, because the coffee shop's heating system had failed. It was well below zero outside and to the roommates it seemed to be heading that way indoors. Lily had an engineer trying to put it right. She knew things could have been worse, that the router might have failed again. Her customers were cold, but still online, which was what really mattered.

Wang was wearing his fingerless woollen gloves, so the roommates decided he should take the controls. He fired up his laptop, the turbo-charged Lenovo, for the initial scouting mission, to see what was out there, checking for potential customers, as they liked to call the targets of their attacks. Liu and Zhang moved their chairs to sit beside him.

A register of Shanghai businesses hosted by a local trade group was always a good place to start. And, once Wang had assembled a decent list of web addresses, he opened another application called a "vulnerability scanner", which went through each website, producing a list of weaknesses and break-in points, which Wang often imagined as being like identifying all the opened windows and unlocked doors of a house.

There were a lot of them.

So he looked again at their names. The best customers were usually small or medium sized, where security was especially bad and where they relied on their website for business. They'd be hit hard if they were offline for long, and they'd also be worried about their reputation with customers. From Wang's experience, they were the ones most likely to pay up quickly for security advice.

Liu pointed to one that the scanner said was riddled with security flaws. Just about all its digital doors and windows were wide open. It wasn't the most vulnerable on the list, but Liu said he had a feeling about it, and they'd come to trust Liu's feelings. That's what made him such an important part of the team.

"Let's try them," he said.

It was a strange site. Pretty basic. The links and buttons on the home page seemed to go nowhere, like there was only a home page. Liu said it must be a work in progress, and they hadn't yet paid much attention to security.

"I like the logo," said Zhang, pointing to the banner across the top of the page with the company's name and a skyline shot of the Bund. It read, "SHANGHAI TT LOGISTICS".

Wang agreed that it was an ideal target.

It took him just six minutes to insert code that gave him control of the site, and a further six minutes to put up their own banner, "You've

Got a Problem", and the bug with the speech bubble saying the company needed better security. Since their usual message site had been compromised by the run-in with the fat broker from Shenzhen, Wang provided one of his own numbered messaging addresses for Shanghai TT Logistics to respond to.

Usually they'd just leave it at that. But Wang was feeling creative, getting a buzz from being back in the security business again. So he called up his stick alien, added a hoody, and placed it in the centre of the company's home page beneath the banner. The typical hacker look. He liked that.

"Nice one," said Liu. "Let's see what happens."

He and Zhang then returned to their smartphones, agreeing that they should just do the one for now, easing back into it.

But Wang wasn't through yet. There was a panel on the Shanghai TT Logistics home page that asked for a login and password, just about the only thing that seemed to be active. And he thought that if security here was as bad as the rest of the site, it can't be difficult to crack.

He opened another tool, a password cracker, which took under ninety seconds to rapidly test login and password combinations before coming up with one of the laziest: 'login', for the login, and the password, 'pa55word'.

The page it took him to was no more exciting than the home page, just an email account and a link for uploading documents. There were no emails, but two documents had been uploaded to the site: one called *The Colonel* and one called *Mr Fang*. He downloaded both to his Lenovo and left the website.

He looked briefly at the cover pages of both documents. The *Mr Fang* one had a list of names of what it called: "Applicants for SK documents". It was a summary of something, with fuller information inside. The second looked more fun, three photographs under the heading "Colonel General Chen Shibo". One was a crusty-looking military guy in uniform, the second a kid, who looked a bit of a mess, like he wouldn't have been out of place in The Moment On Time. The third was a red Ferrari, which would.

He closed the documents without looking any further, powered off the laptop and went back to his phone, pleased that Liu had finally seen sense.

He then opened his *Whack An Alien* app. He was convinced more than ever that digital was his future. Wang Chu the dot-com billionaire. He liked the sound of that. Sure, he was yet to have the Big Idea, but it would come, and in the meantime the game was coming along fine.

He'd placed a beta version in two app stores and already it had been downloaded 50,000 times. It was free for now. He still needed to figure out how to make money from it, but weapons seemed the most promising way forward, charging to upgrade them. He was already experimenting with whacking aliens with a hammer, as well as running them down with a car or crushing them with a steamroller as they emerged with their bags of money from under the portrait of Mao in Tiananmen Square.

Breaking into the Shanghai company's website seemed to energise all the roommates, and Zhang said, "Hey, look at this. We could enter." He had on his screen an advertisement looking for teams to enter something called the Cyber Challenge, a hacking competition between universities. Teams would score points for analysing and identifying hidden weaknesses in computer systems by breaking into them.

"Last year the winning team took control of a car," Zhang said. "They remotely unlocked its doors and changed its settings, sounding the horn, flashing the lights. They even opened the sunroof."

Wang said that was really cool. And Zhang said the members of the winning team had all been offered top jobs with the Government, and that the whole competition had become a kind of beauty contest, a recruiting ground, not only for Government, but for businesses scouting for talent which could help them snoop on their rivals. Looking for guns for hire.

The problem, they all agreed, was that the competition was still months away. They needed their other businesses to come good before then. But they were all smiling now, Wang already checking his messages for any response from the Shanghai company, and Liu kicking him under the table and saying give them a chance, it's only been ten minutes.

Wang said he was feeling good about it, that he was confident they'd hear from the company soon and that they could do a deal, providing their usual package of security fixes. He said he was confident that Shanghai TT Logistics would take a pragmatic and reasonable view of their business proposal.

– 27 –

What the Fuck?

"Fuck. Fuck. What the fuck?"

"Hey Chuck, everything okay?"

"Yeah, yeah. All good, Dave, just a computer glitch," said Drayton, now back at the Shanghai consulate, where he was sitting at his desk, staring at the screen of his laptop.

"I'm heading back to The Facility," said the man called Dave, who still didn't have a second name. "The guys say stuff's happening with their worm."

"I'll follow you over," said Drayton. "Something urgent I need to sort here first."

"Sure thing, Chuck. Don't want to lose your data."

"Too right."

And he might also have added "too late" since he was sitting staring at his hijacked website. The banner was still there, the skyline of the Bund and "SHANGHAI TT LOGISTICS", but beneath it like graffiti on a Brooklyn train were the words "You've Got a Problem", and a bug with a speech bubble saying he needed better security, next to a numbered messaging address. What the fuck?

Then there was another drawing, a character in a hoody. It was a stick character, and when he looked closely, the head of the character looked like one of those classic aliens with the pear-shaped head and big eyes. What the fuck?

At least the website was still responding. It had been defaced, but not disabled. It was impossible to tell if the hacker had got any further than the home page and accessed the email account or the documents.

He signed in and killed all the content, deleting the documents, *The Colonel* and *Mr Fang*, but only after he'd downloaded them again. He made a note of the messaging address of the hacker, took a screen grab of the page; then he went into the settings and deleted the website.

He was angry, with himself as much as the hackers. He felt stupid. He was the Cyber Guy for fuck's sake. He'd set up the website as a kind of Dropbox, as a secure way of communicating with Morgan because that bozo really didn't have a clue. There was to be no more stuffing memory sticks in a Tellytubby's pocket or the like.

Sure, it wasn't the most secure website, but he never imagined it would be targeted by hackers. He tried to reassure himself that the hackers were probably kids, out to extort a buck or two, and most likely hadn't bothered with the documents. But he needed to know for sure.

His first thought was to get Tom and Dick on the case. This would be like child's play for them, tracing the messaging address and finding the hacker. It would take their mind off the dumplings. But it would also be far too embarrassing. They'd think he was an idiot. The Cyber Guy duped like that! He'd never hear the end of it.

So he went to see Ed Wong. Ed, the kid from California, who called himself Ed the Real Geek. He'd even had that printed on his business cards, but the consulate had told him to get them redone, not liking the geek thing and insisting he have a proper name and title like everybody else.

So he was now officially Edmund Wong, Social Media Analyst, though everybody still called him the Real Geek.

"I don't know how you can spend all your time sitting there and sifting through all that crap," Drayton said by way of a greeting.

"It's where you'll find the real mood of China," Ed said.

"Well yeah," said Drayton. "If you can hold your nose long enough while you wade through all the online effluent. There's a ton of crooks and scammers out there. And I see bullshit spreading like digital wildfire."

"I get that," said Ed. "But the internet's holding China's leaders to account like never before. It's much more difficult to be a successful liar in this country."

"But they still try very hard," Drayton said. "And they shut down the online stuff they don't like."

"Sure there's an army of censors, but they can be slow and cumbersome and its awesome the way the kids get round it. Some of the kids are really smart."

Maybe Ed had a point, but all Drayton could think of at that moment was the drawing of the alien in the hoody and, smart or not, he just wanted to get his hands on the fucker who'd done that.

He asked if Ed could do him a small favour.

"You got it," said Ed.

"I'd like to know who this messaging account belongs to," Drayton said, handing over the address. "I'm thinking of buying something from them online and want to be sure who I'm dealing with."

"Leave that with me, Mr Drayton. That shouldn't be a problem."

"Oh, and Ed…"

"Yes, Sir."

"It's quite urgent. And quite private."

"Sure thing," Ed said.

Then Drayton took a regular taxi to the North Bund, getting it to drop him a few blocks from The Facility and walking the rest of the way. That wasn't really protocol, but Dave had gone ahead with Cyril, and they'd relaxed some of the stricter security stuff as the surveillance had continued.

When he arrived he found Tom and Dick, the two NSA analysts, hunched over Tom's laptop. For once they were both smiling, giving each other knowing looks like a pair of kids who'd just mastered the next level of a video game.

"Yeah, yeah, yeah," said Tom to the screen. "Talk to me, baby."

Drayton ignored them at first, since they frequently talked to Tom's screen as if the worm could hear them and needed a bit of extra encouragement as it burrowed into the computer systems in the white building below them.

Dave was playing a game on his smartphone, which he'd downloaded that morning while Tom and Dick's attention was elsewhere. They'd banned any downloading while in The Facility, saying you never know what bugs might be out there. And they should know.

But the way Dave saw it, this was only a game and a great game at that, whacking spindly little stick aliens with a big fly swatter as they appeared from a tunnel under the portrait of Mao in Tianamen Square carrying bags of money. He could play for hours.

Drayton thought Dave looked chilled, and when Dave finished the game he told Drayton he liked Shanghai. That it had kinda grown on him. He couldn't see himself moving from Beijing, but Shanghai was cool.

Then Tom said, "Baby, yes. Thank you. Thank you", almost shouting, but still to the screen.

"You got something there, Tom?" Drayton asked.

"It's starting to communicate. The worm is responding."

They all gathered around the laptop and Drayton asked what it was saying and was it delivering names.

"Nothing that clear. Not yet."

"So it's kinda mumbling incoherently?"

"It's starting to deliver data," Tom said, slowly, like he was talking to a child. "And that data needs analyses, and analyses can take time."

"When can we expect it to say something that makes sense?"

Tom and Dick ignored that, and Drayton took the hint and powered up his own laptop, opening the documents that Morgan had uploaded to the Shanghai TT Logistics website.

*

Morgan had done well, or at least his wife had.

The Colonel was not just a Colonel, but a Colonel General, which was pretty high up the People Liberation Army food chain. Colonel General Chen Shibo had commanded the Jinan and Beijing military regions. He'd been second in command at the PLA's General Logistics Department, controlling a huge budget for housing and feeding the troops. Even buying uniforms. It was a notoriously corrupt part of the military, and Drayton thought it might explain where the good Colonel General generated a bit of extra pocket money.

It was probably also where he first got into computers, though it was still hard to imagine the guy as a hands-on hacker. He probably had his own versions of Tom and Dick, with him standing over their shoulder. Though it had clearly been the Colonel General at the controls when he was photographed poking around the maestro's hard disk.

Morgan's report said that three years ago, Chen was appointed to head something called PLA Unit 61398. But that was where the trail went cold. There was nothing more recent about him or that unit.

Much of the information was sketchy. Morgan had warned Drayton that his wife had found the research tough going, that it had been sensitive, that her usual contacts had been reluctant to open up. But there was still plenty here. The report said this Chen was a life-long member of the Party, with links right to the top, to the Party leader's inner circle.

There was far richer detail about the son, who seemed to divide his time between Hong Kong and Shanghai, fronting several companies described as being in trade and finance, a catch-all for all manner of deal-making. He'd left a rich trail of digital exhaust. A ton of stuff online, some of it linking him to the kids of other top officials. Doing business together. And he usually trailed around with a whole bunch of movie starlets and models.

Drayton reckoned the son had to be leveraging his old man's connections and managing the cash from the logistics job. The front man for the family wealth. But he struck Drayton as being as flaky as hell, which is pretty much the conclusion that Morgan had come to, his final sentence underlined for emphasis.

Mr Chen Huizhi is not to be trusted. The father is powerful. The source of their wealth is dubious. We would strongly advise not going into business with this family.

Then there was the *Mr Fang* file. Morgan had done well there too. Fang's syndicate was so keen to secure an exit route from China that they'd done what they'd never done before and blown their cover, providing Morgan with enough biographical detail to secure their St Kitts passports. There wasn't a lot, that was for sure, and more digging would be needed. But it was a rogue's gallery of Party bigwigs from southern China. All wanting a slice of America. A refuge.

Drayton had felt things were going well after all the missteps with Morgan. He smiled as he watched Tom and Dick at their screen, like two kids. The worm was starting to deliver too, and that hopefully would complete the picture, would give the Bubble Room the names they wanted and confirm what PLA Unit 61398 was up to.

It would be a near-perfect situation, if it wasn't for the hack, the Shanghai TT Logistics website compromised. For sure, that was a stupid mistake on his part. But he'd calmed down now and convinced himself it was probably just kids and saw no reason to believe they'd gone further into the system and grabbed the documents. And even if they'd seen them, they'd be unlikely to realise the significance. And anyway, the site was now deleted.

But he still had a niggling doubt. He'd prefer to know for sure.

So he rang Ed the Real Geek on an encrypted line and asked him whether he had anything more on the chat address.

"Yeah," said Ed. "It belongs to a person called Wang."

"A person called Wang?" said Drayton. "Ed, that's fantastic. How did you get that?"

"Trade secrets, sir. Though actually pretty straightforward."

"Well, whatever, but you've done a good job."

"Hold off the celebrations just for a moment," Ed said. "There's a bit more digging to do."

"How's that?"

"There are ninety-five million Chinese called Wang."

– 28 –

Something Weird

Zhang had started to sound like a recording stuck in repeat mode, which was pretty tedious, but when he said yet again that something weird was going on, something really weird, his roommates agreed that Zhang might just have a point.

No sooner had they all arrived at The Moment On Time coffee shop and got online when Wang received a message from his mother. This time the tone was different, so different that there wasn't enough time for either his itchy knee or trembling foot to click in. There was just plain surprise, and it was a big surprise.

He'd expected more stuff about meeting the non-existent girlfriend, bringing Eu-Meh home to Harbin. But the first thing his mother said was that the girl wasn't good for him, that he should ditch her before she got them all into trouble.

"She's really no good, Chu," his mother wrote. "Think of your father's job at the Party School."

"Wow," he said, showing the message to Zhang and Liu. "What's that all about?"

"I thought your mum was desperate to meet her," said Zhang.

"She was," said Wang. "I even sent her a photograph."

"You sent her a photograph?" Liu said.

"Sure," said Wang. "To keep her happy. I just copied a picture of a Chinese-Australian beauty queen called Eu-Meh, which I found online. Mum said she was gorgeous, which I guess she was."

He said the photograph had just made his mother even more determined to meet her, even saying she'd come to Beijing.

Liu asked to see the picture of the beauty queen, and Wang searched for her online. But he got a lost connection screen. Access denied. His girlfriend had been deleted, and he could no longer find any reference to her on the internet. He did have a copy he'd saved to the picture folder on his smartphone, so he opened that instead and showed it to Liu.

"This is the picture I sent to Mum," Wang said. "My girlfriend, Eu-Meh."

"Miss Australia," said Liu. "It's Miss Australia."

The picture was of a twenty-five-year-old ethnic Chinese woman who had won the Australian crown and become an instant celebrity in China, her country of birth. She'd seemed to Wang to be an ideal girlfriend.

"That's her," he said. "Why?"

"Didn't you hear?" said Liu. "There was a lot of stuff online."

He said Miss Australia had a thing about communists, like she hated them. That's why her family had left China in the first place. And soon after she was crowned she said a whole bunch of things about the Dalai Lama being basically a good guy and that the Party abused human rights.

"Oh dear," said Wang. "She really said that stuff?"

And Zhang told him he should choose his girlfriends more carefully.

Liu said party newspapers had denounced her as a fraud and a liar and she'd been banned from travelling to China for an upcoming beauty competition. There'd been a frenzy online, whipped up by the nationalist bloggers, calling her a "race traitor".

Wang tried not to read those sites, but he was still surprised that he'd missed all the fuss, and he said, "I can see why Mum wouldn't want her as part of the family."

He messaged his mother saying don't worry, and don't let Dad worry, that he'd ditched the girl already, that he knew she wasn't right for him and had never really been serious.

Then he looked back at his mother's message, at the last line, where she'd written, "Things are difficult enough for us as it is, Chu. God bless you, and may God be with you."

Now the itch did start again, and so did the trembling foot. What things were difficult? And what did God have to do with anything? For the first time in weeks he called up his mother's number, but it went straight to voicemail. He did the same to his father's phone, but he didn't pick up either. *They must be working,* he thought.

He was going to ask Liu what he made of that bit of the message, but decided not to bother. His friend had his own family worries. He'd lost touch with his father, the top government official who'd been dismissed from his job. Liu's mother said only that he'd had to go away for a while. That it was a Party thing. She'd tried to sound reassuring, but Liu could tell she was anxious.

Wang went back to his smartphone and searched once again for the fictional girlfriend who was now his fictional ex-girlfriend. She'd definitely been deleted.

The roommates rarely gave much thought to internet censorship, the Party's finger that was poised permanently over the delete button. To them it was just a fact of life. Words were filtered, sites were blocked. That's just the way it was. Not always quick, and there were a ton of ways around it, using pictures, symbols or abbreviations. A whole cyber language. Stuff to replace a word that was blocked, everybody knowing what it really meant. Playing cat and mouse with the censors could be fun.

In a small way, Zhang was part of that censorship machine. He was a member of what the University called its Opinion Guidance Unit, and his role, two evenings a week, was to share in university chat rooms and on news sites popular with students, postings and comments that were fair and reasonable, as defined by daily instructions sent by the Party.

When the Professor disappeared, the Unit defended the anti-corruption crackdown. And when the smog got really bad and the city was gasping under a blanket of toxic air, they were given stories to post about hard-working and public-spirited officials. When a wind swept in from the Gobi Desert and the smog briefly lifted, they credited it to the swift action of the Party. When the wind stopped and the poisonous air descended again, it was a natural phenomenon beyond Party control.

When a discussion got heated or strayed into forbidden areas, their job was just to change the subject.

And there was Brad Maxwell, an American exchange student and a prolific blogger, who thought the foreign media was unfair to China, and blogged about how China needed stability, and why the Party was almost always working in the best interests of the people. He was given prominence in university chat rooms, a foreign voice of reason, insightful and fair minded.

Only Brad Maxwell didn't exist. The Party had invented him, and another role of Zhang's unit was to put words in his mouth, and into the mouths of a fictitious French student called Pierre and a Brazilian named Ayrton. On his last shift, Zhang had been all three of them.

Not that Zhang saw himself as being part of the Party's censorship machine. His main motive was money, since he was paid for each posting. He struggled to take it seriously. As did most of his unit.

"And I'll tell you another weird thing," Zhang said. "The Party's declared war on aliens." He said they were trying to ban them from the internet.

He said his Unit had received instructions that any online references to aliens should be discouraged or deleted. Brad Maxwell was all set to denounce them as the product of a depraved Western imagination. People should be made to understand that aliens don't exist.

"They don't exist?" said Liu. "Wow."

"Very funny," said Zhang. "But they're serious. It comes from the Party's propaganda office and the ban covers time travel, monsters and superstition, which includes aliens."

"Why would they do that?" Wang said.

Before Zhang could answer, they all looked out of the window. As did most others in the coffee shop, as the soupy grey sky of late afternoon began to change colour.

First it turned yellow, a low-level arch of colour on the horizon, just above the railway line. Then the sky turned green and orange, a giant ball of colour which grew into a mushroom-like cloud, high into the sky, before fading back into the deep grey as the sun went down and the sky was drained of light.

There was silence at first in The Moment On Time, where most customers had joined Wang, Zhang and Liu at the window, a wall of smartphones.

"Wow," said Wang. "What was that?"

The strange light in the sky had been seen right across the city and, as photos and videos were posted online, so were hundreds of theories, from a chemical leak to an explosion at a steel plant to a bungled weapons test.

Wang had his own theory, and once again he called up his alien, posting to *The Gasping Dragon*:

The   are weaponising our smog. The ultimate chemical weapon, made from our unique toxins. Battlefield smog, so we can all be secure. Thank goodness for smog!

That's what the   are doing in   And the weapon tests have gone terribly wrong

Within the next hour his posts were shared more than two million times before being deleted. By then there were reports online of long lines of traffic trying to leave the city, a warehouse containing air purifiers looted by a gang chanting "Give us clean air", and shopping malls that claimed to have clean air were besieged.

Riot police were called to one that boasted of being the greenest of them all. It was a new building in the central business district, a triangle of glass and steel, with walkways around and across a giant atrium full of modern art.

Wang knew the building. He'd visited it shortly after it opened and seen a promotional video about its unique air filtration system, which he still remembered. The mall had used that as its main sales pitch. Come and shop and play while protecting your lungs.

Now it seemed like half the city had taken up the offer. It had become a refuge from the toxic air, as the online rumours spread that a weapons test had gone wrong. Official denials and a chorus of experts saying the light was an optical effect, caused by the interaction of the smog, the sun and storm clouds, merely fuelled the rumours.

Wang watched events unfold as a series of snapshots – online photographs, video clips, blog postings and messages – all uploaded from smartphones at the scene.

Security guards attempting to block the doors. More security guards ejecting people from a showroom of Telstra electric cars, one man clinging to a car door. A video panning shakily across the packed atrium and walkways. A chanting crowd. Music still playing in the background, a Western song, "Blame it on the night, don't blame it on me". Crowds outside banging on the windows. An artwork, several porcelain dogs stacked on top of each other, tumbling over and breaking into pieces.

Then the police arrived and there were images of scuffles. A man forced over the edge of a walkway and photographs of him clinging to a red and white bull, another artwork suspended in mid-air, but close enough to the walkway for the man to grab and avoid a plunge to the atrium floor. Frightened-looking children.

The last image Wang saw on his phone was of a large crowd of perhaps a hundred people, standing in front of a row of riot police. Many young children were among them. They just stood there in silent condemnation, holding in the air pieces of paper, some small, some the size of small posters, and all with the same hand-drawn image. Some were better and more distinctive than others.

It was the image of an alien, a stick alien.

*

After a slow start, the internet police soon got up to speed and the images from the mall were erased from cyberspace. Though by that time the roommates had moved on and were gathered round the screen of Liu's laptop looking at a mangled heap of red metal that used to be a Ferrari.

Liu said it looked like it had just been through a stamping machine in a junkyard.

"Says here it happened on one of the elevated highways just outside Shanghai. In the smog,"

"Wow," said Zhang, looking at the picture, and then at several more that had appeared on the website of an official news agency.

"What a mess. Whose is it? Or was it?"

"The report just says there was a high-speed accident, that the driver died, that it happened late at night. But there are other reports here which say there were two women in the car too and that one survived, and that she was naked."

The report and photograph had quickly gone viral, as did speculation and a lot of anger about who owned the car, everybody sure the driver had to be the son or daughter of some high-ranking official, because they usually were.

Wang tried to open the report on his smartphone, only to discover that the official news agency had taken it down, and other photographs were rapidly being deleted, which meant to him that it had to be the offspring of somebody very important. He saved one photograph to his phone, and then reopened it for a closer look, just as Liu said, "There's another posting here that says the driver's name was Chen."

Wang zoomed in on the photo. The Ferrari was definitely red, and for all the damage it was possible to make out the last two characters of the licence plate: a D and an S.

He then powered up his old Lenovo and looked for Shanghai TT Logistics. The site had been taken down, which came as a disappointment to Wang, since it probably meant the owner didn't want to do business, preferring to delete his site and start again rather than pay the roommates to have it put right.

Then he opened the documents he'd earlier downloaded from the site. He looked at the Ferrari on the cover page of the one called *The Colonel*. The last two letters of the plate were D and S. And the guy, the military guy, he was a Chen. The kid had to be his son. It had to be more than coincidence. The kid must have totalled the Ferrari. This must be the same one as the crumpled pile of metal in Liu's photograph.

He decided to share the cover page of the document on *The Gasping Dragon*, his main Twitter-like account, but couldn't open the account. Instead he posted it to another news-sharing site. For good measure, and because he was feeling angry at Shanghai TT Logistics for not responding to his offer of help, he shared the cover page of the

Mr Fang document too. Beside both he posted an image of the stick alien.

Then he tried again to get into his *Gasping Dragon* account. It didn't seem to be there. So he phoned the internet provider and after waiting in a queue for what seemed forever and listening to an annoying high-pitched voice rattle off all their promotions, he was connected to a man on the help desk. The man told him *The Gasping Dragon* account didn't exist, and according to their records it never had.

Wang hung up and only then for the first time did he wonder whether there was any connection between all the alien fuss and his own postings, his own stick alien. But he quickly discounted the idea. It was just too silly. His was just an online thing. It wasn't real. It was just some fun.

But when he went to look at his game, *Whack An Alien*, figuring it was time to start charging for all the add-ons, all the new weapons, that was gone too. It had been removed from both the app stores on which he'd listed it. He sat back in his chair and looked out at the thick smog and the frozen bare branches of a skeletal-like tree brushing against the coffee shop window, and he realised that his online world had just been deleted. He'd been eliminated from cyberspace.

– 29 –

The Red Ferrari

Chuck Drayton didn't immediately see the Ferrari report. He was reading about the sudden death of the head of the Communist Party's anti-graft unit. A brief statement on state media said he'd passed away after a short illness and that his work would continue.

Drayton was back at the consulate, on his iPhone, his VPN enabled. He saw the news while he was checking out the *@Beijing_smog* Twitter account, which had shared the story, and was making a bit of a joke of it, saying the guy, this big-shot graft-buster, must have been under a lot of stress, with a job like that.

Chill. Overwork can be the death of you. Must have been something really shocking he discovered.

The original story was short, almost an afterthought in a Party newspaper, and Drayton didn't give it much thought. Until he saw the photograph published alongside. He looked long and hard. Whether it was the big pair of thick-rimmed glasses with their tinted lenses or the child-like face betraying not even a hint of feeling, the face was somehow familiar.

There was something about that face, something that made Drayton feel uneasy.

He decided to talk to Ed the Real Geek, see what the word was on Chinese social media, find out what Ed had been wading through down in the sewer. But as soon as he got to Ed's desk he forgot about the graft-buster because Ed had another photograph open on his computer's desktop.

It was the wreckage of the red Ferrari.

"Man, pretty torrid stuff," Ed said, showing Drayton some other photos he'd downloaded, and telling him about the two girls reported to have been in the car, one of them naked.

"Jeez. Looks like it's been pulverised. Hit with some giant hammer," Drayton said. "Did it happen here?"

"Yeah, right here in Shanghai," Ed said.

And Drayton said, "Let me see that again."

There wasn't much to go on. The car was a mess.

He asked Ed if there was any more detail, and Ed said, "It's been crazy. Went viral when the pictures first came out, on a regular news website of all places. Then they pulled the story, and have been busy deleting everything to do with it ever since."

"Which tells you what?" said Drayton.

"Which tells me that whoever was in that car was the offspring of somebody very important."

He said there was a firestorm online, lots of anger about spoiled privileged kids of Party officials.

"So we don't have a name?"

"Well, there was this. Again it was deleted, but only after it was shared a ton of times. You okay, Chuck?"

Drayton wasn't okay. He was staring at Ed's computer, at the cover page of the document he'd just been reading at The Facility, at the face of Colonel General Chen Shibo, his son and the Ferrari, which had now been posted online by the hacker.

"And the Ferraris match?" he said.

"Well, two of the letters of the licence plate do. Seems like his name's Chen and he's the son of an army officer. Pretty senior, I guess."

"I guess," said Drayton. "What else?"

"Nothing else on the car. Just this one page. Posted on a news website."

Which came as a partial relief to Drayton, though it didn't last because Ed then showed him a single page from another document that had been shared alongside *The Colonel* on the same site.

"I'm not sure if this has anything to do with the Ferrari, but it was posted at the same time, by the same person. Just some biographical detail of a bunch of officials." It was the cover page of the *Mr Fang* file.

Drayton said he needed to get some fresh air, leaving the main consulate building and dialling Morgan's number as he went. He needed to warn him. The documents were all over the net. They all led to the Englishman. It wouldn't take rocket science to figure that out.

But Morgan wasn't picking up.

So Drayton then headed downstairs to the old wine cellar that was now the secure communications centre, the Bubble Room, by way of the two heavy security doors with their biometric readers checking his retina and the prints of his thumb and forefinger. They didn't hesitate this time, agreed it was him, and the doors clicked open.

He took his usual seat at the edge of the room, which was busy for the regular conference call. He counted thirteen people around the room and at the long table. All five screens were live, and today they included the Defence Department, where the video conference room looked a bit more colourful than the others, with bookshelves and pictures on the wall. And where they introduced a tall academic-looking man in round spectacles, Professor somebody-or-other from Harvard. A chemical expert.

"We are dealing with a nasty cocktail here," the Professor said, placing a large display board upright on his table with the title *Beijing Smog*, and then a pie chart showing its chemical makeup.

"We have particulate matter, the most dangerous of which are the tiny bits. We also have sulphur dioxide, nitrogen oxides, carbon monoxide and ozone. All nasty in themselves, but with complex, poorly understood and potentially dangerous interactions."

He said that although the samples had been collected in Beijing, the combination was similar in other Chinese cities.

"We know that it's already having a devastating health impact, cutting life expectancy by an estimated five years in northern China. An estimated one point six million people die each year from heart and lung disease and strokes as a result of the pollution. Now imagine for one moment if it can be harvested, concentrated and possibly liquefied."

"So you're saying it is possible, to build a smog weapon?" said a woman from the CIA screen.

"From the perspective of chemistry, yes. It's a lethal cocktail," said the Professor. "We are dealing with a very nasty poison with immediate and long-term effects, and if concentrated and released in a highly populated area it would have a potentially very high morbidity rate."

"What he's saying is that this stuff kills. It could make a potent weapon in the hands of a hostile state," said a person sitting alongside the Professor.

"That's scary," said a voice from around the table in the Bubble Room.

"So it's deadly. But even if it could be harvested, could you realistically make a weapon out of it?" asked the CIA woman.

"It's like any chemical weapon. You could put it on a missile or a bomb. Or maybe a stealth weapon smuggled into an enemy's city," said a woman at Defence.

"But is that really plausible?" asked somebody around the table in the Bubble Room.

And the woman at Defence said, "We have to be vigilant. We can't afford to ignore that possibility. We have to take it seriously. Especially with all the internet chatter. Let's see the postings again."

The central screen went blank and then showed two internet postings, enlarged to make them clearer.

The ⚇ are weaponising our smog. The ultimate chemical weapon, made from our unique toxins. Battlefield smog, so we can all be secure. Thank goodness for smog!

That's what the ⚇ are doing in 🚬 And the weapon tests have gone terribly wrong

"They were posted at about the same time as the strange light in the sky over Beijing," said another voice from around the Bubble Room table.

"Didn't we conclude that the light was a natural thing?" said the State Department.

"We did," said Defence. "But can we *totally* discount that it wasn't a bungled weapons test?"

"What does that *mean* though, those images? What's the alien that's supposedly mixing the gases? And the cigarette? Is that your smoking gun?" said State, not convinced.

"It could be a threat, a warning, some sort of code. Whichever way you look at it, this isn't something we can simply ignore," said a man from the Defence Department screen.

"Chuck, what do you make of it? You're the Cyber Guy," said a voice from the State Department.

But Drayton didn't immediately hear him. He was looking at the alien. Looking hard. It was familiar. Minus the hoody.

"Chuck. What's your take?"

"Sorry," Drayton said, tuning back in.

"Well, the cigarette. There's a brand called Zhongnanhai, which is the same name as the Communist Party's leadership compound next to the Forbidden City in Beijing. Netizens, as regular internet users are called here, they sometimes use it to sidestep the censors, when they want to talk about that place."

There was a sharp intake of breath around the table. Then silence before a man from the Defence Department said, "Jesus."

"This is serious," said the CIA screen. "This could be a warning, saying that something or someone in that compound is developing these weapons."

"And the alien? Where does that come in? Who does that represent?" said another Defence Department voice.

Drayton said it was hard to say for sure, but the alien might be the signature of a hacking syndicate. A calling card used for bad guys breaking into computers. He said it could also represent a hardline nationalist group, remembering the Alcatraz stuff, the alien looking through the wall where Clint Eastwood should have been.

"Wow," said the CIA screen. "Hackers and nationalists dabbling with poison gas. This is looking far worse than we'd thought."

Then the National Security Agency screen came to life, and a voice from its conference table said, "What are we dealing with here, Chuck?"

Drayton said it might just be a prank. Probably was, that there was a lot of strange stuff on the internet, and that we perhaps shouldn't jump to conclusions.

But the screens in front of him had already jumped to one big conclusion. That at that very moment deadly vials of concentrated smog were being cooked up by an enemy in a hoody and draped in a Chinese flag. And it was possibly happening in the Chinese leadership compound.

"Aren't we getting a little ahead of ourselves here?" said a lonely voice from State.

But the others were no longer listening.

"The alien must be the key," said the CIA screen.

And Defence said, "We have to identify that alien."

"I'm on the case," said Drayton, excusing himself from the room, where the screens gave him a rousing send-off.

"Good one, Chuck."

"Go for it."

"Whatever resources you need, they're yours. Just ask."

He said sure, I'll do that. Leave it with me, guys.

When he reached the top of the stairs, Ed was waiting for him, saying could he have a word, and the two walked outside to the consulate's carp pond.

"There was one more thing I forgot to mention, Mr Drayton."

"What's that?" asked Drayton, irritated that the kid had been hanging around outside the Bubble Room, waiting for him.

"Your Mr Wang, the one you asked me about."

"Tell me, Ed," said Drayton, now a good deal more interested.

"Well, I've found him. I've found your Mr Wang."

– 30 –

Subverting State Power

Soon after Wang Chu disappeared from cyberspace they came for him in person. He saw the minivan as he was leaving The Moment On Time in the early evening. It was parked opposite, a dark Buick with five doors and tinted windows. One of the rear doors slid open and two uniformed police officers climbed out, one throwing down a cigarette as he did. Another two men in plain clothes joined them, quickly crossing the road, straight towards Wang.

Without speaking a word, they snatched the bag containing his laptop, pinned his arms behind his back and handcuffed him. They pushed his head forward and, gripping his arms, they marched him across the road and pushed him into the back of the van, placing a heavy cloth hood over his head as they did so.

The road was busy, but few people noticed. It was dark and the smog was thick. Streetlights and the glow from the coffee shop window struggled to penetrate the gloom. And it all happened so quickly, like the sharp movement of fuzzy shadow puppets across a dirty screen. Those who were closer and did see knew better than to show it.

The police sat Wang on a bench seat in the Buick, a man either side. He slumped slightly forward because of his shackled wrists and struggled to breathe through the heavy cloth of the hood, which also muffled any sound.

They drove for twenty minutes, though it seemed much longer to Wang, gasping for air, his wrists and shoulders beginning to ache. The policeman to his left adjusted the hood slightly, allowing a little more air to seep in.

The van slowed and sounded its horn. He heard a whistle. Some words were spoken, though it wasn't possible for Wang to make them out. Then he heard a metal gate opening. They drove a little further and then stopped again, the van door sliding open. A hand gripped Wang's arm and guided him out of the van. He was led along what seemed like a pathway that was slippery in places, ice most likely, since from time to time it cracked under foot.

He coughed as they entered a building, the hood seeming to trap inside a layer of sooty air. He was led up concrete stairs, which was awkward at first, until he got into a rhythm, though he almost fell when he reached the top and stretched his foot for a step that didn't exist.

They paused and he heard the sound of a key in a lock and a door opening. They led him through the door and sat him in a cold metal seat.

One of the policemen removed the hood and the cuffs, took his belt, shoes, phone and watch. He told Wang not to move and not to speak.

It took a while for his eyes to adjust to the light, not that there was much of it. Just a single bare bulb hanging from the ceiling. The room was small and without windows, with bare yellowing walls. There was a metal table in front of him and along the wall to his left was a long narrow bed with a single folded blanket. There were cupboards along another wall. A door led to what appeared to be a bathroom. There was a small heater in the corner, but if it was working it wasn't having much impact. The room was cold and damp, but it struck Wang as more cheap hotel room than prison cell.

Two men in military-style uniforms, possibly policemen, possibly soldiers, sat the other side of the table. They just sat, watching. Cropped hair, severe-looking and young. Probably not much older than Wang. Bolt upright, expressionless, never taking their eyes off him, like the inanimate guards at the Forbidden City.

At first Wang said nothing, as he'd been instructed.

Then he asked where he was. Why he was there. His guards didn't respond. Never turned a hair. He asked for water. Still nothing. Only when he raised an arm in the air, waved it around, and said please, can I have water, did one of them stand, go to the bathroom and come back with a small plastic cup, half filled. All with military rigidity, every movement slow and deliberate.

He said thanks, appreciate that. The guard said nothing, still showed no response at all, just sat back down next to the other one and carried on watching him, impassive.

But that had been a breakthrough. And so when he needed to use the toilet, he raised his arm and asked ever so politely. They ignored him the first time, and the second. And only on a third attempt, when he said, please, I am really desperate, did one of the policemen stand and gesture towards the bathroom door. Then the second one stood, and both followed Wang to the bathroom, standing to attention in the open door and watched him piss. They returned to their seats as he did.

He ate when they did, and what they did, some sort of soup and rice. And when he needed to sleep because he could not keep his eyes open any longer, he raised his arm again and they nodded towards the bed, still without speaking.

He wasn't sure how long he slept, but by the time he woke they had changed shifts and two more young guards sat in the same seats, with the same fixed expression, eyes still trained on him. When they saw he was awake they gestured for him to return to the metal seat.

So he sat back down, looked at the table, looked at the floor, at the walls, anywhere but at them. But it was impossible to avoid those eyes, which never seemed to blink. He smiled, raising an eyebrow, stretched his arms, gave an exaggerated yawn. He tried a bit of small talk saying it must have been a long day for you guys too, did they know how long he would be staying there? Anything to provoke a response. But he might as well have been talking to the wall.

Only when it was time again for a change of shift did his guards show an inkling of emotion, or maybe relief as they handed duties back to the original two. One appeared to glance at his watch. Perhaps they were human after all.

He quickly lost all sense of time, becoming disorientated and exhausted. It was made worse by not having access to his phone, depriving him of the screen that was his access to a world he understood, a friendlier world; sometimes he instinctively felt for his back pocket, or woke up to imaginary message alerts.

The only natural light came from a small air vent high on one of the walls. He thought he heard distant marching feet, the yells of a drilling exercise, which made him think it must be some sort of army or police camp. But mostly it was silent.

He wondered whether he was inside that building, the building near the coffee shop that didn't exist on any map, and he shivered as he remembered Liu's joke about people never coming back out once they'd gone through that gate. But his car had travelled further. Unless it was a trick and they were trying to confuse him.

He didn't know what to think.

He tried to keep track of time by counting the shifts. Maybe each was for eight hours, maybe ten. But soon he stopped noticing those as well.

He slumped in his seat, overcome with fatigue, too tired almost to raise his hand and ask for permission to go to his bed. Then the door of the room opened for what he assumed was another change of shift. Though it hadn't been long since the last one.

He looked up to see his guards standing to attention and then moving to the back of the room to make way for two men in regular clothes, one carrying a laptop computer, the other a file. They sat at the table opposite him.

The one with the file seemed in charge. He was smartly dressed, wearing a blue blazer over a buttoned-down shirt. He reminded Wang of one of his teachers. The kind of guy you'd hardly notice in the street. In his thirties, early forties maybe with thinning black hair, neatly brushed back and glasses with a fashionable rimless frame.

The other was younger, wearing dark jeans and sweatshirt. He was carrying clothes, which looked like a jogging suit, which he placed on the bed.

"Those are for you," said the one in the blazer. "You might be with us for a while. Although really that's up to you."

Wang tried to focus his thoughts, to clear his head. He sat up on the metal chair, thanked the man for the clothes and asked if he could make a call, tell his family what had happened.

"It's really in your interests and those of your family to cooperate with this investigation," the man said, ignoring the request and opening his file, which contained a pile of papers, which looked like they had been printed from the internet.

Wang said that of course he wanted to cooperate, and that he would never do anything to damage his family.

"Sir, what are you investigating?" he said.

The man ignored the question and said that Wang's family was a good family, a family that had served the Party well, and he should think about how his actions might affect them.

Wang said he always thought about his family, but it would help enormously if they could tell him why he was here and what actions they were talking about. He said he was confused.

At which point the man in the blazer got a little agitated. He looked at the other one, the one on the laptop, who was banging away on the keyboard, presumably making a transcript of the interrogation, and then he told Wang it was precisely that attitude that had got him into trouble in the first place and could only make matters worse for him.

Wang asked what attitude that was, but the men ignored him, the one in the blazer then saying, "Are you enjoying university, Wang?"

"Very much, sir. It's a good course, at a good college. And I have always enjoyed computers."

The two men looked at each other again, the one in charge then having another look at the file.

"The accusations against you are very serious," he said.

Wang said he was very sorry to hear that.

"I'd be very grateful if you could tell me those allegations," he said. "It will help me to better understand just how serious they are."

The man said nothing. He then began sifting through the papers in front of him.

"You know, Wang, everything you do on the internet is logged. Everything you click on, to buy things, watch videos, follow blogs or view websites. It's all in the log. As well as who you message and call, and what you write and say. Everything you post, too. Even where you go, because when are you ever without your smartphone? It's all logged. Everything.

243

"Wonderful thing technology, isn't it Wang?"

He paused for effect and to make sure the one on the laptop was keeping up.

"Mostly its done to sell you stuff online, or else to sell the data to others who want to sell you stuff. The data are very valuable. And you know something else? They can also show what sort of person you are, what sort of citizen. Are you a patriot, Wang?"

Wang said he was very proud of China and being Chinese.

"Well, that's strange, Wang, because you score very low as a citizen, and that has been drawn to the attention of the relevant organs."

"Which organs are they?" said Wang.

"The relevant ones."

Then the man stood up, as moments later did the one on the laptop, telling Wang to think very carefully about his situation.

Wang promised that he would, but said that he was having trouble understanding that situation.

Then as they were leaving, the one in the blazer turned and said, "When was the last time you saw Yang Eu-Meh?"

Wang was so startled by the question that he almost fell off his seat.

"I've never met her."

"You've never met your own girlfriend?"

"No. Never. I mean she's not my girlfriend. Never has been."

"Your girlfriend's a very bad person, Wang, who's said some treacherous things about her motherland."

"I swear I've never met her. I made it up to please my mother," Wang said, rambling now.

"And you thought that seeing a girl with a bad attitude would please your mother?"

"But I never saw her."

He started to explain about the pressure he was under from his parents to find a girlfriend, but the man in the blazer raised a hand, not wanting to hear any more, and said, "Your situation is very bad, Wang. You'll have to do better than that."

Then the men left, and the two guards resumed their positions in the chairs across the table, just watching him.

"Do you understand my situation?" he asked the one nearest to him, who said nothing and continued to show not the slightest emotion.

244

Wang then raised his hand and said he'd like to take a shower, have a dump and change into his new clothes. One guard nodded, and then both followed him to the bathroom and again took up their positions at the door, watching him as he squatted and then showered. He was beyond caring.

The man in the blazer and his sidekick returned the following day, and again sat at the table opposite Wang. The one in the blazer opened his file and this time removed several pieces of paper, placing them on the table in front of him.

Overnight, Wang had thought a lot about his situation, as he'd been told to, and he decided that if this was just about Eu-Meh then he really could explain, that perhaps his situation wasn't so bad after all. And he'd practised that explanation in his head, rehearsing what he'd say over and over.

But this time the man in the blazer didn't even mention the Chinese-Australian beauty queen, and for the first five minutes he just sat there slowly shuffling the papers in front of him and staring at Wang.

Then he pushed one of the papers across the table towards Wang before sitting back in his chair and crossing his arms.

"Look familiar, Wang? You posted it to your account, the one you call *The Gasping Dragon*. Nice name. Snappy name. Tell me about this, Wang."

Wang looked down at the paper in front of him, which was definitely a printout from the internet, and which contained words and two images.

Under the cover of smog   *have landed and taken control of*

"Tell us, Wang. Who exactly is under cover of smog and what have they taken over?"

Wang said nothing at first, not sure how to respond. It was definitely his, but he'd pretty much forgotten about that posting, and why he'd done it. Surely this couldn't be why they'd brought him here?

"I can't really recall," he said. "It must have been a joke about the smog. That the smog was so thick aliens could land and we'd know nothing about it."

"Aliens that could take over the Government, Wang? Do you believe in aliens?"

Wang said he didn't believe in aliens, that he was just having fun.

"Fun, Wang? You were having fun?" said the one in the blazer, looking again at the sidekick on the laptop, to make sure he'd got that, and who then also looked up, a vague smirk on his face, like this was the most fun he'd had all week.

"Well, tell me about this one," the one in the blazer said, taking out from the pile a second sheet of paper, another printout from *The Gasping Dragon*.

The are weaponising our smog. The ultimate chemical weapon, made from our unique toxins. Battlefield smog, so we can all be secure. Thank goodness for smog!

"Making weapons out of smog. That's an interesting concept, Wang," said the man. "You think that's possible?"

Wang said he wasn't sure, but the smog could be very bad at times.

The man ignored that and showed Wang a third piece of paper, this one with a stick alien wearing an outsize pair of spectacles and a Twitter-like posting beside it, about Chinese officials.

"So you think Chinese officials lack imagination, foresight or intellectual insight?"

Wang didn't know what to say. His anonymous postings had clearly been less anonymous than he'd thought, but surely they can't be taking them seriously?

"They were jokes," he said, pleading with the man now, his voice cracking. "They weren't supposed to be serious."

The man pushed his seat back and looked at Wang like he was some sort of strange object in a museum or a child who really didn't get the simple and self-evident words of a parent.

"Are these a joke?" the man said, showing a series of photographs: Protesters outside some building, facing off with police and holding high big drawings of the alien, the same alien. Wang's alien. The alien scrawled crudely on the door of a charred police car. Another on a poster carried by a protester with only one foot. Then the stick alien in graffiti on a wall near a demolition site.

Then again on a soiled greetings card alongside the words "Keep up the fight".

"Tell me about 'the fight', Wang. Which fight are we talking about here?"

And Wang said he'd never seen that before, or the others, that he had no idea what fight it was referring to.

"But it's your alien is it not?" the man said.

Wang said not necessarily, that there were probably a lot of aliens.

"Let me tell you what I think," said the man. "I think that by ridiculing our leaders you are trying to start some sort of uprising. You really think you could do that in China?"

Wang started to say that he wasn't trying to start anything, that the pictures, those aliens, it had to be a coincidence. But the man interrupted him and asked whether Wang was aware that China faced infiltration from hostile foreign forces, that the country needed to be vigilant.

Wang said he wasn't aware of that, but promised he'd make it a priority to look out for infiltration just as soon as he got back home.

The man said infiltration took many forms, but sometimes ideas were the most dangerous. He said it was happening all the time, all around us, trying to undermine our socialist values. He said that after a century of humiliation, China under the leadership of the Communist Party was standing high again and had to keep permanently on its guard.

"I want you to think about that, Wang."

Wang said he would, and nodded as if he understood.

Then the man said, "Who else is in your organisation, Wang? Who else is involved? Are you receiving foreign funding?"

Wang said what organisation? And the man started banging his finger hard on the picture of the alien and saying, "*This* organisation, Wang, *this* organisation."

He said Wang had allowed himself to become a tool of foreign powers.

That the Communist Party brought stability and order.

"And you know what the alternative is Wang?"

247

Wang said he wasn't sure. Possibly instability and disorder?

"Chaos Wang. It's Chaos."

Then the man asked whether Wang knew the punishment for subverting state power and Wang said he didn't, and said again that he was just messing around, that he'd only been joking with all the online stuff. That it wasn't *real*.

"Subverting state power is no joke. It is deadly serious, Wang. Do you really want to spend the rest of your life in prison? We have treated you gently so far. You come from a good family. Your father is a good man. There could be consequences for them too. Do you understand? Our patience is wearing very thin."

Wang began to ramble, close to tears. He said he understood subversion was very serious, but how could a few posts of a spindly alien, a few silly posts, a bit of fun, possibly be a threat to the Communist Party?

"You really don't get it do you, Wang?"

And Wang said, no, perhaps he didn't.

– 31 –

Macau

For twenty-four hours Anthony Morgan had remained in his Hong Kong hotel, mostly in his room, his curtains drawn and the do-not-disturb sign lit up by his door. He was not sure what he should do next.

He had his *@Beijing_smog* Twitter account open on his laptop, retreating to the comfort of his alter ego, trying to distract himself with some fresh posts. The Hong Kong haze. The protesting lawyers and their alien. A dead graft-buster. The last was the strangest and he'd almost missed it. He'd found the report, just a few words, buried right down the bottom of an inside page of the *People's Daily*, which he'd read online. The Party's mouthpiece was always a good source of slightly surreal stories.

He decided to make a joke of it, sharing the story with a comment about overwork, which made him smile, but only very briefly. *@Beijing_smog* had always been his own private world where he could say what he wanted to say, be who he wanted to be. But that bubble of anonymity had burst, and he kept returning to the message from his wife:

Stay in Hong Kong. Do not come back, and do not try and contact me or Robert. Robert should be fine. My parents are helping. Cindy

There could only be one explanation. That she'd seen the video. That she knew. That would explain her strange tone of voice on recent calls, her reluctance to let him speak to Robert. She also knew about his alter ego, his private Twitter account. What else did she know? She could dig up the most intimate details about the targets of their investigations. So why not about him too? Mimi the masseuse had not been the only one.

He decided he couldn't hide from it. He needed to talk to her face to face.

So he checked out and took a taxi to Hong Kong airport, checking in for a late morning flight to Beijing. He didn't phone Cindy Wu, or reply to her message. He didn't want to give her any advance warning.

He was at the gate, preparing to board, when his phone rang. It was the man from Mr Fang's office saying Mr Fang needed to see him, and that it was urgent.

Morgan said he should be able to get to Shenzhen the following week, but the man interrupted him and said that was too late, that Mr Fang wanted to see him today, in Macau, where he'd meet him for a late lunch on the Cotai Strip. He gave Morgan the name of a restaurant, asking him to text when his ferry arrived.

Then he hung up.

Morgan sat back down on a seat close to the boarding gate, thinking this was strange, even for Mr Fang. But he was an important client. Maybe even more so now. If he was going to get into a scrap with Cindy Wu over their assets, then Mr Fang's money would be very useful. And he had a lot of it. And the way Morgan saw it, he needed to move quickly to seal the deals, and his own commissions, before Drayton had the deals blocked.

So he went to the airline desk and said he could no longer fly, that some urgent business had come up. The woman behind the desk looked irritated, studying her watch for what seemed to Morgan like an eternity before taking back the boarding pass. There were only thirty minutes until the flight was scheduled to leave, but he had no check-in baggage to retrieve; he rarely travelled with check-in luggage.

Then he retraced his steps back through the airport, wheeling his battered black bag to an exit marked Mainland China and Macau. He bought a ticket for Macau, and an hour later he boarded a blue catamaran ferry, climbing a staircase to the Superclass cabin, where he sat in a fading blue leather seat beside the window. He took off his jacket, laying it neatly on the empty seat beside him and rubbed his eyes.

He thought about Drayton, since he had several missed calls from the American. In Lamma, Morgan had demanded to know more about what he was getting into, but Drayton had given him nothing apart from some vague stuff about there being a bigger picture and promises to protect his anonymity. From what? He'd decided he couldn't trust a man who wrapped his iPhone in kitchen foil, wouldn't sit with his back to a restaurant, and had a side job with some obscure Shanghai trading company.

What sort of Economic/Commercial Officer was that?

Morgan wanted nothing more to do with him, and when his phone rang again, he ignored it.

A large screen at the front of the cabin was looping rapid-fire images of his destination. Bright lights, gambling tables, a cabaret troupe in sparkling bikinis, and a preview of a world title boxing match, days away. Macau, the world's biggest casino city, it boasted, now outstripping by far the tables of Las Vegas, and a magnet for big-spending Chinese from the mainland.

Men like Mr Fang.

The ferry pulled away from the airport jetty, heaving and swaying in the wake of a larger passing ship laden with containers. The control tower was barely visible through the haze, below it the smudgy outlines of taxiing aircraft.

It had been a wretched few days in Hong Kong, what with that massage video, and then the disappearance of Sam Ching.

Before the message from his wife, he'd tried to reassure himself that the video was nothing, just a bit of spite on Mimi's part, not liking being shouted at, and that the whole thing would blow over. And Geraldine MacMaster seemed reassured.

And he'd convinced himself that Ching's detention couldn't possibly be about La-La and that stupid sperm machine. That would be ridiculous. It must be something else Ching was into. And he'd continued to reassure Ching's increasingly desperate wife that all would be well.

He began to read that morning's edition of the *South China Morning Post*, a Hong Kong newspaper, a front-page report saying Macau gambling revenues were plummeting, and blaming the Communist Party's crackdown on corruption.

Then his telephone rang again, this time from a number he didn't recognise. After a moment's hesitation, he answered the call. It was Sam Ching.

"Hello there, Mr Morgan, Sam here."

Morgan jolted up in his seat and asked how he was. He said he'd heard some terrible things from Su.

Ching laughed, but it was an awkward laugh.

"Everything's fine. A lot of fuss about nothing. Just a silly misunderstanding. But I do need to see you. It's quite urgent."

Morgan thought for a moment, then he said, "I'm not sure I can come immediately to Shenzhen, Sam. But I will be in Macau later today. I have a late lunchtime meeting with a client at the Cha Chaan Teng restaurant on the Cotai Strip. Can you slip over to Macau?"

There was a long pause, and then Ching said, sure, he could make it, that he'd see him there, and he asked Morgan to text this number when he arrived. Maybe they could get together just before or just after his lunch. There was another silence, and then Ching asked, "Is that Mr Fang you are meeting?"

And Morgan said yes it was, thinking it was a strange question to ask.

He said he was glad Ching was okay, that he was looking forward to talking, and then they hung up.

Morgan slumped back in his seat, an attendant in a soiled grey jacket serving him a plastic tray with lukewarm jasmine tea and stale biscuits.

He should have felt relief, but instead he felt unease. Ching had sounded awkward, stilted, almost like they were not his words he was speaking. It certainly wasn't the Ching he knew. He never called him Mr Morgan. Anything but that.

But he pushed back the uncertainties, feeling duty-bound to try and meet him. Ching had been loyal to him over the years, and he felt he owed it to him.

Midway between Hong Kong and Macau, the ferry entered a dead zone, where the phone signal from neither place was strong enough to register on his iPhone. The ferry slowed, an announcement saying there were speed limits because of the bad visibility. Morgan looked out at the grey nothingness, as the ferry crawled on for another forty minutes before cutting its engines and cruising into a terminal beside Macau's airport on Taipa, an island off the main peninsula of the former Portuguese colony.

The Superclass passengers, a dozen at most, were the first to get off the ferry. Casino earnings may have been down, but the lower deck was packed and they seemed to Morgan to be lining up for a race to the Baccarat tables.

A bored-looking immigration official barely looked at his passport, and he was quickly out of the terminal and into the middle of a frenzy of touts and guides. Groups of young women in shiny gold mini-skirts pointed the way to colourful shuttle buses bound for the casinos.

He boarded a green bus for the Cotai Strip.

It was almost two in the afternoon, and he texted both numbers: Mr Fang's sidekick and the one that Ching had used. "Arrived and heading to Cotai."

A message came back quickly from the Fang phone. "Mr Fang will be there at 4." And he texted the Ching phone again saying that was the time he'd be dining. There was no reply from that phone.

It took fifteen minutes to reach the Cotai Strip, a series of massive gambling complexes. Tall, sprawling hotels built around cavernous casinos.

He left the bus, passed through a revolving doorway and into a reception area lit by enormous sparkling chandeliers. He had time to kill, so headed down a wide corridor lined with luxury brand shops, past an indoor forest and a fountain that changed colour from a deep blue to a violent red. The corridors formed a vast perimeter around a casino that never closed, its constant murmur and pings punctuated periodically by the ecstatic roar of a winner.

Morgan was almost knocked over by one tall heavily made-up young Chinese woman as she came out of a shop, laden down with shopping bags bearing designer labels, four in each hand. Prada, Gucci, Versace, Louis Vuitton were the ones he noticed.

She struggled trying to press a button for a lift, so Morgan pressed it for her. He smiled slightly. She ignored him. She was wearing a bright red skirt so tight that she appeared to waddle into the lift.

If Macau was falling on hard times, nobody had told her.

It had been a while since he'd been in Macau, but it was popular with a lot of his clients.

Ten minutes before four he entered the Cha Chaan Teng restaurant, which was largely deserted, it being well after its lunchtime peak, and gave Fang's name to the woman at a desk near the door. She took him to a semi-private alcove at the back of the restaurant where he sat and ordered a glass of red wine.

He continued reading the newspaper from the ferry as four o'clock arrived. Then four fifteen. Four thirty. Four forty-five. He messaged the number for Mr Fang's assistant, and when he didn't receive a reply he tried ringing the number. It was unobtainable. Power off.

At five o'clock, a tall Chinese woman in tight purple silk *cheongsam* entered the alcove and said that she had messages for him, and would he like tea. He said yes, and asked for a jasmine green tea. The woman left the table, returning five minutes later with the tea and one cup, which she filled.

She said he had two messages.

"Mr Fang sends his apologies, but he can no longer meet you."

"That's too bad," said Morgan, feeling a strange sense of relief, sipping the tea.

"And the other message?"

She gave him a small red decorative envelope, with the characters for 'good fortune' on the front. Inside was a playing card, an ace of spades. There was tiny writing just above the spade on the front of the card, which he recognised as Ching's writing. It said, "Fisherman's Wharf", and then the name of a Thai restaurant. There was also a small drawing.

It was a stick alien.

"Anything else?" said Morgan to the woman, who was still standing near the table.

"Mr Ching wants you to text when you arrive," she said, refilling his cup.

Morgan placed the playing card in the inside pocket of his jacket along with his iPhone, then left the restaurant, passing a group of gamblers posing for photographs in front of a sculpture of four large silver polar bears near the casino entrance. A woman with a green painted face handed him a leaflet advertising "Breakfast with Shrek". He waved her away, and headed towards a taxi, pulling his bag behind him.

The taxi took him across a long low bridge connecting Taipa Island with the Macau peninsula. The casino lights were coming on now – purples, blues, whites and yellows, reflected in the water.

He'd heard about Fisherman's Wharf, knew some of the investors. It was a waterside development of shops and bars, a bizarre mishmash of styles from Rome to Tibet, with a good number of places in-between.

The taxi dropped him next to the Fisherman's Wharf version of the Roman Colosseum, which sat in the shadow of another Casino, dominating the waterfront.

A craft market was in full swing, as was a children's grand prix, toddlers guiding small electric-powered racing cars around a short track. Morgan was now pulling his wheeled luggage in a more haphazard fashion than the young racers were driving their cars, and almost collided with one who'd strayed from the track, drawing angry looks from half a dozen racing mothers.

A warm day was turning into a cool evening, a light breeze blowing from the bay. But Morgan removed his jacket and placed it over his arm. His blue buttoned-down shirt was by now soaked with perspiration. He was feeling dizzy.

He reached the waterfront beside the Thai restaurant. He sat on a wooden bench close to the water's edge, leaning on the long arm of his wheeled bag, and texted the Ching number saying he'd arrived.

Then he fell off the bench; a server from the restaurant helped him up, asking if he was okay, saying she'd get him water.

He felt lousy. He looked again at the Twitter message from his wife, and then at the playing card, staring at it, before putting it and his phone back in the pocket of his jacket, which fell to the floor. He was struck with a sudden and overwhelming feeling of panic.

He pulled himself awkwardly to his feet and began to run, tripping again and then colliding with a barrier near the waterfront.

He managed to avoid falling over it, but the force of the impact sent his bag hurtling over the edge and into the water.

He kept going, not looking back. His vision was fuzzy and he struggled to see ahead of him. He felt like a huge weight was crushing him, forcing him toward the ground. But he willed himself on, weaving, staggering as fast as he could, desperate to get away from that area and to the one place he knew he would be safe.

– 32 –

The Harbin Express

Wang Chu's detention ended after five days, almost as abruptly as it had started, when a uniformed police officer came to his cell and told him to sign a confession and what he called "certain undertakings".

The officer was carrying a thick wad of bound papers, which included a transcript of his interrogation, which said he had admitted to inciting subversion, as well as spreading malicious rumours and malicious hyping online, but was being released pending further investigation.

Wang said he still didn't understand. The officer said he didn't need to. The man seemed to know little about the case, and care even less. He opened the confession at the back page, where there was a place for Wang's signature, just below a paragraph saying he had fully read and understood everything. He signed the document.

Then the officer produced another document, which he called a guarantee, and which said Wang must follow police instructions and not discuss politics online. It specifically barred him from any online activity that depicted aliens or other abnormal live forms. He signed that one too.

Then the officer returned his phone, shoes, belt and watch before placing the hood back over his head and leading him down the stairs and across the icy path to a vehicle that felt smaller than the one they'd arrested him with. The engine spluttered to life after three attempts, the driver swearing about the cold, and half an hour later they dropped him at the railway crossing close to The Moment On Time. Though after they removed the hood it took a while for him to see where he was, as his eyes adjusted to the sudden harsh light.

He took a deep breath, then coughed. The smog was still bad, but the grey silhouette of the coffee shop was a welcome sight; only when he arrived he found the door was sealed, and there was a pasted hand-written note saying it was closed until further notice. Two police vans were parked just along the street.

He couldn't make any calls because the battery on his phone was dead, so he walked back to his room. His roommates weren't there, but on his bed was a note, which he thought might be from them. Instead it was an official letter from the University saying he had been expelled for gross breaches of discipline and disregard for regulations.

He found a portable battery charger in a drawer that was usually full of hard drives and other computer stuff, mostly related to their online shop. The drives had all gone. He plugged the charger into his phone and then ran to the University, thinking that if he could explain himself to his supervisor, Mrs Jiang, he might yet salvage his place.

When he reached the office to which he'd earlier been invited to tea, he found the same elderly woman, wearing another poncho-type woollen top, though this one was brown. She was making tea.

"I'd really like to see Mrs Jiang," he said, breathless. "It's an emergency."

"Mrs who?" said the woman.

"Mrs Jiang. My supervisor. You'll recall I was here for tea just the other day."

But the woman said she couldn't recall Wang being there, or a Mrs Jiang for that matter, and continued with her tea-making ritual without looking up.

Wang noticed that the door into the main office was open. He took a step towards it and saw the same big desk on one side, the crumpled sofas around the stained coffee table, and the old poster for an academic conference on the wall. But behind Mrs Jiang's desk there now sat a wiry man with small round glasses.

"You'll need an appointment to see Mr Zhou," said the woman in the poncho.

Wang moved closer to the door and hesitated, trying to catch the attention of the man called Zhou, who was looking down at his desk. He took another step, right to the door and was about to knock, when the woman in the poncho pushed past him carrying the tea into the main office and closed the door in Wang's face.

Wang left the building, heading back towards his room. There was now some life in his phone's battery, so he tried to call Liu and Zhang, but neither picked up.

When he got back to his room he lay on his bed and fell asleep, finally overcome with exhaustion built up over his five-day detention. But he was woken up well before dawn when a pile of noodle boxes fell to the floor. They were still overflowing from the sink, but had become unstable from the growing colony of cockroaches.

He was soon wide awake again, and the more he thought about it the more puzzled he became about why he'd been released. Perhaps they'd believed him, that the alien thing was just a joke. Perhaps his father had helped, making calls on his behalf.

The thought of his parents filled him with guilt. How would he tell them about the expulsion? They had huge hopes for their only child and he was sure they'd be angry and heartbroken. He checked the messages on his smartphone. There was a bunch from Zhang and Liu, trying to figure out where he was. There were also several from his father. Brief, but with an urgency he wasn't used to hearing, asking him to ring home.

Did they already know? The police had threatened to make life hard for his family. He'd thought they were bluffing, but now he wasn't sure. Though it was early, he tried ringing his mother and father, but both went straight to voicemail. He didn't leave a message. Didn't know what to say.

Unable to sleep anymore, he gathered some warm clothes and took a taxi across the city to Beijing South railway station, a vast and cavernous terminus on the other side of town that served as a gateway for high-speed trains.

When he reached the station it had only just opened. He had never seen it so quiet and empty. He and his bag were scanned at the entrance, and he flinched as a uniformed security official patted him down. He bought a second-class ticket to Harbin, on the eight o'clock train; he then went to find something to eat, with nearly two hours to kill.

The oval-shaped building was so big that the smog hung inside, and he looked down the concourse at the fuzzy neon of fast-food outlets opening for business. He found a noodle shop, which served him a steaming bowl of something with only a passing resemblance to the picture he'd pointed to when ordering.

He held his chopsticks in his right hand, scooping noodles, while with his left he worked his smartphone, opening a game which put him in the saddle of a horse, galloping across a land of snow-peaked mountains and dark valleys, zapping the monsters that appeared all around him.

He didn't notice the two men who entered the noodle shop, ordered tea and took a table near the door, where they sat watching him.

When Wang left, still working his phone and having reached a level higher on his game thanks to a bloodied trail of dead and dismembered monsters, they left too, following him across a station now quickly filling with people, and when he boarded the train they boarded too, taking seats a few rows behind him.

The train to Harbin was packed. It always was. Wang had a window seat. A woman with an overweight toddler sat next to him. And as the train slowly pulled out of the station, the toddler stood on its mother's knee, where it bounced, kicked, coughed and screamed for most of the first hour of the eight-hour journey.

When Wang opened the game on his phone, the toddler took a lunge for it. The mother apologised half-heartedly, but did little to stop it. Wang put the phone away and was soon in another deep sleep, in spite of the best efforts of the barrel-like child.

When he woke, hours later, the toddler was asleep.

He again tried ringing his parents, but there was still no response. He listened again to his father's voicemails. They were short, hurried and anxious. Which was unusual. His father usually left long rambling messages, so long they were often cut off when he reached the voicemail limit, only for him to phone again and pick up where he left off.

His father often said he was able to have a much better conversation with his voicemail than with his son in person. Wang thought he was joking.

He needed to use the bathroom, but leaving his seat required an almost acrobatic skill to avoid waking the toddler and its mother, who was now also asleep. He clipped the toddler with his shoe while making the final vault to the narrow aisle beyond. The toddler yelped but didn't wake up.

The aisle was an obstacle course of bags and cases. It was then he saw the two men, big men with closely cropped hair, almost comically squeezed together in seats that looked way too small for them. And he saw the scar on the head of the one by the aisle, a long pink scar that stretched from beyond his hairline and down to just above his right eye. Wang quickly looked away and was shivering by the time he reached the bathroom, where he stood, leaning against the door, trying to calm himself. It was the way they'd looked at him, hostile and knowing. Yet they didn't look like police, not like the ones who'd detained him in Beijing.

He returned to his seat, avoiding eye contact with the men, while trying to convince himself he was being stupid and paranoid. He ordered some dried fish and a bottle of water from an attendant.

There was now a sprinkling of snow on the passing fields. Irrigation canals were frozen. The snow got thicker as they approached Harbin. The tall cooling towers of power stations and factories grew more numerous, belched huge white plumes of smoke and steam, welcoming Wang back home. At times the smog here could be worse than in Beijing.

But it was the cold that mostly put Wang off Harbin. He hated the cold. A digital thermometer at the front of the carriage showed the outside temperature at minus twenty-three degrees centigrade and falling.

As the train came to a standstill, Wang sat and waited, thinking he'd let the train clear first. He didn't reach immediately for his bag or coat in the rack above. When he looked back the two men had put on their own thick coats. The one with the scar was wearing an orange padded jacket and black ski hat. The other, a black woollen coat and a woollen hat with earflaps. They were waiting too.

Wang now moved quickly, snatching his things, and headed down the aisle. The men followed.

The platform was a crush of people, funnelled down a series of stairs and escalators to the main station concourse and exits below. The crowd swept Wang along, and he could hear the shouts and complaints from behind as his pursuers, big and ungainly, bulldozed their way after him.

When Wang reached the top of an escalator he abruptly changed course, taking the stairs that ran alongside. The men were carried by the human tide onto the escalator, and for a while moved parallel to Wang, watching him.

Halfway down Wang turned and began to climb back to the top. It was hard going, but there was more room on the stairs. The men tried to turn too, but were trapped on the narrow escalator. They yelled and pushed, but there was nowhere to go but down.

Back at the top, Wang waited. He figured his pursuers would expect him to use a different exit, so after ten minutes went back down the same way. There was no sign of them.

He crossed the station concourse to a long taxi line. He still couldn't see the men. So he raised his collar and headed to the front of the line, waving as he got closer, as if there was somebody there he knew. At the front he told an elderly couple that he was sorry, it was urgent, that he needed to get quickly to see his sick mother. The couple shrugged and let him take their taxi.

He told the driver to take him to his parents' place, in the centre, but then changed his mind, still not knowing what to say to them. He asked to be dropped at Saint Sophia Cathedral, a few blocks away from home. He walked aimlessly in the square beneath its huge onion dome and crosses, until he could no longer feel his fingers. Then he went inside to thaw. It was Russian Orthodox, dating from 1907, but was no longer a going concern, now being a museum.

Once some life had returned to his fingers, he decided he couldn't put off seeing his parents any longer. He left the cathedral and walked several blocks to the south, crossing a central walking street, picking his way through the stream of huddled figures, who moved slowly in the cold, their breath turning to clouds of steam.

He passed the city's old synagogue and through a rusting gateway that led to a small courtyard surrounded by low-rise apartment blocks. He paused in front of a five-storey red brick building, and looked up at the windows of his parents' place on the third floor. He saw a faint light. They must be at home. That was a good sign, but he was feeling so nervous that he almost retreated. Eventually he steeled himself and entered the dark doorway, climbing stairs so icy that he had to feel his way along the wall for support.

When he reached the door of the apartment he could hear what sounded like the television. He rang the doorbell and stood back. But nobody answered the door. Nobody moved the other side. He rang again. Still nothing. So he reached under the doormat feeling for the little pouch that his parents had stitched into the mat for a spare key. The key was there and he let himself in, bolting the door behind him.

He called out. There was no reply.

It was a small apartment, just three rooms: a bedroom, kitchen and a living room, where his father had blocked off a small area as a study. It had a homely feel about it. Shelves stacked with books. Pictures, landscapes mostly, but also old photos of the family together, the three of them in Tiananmen Square, in Harbin, on a visit to Shanghai. Mostly from before university, when Wang could be bothered to make the effort.

The kitchen light was on, and there was some sort of quiz show on the clunky old television in the corner, a bunch of kids shouting answers at a host with a permanent grin as wide as the big wheel he was spinning.

Wang sat down, and it was then he saw the bible on the floor beside the sofa, which he picked up and opened to find a written inscription to his mother on the inside cover, urging her to be strong, to keep the faith. Which surprised him. He always saw his mother as a strong person, and never knew she had any faith.

The apartment smelt of tobacco. Another odd thing. Neither of his parents smoked. He saw two cigarette butts ground into the wooden floor. There were two more in a half-filled coffee mug by his feet.

He walked over to his father's desk. There were papers spread on the desk, course notes, and lecture preparations for the Party School, that sort of stuff. One was entitled *Communist Ethics* and was blank apart from the title. Another was called *Returning Frugality to the Party*. That appeared to be a work in progress too. Beside it was a thick book by the Party leader. It was open at a chapter headed, "Towards a Law-Based Society". He thought about the Professor who had disappeared, The Girl In The Corner, the old holdout, and his own detention; he assumed something must have been lost in translation. Did his dad really believe all this stuff?

Then he saw a much bigger document on a shelf above the desk, roughly bound. He took it down and began to leaf through its thick wad of hand-written pages, his father's writing. He took it back to the sofa, where he lay down and began to read, quickly finding himself immersed in a harrowing story of cruelty and suffering, starvation and cannibalism. And death. Death everywhere on an unimaginable scale.

It took him a while to realise that what he was reading was not some grotesque piece of fiction, but a series of transcripts of interviews by his father with the survivors of a terrible catastrophe. And it was all set in his father's hometown, which would have been little more than a village when the events took place, between 1958 and 1960. It was an attempt by his father to construct a village history of those terrible years, though it wasn't a history Wang recognised. In school, the famine of that period had been largely glossed over, and if it was mentioned at all it was as a natural disaster, all the result of bad weather.

Yet what he was reading was not an accident of nature, but the direct result of a Party policy that herded people into communes and killed and tortured those who resisted. His father estimated that half his village had died, including many of his own relatives.

And in Wang's mind it led to all sorts of other questions. His father had been born ten years after the events he was describing, though Wang's grandparents would have lived through it. Why had his father set out to investigate those years? It wasn't clear when he had started his interviews and began this massive undertaking. Wang wondered whether that was the reason his parents had moved from the area so suddenly when he was a child, that perhaps his questions had hit a raw and powerful nerve.

Yet his father continued to serve the Party, even after all that he'd learned about his village. That made no sense either. With each turning page, the suffering was unrelenting. Yet he read on until he was close to finishing but could no longer keep his eyes open. He fell asleep on the sofa, his father's harrowing manuscript on his chest, thinking how little he really knew about either of his parents.

– 33 –

Ice City

Wang was woken by a noise outside the apartment door, something heavy and metallic dropped on the concrete floor. Then voices, angry but trying to keep the volume down, and in a dialect he didn't immediately understand.

Then he heard tapping, the door straining.

They were trying to force their way in.

He sat up on the sofa, his heart pounding. His father's manuscript fell to the living room floor, hitting it with a thud, but the sound was drowned out by the creaking of another door opening on the landing outside and a voice shouting, wanting to know what was going on. The men outside Wang's door said to take it easy, they were friends of the family.

Wang edged slowly to the door, silently opening the peephole, its tiny fish-eye giving him a wide view of the gloomy hallway outside. The first thing he saw was the back of a padded orange jacket, the man from the train, and to his left the other one, in the black woollen coat. The man from the neighbouring apartment was standing in his doorway yelling that friends don't break into apartments.

An elderly woman then appeared on the stairwell. She'd come up from an apartment below and immediately threatened to call the police. She had a smartphone in her hand, which she raised to photograph the intruders. The man in the orange jacket grabbed it from her hand and threw it hard to the concrete floor, where it smashed into several pieces.

But the woman was quickly in his face, yelling, a finger prodding the orange jacket.

"You think you can just walk in here and force your way into somebody's home?"

Which the man clearly did. He just sneered and pushed her aside. She fell to the floor beside the remains of her smartphone, and the two men walked past her and back down the stairs as if they didn't have a care in the world.

The man from the neighbouring apartment helped the woman to her feet. She'd grazed her arm on a sharp corner of the stairwell as she fell, but insisted she'd be all right, refusing his offer to take her to hospital.

"But we should call the police," she said.

"Suppose they are the police?" the man said, and the woman said he had a point.

Wang silently closed the peephole and sat back on the sofa.

He doubted they were cops. Otherwise why leave? Cops could do whatever they wanted. And the dialect they'd spoken to each other, he was sure that was Cantonese, from the south of China. Why would they follow him all the way to Harbin?

The one thing he did know for sure was that he needed to leave his parents' apartment, and quickly.

He glanced at his phone. It was six thirty in the morning and still pitch black outside. He gathered his things and replaced his father's manuscript on the shelf where he'd found it. Then he looked again through the papers on his father's desk, finding a sheet of headed paper for the Party School with no address, but a phone number.

From a table beside the sofa he picked up a leaflet with a child's drawing of a dragon on the front beneath the words "Donfeng Road Kindergarten Welcomes You". Inside were pictures of kids playing in the snow, kids drawing, kids singing. It was the place his mother worked and the leaflet seemed to have been produced for an open day. There was no phone number, but still Wang figured there was enough for him to find it.

He put it in his pocket with the Party School headed paper and, after checking that the hallway was clear, he left the apartment, replaced the key under the mat, and went slowly and silently down the stairs. He waited for a while just inside the main entrance of the block. He couldn't see clearly out of the compound, but figured he'd have to take a chance. He pulled his woollen hat low over his ears, raised his collar and adjusted his scarf to just beneath his eyes. Then he walked out of the gate and onto the dark street beside the old synagogue.

He had no real plan. It was too early to visit the kindergarten or to try phoning the Party School, and he was still not sure how he would approach either. So he walked towards the river, along a road lined with darkened low-rise buildings. The traffic was still light and he paused in doorways each time a car or bus passed, belching clouds of exhaust.

He then went down into a wide underpass, and as he walked he heard a strange tapping, like a misfiring engine or the frantic typing on a keyboard. It got louder as he walked. Then he heard the sound of running, though in fits and starts. He stopped, close to a sharp turn in the underpass and jumped as a hand gripped his shoulder.

"Hey, sorry to startle you," said a young man wearing a heavy grey coat over a jogging suit. "Are you coming to play?"

Wang followed the man around the corner, where the tapping was getting louder and faster. Dozens of people stood in circles, bats in hands, tapping small balls back and forth to each other, cheering as they kept the balls from hitting the ground.

"It's the best place to play right now," said the man. "Where you won't freeze to death. Come and have a game."

Wang said thanks, some other time, and continued through the underpass, exiting onto the broad bank of the frozen Songhua River, now a vast expanse of ice and snow. There was now some light in the sky, a cloudless morning, a dull blue above, and a rusty-coloured haze on the horizon. Smoke and steam from a power station on the distant far bank rose in a near vertical plume in the still and frigid morning air.

Wang walked along the bank, which was lined with makeshift ice rinks and slides. Two young boys were already on one slide, hurtling across the ice on plastic sledges, braving the bitter pre-dawn temperatures.

He was startled by a chain saw, wielded by a man in a coat so thick it made him look twice his size. He was carving big slabs of ice, pulled from the river, to be used to make the ice sculptures for which Harbin was famous.

Shortly after he'd moved here with his parents, when he was eleven, the river had become so contaminated that the water supply was shut down for days. There were rumours of an accident at a chemical plant. But back then not so many people were online, and nobody ever knew for sure what had happened. Wang reckoned that if it happened again today then everybody would know, or at least they'd think they knew.

Wang's fingers and toes were beginning to ache and turn numb from the cold when he found a small dumpling restaurant, a simple place of plastic tables and ugly strip lights. He took a seat at the back and ordered a dozen dumplings with pork and leek, which he smothered in vinegar and chilli.

Then he phoned the number he had for the Party School.

The phone rang five times before it was answered.

"Yes," a woman said.

"Is that the Party School?" Wang asked.

"Who is this?"

"I am looking for my friend. I believe he works there. A teacher. Mr Wang Lixian."

"We no longer have a Wang Lixian working here."

"Really?" said Wang, taken aback. "Are you sure?"

The woman said of course she was sure, and who is this?

And Wang said, "Just a friend", and hung up.

He then opened a navigation app on his phone and was pleased to find that Donfeng Road was close by. So he paid for the dumplings and left the restaurant, guided by the app.

The kindergarten was in an old turn-of-the-century building with chipped columns and a weathered brown facade. A plaque near the door said it was Heritage Architecture, built at the turn of the century by the Russians, when they were in control of Harbin.

He entered through a metal blue door close to where an old caretaker was pasting a notice to the wall. Wang said good morning and asked about his mother. The man continued with the poster,

269

which was for a student ice sculpture competition and showed a big bear carved from ice. Wang guessed the man was just hard of hearing, tapped his shoulder and repeated his question.

"She's my mother. I am trying to find her. I'm visiting from Beijing."

"Beijing?" said the caretaker. "Is it cold there too?"

"Not as cold as here. Nowhere is as cold as here," Wang said. "My mother?"

The caretaker shrugged, turning his face towards the door. In the light he looked as weathered as the building.

"They've all gone to the ice," he said. "Everyone's at the festival today."

Wang thanked him and left.

Harbin might be lacking in a whole lot of other ways, but they knew how to make the most of their snow and ice. The winter revolved around it.

Wang soon reached a park by the river, where he followed a path along a line of intricately carved ice sculptures of animals, musical instruments and wild mythical creatures.

He stopped at another made from packed snow, a boy sitting on the trunk of a sports car and working his smartphone. Wang thought that was pretty cool.

Nearby, visitors were posing for selfies at a grand piano carved from the ice, alongside a big ice chariot drawn by four galloping ice horses.

That's where he saw a group of children, kindergarten kids he guessed, though they were so heavily wrapped up they looked like they'd been pumped full of air. A teacher was carrying a little flag on which was written "Donfeng Road Kindergarten".

Wang introduced himself and the teacher said she was sorry but his mother hadn't been to work for at least two days now and she had no idea why. Perhaps she was sick. Wang said thanks and gave her his phone number, asking her to phone him if she heard anything more.

"Sure," said the teacher, looking anxious beneath a big fluffy blue bobble hat. She turned away quickly because her kids were now throwing snowballs at passers-by and rolling in the snow, taking advantage of the teacher being distracted.

Then somebody grabbed Wang from behind, gripping his left arm so tight he wondered if a dog had snapped its jaws around him, just above the elbow. He spun round and was looking into the eyes of the man with the orange padded coat. The cold had turned his scar a bright pink. With all the strength he could muster, Wang pulled his left arm away and pushed hard with his right. The man slipped and tumbled backwards, knocking over a cart of steaming toffee apples.

And Wang just ran. First up a series of steps made of ice, leading to the sculptured ramparts of a giant ice castle. He pushed to the front of a line of kids waiting at the top of an ice slide, the quickest way down. He turned to see the two men from the train, the men who'd tried to break into his parents' apartment, following him up, though struggling to keep their footing on the ice.

Wang slid back down to the bottom. The two men pushed through after him, but hesitated at the top, mothers glaring at them. They decided to take the steps back down; the one in orange slipped again and bounced down on his backside.

"Are you okay?" said three women at the bottom, waiting for their kids to come down the slide and stretching out hands to help him to his feet. He waved them away, saying of course he was fucking okay, but when he went to stand he slipped again, by which time his sidekick in black was by his side and doing the helping, which he found more acceptable than having the women help him up.

"How can anybody live in this fucking climate?" he said.

Wang entered a coffee shop to one side of the sculptures. It was a long narrow building packed mostly with groups thawing out, and he took a seat on a bench among older students. But the two men had seen him and followed him in, needing some thawing themselves, sitting a few benches away, near the door, removing their hats and gloves.

As the students got up to leave, Wang moved with them, and as they passed the bench where the men were sitting, Wang pushed one of the students, who fell on the man in the black coat, who swore and tried to push him off. At the same time Wang made a lunge for their gloves and hats, grabbing them and racing to the door, throwing them in a garbage bin just outside.

He figured that as southerners they'd be struggling with the cold anyway. Without gloves and hats they wouldn't last too long in the open.

At least that's what he hoped.

They followed him out, and after passing a giant ice mosque, a ship and a towering image of the Buddha made of packed snow, Wang joined a tour group, pushing his way to the middle of them, hoping he'd be concealed in the crowd.

The tour guide was explaining how they used only artificial snow for sculpting because it was firmer and whiter. Natural snow is dirtier, she said.

"Is that because of the pollution?" one person asked.

The tour guide ignored the question and said it was time to move on, that she wanted to show them an incredible maze, and to follow her because she didn't want them to get lost.

Wang moved with them into the maze, its walls made of waist-high blocks of ice, and by following the group he was soon in the middle and beside another big sculpture, this one a kind of ship-like chariot topped by a warrior with six arms wielding spears and swords.

His relief was short-lived. The two men had seen him and now they were trying to find a way through the maze. They looked so cold, with hands in their pockets, red faces sticking out of flimsy hoods, that Wang reckoned it might not be long before they became another sculpture.

They were quickly frustrated by the maze and began to climb over its ice walls, making it over one before the man in orange slipped again, and hit his head on the sharp edge of the ice. Blood was seeping down his face and the one in black again lifted him to his feet.

Then another group of children entered the maze. They looked like they'd done it before, quickly finding a route to the centre. The two men followed them in.

Wang needed to get out fast, but the tour group that he'd hoped would save him were now an obstacle, as the guide invited them to see if they could find their own way back out, and they didn't seem to have a clue.

The men now reached the centre, blood splattered down the orange coat of the one in front. So Wang entered a tunnel beneath the big ship-like chariot at the centre of the maze. He then followed children up yet more ice steps and onto its deck, beneath the swinging arms of the warrior.

More ice steps led to another slide, which twisted back down through the body of the chariot. Wang followed more children to the top, where he waited, doubting the men would follow. He looked over the edge, but couldn't see them, then looked back down the stairs to find himself face to face with the man in the black coat, the blood-spattered orange coat not far behind.

The man lunged at Wang, who slipped, but was quickly back on his feet. This time it was his turn to push the kids out of the way, throwing himself onto the slide and hurtling down so fast through the chariot that he almost collided with a wall where the slide made a sharp turn near the bottom before dumping him out on the snow.

The two men had now reached the top of the slide, where they were hesitating.

"Best take the steps," said the one in black, thinking it would be a tight squeeze for them.

"That's just what I'm going to do. You take the slide," said the one in orange, holding a tissue over his gashed forehead. He shoved the other one so hard that he tumbled backwards onto the ice, and shot headfirst down the slide, hitting the bend near the bottom with such force that the whole sculpture shook.

It vibrated so strongly that the warrior's arm cracked where its hand was holding a long ice spear, which plunged to the ground impaling the man in black as he emerged at the bottom of the slide.

The man writhed and screamed, pinned to the ground, the ice spear clean through his chest. Blood oozed around his body onto the snow. By the time he stopped twitching he was lying in a big red puddle.

Children gasped. Some of them screamed. The tour group turned back to see what had happened and several took photographs or posed for selfies in front of the now motionless body. Then they went back to the coffee shop, which had a Wi-Fi connection, meaning they could more quickly upload the photos to the internet.

– 34 –

Tigers

Wang didn't see the one in the black coat get speared by the ice warrior. He was too focused on getting away as fast as his legs would carry him through growing crowds of children and along a path with about as much grip as an ice rink.

But he figured that at least he could keep his balance better than the duo chasing him. As he got to the exit from the park he was confident he'd lost them. What he hadn't anticipated was their having local help. He was grabbed from behind as he left the main gate and for the second time in just over a week he found himself sandwiched in the back of a car with a hood over his head.

When they removed the hood the sudden light was so intense he squeezed his eyes closed and looked down. A hand pulled his head back up, and his sight slowly adjusted to what at first looked like a kind of blob with two big panda eyes on top.

The blob became a face, and the panda eyes above it were part of a white fur hat it was wearing with two floppy white earflaps. The panda eyes were a good deal easier to look at than the real ones, narrow and cold, staring at Wang from the passenger seat. There was a fresh gash above one eye, just below the other pink scar, and the man was dabbing it with a cloth, held between the forefinger and thumb of a pair of big white mittens.

There were bloodstains down the man's orange coat.

"You like the gloves, the hat?" the man said. "Got them at the festival, because you know what? I seem to have lost the others."

Then he leaned over and cuffed Wang so hard around the head that his ears rang. He ducked to try and avoid a second blow, which caught the top his head. The man to his left pushed him back upright and into the path of a third punch, straight in the face this time.

The man in the panda hat then sat back in his seat.

The car was a medium-sized saloon, its windows tinted. The men beside Wang were wearing near identical padded black jackets and dark woollen hats, pulled low over their ears. The driver was an older man in a Russian-style fur hat and red jacket. He was smoking. For a while none of them spoke.

They were driving across a long bridge over the frozen Songhua River, leaving the city, Wang guessed, because there was less activity on the ice below, just a trail of people crossing, single file, like tiny black ants.

The road itself was busy, and very icy. The driver seemed experienced with the conditions, driving slowly amid the white clouds gushing from exhausts and engines, careful with the brakes.

"I think you have something that doesn't belong to you," the man in orange said, turning again to Wang.

Wang said he didn't understand.

"Well, let's start with this," the man said, removing from his pocket a folded piece of paper, a printout from the internet, stained with the man's blood, and which he opened to show a picture of a stick alien.

"Looks familiar?"

"I've already told you," Wang said. "That was just a bit of fun. Just an online thing. It's not real. I've never been to a protest in my life."

The man cuffed Wang again.

"You've told me nothing. I really don't give a shit how many protests you've been to. And do I look like I believe in aliens?"

Which told Wang what he already suspected, that he was dealing with something different, somebody different from the people who had detained him in Beijing.

"Let's try this one shall we?" said the man in the orange coat.

And he opened another piece of paper, a screen shot, the cover page that Wang had shared online from one of the documents he'd

275

downloaded from the Shanghai company. It was from the document called *Mr Fang*, the summary of names and brief biographies under the title "Applicants for SK documents".

"You posted it alongside your friend, the alien," the man said.

"I don't know what it is. I swear. I didn't even read it," Wang said. "It was a thing I downloaded from some Shanghai company. We cracked their website. I was trying to get some security business from them, wanted to show their cyber defences were vulnerable."

"Cyber defences? What the fuck are you talking about?" said the man, totally lost by the geek-speak of this annoying, thieving kid trying to sound clever.

Wang was pleading now, but might as well be speaking to the panda on the man's head.

"Look. It's simple," the man said. "You have information that doesn't belong to you. My employer would like to know where you got it, and what you've done with it. And he'd like it back."

Wang asked him if he worked for Shanghai TT Logistics, and the man cuffed him again. Wang rolled sideways onto one of the black-jackets beside him who pushed him back up, repositioning him like a bowling pin ready for the next strike.

"I don't have it, and I really have no idea what it is," Wang said, repeating that he'd never read it. He was about to say the downloaded document was on his laptop, which had been taken in Beijing by the police, but figured that might just make things worse.

"You little fucker," said the man who wasn't police, and wasn't from Shanghai TT Logistics, but was getting really mad. "You really don't understand what you're dealing with here, do you? What sort of trouble you're in."

And Wang really wished he did understand, and that someone would tell him just that, what he was dealing with.

"Have you got my parents?" he said.

The man looked at him like that wasn't a bad idea. Then he said, "We haven't touched your parents. Not yet. The question you need to consider carefully, very carefully, is what we might do with you."

They were on the far bank of the river now, driving away from the city along a wide road lined with fields of thick snow. A drunk was being helped across the road ahead, but not making great progress.

The driver blasted his horn, making no attempt to slow down. The helper slung the drunk over a shoulder and lurched for the sidewalk, where they both fell in the snow.

Which the man in orange thought was pretty funny.

They entered a new district of half-built houses, hoardings along the road showing pictures of what the area was supposed to look like when it was finished. If it was ever finished. It looked like a Harbin version of Versailles. There was a picture of a butler serving drinks in an ornate room full of columns and hung with classic old paintings. Another showed ballet dancers.

Then they turned right, beside a sign for the Siberian Tiger Park, under which were several larger-than-life models of snarling tigers. "The world's biggest collection of Siberian tigers welcomes you", said another sign.

"Well, I guess you've been here before," the man in orange said. "You're from Harbin."

Wang said yes, as a kid, but he was barely audible, terrified now and wondering where this was all going.

"I think it's cool," said the man, telling Wang that the other men in the car were good friends of the owner. "More than 600 hungry Siberian tigers, the world's biggest collection of the world's largest and nastiest species of tiger. My friends here say it's just like Jurassic Park. Very dangerous. You know what I'm saying?"

They drove slowly through a busy car park, groups climbing from buses to go and see the tigers. Some were posing in the open jaw of a giant model of a tiger's head, holding the fangs.

They stopped close to the ticket office, a line waiting to buy tickets and maybe buy some food for the tigers. The tiger menu board was next to the office – a list of animals and the price visitors could pay for watching them thrown live to the tigers.

Price for Live Animals of Siberian Tiger Park

Chicken	*120 Yuan*
Guinea Fowl	*120 Yuan*
Pheasant	*150 Yuan*
Sheep	*1500 Yuan*
Cow	*2000 Yuan*

"Don't you just love this place?" said the man in the orange jacket, adjusting his panda hat.

"Let's take a walk."

*

By late morning the park was getting busy. One tour group lingered at the ticket office, taking its time, looking at the menu for a while before deciding they'd go for a cow, because that would be pretty cool, watching it get eaten alive by the tigers.

Then they boarded a small bus with grills across its windows, to go inside the enclosures with the tigers, to take a closer look.

The bus entered the park via a series of heavy electric fences. They went through one gate, waited, and only after that gate had closed did the second one slide open. It was the same process as the bus passed from one icy enclosure to another, each surrounded by a thirty-foot-high fence.

There was also a long viewing platform that snaked through the park, and from which visitors could pay to dangle live chickens for the tigers, teasing them, driving them into a hungry rage. But the bus gave the best view. Up close and personal with the tigers.

Mostly, though, the tigers lazed around in the snow looking bored, picking fights with each other from time to time, each roar raising a cheer from visitors on the walkways. The bus stopped when it came across a bigger group of tigers, the tour group crowding at the windows with phones raised and asking when the cow was going to come to the party.

The driver said it was on its way. The tigers rose to their feet and circled the bus. Others ran over to join them.

Then a small truck entered the enclosure, about the size and shape of a horsebox. It paused near the tigers, which were now getting excited, snarling at each other, clawing at the side of the truck, knowing it meant fresh food.

On their bus, the tour group pressed closer to the window, cameras at the ready.

The truck was a dump truck with a flap at the back, and slowly its rear platform began to tip backwards until the live food came tumbling out.

There were screams and gasps on the bus.

"Oh my God, it's a person."

"Do something. Do something," others shouted at the driver, who just froze at the steering wheel.

Mostly the tour group just carried on taking videos and photographs.

The person dumped from the truck wriggled and tried to kick, but he was bound and gagged. The tigers seemed to hesitate at first, seeing something that wasn't usually on the menu. Maybe the panda eyes staring at them from the man's hat put them off. Or the bright orange jacket, which wasn't like any cow they'd eaten before. But they didn't hesitate for long, deciding this was a real treat. One sunk its teeth into the man's neck, others tearing at his legs and arms. And soon a shark-like feeding frenzy exploded before the bus.

The driver tried belatedly to force the tigers away with his bus, sounding his horn.

But the tigers weren't in the mood to let anything spoil their lunch, and there was soon little left but a bloodied and shredded orange jacket. The tigers dispersed to different corners of the park where they scrapped over body parts.

While the tour group went online to upload their images.

*

By the time Wang regained consciousness he was in the back of another car, a bigger one this time, an SUV, squeezed between two more men in thick jackets and ski hats.

Everything had happened so quickly. He recalled being led from the other car, the guy in orange gripping his arm and saying they were going to meet some hungry tigers. Then another group had confronted the man in the orange jacket. The last thing Wang remembered was shouting, a scuffle, and a foul-smelling cloth over his mouth. Then nothing.

There was a foreigner in the passenger seat of this, his latest car, and he was speaking to another beside Wang.

"What a fucking place, man. This has nothing to do with conservation. Nothing. These things would never survive in the wild.

Tigers don't hunt in packs. They must be breeding them for their body parts."

And the one beside Wang said yeah, too right, and told the one in the passenger seat there was other weird stuff.

"Chuck man, did you see the ligers? They were breeding tigers with lions? Can you believe that?"

Then the one called Chuck saw that Wang had woken up.

"Oh, Wang. Welcome back. Pretty wild place, eh?"

"What happened to that other guy, in the orange," Wang said, sounding confused. And Drayton said he'd gone to take a closer look at some of the conservation work, improving the tigers' diet.

"And who are you?" said Wang.

"Well," said Drayton, "I'm the idiot with the computer security problem. Remember? Shanghai TT Logistics. I think you wanted to help me out. But before you do that, I have one thing I'd like to know. Tell me a bit more about this guy. He's sure been busy."

He was holding up his iPhone with a picture of the stick alien.

Wang began to cry.

– 35 –

Baccarat

Drayton dropped the kid called Wang back in Harbin, giving him US$100 for his security consultancy. He told him that hacking a website was not the best way to win business and to keep away from Shanghai TT Logistics because its directors were not a very forgiving bunch.

Wang had spent most of his time with Drayton just whimpering in the back of the car. He'd clearly had a tough few days and was bewildered and frightened, not really getting all the fuss his alien was causing. He was just a kid with a vivid imagination and some dubious computer skills who spent too much time online. At least that's the way Drayton saw it.

Whether that was what the Bubble Room would want to hear was another thing, but he'd deal with that when he had to.

He then headed to the airport for a flight back to Shanghai.

He was worried about Morgan, thinking that maybe the Englishman already had been fed to some hungry tigers. Maybe worse. He'd been trying to reach him but he never picked up. He tried again, and this time Morgan's phone didn't even ring, just went to voicemail. Drayton didn't leave a message.

When he reached Harbin airport his phone rang. It was a voice from the past.

"Hey Chuck, Luis here. Luis Acevedo. How you doing?"

"I'm doing good, Luis. Been a long time. How's Macau? Still chasing the bad guys?"

"It's still keeping me busy," Acevedo said. "Which is why I'm calling."

"Tell me."

"We fished a body from the Pearl River, badly cut up, hard to identify. There was a bag in the water too, with documents and a passport belonging to a Brit called Anthony Morgan, a finance guy by the looks of what was there. You know him?"

"Maybe," Drayton said. "Should I?"

"Well, in the bag with his other stuff there was a business card of one Chuck Drayton of a company called Shanghai TT Logistics. I wondered if that was the same Drayton that I used to know, the one that worked for the US Government."

Drayton was silent for a moment, then he said, "It's a long story, Luis. I'll be on the next flight down."

*

Drayton met Acevedo in a noodle restaurant that was a small island in the middle of the vast gaming floor of the biggest casino in the world. The first thing they talked about was Baccarat, a card game, and the most popular in Macau by far.

"It makes no sense, Luis," Drayton said. "What's the point?"

"Chuck, it doesn't have to make sense."

"There's no skill involved, absolutely none."

"It's not about skill. It's about luck."

"That's my point, Luis, it's a game of pure chance. Like the toss of a coin."

"Luck, fortune, that's what matters here. That's what brings more than one and a half million Chinese to these tables every month, and you know what?"

"What?"

"Most of the near US$40 billion a year they blow here goes on the game you say makes no sense."

They were drinking the local Macau beer. It was early evening and the place was quiet.

They'd chosen a secluded table by a glass wall covered in dragons and giving them a grandstand view of rows of curved Baccarat tables, mostly empty apart from bored-looking dealers. Just one was busy, standing room only, the crowd hanging on every turn of a card. Acevedo said somebody on that table must have won big, because winning attracted a crowd that wanted to share the winner's good fortune.

Acevedo understood gaming, since he'd worked around the casinos for more than thirty years. He still had the title of Special Investigator in the Public Security Police of Macau, though he told Drayton that nowadays he did little investigating and nothing he'd describe as special.

Acevedo had once been the go-to man on the Triads, China's organised crime syndicates, and had the scars to prove it, shot in the stomach and almost killed during Triad wars that gripped Macau in the mid-1990s, fighting for control of the casinos. He'd been attacked by gangsters with meat cleavers a couple of years before that, nearly losing an arm.

Acevedo was almost twenty years older than Drayton, and the American had been enthralled by those stories when the two men had first met in the late 1990s at a conference in Washington DC on organised crime. Drayton had been a State Department rookie back then, still learning the ropes.

They'd worked together a few years later in Lyon, France, when both had been on assignment to Interpol, an organisation supposed to track down international crooks, but mostly getting in the way. At least that's how Drayton had seen it.

By then Acevedo had been pretty much side-lined back in Macau. He was Portuguese and when the place was handed back by Portugal to China in 1999 he was pushed to one side along with many other colonial-era officers. But he didn't see much future in near-bankrupt Portugal. So he took his chances and stayed, consigned to a desk job in the police force of China's new Special Administrative Region of Macau.

Drayton looked at his old friend and could feel his frustration. There was much that hadn't changed about him. He still wore an old black bomber jacket over blue polo shirt and blue jeans. His hair was grey now, but still slicked back behind his ears, and there was still that indelible tan Drayton had always envied.

Lines were now spreading across his face like cracks in drying mud.

Acevedo said it had been coincidence that he'd been the one who took the call the day the body washed up on the coast of Taipa Island, not far from the airport.

"Who found him?" Drayton said.

"Old woman, exercising at dawn. Morgan's bag was found near a place called Fisherman's Wharf."

"How long had the body been in the water?"

"One, two days at most. It was badly cut, like a Triad attack, except when the Triads do that, when they chop you, it's usually to mutilate, to maim. As a warning. They usually leave you alive, if only just."

A cheer went up at the crowded Baccarat table, where more people were jostling for a place. The good fortune seemed to be lasting. Other tables were filling up, and Drayton watched how the players handled their chips, some nervously rotating them or tapping them on the table, pushing them gently into position. Others banging them down with a theatrical grunt.

"Boy, they take that stuff seriously," Drayton said. "Like their life depends on every turn of the card."

"Sometimes it does," said Acevedo.

Then Drayton said, "The body, Luis, were there any identifying marks?"

"Well, here's the thing, Chuck. They pulled me off the case before I got to see it, then sent the body to the mainland. The initial report went with the body."

They stopped talking as their food arrived: a double-cooked pork rib soup with seaweed and sea coconut for Drayton, because he liked the sound of that, and shrimp and noodles for Acevedo, who'd eaten there before.

"Why would they do that?" Drayton asked. "Pull you off the case like that."

"I'm guessing it's pretty sensitive. And was rather hoping you might be able to help there, Chuck. You knew the guy."

Drayton took a piece of paper from his pocket with a photograph on it.

"You know this guy, Luis?"

Acevedo sat back, drank some beer and started to laugh, a laugh of weary recognition.

"Sure. Fang Sau Kei. That's Three Finger Fang."

"Three Finger Fang?"

"He was a leader of one of the most powerful Triads here in the mid-90s, which is when he lost the little finger of his left hand, during the gang wars. Then after the handover he reinvented himself, became a big power broker in southern China. Very close to the Party leadership there."

"That's a pretty big career move," Drayton said.

"Not really. Don't forget the Triads liked to think of themselves as patriots. They often had strong links across the border, with the Party. We always suspected Fang had protection over there, and after the handover he became untouchable. This guy's nasty, Chuck. In his day he was the most violent of the violent, and I don't suppose he's a completely reformed character. How come he's on your radar?"

"Let's take a walk," Drayton said, and they headed out of the restaurant and across the gaming floor, weaving around the tables and slot machines designed, as Drayton saw it, to extract every last cent from you. Acevedo told him there were 1,000 gambling tables and 3,500 slot machines in that one casino alone.

"A British finance guy, probably dead, and a Chinese Triad. What's the link, Chuck?"

But Drayton ignored the question and asked whether Three Finger Fang was still doing business in Macau.

"Look around you, Chuck. At last count we had thirty-five casinos in the thirty-five square miles that's Macau. Nothing else really matters in this place, but the real action is not here, on the floors, it's in the VIP rooms, the private rooms, which you don't see and to which you'll need a special invite. That's where the high rollers go. Up there they gamble millions."

"Who are the high rollers?"

"The big gamblers. Party officials, the heads of state-owned companies. Which is where Three Finger Fang comes in. He runs one of the biggest junkets."

"Junkets?"

"Yeah. Think of them as travel agents with a nasty streak. They organise things for the high rollers. They're also informal bankers, providing credit here in Macau and collecting the debts back home in the mainland."

Drayton said he didn't see why you'd need to use a junket, and Acevedo said that since gambling is illegal in mainland China there's no legal way of recovering gambling debts.

"And there's another thing," Acevedo said. "You know how much money a Chinese person is legally allowed to take out of China each year?"

"Must be a lot, looking at the way they spend."

"It's US$50,000. Half a *trillion* dollars a year flows out of China illegally. And it's speeding up, with a good chunk of that through Macau and Hong Kong. Let me give you an example, Chuck. You must have noticed all the jewellery shops here?"

"Can't miss them," Drayton said.

"Officially Macau sells US$250 million of luxury watches alone each year."

"That's a lot of watches."

"Not necessarily."

Acevedo told him it was just another money laundering scam.

"I go into a jeweller and I buy, say, a US$75,000 Bernard Dupuis Aquamarine."

"That's a watch?"

"That's a very nice watch."

"I put it on my Chinese credit card, which is accepted here. Then immediately pawn it to the same jeweller for US$70,000 cash."

"The five k being the commission?"

"Yeah. The Bernard Dupuis never even leaves the display cabinet."

"Nice. But why not just bring it all in a suitcase across the border?" said Drayton.

"Oh, they do that too, but can be risky. There are lots of other tricks. The really big players can use shell companies, in Hong Kong say, and issue fake invoices for non-existent imports to China. But that way you miss out on the Baccarat."

"So there are lots of ways of shifting money from China. What are you trying to tell me?" Drayton asked.

"I'm saying first that the money flows have jumped sharply as the Chinese economy has wobbled and the Party's cracked down on corruption. I'm also saying that some of the big players, like Three Finger Fang, couldn't do what they do without the help of Western bankers. Now tell me about Mr Morgan."

– 36 –

Fisherman's Wharf

They left the gaming floor and walked along a broad bright passageway lined with luxury shops, and into the heart of Venice, or at least Macau's copy of it.

They paused on a bridge over a canal as a gondola passed below, navigated by a stout Chinese gondolier in a striped T-shirt and straw boater, while wisps of white cloud moved slowly across an impossibly blue sky projected on the ceiling above. Drayton couldn't recall the last time he saw a sky like that in China.

"As knock-offs go, it's pretty impressive," he said.

"Some say it's better than the original," Acevedo said. "The sun shines twenty-four hours a day, it never rains, and there are no pigeons."

"Too bad. I like pigeons."

Opera music was playing gently in the background too.

"Okay, I will level with you," Drayton said. "You guessed right. The English guy was advising Fang on his overseas investments, but not just his. Fang represents a syndicate, top Party officials mostly. They've been buying real estate in the US, and are looking for more."

Then he told the Macau investigator about the St Kitts passport scam, and Acevedo said, "Now I see your interest. And the Englishman, did they have some sort of falling out?"

"Hard to say," Drayton said. "It's a long story, but some of Morgan's documents about Fang's syndicate got posted online."

"That's not good," Acevedo said. "He's very private, and not the forgiving type."

"I know," said Drayton. "I've met some of his associates."

"There's something else you should know," Acevedo said. "The heat is really on these guys, which probably explains why they want to get so much cash out of the country, hoover up overseas assets."

"How's that?"

"A whole bunch of officials in the south have been targeted in the Party's corruption crackdown. But this is about more than corruption. It's bigger than that. They're on the wrong side of a vicious power struggle."

Acevedo said officials in the south had always done their own thing.

"There's a Chinese saying, 'The mountains are high, the emperor is far away'. But not anymore. A lot of them have been swept up in the crackdown."

He asked Drayton whether he'd heard the coup rumours in Beijing, and Drayton said yes, but the guys at the embassy there didn't really take it seriously, saying it was just a piece of internet hysteria.

Acevedo said security guys he talked to in Macau and Hong Kong really believed that something was going on.

"They say the anti-corruption guy, the one they said died after a short illness, was shot, at a concert of all places."

Which got Drayton thinking.

"What concert was that?" he said, and Acevedo said he didn't know, some concert at the big cultural centre in Beijing. Then he asked Drayton if he was okay, because the American seemed distracted.

"But who really knows what's true or false?" Acevedo said. "Welcome to the Matrix."

Another gondola passed below, the gondolier singing what sounded to Drayton like an ice cream commercial. His passengers were busy taking selfies, living their Venetian moment.

Drayton said he should really go, since he could still get a late flight from Hong Kong back to Shanghai.

"Your sources, they really think the anti-graft guy was shot?" he said.

"That's what they say. But, hey, who really knows what's going on in this place?"

And Acevedo said there was one more thing.

"Your Englishman, he was last seen at a Thai restaurant at Fisherman's Wharf, close to where his bag was fished from the water. He was pretty groggy, according to a server there. She helped him to his feet when he fell off a bench. And he left his jacket, on the floor."

Acevedo then gave Drayton an envelope.

"His iPhone and a playing card. They were inside Morgan's jacket pocket. There were several missed calls from you, and messages and calls with Chinese numbers, now unobtainable, though I'm sure your experts can dig further."

Drayton went to open the envelope, and Acevedo said no, not here, the casinos have eyes.

"And the card?" Drayton said.

It's an ace of spades," Acevedo said, "with the words 'Fisherman's Wharf' written in very small letters above the ace, together with the name of the Thai place and a funny little drawing."

"A drawing?"

"Yeah. Strange. A stick alien."

This time Drayton smiled, shaking his head.

"A stick alien?"

"That's right. You know, matchstick man with big head, big sloping eyes. Classic alien. You know, little spaceman from another planet."

"I know. I'm familiar with them."

"So maybe the aliens got him," Acevedo said. "We may never know. Maybe it's some sort of signature. Perhaps this guy just liked aliens. Who knows?"

"Or a warning," Drayton said.

They walked along a walkway and through a tunnel of swirling changing lights that led to another casino, the entrance marked by a big snarling golden dragon coiled around a silver ball.

"So how come you have these," Drayton said, "seeing you were pulled off the case?"

"I was on the case for one whole morning."

"And you never told the new investigators from the mainland about this?"

"They never asked," Acevedo said. "That's the shuttle bus that will take you to Fisherman's Wharf, if that's what you're thinking."

And Drayton said he did have a sudden craving for some Thai food, thanked Acevedo, and asked him to be in touch if he learned anything more about the identity of the body.

"Keep me honest," he said. Then he headed for the bus.

"Oh, Chuck," Acevedo called after him, "the server, her name's Angelika Rosales. From the Philippines."

The bus was half full. The hardcore casino-hoppers were only beginning to get into their stride, though the stories of the night so far, the ups and downs, wins and mostly losses were all over their faces.

Two men with cropped hair and leather jackets got on the bus and sat near the back. Drayton, who was sitting near the front, watched them in the driver's rear-view mirror, as they toyed with their smartphones, heads down, saying nothing. To him, they didn't look like winners or losers, or gamblers at all for that matter.

The bus crossed the low bridge linking Taipa with the Macau peninsula, ferries moving below, picking up pace as they left, the waterfront casinos a blaze of colourful neon. The bus pulled up, its first casino stop, and Drayton made sure he was first off, well ahead of the buzz-cuts.

He quickly entered the lobby, and into a coffee shop, taking a seat in a far corner, away from the door and out of view of the lobby. He waited there for ten minutes before abandoning his coffee half drunk, leaving the building from a rear entrance, and heading across a busy road to Fisherman's Wharf.

Then he was in Rome, confronted by a big floodlit copy of the crumbling colosseum. A bored-looking security guard was slumped against a tall pillar, which was topped with the figure of a prancing horse. He was struggling to keep his eyes open. Three young children startled the guard as they ran, shouting, from one of colosseum's arches, disappearing into another.

There was nobody else to be seen. Fisherman's Wharf boasted dozens of upmarket shops, restaurants and bars, sitting in copycat architecture from across the world. But even for a Monday, close to nine in the evening, it was unusually dark and deathly quiet.

Drayton walked to the waterfront, pulling his coat closer, his collar higher, to protect against a cold breeze from the bay. The long low bridge which he had crossed just half an hour earlier, brightly lit, spanned across the water in front of him. A ferry manoeuvred into a terminal to his left.

The waterfront was lined with houses built in old European style.

A few minutes later he reached the Thai restaurant, more than a dozen outdoor tables dominated by two big television screens. There was a small stage, presumably for a band, but not tonight, with only one table taken by a young couple, huddled together for warmth, and looking like they regretted their decision to eat there.

The only thing obviously Thai about it were two life-sized wooden carved figures in traditional dress, hands clasped together in welcome, and standing either side of the main door.

Drayton took a seat overlooking the water and ordered a beer from a tall server in long silk dress and a woollen jacket, her dark hair pinned up. She brought back an ice bucket containing two bottles of Thai Singha beer and told him it was two for one tonight. She opened one and went back inside.

The quiet was broken by the clatter of a helicopter taking off from the roof of the ferry terminal. The VIP route from Hong Kong to Macau, more time on the tables, and a little more discreet.

Drayton finished his first Singha, and gestured to the server to open the next.

"You're Thai?" he asked her, with what he hoped was his broadest of reassuring smiles.

"Philippines," she said.

"So you must be Angelika?"

That startled her, and she looked away, fumbling with the bottle opener, spilling beer as the top finally popped off, retreating to the restaurant without a word.

A few moments later, a young Chinese man came to the table, and introduced himself as the duty manager.

"You were asking about Angelika Rosales?" he said brusquely.

"Yes, I think that was her name. A really great server. I met her last time I was in Macau. I think it was here."

"Not here," said the duty manager. "We've never employed anybody by that name," telling Drayton that the restaurant would be closing soon.

"Must be my mistake then," said Drayton apologetically, paying for the drinks.

He left the table and started to retrace his footsteps along the largely deserted waterfront. He crossed over a small bridge and followed a dark path under an awning covering what on a busier night would have been an outside drinking area for several bars.

He turned another corner, heading inland on a wider tree-lined path towards the colosseum. It was then he heard the footsteps. He stopped and pulled out his phone, as if to make a call, turning to look behind him. He saw nothing, and the footsteps stopped.

He started walking again, phone to his ear for effect, to look like he was distracted by a non-existent conversation, but more aware than ever. The footsteps resumed. He turned another corner, and into a doorway, putting the phone back in his pocket.

A tall figure turned the corner.

"Hello Angelika," he said.

The server was startled and retreated a few paces.

"How did you know?" she asked.

"When your boss came over, a charming man by the way, telling me you don't exist, and asking me to go away, he referred to you by your full name. I never did that."

She looked away.

"And anyway," Drayton said, "it's on your name-tag."

She instinctively lifted her hand to her shoulder and ran her fingers over the badge on the lapel of her jacket.

"Are you a policeman?" she asked.

"Sort of," he replied. "I am a friend of Inspector Acevedo, the man you handed the jacket to."

She told him she was sorry about what happened.

"You wanted to talk to me? That's why you followed me here."

"I have to meet customers by the colosseum, show them the way," she replied with no great conviction. "The Inspector, your friend, he said he'd be back in touch."

"The case is closed. The man drowned."

They stood in silence for a moment.

"There was more," she said, so quietly Drayton had to ask her to repeat it.

"Tell me, Angelika. Did you see him fall in the water? You said he was drowsy."

"He didn't fall in the water."

She was sobbing now, wiping her eyes with the long sleeve of her dress.

"When I found the jacket, just after he left, I walked along the waterfront trying to catch him, but couldn't see him anywhere. Then I saw a group of men. Big men. Looked like the men that stand in the doors of the clubs and bars here, throwing people out. Mostly wearing jeans and dark jackets. There were some in uniform too. They were looking in the water. But not just the water, looking everywhere."

"They didn't see you?"

"I'm sure. I hid amid the trees down there."

"You didn't tell the Inspector?"

"I was afraid. The boss was furious that I'd given him the jacket."

That's when Drayton noticed the fading bruises on the left side of her face, disguised, but not completely, by make-up.

"The boss did that?"

"Mister, please understand, none of us, the Thai and Filipino servers, have proper paperwork. I need that job, not for me, for my family."

"Don't worry," he said, moving closer and touching her arm. "I am not the immigration police."

She looked nervously down the dark street at the sound of muffled laughter from inside one of the distant bars.

She said a lot of people had come to the restaurant asking questions.

"The boss told me never to talk about it again."

Drayton told her she was brave, that he was grateful and that she should get back to the restaurant before the boss got suspicious.

She nodded.

"What about those customers you are supposed to be meeting?"

"They never turned up," she shrugged.

"One more thing," he said, "do as your boss asks, and please don't mention any of this to anybody else."

He waited and watched as she walked back down the dark street lined with mock-European buildings until she turned onto the waterfront. Then he left, heading for the ferry terminal.

– 37 –

Macau Rubdown

Chuck Drayton bought a ticket, first class, for a ferry direct from Macau to Hong Kong airport, from where he planned to take the first available flight back to Shanghai. He'd received encrypted messages about a breakthrough at The Facility.

There was a ferry leaving in fifteen minutes, but the woman behind the counter said he was too late for that, even without checked bags. Her look told him not to even think about arguing. Indifferent, robotic. Like the croupiers in the casino. Maybe that's what you became when you were dealing with psychotic gamblers day-in, day-out.

That gave him an hour and a half to kill.

The dreary ferry terminal was spread over three floors. At the bottom, the pick-up and drop-off area, from which fleets of buses shuttled between the main hotels and casinos, the punters guided by girls with tight dresses and plastic smiles. The sales counters and check-in area were on the floor above, and there was a top floor of unappetising-looking restaurants and shops. All built around a central atrium linked by stairs and escalators.

Drayton headed up an escalator to a small coffee shop and ordered a latte. He'd just taken a seat when his phone buzzed with a short message that said, "Casa do Prazer. Don't leave Macau without visiting." It was from a local number he didn't recognise, and he immediately deleted it, thinking it was a fucking imposition, spam like that, but not entirely sure where they'd got his number.

Then another one: "Really. You should visit before leaving."

Which got him thinking.

He went back to the coffee shop counter and asked the women who'd served him the latte about the Casa do Prazer and how he could find it. She ignored him at first, and then shot him a look that made the ferry girl seem friendly.

"I'm sure *you'll* find it," she said, like it wasn't really a question she cared to answer.

"I don't think so," he said. "Is it nearby?"

"It's on Rue Francisco Fernandes," she said. "Follow the harbour, then it's on your right."

He asked if it was far from Fisherman's Wharf, whether somebody could walk to it from there, somebody who was unsteady on their feet.

And she said sure, if that's their thing.

He went back to his seat, which was when he spotted the two men from the bus, sitting in the middle of a cluster of seats at the bottom of the escalator and doing a bad imitation of reading a newspaper.

Drayton finished his latte and walked around the shops, but close enough to the wall of the atrium to be able to see what was going on below. The men were no longer there, and for a moment he thought that perhaps he was deluding himself. That maybe they'd gone to catch their ferry.

There was a long corridor to one side, a McDonalds at the end of it, which was taking a delivery, stacks of blue crates on trolleys being wheeled in. The deliveries were coming through a pair of heavy metal swing doors to one side of the corridor, with a sign saying "Service Area".

He went through the doors, which led to three battered service lifts. He took one to the ground floor and after a short wait he left by another pair of swing doors to find himself at the far end of a dark delivery area, with giant garbage bins, several cars and two trucks that were servicing the McDonalds.

He saw the flash of light on the blades of their meat cleavers before he saw the men wielding them, the guys from inside, smiling now as they approached. Separating slightly and raising the blades. Eyeing their prey, almost casual. If he'd learned one thing from Acevedo it was that in Macau men bearing meat cleavers were very bad news. His friend had the scars to prove it.

He could still hear Acevedo's words. "When they chop you, it's usually to mutilate, to maim. As a warning. They usually leave you alive, if only just". Some comfort.

Drayton started to back away when the double metal doors burst open followed by a trolley laden with empty blue crates. He pushed the crates, which crashed to the ground in front of the Triads. The delivery guy shouted, but quickly retreated back inside when he saw the meat cleavers.

Drayton ran down a narrow gap between the two trucks, slipping on some slimy leftovers from an earlier delivery. He clamoured over the hood of a car parked behind the trucks and then over a metal fence, tearing his jacket. The fence lined a narrow drainage canal, and he slipped down its bank and into the water.

The water wasn't deep and he was able to wade across, though it was slow going as his feet sank into the deep sludge below. He glanced back to see the two men pausing at the fence beside the canal. They didn't follow but instead began to run along the fence and towards a path that crossed the canal at the far end of the car park.

Drayton knew he didn't have long, but it still took him three attempts to climb the bank on the far side of the canal, over another fence, and into the ferry terminal's main pick-up and drop-off area.

A ferry must just have arrived because the area was packed, the girls in tight dresses frantically waving signs at punters pushing or pulling their wheeled bags. Drayton wondered if they were full of cash, but mostly he thought about the meat cleavers. He bulldozed his way through, stumbling over cases and sending one woman tumbling into the luggage hold of a bus. Which gave him an idea. He paused near the back of one bus, which seemed about ready to leave, then quickly climbed into the hold amid the bags just before its hydraulic door swung closed.

As the bus pulled out Drayton could feel his heart pounding. His legs were aching. And his toe, the one bitten by that wretched pug, felt like it had been broken in two. He sat against the side of the hold. The bus braked hard and bags slid, pinning him against the cold metal. As the bus moved again, it took all his strength to push the bags away.

It took five minutes to reach the first stop. The door swung open and Drayton found himself face to face with a hotel luggage boy who, after his initial surprise, asked Drayton if he could be of any assistance. Sounding all chirpy, like he regularly found dishevelled passengers in the belly of the bus.

Drayton said yes, actually, and as the luggage boy helped him out of the hold he asked him about the Casa do Prazer, which the luggage boy said was quite close, giving directions and saying, "I think they'll take good care of you there."

The bus had stopped at another vast casino, and even with the directions it took Drayton a while to find his way out of the place. He stayed in the shadows, close to buildings, away from the glare of the neon, looking all around him. There was no sign of the cleaver-wielding pursuers.

He was limping badly and he realised that his jacket had been ripped right down the back, almost in two. He was caked in mud.

It was hard to miss the Casa do Prazer, which announced itself in multi-coloured neon and flashing lights, big red lanterns above the entrance, and the sign, Sauna and Massage Casa do Prazer.

Drayton entered through sliding glass doors and into a plush carpeted hallway, with a broad staircase leading to a reception area that would not have looked out of place in any five-star hotel, all marble and dark wood. Except for the pictures lining the walls, which were all of smiling masseuses with movie-star looks.

A young woman in a long, tight *cheongsam*, hair pinned up neatly, and with a white fluffy scarf around her neck met him at the top of the stairs and said, "Mr Drayton. This way, if you would. Your friend is waiting."

She directed him towards another door and into a locker room, where a tall, thin, uniformed attendant, a man this time, stood beside him and took his filthy and shredded clothes, hanging his jacket in the locker like it was a pristine Armani. When Drayton hesitated at his underwear, the man gave him a weary look and said, "Everything, please."

Once Drayton had complied, the man handed him a towel and directed him into another room, this one ornate with a high ceiling and with three giant Jacuzzis in the centre, a sauna on the far side. Several naked men were in the Jacuzzi. Two more were in the sauna. Others sauntered around the edge of the bubbling water.

Drayton took a shower, as directed and then entered another reception area where a young woman dressed him in a robe and shorts, and escorted him to a room full of large leather armchairs, where he took a seat. There were several television screens overhead.

About a dozen girls were lined up down one side of the room, wearing skimpy uniforms of tight black skirt and jacket over a white T-shirt. Drayton guessed they were Vietnamese or Thai. They didn't look Chinese.

He was then handed two menus. Food and drink, from which he ordered tea, and one for the services on offer, which ranged from a pedicure and ear cleaning to various massages, which Drayton assumed from the price involved different levels of additional service.

Two girls were quickly at his side, telling him they did a very good thigh massage, which he initially mistook for Thai massage, until one of the girls corrected him with hand signals that left him in no doubt what she had in mind.

Drayton said he'd have his ears cleaned, and a bucket of warm water for his foot. He sat back, closed his eyes and as cotton wool started working its way around his ear lobe he heard a familiar voice.

"I guess there are worse ways of spending the evening."

"Hello Tony. You look very good for a guy that's just been fished out of the Pearl River."

They told the ear cleaner to take a break, and Morgan said, "Somebody's been fished out of the Pearl River?"

Drayton explained how a drowned man, badly cut, had been found and taken to the mainland, without being identified, and how the local cops thought it was Morgan when they found his belongings in the water.

"Oooh, nasty toe," said Morgan, looking into the bucket in which Drayton had now sunk his foot. "How did you do that?"

"Old war wound," said Drayton.

"Iran? Afghanistan? I didn't realise you served in either."

"Japan, actually," said Drayton. "But it's a long story."

Then Morgan told Drayton about the summons to Macau from Mr Fang, Sam Ching's arrest and the call from him. He told Drayton about the Fang meeting at the restaurant that never happened, and Ching's ace of spades directing him to Fisherman's Wharf. He said he suspected they'd spiked his tea at the restaurant and wanted him at Fisherman's Wharf because whatever they had in mind it was more private.

"So they likely did want you to take a dip. How did you end up here?"

"The card, the ace of spades, it was definitely Ching's writing," Morgan said. "But there was something else. He'd drawn a figure, a stick alien. I remembered Ching telling me that the alien was all over the place, that it was becoming a kind of symbol of protest. Representing the out-of-touch authorities, I guess. Something like that. So I thought it might be a warning. But by the time that dawned on me I was at Fisherman's Wharf and could hardly walk. That's when I dropped my bag in the water. I then remembered this place was nearby."

Which got Drayton thinking about the alien. It made a lot of things a lot clearer. But he let that pass for now, while Morgan told him he was unconscious for most of his first six hours in the sauna, but that wasn't a problem since they knew him and saw all sorts of things there.

Drayton said he was sure they did, dismissing another proposal for a thigh massage. He said that Ching might be the least of Morgan's problems, that the documents about Mr Fang and the Colonel had been leaked on the internet, and neither would be impressed.

"Well, that's just great," said Morgan.

"I'll spare you the details for now, but it turns out that Mr Fang has serious Triad connections. The Colonel's connections are just plain serious. And they represent two Party factions that are virtually at war with each other."

"You're right," said Morgan.

"About what?"

"To spare me the details."

Morgan said there was something else that Drayton needed to

know. And he told him about the message from his wife, sent as a private message to his Twitter account, though without identifying the account to the American. Still wanting to protect his alter ego.

"I thought at first that she must have seen the massage video, that somebody had sent it to her. But now I'm not so sure. I know it sounds a bit silly, but I think the authorities, the public security people, they might be holding our son and using him to get information from my wife. Information about our work for you, Chuck."

And Drayton said that didn't sound silly at all, his mind racing.

Then Drayton said the priority had to be to get Morgan somewhere safe, maybe to the consulate in Hong Kong; Morgan replied that right now he was in the safest place he could be.

"How's that?"

"This place is open twenty-four hours a day. It is extremely discreet. No registration. Generally, they prefer you not to stay for periods of more than twelve hours at any one time, but they are highly flexible and have plenty of rooms for hire, comfortable rooms by the hour. They're happy just as long as you are availing yourself of the services and tip generously."

"Which you are?"

"Naturally."

"So the ideal way to disappear."

"For the moment."

Drayton said he needed urgently to get back to Shanghai and that he'd be in touch. Then he eyed Morgan in a way that made the Englishman a little uncomfortable, sizing him up, then saying, "Can I borrow your trousers, shirt and jacket?"

Morgan said sure, he could keep them, and gave Drayton his locker key. He said that the Casa do Prazer would order in some more for him.

Morgan said he could be reached on the number from which he'd sent the message about the sauna. It was an old Nokia with a local pre-paid card, anonymous, which he showed to the American.

"Very good," said Drayton. "You're learning."

"Otherwise call the sauna and ask for Gerald," said Morgan.

"Gerald?"

"Yes. That's how they know me here. Who would you like to be?"

Drayton said he'd stick with Chuck.

"One more thing," Drayton said. "When you sent that message, how did you know I was in Macau?"

"I didn't. But I figured that if you weren't you would be soon."

"Are you sure you'll be okay here?" Drayton asked.

And Morgan said yes, he'd cope.

– 38 –

Up the Garden Path

Drayton had to assume he'd been compromised, that Chinese security now knew about him and his interest in Colonel General Chen Shibo and his recently deceased Ferrari-loving son, and that they were aware of the information he'd been given by Morgan.

He didn't discount the possibility that the message Morgan had received from his wife was just something personal, that somebody had shown her the video, that she'd done the due diligence on her husband and didn't much like what turned up.

But if that was the case, she probably wouldn't have cared less who saw the message. Instead she'd used the most secure messaging she had available. He had to plan for the worst. He couldn't afford to take any chances.

What was harder to judge was whether the wider operation had been compromised too, whether they'd discovered The Facility. He'd need to talk to Dave, have a round-table with the other agencies. He'd have to fill them in and they'd have to make the call on whether to wind it up.

Cyril was waiting for him when he landed back in Shanghai and they headed immediately towards the North Bund. Drayton's phone rang just as soon as they hit the expressway to the city.

It was Luis Acevedo, the Macau investigator, sounding upbeat.

"I've got some news for you, which I think you'll be pleased with."

"Tell me," Drayton said.

"The body fished from the water, it wasn't your friend," Acevedo said, telling Drayton he'd got sight of the original report.

Drayton didn't mention that he'd just seen Morgan, thinking it was unnecessary detail and not really trusting the phone line. He just said thanks, that's really good news and did he have anything on who the drowned guy was?

"Three Finger Fang," Acevedo said. "Badly chopped, but definitely Fang."

Drayton asked who might have done that, and Acevedo said well, where do I start? The guy had a shed-load of enemies. But he said it was most likely Fang's associates, none-too-happy about having their names and Caribbean plans plastered all over the internet.

"Maybe somebody wanted it to look like a Triad attack," Drayton said. "It was you who said they usually maim, not kill."

"Usually, not always," Acevedo said and hung up.

"Sounds like a fun time in Macau," said Cyril, which Drayton ignored since, the way he saw it, that was none of Cyril's business and he couldn't recall ever telling the driver that he'd been to Macau.

Instead he borrowed Cyril's phone, which he then used to call the Casa do Prazer and asked to speak to Gerald. A woman told him that right now Mr Gerald was receiving therapy. Drayton said he didn't want to disturb that, but could she pass on a message. From a friend.

"Tell him Mr Fang won't be swimming in the Caribbean. That he took a dip in the Pearl River Delta instead."

"Is that it?" said the woman, expecting more.

"That's it," said Drayton. "He'll understand."

Cyril dropped him at the usual spot near the river where, unseen by Drayton, a newly installed surveillance camera, high on the roof of a riverside warehouse, followed him as he crossed the road and into the narrow streets leading to The Facility. Another picked him up as he approached the old twelve-storey building that was home to Shanghai TT Logistics, and where he took the creaking lift to the top floor.

When Drayton arrived at The Facility, he was surprised to find it was all high-fives and back-slapping. Even Tom had cracked a beer. Team Panda was moving out, closing down, and the NSA duo would soon be on a plane home. Job well done.

They told Drayton that events had moved fast since the worm began to talk, and Tom and Dick had quickly come up with four additional names of military officers working out of the white low-rise, which they were now calling Shanghai Cyber Command. The US government had moved with uncharacteristic speed too. The President's visit was fast approaching, and a US Grand Jury had just indicted the four plus Colonel General Chen Shibo for computer hacking and economic espionage directed at a string of US companies.

"For too long, the Chinese Government has blatantly sought to use cyber espionage to obtain economic advantage for its state-owned industries," said the FBI Director when the indictment was announced.

For good measure, an overseas Chinese website with close links to US intelligence reported that Chen was the father of the dead Ferrari kid. The detail about Chen's political links and the business dealings of his son left Drayton in no doubt that the site had been given access to Morgan's document.

It was quickly picked up by the mainstream media, starting with a lengthy front-page article in the *New York Times* under the headlines, "Saga of Cyber Espionage" and "Sleaze Goes to the Top".

Drayton admired their tactics. It was clever politics. A shot across the bows before the President's visit. The charges would never stand up in court. The attacks had been routed through computers across the world. Digital forensics was tough, and he knew the NSA would be reluctant to provide what proof it did have, not wanting to reveal its methods and capabilities.

And in any case, China would deny it and would hardly hand the men over.

The indictment was a way of sending a message saying, we know what you're up to, rein it in. And the Chen sleaze stuff would just rub salt into the wounds.

Dave said there was something else. Based on information from the worm, they'd been able to block on national security grounds the takeover by a specially created Chinese shell company of a strategically important company in Montgomery, Alabama. Dave said the company made garden gnomes and light fittings.

"How are garden gnomes strategically important?" Drayton asked.

Dave said the gnomes weren't important. That China was after the advanced engineering processes they used. 3D printing and all that, which had been licensed by the Alabama company to several defence contractors. He said the company's computers had been hacked, and they in turn had passed on the infection to the defence boys.

"Wow," said Drayton. "Do we know how the Alabama company got infected in the first place?"

Dave said he wasn't sure, that the company wasn't cooperating.

"The owner, a guy called Bud, he's in denial. Says it wasn't him that was hacked. Thinks we are all paranoid, and it's some giant conspiracy by the US Government."

"Sounds familiar," said Drayton.

He then looked at the new information on the other four hackers. It seemed pretty thin. Sure, the worm had delivered their names, but there wasn't much else to go on. Dave said they'd not been able to find anything more about them online. Commissioning Morgan and his wife to do some further digging would have been the way forward, but that was no longer an option.

Drayton could understand the urgency, DC wanting the indictment out before the President's visit, to focus minds, but he'd have preferred to have more before going public. Instead there was nothing on their military careers or anything else for that matter. It was as if they didn't exist.

And he had a gnawing feeling that something wasn't quite right. That the worm might have been led up a very muddy garden path. But that wasn't something that could be easily brought up with Tom and Dick, for whom the worm was infallible, almost family.

And that wasn't all. Perhaps it was because he'd been away for a few days, which had heightened his paranoia, but the outside office looked a little different too. The picture of the Bund was hanging at an angle and the fish tank had been moved, just slightly.

There was a toy in the tank too, which Drayton hadn't noticed before, a shark with big jagged teeth, its open mouth above the fetid water that contained no fish to chase. Drayton looked at the shark, then picked it out of the tank, shining a light from his iPhone into its mouth. Which is when he saw the lens of a tiny camera.

The watchers were being watched.

Drayton placed the shark back in the tank, this time pushing it face down and deep into the filthy water from where it wouldn't be seeing much at all. There was no evidence that whoever had planted the camera had got into the back room, which was now being cleaned up by a pair of technicians from the consulate, returning the office to normal.

Drayton told the others he'd make his own way back to the consulate, deciding to keep the discovery to himself for the moment. It wasn't exactly what anybody would want to hear right now. Not in the Bubble Room. But he'd have to tell them. Team Panda had been compromised.

Tom and Dick met Cyril in the old taxi at the usual rendezvous point near the river and they drove back down past the Shanghai Glorious Shipping Company building where a protest seemed to be flaring up again. A big one this time. Tom lowered his window for a better look as the car slowed, traffic forced into a single lane on the far side of the road by the swelling crowd. Police were trying to force the crowd back.

"Wonder what that's all about," said Tom, more to himself and not really too interested in an answer, just focused now on getting home.

Surveillance cameras followed the taxi's progress past the protest and down the Bund.

Once back at his hotel Tom told Dick he was whacked and would take room service. He lay back on his bed and reached to his side table for his iPhone charger, which wasn't there. He thought that maybe he'd left it at The Facility. He looked for his spare and couldn't find that either, so he rang Guest Services, and five minutes later a uniformed butler delivered a new charger. A local make, but it would do.

But when the charger was plugged in, it delivered a lot more than power, installing on Tom's phone a piece of malware designed to monitor and take control of his emails.

Initially at least, the bug found itself in hostile territory: an NSA-issued phone with some of the best defences available.

While Tom slept that night and Washington DC worked, it being daytime there, Tom received an email from a White House assistant passing on the President's personal thanks for all his efforts on what she called "vital matters". The assistant said she was travelling with an advance team for the visit and could Tom recommend any good places to eat near the consulate. "I *love* Chinese food," she said. "Especially crispy prawns."

She sent it to his personal email, where his defences were much poorer, and where it was immediately grabbed by the bug.

By the time Tom woke, the bug had already organised a reply on his behalf, complete with attachment, a good-eating guide to Shanghai containing a smorgasbord of malware. By morning Shanghai-time, the attachment had been opened and shared by several of the assistant's team.

For good measure the reply also recommended a takeaway near the consulate, for some of the best food in the area, and where Chinese cyber experts were already at work on the menu, infecting the crispy prawns.

*

When Drayton got back to the consulate he went straight to the Bubble Room, where a conference call was just starting. He wanted to raise his concerns about the cyber operation, that it had been compromised. He'd been rehearsing what to say on the way over, knowing it wasn't what they'd want to hear.

"Hey Chuck," said a voice from the NSA screen as he entered the room. "You guys must be pleased with yourselves. You certainly deserve to be."

"Thanks," said Drayton. "But about the other four names provided by the worm, I'd have preferred if we had a bit more on them."

"For our purposes it's enough," said a voice from the CIA screen.

"We've sent them a clear political message," said the White House screen. "The indictments are a great curtain-raiser for the President's visit. And the President can follow that up. Put them on the spot about cyber spying."

"You guys did a great job," said the State Department screen.

Drayton said he had an uncomfortable feeling, and started to talk about the fish tank, but he was cut short by the CIA screen, from which a voice said, "Has The Facility been cleaned up and closed down?"

"All done," said Drayton.

"Then relax. You delivered what we needed."

"Let's move on," said the State Department. "The protest is really worrying. What's it about?"

The consulate's political guy said it was paralysing the North Bund, and was one of the largest the city had seen in years.

"So what's their beef?" said the CIA.

Drayton said perhaps he could help, since it was close to The Facility and he'd witnessed it building up.

"It's a shipping company, the one that owned the cruise ship that sank on the Yangtze," he said. "It killed more than four hundred people, most of them children."

A couple of voices said yeah, we remember that.

"Families of those who drowned have been going there every day for weeks demanding compensation and answers about what happened, but not getting either. They tried to occupy the place. Been getting pretty tense."

Drayton said he could check it out, keep across it, and the State Department screen said sure thing and keep us honest on that, Chuck.

Which made him feel good, because Chuck Drayton was the man again. The shark with the camera between its teeth could wait. And his concerns about the names provided by the worm could wait too. The CIA was right, The Facility had now been closed down and cleaned up.

He got Cyril to take him back along that familiar route, but they couldn't get near the besieged office of the shipping company; he had to get out on the main part of the Bund, where crowds were already backing up.

The families of those who'd drowned suspected negligence, with pretty good reason, since the ship had technical issues, and had sailed on into a storm while just about everybody else had taken shelter. But the company blamed the bad weather. It was rumoured to have links to local government officials, who'd promised an investigation and answers, but had delivered neither.

And now the families who at first had been welcomed and treated with sympathy were being ejected as troublemakers. Though it was proving hard to label distraught mothers and fathers that way, and their plight generated huge online support.

When parents were forcibly kicked out of the building, some beaten by police as they left, even state-owned news organisations called it a disgrace. And the images, captured by dozens of smartphones, went viral, shared by millions.

A social media site, *We are all fathers and mothers of the drowned*, was for a while the most popular on the internet, attracting millions of followers and comments. Mug shots of those who'd drowned were posted there, together with messages of sympathy and of anger. It quickly went from being a platform about the sinking to a broader call for social justice. Which is when it was shut down.

Drayton had followed highlights via the *@Beijing_smog* Twitter account he followed, though that account had suddenly gone quiet.

He found it tough getting through the crowd. The road was now completely blocked. There must have been tens of thousands of people, stretching for at least a mile. Drayton couldn't see where the crowd started or ended. There were a lot of police, but they seemed frozen, unsure of what to do. This wasn't the sort of crowd you could easily bully.

But what was most striking for Drayton was the mood. It wasn't anger. It certainly wasn't confrontational or violent. They just stood there in silence, holding drawings and pictures high in the air above them.

Some were hand-drawn and some were printed.

All were of a stick alien.

− 39 −

The Alien Revolution

It was only after Wang Chu got back to Beijing that he learned what had happened to his parents. The teacher rang him, the one who worked with his mother, and who he'd met at the ice festival guiding her kids around the sculptures. She said the police had come to the school and taken his mother away two days before Wang had turned up, and that she was so sorry she'd not told him when they met. It had all been such a shock. She'd not known what to say.

She said she thought it was because of his mother's work with the church.

"What work with the church?" Wang asked, remembering the bible on the floor of his parents' apartment, but not knowing his mother was religious. But the teacher had said as much as she wanted to, and told him she couldn't really explain right now, saying again that she was sorry before hanging up.

Then a little later, Wang's mother herself rang, and much to his surprise she sounded happier than he'd heard her in a long time and hardly allowed him to get a word in. She said the police were raiding what she called house churches, unofficial churches, removing and destroying crosses and even demolishing some of the buildings.

She said she'd been at a service at one of those informal churches when the police arrived with what she described as a bunch of thugs.

312

She said she'd helped block their way, pushing them back, singing and defending the cross.

The following day the police had come to the school and arrested her, accusing her of picking quarrels and provoking trouble. They'd released her after three days, though only after she'd signed a confession and a promise not to attend any more religious meetings.

"So you can't go to church anymore?" Wang asked, and she replied that promises to those people meant nothing.

Then she began to praise his father, saying she was so proud of him. She said he'd quit his job at the Party School in protest at the treatment of his wife, saying he could no longer work for an organisation that violated its own laws and constitution.

"So he's quit, he's really quit?" Wang said, finding that more shocking than news of his mother's faith. Communists violating their own laws were nothing new and would hardly come as a great surprise to his father. But he guessed it was because the abstract had just become very personal.

His mother said that wasn't all. That Christians had gathered in the square beside Saint Sophia, the old Russian Orthodox Cathedral in Harbin, to protest against the raids. The police had tried to clear them, but then hundreds more people began to arrive, to support the Christians. And those hundreds became thousands. She said the square was now packed, that the protest had spilled into the streets nearby.

She said she was there now, and so was his father, that she would send a photograph. Then she hung up promising to phone again soon. Only then did Wang realise that he'd forgotten to tell her he'd been expelled from university.

It no longer seemed to matter.

A message with the photograph arrived within a minute and showed the packed square, filled with people standing in silent protest.

Some were holding crosses. Mostly they were holding drawings and pictures of a stick alien.

He shared it online. Though *The Gasping Dragon* had been shut down, he'd opened another account, this time in his own name. His mother was right, promises made to those people meant nothing. He was back online, in the world he understood best.

He was standing near the train crossing, the one close to the coffee shop. The barrier was down, but there were no police supervising it, so it was being ignored by pedestrians and cyclists going around, over and even under it. An elderly woman selling headphones nearby had appointed herself lookout and shouted a warning when she saw a train coming.

Wang shared more photos and videos from Harbin. And also from Shanghai, where another big protest was happening, this one supporting parents who'd lost kids when a ferry sank on the Yangtze. It was big online. The crowd looked huge. And again there were the pictures of the alien, held high in the air. The crowd just standing, silently.

Moments later the train rattled by, after which the barrier was raised and cars began to move across the railway line. Wang almost bumped into a red-faced Fatso heading in the other direction, totally absorbed in an angry conversation on his phone, yelling and waving one arm around.

"Hey," said Wang.

Fatso stopped, but only briefly, saying, "They think they can steal people's money. They'll pay for this."

Then he stormed away and resumed the angry tirade. Wang noticed he was carrying a poster mounted on a board. It appeared to be a very rough drawing of a stick alien. Art had never been one of Fatso's stronger points.

Wang found his roommates Liu and Zhang at their usual table in the coffee shop, which to his surprise had reopened. Liu said Fatso had sunk a ton of money into an investment fund promising big returns. But it turned out to be a scam with no real investments other than cars and property for the owners, who had disappeared, along with Fatso's money. And a lot of other people's money too.

Liu said the office of the company was being besieged by angry investors, including Fatso, though their real anger was at the Government, which was refusing to bail them out. He said the owners were rumoured to have links with the Party.

"But the Government always bails these things out, don't they?" said Wang.

Liu said that's what everybody expected. But there were now so many of these funds going under that the money was huge. Billions.

Liu said his father had told him there was a massive industry in what he called shadow banking and it was creaking under a mountain of bad debt. He said schemes like the one Fatso was involved in were just the tip of the iceberg, and that the Government could no longer afford to bail them all out.

"He's okay, your dad?" asked Wang.

"Seems okay."

He said his father wasn't his usual self, seemed very quiet, but at least he was now back in Beijing. He wouldn't reveal where he'd been for two weeks, just that he'd had no choice but to go away for a while. At one point he'd said he'd been "held" outside the capital, but then corrected himself, saying he'd been "staying" at a Party facility. He'd also said, "Things are changing", though without ever explaining what that meant.

There were online reports that trading had been suspended on the Shanghai and Shenzhen stock exchanges, which had collapsed even more dramatically than usual. Wang shared photographs of investors rioting in several cities.

The rioting had been particularly bad in Shenzhen, from where reports said the police had just stood by and let it happen. There were online rumours that the local police chief had been too busy liquidating his own investments to crack down on the protests. Others said it was part of a power struggle within the Party, Beijing having targeted the leadership in the southern boom areas, who'd responded by allowing the protests to happen.

At which point Lily came to the table, smiling for once, back in business and proud of her own little act of defiance. She said the police had ordered the coffee shop closed, giving no real reason. She said they'd sealed the door and put up a big notice saying it was shut down for the foreseeable future for violating unspecified hygiene regulations.

They'd parked a pair of vans just up the road, watching. But the cars left abruptly after two days and she quickly stripped their seal from the door, pasted over the police notice with a picture of the alien and reopened. She said the place had never been busier.

And a strange thing had happened. Though most of Lily's customers quickly logged in to the world beyond their screens, conversations were breaking out, many political, on subjects that had been treated before with caution or kept online and cryptic. The far corner of the coffee shop had become a little workshop, turning out posters and banners of stick aliens.

Zhang said it was hard to tell what was going on at the University. That there'd been protests there too. For more protection against the smog. Against the new rules on patriotic education. In support of the parents of The Girl In The Corner. For the reinstatement of Professor Huang. A whole bunch of things.

Zhang said the university authorities seemed paralysed, which had encouraged the protesters. He said they'd tried to deflect the anger by laying on buses to carry students to a spontaneous anti-Japan protest, followed by a spontaneous anti-American one, handing out banners saying, "Keep out of the South China Sea" and "Alcatraz belongs to China".

But Zhang said most students didn't even bother to leave the campus on the buses to the Japanese and US Embassies, and the official slogans had been overdrawn with images of the stick alien.

That, and pictures of a smashed red Ferrari with a caption, "Where's the Justice?" Liu said the crash in Shanghai had made people really angry, especially when the driver turned out to be the son of a high-ranking military official.

He said there'd been a news blackout, and censors had blocked the words 'Ferrari', 'red', 'crash' and 'naked', the last one referring to one of two girls in the car. The other one died.

Zhang said that initially he'd been really busy with the University's Opinion Guidance Unit, since there were an awful lot of opinions that needed guiding. But those running the Unit began to suspect that the opinion guiders were not taking their task seriously enough.

Especially after a mix-up with party slogans.

One slogan, "We must firmly uphold the unity of the people," was posted by Zhang as "We must firmly *upload* the unity of the people."

He told his supervisor it was a genuine mistake, but that it might sound better to a younger audience.

Soon afterwards it went viral, the first time anybody could remember that happening with a Party slogan. And alongside many of the postings was an image of the stick alien.

316

Soon after that, Zhang and his fellow opinion guiders where told that the work of their unit was being temporarily suspended.

The University then announced a two-week closure, for what it called urgent repairs to the main buildings.

Elsewhere the online censors were busy but inconsistent. The sheer volume of pictures and videos from protests now spreading nationwide was a challenge for sure. But their response veered from one extreme to another. One minute leaving the posts, perhaps hoping the anger and ridicule would burn itself out, the next deleting anything about protests and blocking everything that contained the words 'protest' or 'alien'. To this was added 'Yangtze', 'sinking', 'compensation', 'church' and 'investment'. For a while even the words 'Harbin' and 'Shanghai' were blocked.

Dozens more sites were taken down and there were at least a hundred arrests for malicious rumour-mongering.

In reality it was impossible to turn back the tide of anger without pulling the plug on the digital world completely, though that's what happened for a while in some areas of Harbin and Shanghai, where the authorities turned off the internet and digital services.

But that merely delayed the uploading of images until protesters found an area with a signal.

As he jumped between social network sites, sharing and commenting, trying to make sense of what was going on, Wang began to feel that he knew everything but nothing. The only constant was that spindly figure with the big pear-shaped head and angled eyes. His stick alien.

– 40 –

Ritan Park

When the Chinese Government abruptly cancelled the President's visit, it was seen initially as a snub, a reaction to the cyber indictment, though it soon became clear to the Americans that Beijing had bigger things to worry about.

Privately there was relief at the Shanghai consulate. Top-level visits were always a pain. And even the President's advance team found a silver lining, able to switch their attention to sightseeing. And plenty of crispy prawns from the great takeaway they'd been recommended.

The daily conference calls in the Bubble Room were now dominated by efforts to make sense of the protests sweeping the country. To Drayton the only common thread appeared to be the images of that strange little stick alien, held high by waves of mostly silent and peaceful protesters.

The protests had now crippled a large part of southern China too, across the border from Hong Kong, and China's industrial heartland, triggered by the collapse of an over-stuffed landfill near the city of Shenzhen. Construction companies building a vast new suburb nearby had used it as a dump, and it had given way after days of heavy rain. A river of mud and rubbish had swept downhill from the site, engulfing villages, two schools and workers' dormitories, burying hundreds of people, including scores of children.

The authorities called it a natural disaster. But there'd been warnings and small protests for months. Online they were accused of negligence and a cover-up. Images of desperate and distraught families searching for loved ones went viral, as did videos of security agents dragging a crying elderly couple, grandparents of some missing children, from a construction company's office where they had gone to demand answers.

Thousands took to the streets, but this soon became tens of thousands and then hundreds of thousands.

Across the border in Hong Kong, pro-democracy protests flared up again. They'd been led by lawyers and judges at first, accusing Beijing of eroding the former British colony's independent legal system. But they were growing bigger by the day.

The only violence appeared to have been at protests by investors, as they watched markets collapse and investment funds go under, and demanded their money back. That was already spooking world markets, and a trusted American financial expert from a leading bank in Shanghai was invited to the Bubble Room to brief them about the mess.

"What is a Ponzi Scheme exactly?" asked a voice from the darkened State Department video screen.

"It's a fraudulent investment operation where the operator pays returns to its investors from new capital paid to the operators by new investors, rather than from profit earned," said the expert.

"You what?" said a trio of voices.

"Can we have that in plain English?" said another.

"Basically it's a scam investment designed to separate investors from their money," the expert said. "And they do have a tendency to collapse eventually."

"And remind me, what's the name of the one that's giving us most worry right now?" asked a voice from another screen.

"Well," said the expert, "I'd call it the Chinese economy."

*

319

The foreign media had started to call the protests the Alien Revolution or the March of the Aliens, likening the Chinese protests to the "colour revolutions", the uprisings that had once swept parts of the former Soviet Union and the Balkans.

Diplomats struggled to figure out what it all meant, and the dark silhouettes around conference tables on the Bubble Room video screens demanded answers. Who was behind the uprising? What was the organisation? Because surely there must be one. What did they want? And how should we react?

Mostly it came down to the alien. Who was it and what did it represent? This sometime hacker, nationalist, brewer of deadly smog weapons, and now possibly the force behind the uprising.

Drayton came under pressure. The Bubble Room screens wanted answers. And he was the Cyber Guy. He had plenty of reason to doubt that the alien symbol was anything other than that, a symbol, but for the moment kept those thoughts to himself.

The search for the hand behind the uprisings, the conviction that there must be one, was shared by the Party, which saw a dark foreign hand, what it called a conspiracy against the Chinese people, orchestrated by enemies abroad.

For good measure, security agents rounded up hundreds more lawyers, as well as civil and labour rights activists, accusing them of subversion.

In Shenzhen they paraded on television a factory owner called Sam Ching who tearfully confessed to inciting unrest. The police released a photograph that they claimed was Ching meeting villagers near the collapsed landfill. Much was made of Ching's Canadian passport, and he apologised in a faltering on-camera statement for hurting the feelings of the Chinese people and allowing himself to become a stooge of unnamed foreign enemies of China.

His wife, a feisty woman from Hong Kong, condemned the confession as being forced, calling it a grotesque piece of totalitarian theatre. In a written statement, she said her husband had been wrongly arrested, possibly for counterfeiting goods, and attached a picture of what was later identified by its original Japanese inventor as an automatic sperm extractor.

Most journalists and diplomats following the story didn't really get the significance of that. It was just plain weird. So they stuck with the line about the grotesque piece of totalitarian theatre. That was a far better sound bite.

When he read the wife's statement, Drayton did raise an eyebrow of recognition, but decided this wasn't something he needed immediately to be taking to the Bubble Room. He mentally filed it away, along with the aquarium shark.

In Hong Kong, the protests were inflamed when democracy activists disappeared. Chinese security agents were accused of abducting them in violation of local laws. They turned up two days later on the mainland, confessing to inciting protests and saying they'd made the trip voluntarily, having felt a sudden need to atone for their wrongdoing.

The abductions brought thousands more to the streets, crippling several areas of Hong Kong Island and neighbouring Kowloon. The image of the stick alien hung from buildings and walkways across the territory as waves of protesters blocked the roads below.

Hong Kong's internet connections collapsed and one of the World's most important financial centres went blind. It followed cyber-attacks on pro-democracy targets, crippling their websites with a flood of requests in what was called a denial of service. Only the attack was so big the territory's entire network came crashing down.

Hong Kong's tech-savvy students had already shut down China's top official in the territory, a man known as Two-Phone Ma on account of the two mobile phones he usually had glued to his ears. Students got hold of the numbers and posted them on sex-for-sale websites, offering big discounts. Ma's phones were crippled when they were overwhelmed with calls. Drayton smiled when he heard about that. It was more low-tech than high-tech, but just about the most ingenious denial of service attack he'd come across.

There was a sharp increase in incidents in the South China Sea. A Chinese ship fired shots near an American destroyer. The US Ambassador to China urged the screens in the Bubble Room to stay calm, saying it was simply an attempt to deflect the protests by stirring up nationalist sentiment.

The Ambassador called it a dangerous strategy. He said that even where it succeeded in bringing nationalist protests onto the streets, they soon morphed into something else. And the funny little alien was never far behind.

The Bubble Room wasn't convinced. Calm wasn't something the screens did, and the Ambassador was told to issue an immediate diplomatic protest. A voice from the White House said any deployment of smog weapons to the South China Sea would be a red line for the President.

It was hard to say what was going on at the top of the Party, where a secretive and paranoid leadership saw enemies everywhere. Yet for all the arrests and abductions, and a renewed crackdown online, the authorities seemed at a loss as to how to deal with the big protests, the silent, peaceful protesters with their alien posters and banners, which just seemed to spread and to grow.

*

Drayton decided he needed to get out of the hothouse atmosphere of the consulate, and especially the Bubble Room, and grab a beer. It was all getting a little surreal, the diplomats now under fire from DC for failing to see this coming. Even while they were struggling to figure out quite what *this* was.

Drayton had been in the diplomatic game long enough to know that DC heard what it wanted to hear, saw what it wanted to see. And if a year ago anybody had predicted an uprising built around a strange little alien, and had suggested that far from being the biggest boon to the world economy, China might be about to bring it down, they'd have been laughed out of court.

And diplomats didn't like being laughed out of court.

Drayton walked to the nearby microbrewery run by the guy from Minnesota, where he took his usual seat in a corner, back to the wall as always, and ordered a pint of Airpocalypse Pale Ale. But it was back to its usual name, Shanghai Wallop, and without the discount, because the smog was lifting.

His iPhone rang, a Japanese number he didn't recognise. It was Sakura, telling him she'd had her visa revoked without explanation. She said work had become impossible anyway because their computers had been crippled by something called a service of denial attack, hackers bombarding the system with so many requests that it just collapsed.

"You familiar with that stuff?" she asked.

"Not really," said Drayton. "Though it was probably a denial of service attack. Service of denial happens later, when you accuse China of doing it."

He'd had his fill of the cyber world and changed the subject, saying they should really get together before she left and have some more fun, and she said, "But I've already left, Chuck. I'm back in Japan. Give me a shout next time you are in Tokyo."

Then she hung up.

But Sakura phoned back a minute later, this time sounding a little more emotional, telling Drayton that it had been hard returning to Japan, leaving behind someone that means so much to you.

It was the most affection he'd ever heard from Sakura, and for a moment he didn't know how to reply.

Then she said, "It was a quarantine issue. There was a lot of paperwork, and I had to leave Bobby behind."

She asked whether he'd mind keeping an eye on the pug and gave the name of the Shanghai dogs home where he was lodging.

"Give him a kiss from me," said Sakura.

And Drayton said, "Sure", before they both hung up and he ordered another pint of the Airpocalypse Pale Ale that was now Shanghai Wallop.

He was worried about Morgan. He'd not been able to reach him. When he telephoned the sauna they told him that Mr Gerald had left for now, but they'd be sure to pass on a message if he returned.

Drayton had never met Morgan's wife and had no contact information for her, so reaching out to her wasn't an option.

He'd received two letters that afternoon in the diplomatic pouch from DC, which he'd forgotten about, but now with a moment to himself he took them out of his inside pocket. One was an in-house State Department magazine trumpeting all the latest efforts by US diplomats to bring peace and prosperity to the world.

It had become a lot thinner of late.

The other was a brown A5 envelope addressed to him, but care of the State Department. It had a bunch of strange stamps of exotic birds. Another of a turtle. It was from the Cayman Islands.

There was a smaller white envelope inside, and inside that was a

323

postcard with a picture of a long beach fringed with palm trees on the front and a short message on the back.

Dear Chuck,
Aliens are by nature remote and of another world.
But thankfully some Party functionaries are still reliably corrupt.
Pay us a visit next time you are in the Caribbean.
Take care,
Mr and Mrs Gerald and son

Which made Drayton smile. Morgan and his wife had done a deal, bought their way out. Playing the system as always. And Morgan was right about the alien. That was precisely the message all those different protests were sending. That the Party was of another world.

Drayton then activated his VPN and went to the *New York Times*, which was reporting government appeals to protesters for reason and promising to investigate the landfill disaster and the collapsed finance companies and provide the truth about what happened.

Then he went to Twitter, where he was pleased see that *@Beijing_smog* was tweeting again, back online after a break, and with its own take on promises of honesty from the Party.

When they've always fed you lies then even truth and honesty look tainted.

Drayton smiled. That guy was always spot on. He wished he'd had a chance to meet the person who wrote that stuff.

His phone then buzzed, an encrypted message saying there'd be another conference call in the Bubble Room later that evening, morning in DC. Which hardly filled him with enthusiasm. He already knew what the questions would be.

They wanted motives, conspiracies. But what could he tell them? That the Communist Party was brought to its knees by a viral image, unleashed by a student with a smartphone who thought it was all a joke. That the Party had been undermined by the power of ridicule, indifference and the internet.

His phone buzzed again, saying the world's financial markets were in free-fall and looking for confirmation that he'd be on the call. For the first time in a long time he powered his phone off. Then he ordered another pint of Shanghai Wallop.

*

It had been a busy day in The Moment On Time coffee shop, where they'd stepped up production of stick alien posters and banners. Fatso was lending a hand too, providing the students with one room of his workshop.

There was going to be a protest in Tiananmen Square, right beside the Zhongnanhai leadership compound.

News had spread rapidly online, but cryptically.

5pm at *to meet the*

The Zhongnanhai cigarette as a symbol for the leadership compound, and of course the stick alien for those who lived there. Both as originally posted by Wang. But that was a while back now. The alien had travelled a long way since then. And Wang played no part in the preparations. He was back in the world beyond his screen, working on an idea for another app. Another game, this one a chase. The player pursued by a bunch of crazed zombies through, round and sometimes over giant ice sculptures.

He left the coffee shop with the protesters and took the same train with them into the centre of town. It seemed like almost everybody on the train was heading to the protest, all nursing their aliens. But when they got off at Tiananmen Square, he stayed on for another three stops to Jianguomen, from where he walked to Ritan Park.

He entered the park and walked past a lake, still partly frozen. On a hill beside the lake the trees were still wrapped in green cladding to help them through the long winter. In a pagoda on top of a hill a group of elderly people stretched and turned, going through a series of slow and graceful movements, as they did every afternoon.

In another small clearing more elderly people were bent over low tables playing a board game, focused intensely on the small round pieces in front of them.

The sun was going down fast now. It was a cold, crisp afternoon without a cloud in the sky. And the smog had lifted. You didn't need an app to tell you that.

Wang couldn't remember the last time the air had been so clean. Apart from in the distance, close to where the sun was sinking, from the direction of Tiananmen Square, where smoke seemed to be rising. It was hard to tell for sure.

He sat on a bench and looked for the answer online, where he'd always looked, tapping on the screen of his phone. But the signal had been cut. His world was offline and he sat staring at a screen of lifeless icons.